Quest of the Dicepterons
Volume 1
The Blue People of Cloud Planet

Brian Wolfenden

Published in 2013 by FeedARead.com Publishing – Arts Council funded

First Edition

A CIP catalogue record for this title is available from the British Library.

The events and names in this story are entirely fictitious and bear no resemblance to persons either living or dead.

Dedication:

To Seren and Aiva. I hope that in their lifetimes they will learn of life at another star / planet.

Acknowledgements:

Firstly I must thank my family for turning my 'technical study' into a readable story and in particular my wife, Christine, for patiently pouring over the text to achieve a semblance of English grammar. Secondly I am deeply indebted to my reviewers John Pikoulis, Jean Harvey, Debbie Todd and Suzanne Rees for their invaluable critiques. Nearly all their suggestions and amendments were used in the book. Thirdly I would like to thank and acknowledge NASA and STScl for use of pictures from the Hubble website. Finally I would like to thank John Anthony for editing this book.

FORWARD

Our sun is one of over 100 billion stars in the Milky Way galaxy and there are more than 100 billion galaxies in the universe which was formed about 4.5 billion years ago.

Life on Earth has existed for many hundreds of millions of years and in our humanoid form, for only the last 10,000.

It is the author's belief that considering the vastness of space and the sheer numbers of stars, it is highly probable we are not alone and that parallel or very different life forms have evolved elsewhere. Within our solar system they will certainly be far more primitive than us but as we move out to the stars the chances of life comparable or more advanced increase.

Our nearest star is Proximo Centuari about 5 light years away and at 8.3 light years distant is Lalande 21185 in the constellation Ursa Major. This latter star has two confirmed planets in orbit which are gas giants like Jupiter. It is only a matter of time before we find a star in the Milky Way with an earth size planet orbiting at a distance where heat, light, water and oxygen are optimal for life to evolve, possibly similar to our own.

However, in other galaxies, where conditions could be very different from the Milky Way, who knows what kind of beings may have evolved and what level of intelligence they have achieved?

This story is about one fictitious star in our galaxy called Seren which is 10 light years from Earth. This star has an orbiting planetary system including an optimally positioned world called......

.... Cloud Planet ....

PROLOGUE

'Let me introduce myself. My name is Zec and the incredible story I am about to unfold started well over 100 years before I was even conceived. I can assure you that I have meticulously examined Commander's logs, collated transcripts, and studied video and audio recordings from several sources. I have used my extensive databases to cross reference and double check key happenings during the last two hundred years. These are structured carefully to produce an accurate picture of the events they portray. Further, I, and more importantly several members of my family were actually witnesses to some or all of the remarkable findings on Cloud Planet, 10 light years distant from Earth.

'I am compiling this narrative in the year 2190 but my story spans over two centuries.'

Chapter 1
Cloud Planet, Constellation of Vercingetorix – 2135

The vastness of space is not always deserted and, where there was a constellation of stars, the 'sky' was illuminated by dozens of heavenly bodies in relatively close proximity. One star in this group, Seren, had its own planetary system, with huge giants similar to Jupiter and planets with ring structures like Saturn. From a distance these were lit up by their star and produced a majestic sight, with night and day clearly delineated on their surface.

A spinning satellite hurtled towards Seren on a trajectory between the star and one of its massive gas planets. Although travelling at high speed, it experienced the gravitational forces of both bodies and their combined and opposing vectors caused a significant deceleration. Now the star and the enormous planet competed to capture the tiny object but their forces were very closely balanced and its speed decreased dramatically until, imperceptibly, the gas giant won the battle and the craft started a slow descent.

Then, on the horizon, a smaller planet of dazzling blue with white caps at the poles and an unusual ring of thick cloud around the equator also contributed its pull on the object and yet another tug of war occurred. However, the satellite was quickly gathered by the gravitational field of this planet and it started a very slow descent into the thin atmosphere, surviving the heating process surprisingly intact.

Still some distance from the surface and in complete darkness, the craft entered the deep cloud ring and a world of constant wind and rain, which did little to slow its downward momentum. Then it flew over the mountain tops and penetrated through layer after layer of thick, fleshy leaves and branches, quickly losing parts of its structure until only the body remained. This careered out of the dense forest and crashed to the ground in the centre of a peculiar crater.

The badly-deformed shell of the satellite gave one final lurch and settled. In its last gasp a small gold plaque detached itself and fell to the red surface, its pictorial side uppermost.

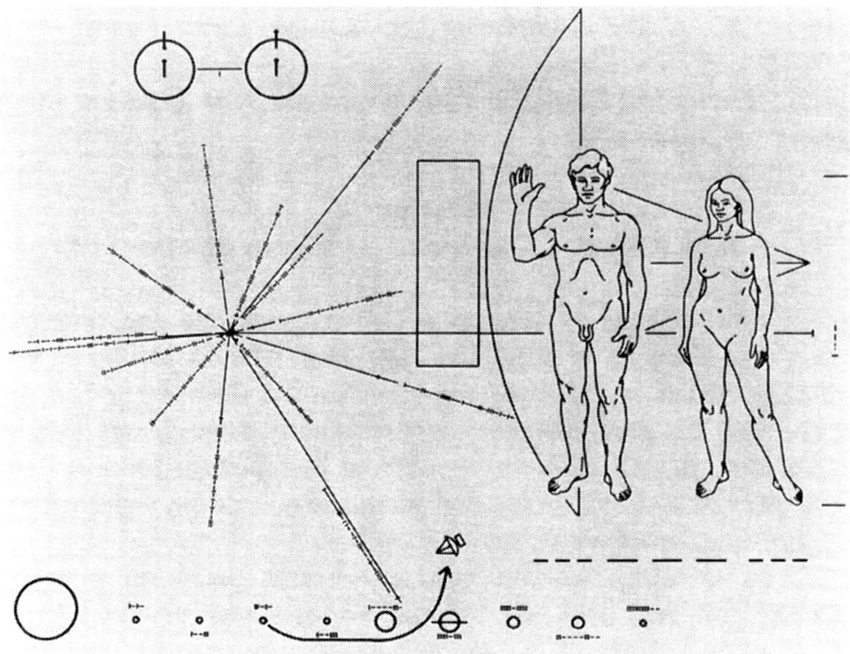

'My research of the World Wide Web, as it was called in the 20th and 21st century, produced vast information on the Pioneer missions. In particular, the NASA website details numerous launches in the late 1960's and early 1970's but Pioneers' 10 and 11 were of interest for two reasons. Firstly, both satellites were scheduled to leave our solar system after completing their primary objectives. Secondly, both spacecrafts had a gold plaque bolted to the main frame showing a picture of a man and woman and the relative position of our planet in the Milky Way galaxy.'

A short time later and equivalent to the period for this planet to rotate through one third of its equatorial circumference, the wreck was bathed in hot sunlight. Hundreds of pairs of piercing green and yellow eyes failed to take any notice of the twisted lump in their midst. Even more surprisingly, and for the next twenty revolutions of the planet, these beings with strangely-coloured eyes continued to ignore the intruder.

Meanwhile, their bizarre world cycled from intense sunshine to one of cold darkness. As the sun set, they disappeared underground only to rise again each day to the renewed warmth of their star.

These unusual forms changed in temperature and colour as they moved between regular-shaped pools of hot liquids. They drank, fed and cleared away fleshy leaves from the floor of their domain.

They mated.

Sadly, deaths outnumbered births.

These peculiar creatures utilised the largest leaves to wrap the cold life-less bodies which had not survived the hostile night. They were placed in an open drainage channel where the hot liquid shrank the fleshy covering. The mummified forms travelled down into a dark subterranean world where hungry predators eagerly awaited them.

Then, one Cloud Planet day later, amongst the hoard of unseeing green and yellow eyes, a pair of the most striking and brilliantly blue eyes swivelled to observe the weird mass at the centre of the structure. They blinked repeatedly as rays of golden sunshine reflected from the ground beside the strange object.

Chapter 2
Events in Space-Time

'The launch of Pioneer 10 in 1972 from Cape Canaveral, Florida was watched by thousands of onlookers including a father and his six year old son, Jack. This was a pivotal moment in time for the Parker family which resulted in generations of space travellers.'

Cambridge University, England, 2003

Jack Parker's head was literally buried in his books. It had to be as he was majoring in honours in both physics and mathematics and exams were a matter of weeks away. Even so, his ears pricked up as the BBC newsreader mentioned a report from NASA and he listened with fascination.

'Pioneer 10 spacecraft sends last signal – after more than 30 years, it appears that the venerable Pioneer 10 spacecraft has sent its last signal to Earth. Pioneer's last, very weak signal was received on 23rd January 2003. NASA engineers report that Pioneer 10's radioisotope power source has decayed and it may not have enough power to send further transmissions to Earth.'

The NASA spokesman continued with the history of Pioneer 10 but Jack's mind drifted back to that day when he saw the launch with his father.

'Was that really thirty years ago?' he mused. He could recall the event as if it were yesterday. He remembered the excitement among the crowd, the flash of light and the noise which bombarded his ears as the rocket crawled into the early morning sky. From that moment he had wanted to travel into space, and he still did.

'And now,' continued the NASA spokesman, 'Pioneer 10 is the most distant manmade object at over 16 billion kilometres from Earth. Pioneer 10 will now continue to coast silently as a ghost ship through deep space into interstellar space heading generally for the red star Aldebaran in Taurus the Bull – a mere 68 light years away.'

Jack sat back and wondered what was in store for the little satellite but dismissed the thought as it was going to be a long, long time before anything significant happened.

Little did he know that it had just changed course and velocity. How could he have possibly imagined the consequences for future generations of the Parker family?

'I have meticulously examined records to try to explain how Pioneer 10 headed in the direction of Cloud Planet. Interestingly, in 2000, NASA reported that the largest asteroid detected to date was on a near collision course with Earth and it was classed as high risk. Then, in 2003, a minute change in its trajectory away from Earth was observed which downgraded the risk to negligible. No reason was recorded for this occurrence.

'I used advanced algorithms, not available to mathematicians at the start of the 21st century, and conclude with 99% certainty that Pioneer 10 and this huge asteroid were on a head-on collision course. My complex modelling shows that the satellite would have experienced a phenomenal gravitational sling-shot changing its trajectory by 90 degrees. The model predicts a huge increase in velocity and a destination in the constellation of Vercingetorix 132 years later.'

Solar Flare - 2125

In this year, the sun spewed out one of the most powerful solar flares in its history. Billions of tonnes of incandescent hydrogen were blasted millions of kilometres from its surface and intense radiation spread at the speed of light through outer space.

Communication systems around planet Earth were badly disrupted but quickly restored after computers reset themselves and continued transmitting as before. Anxious technicians sat at their consoles awaiting messages from distant probes and various spacecraft on journeys to far corners of our solar system.

One by one, each returned a transmission showing that all was functioning satisfactorily.

Only one mission failed to return a signal.

Communications with StarGazer-1 were terminated!

The lone astronaut aboard that spacecraft was sleeping.

In fact, he had been in a deep sleep for nearly five years and would have continued in that state for a further four months had it not been for the severe bombardment of radiation that streamed over his craft.

He knew nothing of this, however, because his whole body was at five degrees Celsius and encased in a strange cocoon within StarGazer-1.

The force field around his spacecraft had deflected nearly all the electromagnetic waves. However, one array of solar cells was burned out by the sheer intensity of the blast and curled over the end of the communications antennae. The damage to this solar panel caused a momentary breach in the spacecraft's defences. Radiation swept through some of the onboard computers and through a microchip controlling a most vital function.

The radio waves passed over a group of transistors etched in the silicon surface and altered their settings. Some that were 'off' were turned 'on' and others that were 'on' were switched 'off'. Thus 'zeros' changed to 'ones' and 'ones' became 'zero'. In the binary system, the numeric value represented by one particular group of transistors was changed from five to fifty. Critically, other algorithms relied on this specific value.

Even more critically, this number was the time in years that the lone astronaut would remain at five degrees Celsius.

Now it had a 'nought' after it and the clock was reset to zero!

Chuck Parker would not wake up until 2175, provided power and vital resources lasted that long and he did not die beforehand.

BOOK ONE
PROJECT OMEGA

'We move forward to the middle of the 22nd century and make a visit to Earth where many of my family members reside. We are not going to meet any of them yet, and certainly not where we are heading. However, we are about to become acquainted with two key characters in my story.'

Chapter 3
Tropical Rainforest, Borneo – 2150

It was midday and the fierce sun was directly over the thick forest canopy, bathing the upper leaves and branches in hot sunshine and drying the remnants of the early morning tropical downpour. Further down, raindrops cascaded from leaf to leaf and branch to branch, so that at ground level it was still raining heavily. The atmosphere was hot and humid and surprisingly gloomy with much of the sunlight filtered out by the mass of vegetation that soared 40 metres above. The whole area was filled with a babble of diverse sound as various species called, warned, mated or merely chattered. Suddenly, the noise stopped as two bodies crashed through the undergrowth and slithered down a wet, rocky incline.

'Shit!' cried Olivia as she stumbled headlong down the shallow ravine, falling face first into the muddy undergrowth and disturbing creatures she didn't want to think about. Her face was splattered with mud while blood seeped from a cut on her forehead.

'Shit! Shit! Shit! – What the hell am I doing in this stinking forest? – I'm a top astronaut!' Olivia vented her fury as a second body slid down the same slope.

Scott Parker landed heavily beside her.

'We're being tested, Livia. This mission, whatever it is, needs the right people or combination of peoples. You're the fourth partner I've struggled through these forests with and you were with Andy two days ago.'

'Tested! I don't do bloody tested! I'll train for any job they want and do it!' she replied, 'And let's get one thing straight. It's Olivia, not Livia, OK!'

Scott raised an eyebrow. This was going to be an interesting couple of days.

'I had planned a two week training course in one of the few remaining forested areas of the Borneo jungle. The candidates were dropped in the middle of nowhere with their first partner and given only a crude map, minimal instructions and a compass with a swinging needle – the sort that became obsolete in the middle 21st century. Each was equipped with a rucksack and the basics for a two day trek, including one overnight stop. Then, when they reached the trainer's tent [and not everyone did] and after a night's rest they were reassigned a different partner, given new instructions and off into the jungle again to repeat the whole process.

'Olivia was the dominant partner on the first two treks which were successful because of her resourcefulness and determination. However, Andy was known to be single-minded and this pairing became a clash of personalities. They arrived late at their destination.

'All four of Scott's pairings successfully completed the missions proving his outstanding leadership qualities. There was an obvious chemistry in his partnership with Olivia. I know because she was delighted when she found out that he was in the same pool of top astronauts selected by me for a major confidential mission.

'However, the trainees were unaware that I was monitoring and recording their every move and utterance.'

'And another thing about that idiot, Andy! Not only did I have to ward off his groping when we camped but he wouldn't listen to me when I knew we should take a left fork. We took a right and got lost – it took us ages to retrace our steps!'

'That's not like you. You should have been firmer, Olivia.'

That was typical of Scott, Olivia thought, always rational in all situations. That's what she liked about him.

'Olivia Medici, 34, and Scott Parker, 38, are both honours graduates in astro-physics who doctored at the McFarland Research Centre on the Moon, which is where they first met. Scott was attracted to Olivia but found her somewhat aloof and difficult to know. Both are fully qualified astronauts with licences to pilot all Roving Orbital Landers [ROL's], shuttles and long-distance rockets.

They have clocked up many thousands of pilot hours between the Moon base and Earth and more recently between the Moon and the new Mars station which was in its final stages of completion.

'Olivia is of British and Italian extraction. She is tall, slim with jet black hair and strikingly good looking. She has a reputation for being serious and very critical if her high standards are not met. She has two younger brothers and a sister 20 years her junior who is studying geology and glaciology.

'Scott is American with a passionate love of space travel and adventure that runs back through the generations to Jack Parker in the early 21st century. More recently, Scott's father, Chuck, was deemed 'lost in space' after the solar flare of 2125. Scott is tall, well-built and handsome in a craggy way. He is the epitome of logic, coolness and rationale and gets on well with all acquaintances. 'A born leader' is recorded in his profile.'

'We need to get off our arses and back on track', said Olivia. 'We've a way to go before camping at this river.' She pointed to a blue line on the rather crude map they were following, 'Which we'll intercept in about four hours on this northerly heading.'

'And then what?' Scott queried.

'Candlelit dinner for two washed down by your favourite red wine.'

'I wish. Lead on,' he replied.

They reached the river after five hours of trekking in the oppressive heat and with the light beginning to fail they set up the two person tent. The candlelit dinner was beans heated on a gas burner and washed down with tea, with chocolate for dessert.

They finally settled in their sleeping bags and Scott fell asleep almost immediately.

'How does he do it?' Olivia thought, disturbed by every sound and movement outside. She finally drifted into a fitful sleep...............

.... the dark cavern entrance was so tempting and Olivia could not resist entering to explore it. But the light dropped quickly and, turning, she ran, not out of the cave but further into the murky depths. It was so black she couldn't see her hand in front of her face and then she bumped into the wet, fetid wall and screamed!....

'Olivia! Wake up. What's wrong?' cried Scott. He could not believe that Olivia was whimpering in her sleep.

'Oh no! No! I'm trapped.'

'Olivia, wake up!' Scott gently shook her shoulder.

She woke with a start. Perspiration had beaded on her forehead and her heart hammered wildly. With horror she realised that, after all these years, the nightmare had returned to haunt her; only this time in company.

'It's OK', she stammered, 'only a bad dream.'

'It sounded more than that – do you want to talk about it?'

'No, I'll be fine'.

Olivia was determined not to let Scott realise how agitated she was. However she was grateful when he gently put his hands on her shoulders and spooned her back into his front. Tentatively, he slid one arm around her waist and was delighted when she lifted his hand and cupped it firmly to one of her breasts. They both quickly fell asleep.

They woke the following morning and got on with their daily routine.

'So what's next?' Olivia queried. 'I seem to remember we follow the river downstream for a few kilometres.'

'Yes, right, but we have to traverse the river first.'

'What!' cried Olivia, 'Are you crazy? Look there's a reasonable path this side, that bank over there looks horrendous. Show me where it says we have to cross?'

'It's not in the instructions but I know we have to get to the other side of the river. Olivia, you have to trust me.'

She looked into Scott's blue eyes. There was a depth and quality that reassured her and also an underlying sadness. Yes, she could trust this man unlike her disastrous partnership with Andy.

'OK buster! – But you'd better be damned right 'cause we're going to get awfully wet crossing that!'

They didn't just get wet but absolutely soaked. The journey down the riverbank for the next half mile was treacherous. Then, they were on a reasonable path and Scott was quick to point out that on the other side of the river the gorge came down to the very edge – there would have been no easy route there. After a further three kilometres they came to a clearing and there was the trainer sitting under his awning.

'You're the first team to get here,' he said, 'well done.'

'So where now?' enquired Olivia, stifling a yawn. 'Which lucky guy has got me next?'

‘Ma-am, 100 metres up the road there’s hot showers, fresh clothes and a three course lunch in a five star hotel for you,’ he answered with a wry grin, ‘and then you’re both on a shuttle to Moon Base leaving at 3 pm sharp – don’t miss it!’

‘Yes sir,’ they replied in harmony. Things were looking up.

Chapter 4
The Moon – 2 Weeks later

'Welcome to the Moon and to my home where I hold a very privileged position. Of all the occupants, I have the single largest residence at the base with the most sophisticated air conditioning system. A large number of my family members reside here with me and many more are constantly travelling through space.

'You are now going to meet one of my family who is about to put our two astronauts through their paces in the Sea of Tranquillity.'

'Emergency! Emergency!' Zec-1's voice boomed in Olivia's ears, 'Return immediately to ROL-1,' the strange sound continued.

'Zec-1 is the latest in artificially intelligent computers which is installed in the advanced Roving Orbital Lander – ROL-1. I am Zec which is short for ZENIC – Zeeman Enhanced Nanotechnology Induction Computer. I control every member of my family, and there are millions of them, through the Safe Solar Protocol, SSP as it is known, which is the replacement for the Internet used during the 21st and 22nd century.'

Simultaneously the heads up display in the helmet of Olivia's spacesuit flashed the same digital warning in red light before her eyes.

'Command received and understood.' She replied and the voice recognition algorithm in Zec-1's vast database confirmed the identity of the astronaut. Twenty metres away, Scott had received the identical instruction and had similarly replied and been authenticated by Zec-1.

With both astronauts initially identified, Zec-1 now started lowering the air lock bay door located on the underneath of the lander and with it the revolutionary through air lock command seats.

Olivia and Scott turned carefully and proceeded in controlled short hops towards the lander thirty metres away. In this low gravity sudden movements could end in disaster and even in emergencies, calm, precise actions were drilled into the astronauts during training.

As Olivia hopped towards the craft, she couldn't help thinking that BUG-1 might have been a more appropriate name as it stood on four huge bent 'legs' in front of her.

'This lander is the most sophisticated craft that I have designed and is multi - versatile for take-off, landing and roving in the most inhospitable of terrains – whether solid or liquid and has the ability to climb up or down ledges of 2 metres. The cylindrical design is 4 metres in diameter and 20 metres in length and it stands 3 metres above ground when its legs are fully extended.

'The most technically advanced feature is the clear hemispherical dome at the front which carries the command module. It is moulded from enhanced cyano – acrylic copolymers and contains multiple layers of programmable liquid crystal displays. I, or in this case Zec-1, can command this half metre thick dome to display any activity or situation both inside and outside the lander. The dome, depending on the level of the emergency, can be blackened from its outermost layers inwards ultimately giving protection from the severest of radiation.

'Also, there is no more scrambling up a ladder into the air lock – the astronaut's command seats are capable of being cycled from the dome through the airlock to a position between the huge caterpillar tracks on the front legs just above the Moon's surface.'

Olivia and Scott arrived at the twin command seats virtually together and sat in their own ergonomically designed positions. They then put their left hand palm downwards on the side arm, where, through a circular clear panel in the hand glove of the spacesuit, the palm print was read by Zec-1 again confirming the identity of the astronauts. Lap belts automatically encircled their waists and their helmets were also clamped.

'Command enter ROV-1,' they said in unison and, satisfied that both astronauts were secondarily identified and confirmed, the telescopic gantry holding the command seats started to rise up into the air lock. As this was an emergency entry, the speed was at maximum capability and the lower door closed behind them and sealed the craft against the hostile outer environment. Once Zec-1 had confirmed that the silicone seals were inflated to optimum pressure, the air lock was quickly pressurised to internal lander conditions and the forward internal door was opened. The seats with their two occupants were moved forward into the command dome and latched. The telescopic gantry detached itself and retracted back into the air lock and the forward door was closed and sealed, thus establishing optimum integrity inside the craft.

Concurrently, Zec-1 had already started the four take-off rocket boosters on the underside of the lander.

Olivia and Scott, still fully suited, again placed their left palms on the registration monitor on the control panel in front of them.

'Command emergency lift – off!' they instructed and Zec-1 took the four boosters from idle to controlled power. This lifted the huge lander quickly into the vacuum above the Moon's surface and pressed Olivia and Scott into their seats with significant g-force. When the lander was one kilometre above the surface the emergency was declared over by Zec-1 who reported that the evacuation had taken one minute fifty five point three two seconds beating the previous best practice by 1.28 seconds.

'Why we have to know to the second decimal place I will never understand,' joked Olivia.

'Precision is the difference between success and failure,' replied Zec-1.

Olivia could only smile at the computer's apt but very correct response.

Now the heads-up display informed her that she could release the helmet from the spacesuit. 'Command raise helmet,' she instructed and it was slowly raised and parked behind her seat head rest. At the same time the pressurised air pack and hand controlled thrusters located across the front of the spacesuit were released and a side clamp swivelled these away from the astronaut and retracted them into a utilities compartment where they would be checked and refilled appropriately for the next use. They could now relax and not for the first time they admired the marvellous spectacle of the Moon's surface through the clear dome.

'Command return to Moon Base!' called both astronauts again with their left hands on the panel.

'Confirm return to Moon Base,' Zec-1 replied.

'This is one of many training exercises that I have arranged during the last two weeks with ROL-1 including a two day 'trip' to Earth. Here they practised gravity landings and take-offs from a variety of terrains including water and ice. In the weightlessness of space they rehearsed space walks around the lander. Normally only

one astronaut is outside the lander as dictated by the safety protocol. However, this rule can be broken in an emergency. To facilitate single walks, the telescopic gantry is commanded to engage either right or left control seats singly and this is a valuable feature for taking passengers on and off the lander.'

Then, when Olivia was spacewalking and gawking through the dome of the lander at Scott in the command seat, her most feared exercise suddenly took place.

'Red emergency!, Red emergency!' commanded Zec-1, *'return to lander immediately.'*

This was the highest level of threat to the astronauts and their lander and Zec-1 immediately commanded Olivia's helmet and the lander's dome to maximum black condition. Olivia shuddered as her world suddenly switched off and would have panicked but for the displays in front of her eyes which gave her a picture of the outside and her relative position to the lander. Almost immediately Zec-1 started issuing instructions to guide her to the outside command seat below the lander and the tether attached to Olivia was slowly reeled in.

Meanwhile inside, Scott's lap belt suddenly clamped in place and he was momentarily shocked as Olivia suddenly disappeared behind the dome of black in front of him. He was then reassured as the internal display quickly showed multiple views of Olivia outside progressing towards the safety of the external command seat. All through this, Zec-1's calm instructions echoed inside the command dome and her replies followed as each order was complied with.

When she reached the air lock and Zec-1 had confirmed the outer door closed and sealed, the lander went into final red emergency mode and a force field was generated around it. ROL-1 then retreated from the crisis situation at full power.

10 kilometres away, Zec-1 commanded an end to code red and the dome and Olivia's helmet cleared.

Scott peered in – Olivia's face was white!

'4 minutes 29.06 seconds for red emergency in spacewalk conditions,' Zec-1 informed, *'well done Olivia.'*

But Olivia was not listening.

Olivia thought of that particular exercise as they were returning to Moon Base on the following morning. A shiver ran through her body as she remembered the return of the nightmare that previous night in her quarters. She feared that another uncontrolled outburst might jeopardise this training and her aspirations for space travel in the future.

'Command, prepare to dock!' Zec-1 announced.

They moved forward to their seats and placed their left hands on the control panel.

'Confirm command to dock.'

Though not yet in view, they knew that the Moon Base would soon appear over the lunar horizon and with the sun low in the sky they were rewarded with a spectacle of light from the multi-faceted 'rooves' of the base.

'It's just like the Eden Project,' Olivia said to Scott, 'but on a larger scale.' Scott had only seen pictures and agreed, commenting...

'Yes, the geodesic design has stood the test of time but there were a few more problems to solve up here.'

'Construction of Moon Base was started by me in 2050 and it was fully operational by 2100. Occupying an area over 500 metres square, it is located near one of the poles where significant deposits of ice lie just below the surface. It is shaped like a cross with the main large dome at the centre and three linked smaller modules on each of the four arms. From the fourth arm protrudes the maintenance hangar with a flat roof to dock space vehicles. Research, accommodation, recreation and utilities are housed in the other three arms of the base. The central dome houses the control and communications centre where up to 500 technicians monitor space missions and flights.'

'ROL-1, you have permission to dock at 3A,' called the lunar flight controller in the observation tower of the Moon Base.

'Confirm docking at 3A.'

The lander was one kilometre above the roof of the base and now descended under Zec-1's control at 10 metres per second. At 500 metres the four main thrusters under ROL-1 increased their power and slowed the vessel to 1 metre per second descent speed.

Scott watched the graphics on the dome head as they showed multiple scenes of the craft and the base. Also displayed were all the vital speeds, distances and vectors. But the view that always fascinated him most was the vertical alignment of the lander above the dock and the oval-shaped locating hatch which grew steadily larger as they descended. This reminded him of the conning tower on the old nuclear submarines. Now 100 metres up and descending at half a metre per second, the mimic showed the multiple outlines of the docking hatch, one above the other but still slightly out of perfect alignment. Zec-1 now carefully applied minute amounts of thrust to the appropriate horizontal rockets until at 50 metres the 'ovals' were synchronised.

'ROL-1, you are correctly positioned and cleared for final landing at 3A.'

'Confirm final landing at 3A.'

Scott now watched as the docking oval loomed large on the dome screen. He knew that it was perfectly aligned with an identically sized shape on the underside of ROL-1. Mating was male on the lander to a double ring on the roof dock. At 10 metres above the roof ROL-1 was slowed to 0.1 metres per second and just before docking the caterpillar tracks on the four legs of the lander touched the reinforced roof around the ring and took its weight. Final mating was as light as a kiss. The silicone seals then inflated and hydraulic locks clamped into place and the craft was now firmly sealed to the Moon Base roof.

'ROL-1, you are now secured at 3A.'

'Confirm secured at 3A.'

'Command astronauts - prepare to disembark ROL-1.'

They clutched their small flight bags and the command seats were retracted and lowered into the air lock. After checks by Zec-1 that pressures were equalised, doors opened and the seats were lowered into the elevator.

Olivia and Scott then left their seats after receiving final instructions from Zec-1 and the flight controller. The seats were retracted into the air lock and both doors above them were closed and sealed. Once confirmed, the flight controller now activated the lift carrying the two astronauts and it descended 50 metres to the floor of the maintenance module of Moon Base.

When the doors opened, a lunar flight attendant made a smart salute to Olivia and Scott and welcomed them back to the base. They made their way through to the reception module where the receptionist handed them envelopes.

'Where are we training next?' thought Olivia.

But when they opened them they found an invitation to attend the main conference room at 10 am lunar time the next day to be briefed on 'Project Omega'. Training over!

Chapter 5
The General

'I particularly remember this day because Moon Base was rife with speculation about this meeting and nobody knew the agenda. They do not even know who is chairing this gathering. I include the detailed transcripts of this discussion because of their vital importance to Project Omega and my story.'

By 09:55 am lunar time, five pairs of astronauts were assembled in the main conference room of the Research module. Olivia looked around her, surprised that only 10 remained from over 50 who had started training three months ago.

She was not surprised to see Alison and Steve in the same room and there were Jane and Tom and Melanie and Angus, but she could not name the fifth couple, only recognising their faces from earlier training sessions.

Scott was staring upwards and Olivia followed his gaze to the lunar sky so perfectly framed in the hexagonal sectors of the module roof. But what held their attention was the lovely sight of Earth, with day and night so clearly defined, and the wonderful blues and whites as sea and cloud gave glimpses of the huge land mass of Africa.

Suddenly the conference room door hissed open and the ten astronauts stood smartly to attention and saluted as, to their astonishment, no less than General Patrick L. McFarland entered the room.

'This must be some serious mission.' Scott whispered knowing that this was the supremo of space travel and exploration.

'The General is Commander-in-Chief of the World Space Exploration Council based here at the McFarland Research Centre at Moon Base. He was the first man to have set foot on Mars with, as it happens, Scott's grandfather Ralph. He also pioneered the establishment of the first Moon Base now named after him. Now in his sixties, the General is an imposing, strong-featured man, still lean and fit, and with a striking head of hair.'

'At ease, ladies and gentlemen, and thank you for your prompt attendance here this morning.' He was always extremely polite with all personnel at the Moon Base and commanded huge respect with the way that he managed people. However, look out if he raised his voice slightly or lifted an eyebrow – you were probably in trouble.

Then, surprisingly, he took off his uniform jacket, put it on the back of a chair and joined the stunned astronauts at the round table.

'Please feel free to remove your coats and make yourself comfortable.' This was unheard of in the presence of the General and none of the teams moved until Scott led by example and removed his.

'Today and tomorrow,' he continued, 'there will be no status in this room and everyone will be entitled to say exactly what they think without prejudicing their rank or position on this Moon Base.'

'So what is going down, Sir?' Scott asked, 'This is highly unusual.'

'You can drop the 'Sir', but I would like you to call me 'General'. You must all be wondering what you are doing here and the reason for the extraordinary training sessions that you have come through.'

The General then pressed a button on the small remote in his hand.

'Shit! Shit! Shit!'

Olivia's head shot up as her voice suddenly boomed out of the multi sound speakers.

'What the hell am I doing in this stinking forest – I'm a top astronaut!'

The astronauts exchanged smiling glances but before Olivia had time to feel embarrassed the General quickly went on.

'What indeed and doubtless you all harboured similar thoughts and before we go on I make no apologies for the fact that you have been monitored every minute of the day and night for the last three months.'

Olivia turned and saw that colour had risen up Melanie's neck. She smiled knowing that Melanie had a thing for Andy. What a relief he hadn't made it through jungle training!

'I know you are the best technical astronauts we have produced,' he continued, 'but we needed to find the best possible teams for Project Omega.'

He operated the remote again and this time Scott's voice reverberated around the room.

'It's not in the instructions but I know we have to cross the river. Olivia, you have to trust me.'

'You were all given common instructions for your teams in Borneo,' the General explained, 'but each of you was also given one piece of vital information which you would know when to use. You were also asked not to reveal how you came by this knowledge but to use your powers of persuasion to get your partner to trust your decision. Trust, respect and finding the couples most suited to one another is vital for this mission because some of you are going to be together for the next 50 years!'

The silence was palpable as the astronauts looked at one another and tried to take in this astounding revelation.

Chapter 6
The Search for Life

'You will not be surprised to learn that Project Omega is the search for life, hopefully intelligent, amongst the star constellations that light up our night sky. What may surprise you is that I have been active in this project for the last 25 years. Back then we focused on stars with known planetary systems and within 20 light years of Earth. We also needed strong evidence that Earth sized planets at the right distance from their star were likely to exist.'

He paused and then operated the remote.

The lunar sky in the dome above them suddenly vanished and was replaced by a myriad of stars and constellations, resplendent in their unique colours. The astronauts adjusted their seat backs and admired the spectacle.

Suddenly three red arrows appeared at different parts of the sky.

'The constellations of Agamemnon, Vercingetorix and Hercules,' the General's quiet voice played over the visual display and each constellation's name appeared beside it, 'have stars with known planetary systems and fall within the distance criteria. In the constellation Agamemnon, the star Capitulan has a very interesting system.'

The overhead display changed to show the detail of this star and its attendants. Gas giants, ringed planets and barren rocks swirled around their central energy source.

The General moved the pointer over a small planet. 'This one has possibilities and it is roughly the same distance away from Capitulan as we are from the sun.'

'However, in Hercules, two stars have very promising planetary systems but they are 20 light years away and at the limit of reachable space travel. But in Vercingetorix, 10 light years away, the star, Seren, gives us the most excitement.'

Then the overhead display filled with Seren and her orbiting family. The astronauts looked up in awe as colourful gas giants, multi–ringed planets and smaller orbs circled around an intensely red star.

'Excuse me, General,' interrupted Scott, 'are these computer simulations?'

'No, they are real time because what you don't know is that 25 years ago we sent high speed ion engine probes to each of these constellations and they are now returning distant but clearly definable images.'

The General now moved the pointer to a small planet with a strange looking ring structure. 'This planet is approximately 140 million kilometres from Seren and its infra-red and x-ray analyses show significant water, ice and oxygen. The ring is not dust or small rocks like Saturn but composed entirely of water, so we think this is a cloud collar, which is most unusual.'

'Are these the most recent pictures and how old are they?' asked Steve.

'Good question, and no they are not the most recent. They were received 15 years ago and subsequently focussed our attention towards investigating this planet. I will tell you later about the programme to build two, yes two star ships and the development of Mars Base which is, in fact, dedicated to Project Omega.'

The astronauts sat speechless at this revelation.

'So that explains the extreme security when we shuttled to Mars?' queried Olivia, 'I thought it was going to be a duplicate of Moon Base.'

'Yes, this project was only privy to the World Council and a handful of senior personnel at Mars Base. Now I want to show you two events that completely changed our plans and timescale for Omega.'

'The images we received 10 years ago started giving a much clearer picture of Cloud Planet as it became known,' continued the General, 'and we could discern the unusual ring more clearly with seas and ice caps to either side.'

The picture above them now changed to a planet of striking white and blue with a collar of cloud around the equator.

'A beautiful sight isn't she and can you imagine our euphoria when we started picking up small points of intense light around the equator?' The excitement in the General's voice was palpable as the display then showed these pinpricks of light in the cloud.

The silence in the room was broken by Olivia, 'Are these points of light real or an aberration caused by signals passing through such vast distances?'

‘Good question and one which we constantly tested ourselves. However, over the next year, and as we got closer, these light specks increased in intensity and smaller ones started appearing alongside the stronger sources. And don’t forget we couldn’t monitor the planet for long periods of its ‘year’ – about 10 of our months - as our probe couldn’t always see its day side.’

‘Are you saying that there were no pin pricks of light on the night side of the planet?’ contributed Angus. ‘So they could merely be reflections of the planet’s sun?’

‘Yes, but look more closely, what do you see?’

‘Why, there’s a pattern!’ cried Scott, ‘They seem to be in equally spaced lines along the equator – how can that be?’

‘Exactly!’ agreed the General, ‘Now, can you see why we got so excited?’

‘But General,’ Olivia persisted, ‘you said two events occurred but you’ve only described one.’

‘Yes, I’ve left the best to last and this occurred 5 years ago,’ he paused and the silence could be cut with a knife, ‘look up now!’

The astronauts stared up and there were audible intakes of breath as one of the stronger points of light started blinking......

–off – on – off – on – off – on– off – on– off – on -

Chapter 7
Message from Space

The astronauts exchanged excited looks, ‘what does it mean?’

‘It means we are going to have a look!’ the General replied and waited for the penny to drop.

‘You mean we are going to this star!?’ Scott responded, ‘How can we? It’s 10 light years away!’

‘Yes, but probably not all of you. However, let me give you the good news, the incredible news and the not so good news.’

The astronauts were all ears.

‘When we discovered Cloud Planet of the star Seren we embarked on a 20 year project to build two star ships capable of travelling at a significant fraction of the speed of light. We also knew that we had to refine, improve and test cryo – hibernation so that astronauts could ‘sleep’ for most of the journey, oh, and wake up OK and with a bit of luck get back.’

The astronauts smiled at this unusual bit of humour from the General.

‘Our goal was to go to Cloud Planet in 2155 and that’s 5 years from now and the good news is that we are on target for this date. We have built our first starship capable of half the speed of light and have cracked cryo – hibernation!’

‘But that’s incredible,’ most of the astronauts retorted together.

‘So why have we been rushing through this training programme when we’re 5 years from take-off?’ Scott enquired still unable to digest what the General had said.

He smiled; Scott was usually the most perceptive of his astronauts. ‘Well, now for the incredible news,’ and he looked up to the display of Cloud Planet, ‘the ‘on – off’ pattern of this one particular light spot started off quite erratically and usually lasted for about 2 hours. Then it repeated every 20 hours which, by the way, is the 360 degree rotation time for this planet on its axis. It is also the same spot of light that blinks each day.’

Then he paused, his audience completely focused on the planet above them with its pulsing speck of light.

‘Now we move on about 20 revolutions of the planet as what you are about to witness happened gradually during this period.’

The General was silent and waited as the astronauts stared, gasped and some even stood up to get a closer view as the random flashing spot of light started to form a repeated pattern of 'offs' and 'ons'.

After a while, Scott leaped to his feet, 'IT CAN'T BE! IT CAN'T BE POSSIBLE!' he yelled,

'That's the Morse Code for SOS!'

Now all the astronauts could see the repeating distress pattern and they sank back into their seats utterly stunned.

Scott then turned to the General more in hope and desperation and as their eyes met the General quietly shook his head and he knew it could not be. Olivia noticed the glance and she realised what Scott must have initially thought of the distress call from space. But now was not the time to dwell on it.

'So fellow astronauts,' said the General, 'that SOS message has been repeating every Cloud Planet day for 2 hours during the last 5 years. Also according to our calculations that's 1 hour either side of the planet's midday sun - yet another fascinating symmetry.

We are convinced that this is no fluke or aberration of signals across space because there are too many repeating patterns, so we believe that this is a genuine message from space and we have decided to respond prematurely.'

'And now,' he continued, 'the not so good news. We are going to send the first starship to Cloud Planet in one month's time. This starship, called LifeSeeker-1, has the capability to reach Cloud Planet...... but not to return.......

........it will be at least five more years before LifeSeeker-2, which is capable of the return journey, leaves to follow the path of LifeSeeker-1......

.....the risks are high, 20 year cryo–hibernation is an unknown factor although ten has been proved and there is good confidence that extending the timescale will have no adverse effect...........'

He looked into the eyes of the ten astronauts before him seeing excitement, bewilderment and, in some cases, even fear. Then he said,

'I'm looking for volunteers for a one way ticket to the stars!'

Chapter 8
The Commander

After the silence, the questions flew thick and fast, and the General held up his hand.

'One at a time, one at a time, please, I can't answer all your concerns,' he consoled them. 'but I hear a common question........ 'why did we build a starship capable of only the outward journey?'...... Well, as I told you earlier the plan was to send two ships in 2155, perhaps up to 1 year apart. The first, LifeSeeker-1, would have a crew of seven, two ROL's and four emergency shuttles. The nuclear power plant feeding the ion engine would have a capacity to reach the star, Seren, and start initial investigation of Cloud Planet. Then LifeSeeker-1 would remain in permanent orbit and await LifeSeeker-2, a ship twice the size with a crew of 21, eight ROL's and 28 emergency shuttles. Its power plant would have the capacity for the return journey accommodating all astronauts from both starships if necessary.'

He paused, 'But the astounding SOS message has changed all that and we are sending LifeSeeker-1 at least 5 years before LifeSeeker-2 and,' pausing again, 'LifeSeeker-2 is only 50 per cent completed as I speak.'

It was Angus who broke the silence. 'This is crazy! To send a starship on such a high risk mission with the backup not even built!'

'Not crazy, but yes, very high risk which is why this mission is volunteers only.'

'But General,' continued Angus, 'this sounds like a suicide mission. Who would be foolish enough to put themselves forward?'

He smiled, and reached for the remote, 'Well, we've actually got our first crew member.'

Part of the night sky behind the General suddenly changed and the head and shoulders of Commander Abraham Joshua Stewart dominated the astronauts' attention.

'It's Commander AJ!' Olivia gasped, 'Where's he been for the last 5 years?'

'Commander Stewart was known as AJ to his fellow astronauts and was the first astronaut to go to the moons of Jupiter. He is iconic in the space world as he volunteered to fly to the outer

regions of our planetary system under full cryo – hibernation in an ion-driven spacecraft. AJ came back after 5 years in space and was successfully resuscitated with no ill effects and looking remarkably unchanged.

'However, communications with an earlier similar mission were lost after the massive solar flare of 2125. This was piloted by Chuck Parker, Scott's father.'

These facts flashed through Scott's mind and painfully reminded him that it was his Dad that had not returned from space, but he quickly controlled his emotions as AJ started to speak.

'The General has briefed you on Project Omega, and the remarkable message from Cloud Planet and you will soon be asked to volunteer for what must seem to you to be a most risky mission. I have been involved full time in Project Omega for the last 5 years and my main role has been putting LifeSeeker-1 through its paces and, believe me, she is the most stunning starship as some of you, I hope, will see tomorrow. The General has asked me to volunteer as mission commander, which I have, and I have closely watched your training and would be delighted to have any of you join me for this mission. But now I will pass you back to the General.'

The night sky returned to the dome display.

The General raised his hand, 'Fellow astronauts, we have had a long four hour session without a break and I am going to suggest that we reconvene for dinner at 5 p.m. moon time, when I will be happy to answer more questions.

'As I said earlier, I am looking for volunteers to man ROL-1 and ROL-2 on LifeSeeker-1 but I don't want any decisions from you until tomorrow at 10 a.m. This evening you are all booked into the executive hospitality suites where you will enjoy complete privacy – no bugs I assure you! – to make up your minds. Finally, whatever you decide will not be held against you and you can walk away from this with no effect whatsoever on your career.'

He moved to his coat and pulled out a wad of envelopes. 'Each of you has proved themselves exceptionally in the last three months and you are all promoted to Senior Rank Astronaut, effective today. You are the elite of our profession.'

He handed out the envelopes amongst murmurs of thanks, surprise and appreciation and continued.

'However, you must make your choice as a team – I cannot accept one person from one pair and one from another and you must both freely volunteer in each of your groups. Tomorrow, I will be back in this conference room from 10.00-10.15 a.m. lunar time and whichever teams walk through that door will be considered for the mission. Any final questions?'

'What if no one turns up?' queried Angus.

'I hope that will not be the case, but if so we will wait for LifeSeeker-2 and then proceed with the mission.'

'And if more than two teams volunteer?' this from Scott.

'Then I will have a difficult decision to make. See you all at five.'

The General gathered his jacket and left the room.

Chapter 9
Decision Time

During dinner they discussed Project Omega at length but Scott could hardly keep his eyes off Olivia's stunning dress. Made of creamy satin with a plunging back, it moulded itself to her perfect figure.

After coffee, the General excused himself and reminded everyone of tomorrow's deadline. The teams started to disperse and Olivia picked up a nearly full bottle of red wine from the table along with their glasses.

'We've got a decision to make,' Olivia whispered to Scott, 'let's make it in my room.'

Scott did not need any persuasion.

Later they luxuriated in the large bath facing each other with legs entwined and completely at ease. Olivia noticed a sad look on Scott's face.

'You thought it might have been your Dad when you heard that distress call, didn't you?' Olivia said softly.

'For a moment yes, but the General shook his head when our eyes met and I knew it wasn't. And how could he have been 10 light years away?'

He paused and looked into Olivia's eyes, 'I was six when, with my Grandfather, I watched Dad take off for the stars. At least that's where Gramps said he was going and that he would be back for my 12th birthday. But all contact was lost 5 years later after that huge solar flare in 2125 and that was 25 years ago.'

She was touched by the sorrow in his voice. She sat forward, soapy water draining from her shoulders and breasts, and cupped Scott's face. 'Never give up hope,' she said and kissed him tenderly.

Scott regained control and looked at Olivia. 'That was more than a bad dream in Borneo, wasn't it?'

'Yes, it was my recurring nightmare,' Olivia paused and then continued. 'I've never told anyone but when I was six, that's funny I was six too, I was on holiday with my parents in Italy. We were having a picnic and I wandered away towards the edge of the forest where there were huge rock formations. A dark hole in the rock caught my eye and, being the adventurer, I entered the cave entrance. Even though it grew dark quickly I wandered on and turned left and then right.' Olivia shuddered and now Scott gently held her shoulders as she continued. 'And then it was black, I couldn't see my hand in front of my face and then, ...then, I tried to retrace my steps and banged my face against the wet, foul-smelling cave wall – and I screamed and shouted until eventually my parents found me – a quivering, lump of jelly!'

'I only found this out recently. I have all Olivia's records - academic, medical, psychiatric. I find it difficult to believe that this inner fear did not reveal itself at the many demanding interviews during her training programme. It is another factor demonstrating her strength and resolve to become an astronaut.'

'So a fear of black holes – how ironic is that for an astronaut!' Olivia continued, 'You're hardly going to want to go to the stars with me.'

'I'd go to the end of the universe with you, Olivia,' Scott said tenderly and in that moment they knew they had made their decision.

At precisely 10 a.m. lunar time, the conference door hissed open and Olivia and Scott entered. The General smiled. He would have bet a fortune that these two would be the first to volunteer. Five minutes later Alison and Steve entered but the door did not open again by 10.15.

However, the General was delighted with his two teams.

Chapter 10
LifeSeeker-1

Both ROL's had lifted off around midday lunar time and Zec-1 had set a course for the far side of the Moon which was always hidden from Earth.

'Emergency! Emer.'

Zec-1's instruction was cut short and Olivia and Scott were startled as Commander AJ's face appeared on the dome in front of the command seats of ROL-1.

'Zec-1 doesn't know we exist,' AJ continued, 'but he does now as I've downloaded LifeSeeker-1 into his memory. With a bit of luck Zec-1 will now see us as friend and not foe!'

'Because of the high security attributed to the project and LifeSeeker-1, I must keep secrets even from my own family. Now Zec-1 and Zec-2 are privy to Project Omega and the two starships.'

'But Zec-1 couldn't pick you up before,' Scott replied, 'you must have a pretty good screen around you.'

'Yes, we're only just over your horizon – you would have bumped into us before you saw us!' AJ said with a smile, 'and now Alison and Steve in ROL-2 are on-line.'

'We need to be precise with our computer identity,' AJ explained, 'so ROL-1 is Zec-1, ROL-2 is Zec-2 and LifeSeeker-1 is Zec-C for Control. I'm putting up some images of LifeSeeker-1 on your domes so you will have a better picture of us before you make visual contact.'

A large section of the dome then showed several line drawings of the starship.

'LifeSeeker-1 is 150m long and 80m diameter at the ion drive. The command, accommodation and all utilities are contained within a 30m diameter by 80m long tubular front section. It was a huge undertaking to build a starship in space and I managed the whole process through inventory, materials procurement, sub-assembly, transport logistics, final build and test.'

The astronauts in the two landers looked through the clear dome to the horizon and sat back in awe as the huge starship started to appear with its vast arrays of solar cells glistening in the low sunlight. The ion drive dominated the skyline and the huge fins seemed to curve perfectly into the relatively small forward body of the ship.

Olivia and Scott were transfixed by the sight. They watched in silence as the twin lander bay doors on top of the ship started to open.

'Each door is 10m wide by 30m long and positioned either side of the vertical fin. Between the doors and the ion drive are four emergency escape rockets. At the front is a 30m diameter command centre made from the same cyano-acrylic building blocks used at Moon Base, the lander command domes and the astronaut's helmets.'

'ROL-1 is seeking permission to dock with LifeSeeker-1.'

'ROL-1 confirm identity,' Zec-C commanded.

As previously, Olivia and Scott put their palms down on the control panel. Now it was LifeSeeker-1 that checked the identity of the astronauts and gave permission to start the docking procedure to bay door 1. LifeSeeker-1 was in geostationary orbit behind the moon but even so it was travelling at over 1,500 kilometres per hour so ROL-1 had to slowly catch up with the starship and then begin the intricate procedure of exactly matching speeds whilst positioning itself 100 metres directly above the door.

As the lander started descending it was dwarfed by the huge starship below. The astronauts looked back and forth excitedly from the starship to the mimic displays in the dome. They were now just below the outer rim of the ion engine and descending between the two graceful fins. Then the bay door appeared level with their right side. Meanwhile, Zec-1 and Zec-C constantly confirmed speeds and height and alignment until the caterpillar treads on the lander touched down on the bay floor and the locking ovals mated and sealed. The huge door now closed and sealed but there was no necessity to pressurise the lander compartment as the astronauts could deplane using the through airlock command seat system as they had done on the roof of Moon Base. As they stepped out of the lander's seats and took their first weightless steps on the starship, Commander AJ greeted them and led them into a four seat maglev buggy.

'Weightlessness might be fun but getting around this starship is by taxi only.' AJ instructed and when they were seated and 'belted up' he touched the screen for dome and the buggy silently moved forward to LifeSeeker-1's command centre.

The bulkhead door hissed open and the buggy containing AJ, Olivia and Scott stopped and the two astronauts stared out into the dome.

Nothing, absolutely nothing could prepare them for the spectacular vista and they gasped as they slowly moved forward from the rear of the 30 metre diameter hemisphere. On either side were wide walkways with banks of controls and instruments and lights of varying colours blinking status of unseen charges. Ahead and seemingly suspended in space, the maglev docked with a slightly downward inclined cantilevered walkway which connected to the wide arc of the seven seat control panel. The two astronauts carefully moved to seats labelled with their names, connected their lap belts and stared out through the huge dome. The view was magnificent.

Meanwhile Commander AJ had picked up Alison and Steve, who, equally stunned, moved to their positions while AJ took his place in the centre. The arc of the command seats curved outwards and forwards towards the clear dome giving everyone a panoramic view of the outside world.

'Astronauts!' AJ commanded, 'Confirm decision to fly to Mars Base.'

The four astronauts and AJ put their left hands onto the control panel and Zec-C confirmed their identity.

'Setting course for Mars Base.'

Almost imperceptibly the Moon's horizon dropped away and LifeSeeker-1 started her relatively low speed journey to Mars. This would only take an incredibly short 14 days.

Chapter 11
Mars Base

'Mars Base is Project Omega. It was designed along similar lines to Moon Base and it has five large modules in total – two for fabrication and sub – assembly, one each for utilities and accommodation and a special module. I had co-ordinated a constant stream of shuttles between Earth, Moon and Mars for the last 20 years. Then I took completed sub – units into Mars orbit to assemble and complete LifeSeeker-1. Now I am continuing the task for the half completed LifeSeeker-2.

'But there is one very unique module on Mars Base and our four astronauts are about to learn a surprising secret.'

'I'd like you to meet Dr Astronaut Martha Baker,' said AJ introducing the four astronauts by name, 'Martha runs the cryo – hibernation unit here at Mars Base and she is going to show you around.'

Martha was in her late 30s with a small neat figure and smooth dark skin encompassing large eyes. She looked very striking in the white hygiene clothing which they had all changed into before entering the air lock.

The inner door hissed open and AJ and the astronauts followed Martha into the cryo-unit. They had seen many strange sights but this white floor- tiled, white-ceilinged, igloo-shaped room shrieked cleanliness and the astronauts felt almost afraid to enter. There was a constant noise of equipment beeping, valves opening and closing and the hiss of air and other gases pressurising and venting.

Martha beckoned them towards the middle of the room where seven lozenge shape units stood on complex support machinery fed by a multitude of pipes and wires. Behind each an LCD screen bristled with data, graphs and various coloured lights. Six of the structures were closed and the seventh stood open with its upper half retracted.

The four astronauts peered closer into the dark translucent upper halves of the closed units and saw that each contained a body!

'My God!' Olivia gasped, 'Are they alive?'

'Very much so,' Martha replied, 'let me introduce you to our six cryo – hibernation volunteers.'

'Who on Earth would volunteer to be frozen?' Steve queried.

‘Well, firstly they’re not frozen but kept at exactly 5 degrees Celsius and secondly on Earth there are still some really bad human beings.’

Martha paused for effect and then moved closer to the first unit.

‘Let me introduce you to Freddie Riggs, 20 years for armed robbery, killed a security guard – no parole. We offered him 15 in cryo and he’s done 10, five to go – he’ll soon be our longest serving cryo.’

Before the astonished astronauts could respond, Martha moved to the second unit. ‘Lisa Greenfield, killed her young child, very sad case, 10 years but could be out in seven for good behaviour – accepted five from us – one down four to go.’

Martha detailed the next four criminals and then stood before the last open unit. ‘Joe ‘bully’ Saunders, 10 years for serious aggravated assault, no parole, accepted seven from us – went home 4 weeks ago in surprisingly good health and hardly looking a day older!’

‘My biggest concern using criminals was maintaining the secrecy and security of the operation at Mars Base. Therefore I chose only those candidates susceptible to hypnosis so that all memories of their stay at Mars Base were erased before returning to Earth.’

‘Is this legal? Is this moral?’ Alison asked. She looked a bit shaken. Olivia was also looking very concerned and Scott wondered if she was thinking about having to go into one of those dark units. They had all heard about cryo – hibernation and that AJ had been through it and survived OK; but now they were confronted with the reality!

‘Oh yes, approved at World Council, ... moral, well, I will let you judge, I’m sure you wouldn’t want to go through this without full and realistic testing and we’ve successfully cryo’d 18 criminals over the last 15 years – and not lost one – Oh, and of course, AJ has been through it out there! But let me give you some of the technical stuff.’

‘It is not possible to freeze someone and then thaw them out in some years’ time – the body is 75% water and when that turns to ice it expands – think of the damage to delicate nerve ends, capillaries. If you cool someone down, they start shivering in an attempt to generate heat and if they can’t generate enough they die

of hypothermia. The key to cryo – hibernation was to cool the body very slowly and at the same time to slow the body functions so that they required very little heat to maintain life. The breakthrough in animal testing 30 years ago was the use of new strains of genetically engineered DNA which were introduced into the body as it cooled. These controlled the slowdown of body functions, pulse, brain activity etc. and through an exothermic reaction produced minute amounts of heat right at the key points of activity. Provided that the cooling and warming periods were long enough, the infused DNA balanced the bodily rates and the amount of heat required.'

Martha continued, her audience quite spellbound. 'In two words, it works, particularly when combined with these sophisticated cocoons which maintain a perfect environment and gently exercise all parts of the body during the cryo. And what you see here is duplicated in LifeSeeker-1.'

'How long could someone remain in cryo?' Scott queried, 'And wake up OK at the end, of course.'

Martha considered her reply very carefully, well aware that the only cryo 'failure' was the loss of StarGazer-1 with Commander Chuck Parker on board.

'I am confident that we could cryo for 50 maybe up to 100 years and certainly for 20 which would get you to Seren. Also, at 5 degrees Celsius, the amounts of gases and drugs consumed are infinitesimally small. These units and the older ones from the Stargazer missions carry enough materials for a hundred year journey – as long as the power source remains active.'

'All very well for you to say that – you haven't got to go into one of your pods.' Steve mused sceptically.

'Oh, but I am, hasn't AJ told you? – I've volunteered to be doc astronaut for this mission and my husband, Pete, is coming as chief engineer!'

AJ smiled; the seven person team for LifeSeeker-1 was now completed.

'A risk assessment is carried out for every new mission and again when any unforeseen changes occur during the operation. I carry out this process against strict criteria, dependent on the type and complexity of the operation, and assign a success rate percentage. Below this number, I, or a member of my family can

abort or modify a mission. Even the commander of a starship cannot override me or one of my team.

'At the time, I assessed this journey to Seren at well below the acceptable value, influenced mainly by the absence of the backup starship which would not be ready for another 5 years. However, because of the unprecedented SOS signal and the voluntary crew, the General takes the decision to go early against my documented advice.

'Even I am overruled!'

BOOK TWO
JOURNEY TO A STAR

Chapter 12
LifeSeeker-2

'Provisioning a starship for a 20 year voyage and then the unknown is a huge undertaking. I ensured that every necessary spare part was carried in sufficient numbers and that all materials and fabrication techniques were available to the crew. The most vital of my tasks was storage of the key gases viz. hydrogen, helium, oxygen, nitrogen, carbon dioxide, chlorine and other specialised gases which were required by the sophisticated equipment aboard LifeSeeker-1, in particular the cryo – hibernation unit. Water is synthesised on demand by the astronauts using hydrogen and oxygen. The aft section of the central tube of the starship is dedicated to gas storage using a concentric arrangement of reinforced high pressure cylinders to contain the precious gases.

'LifeSeeker-1 can generate a significant force field in order to defend itself and, in 'emergency red' condition, can divert most of its power to protecting the starship and its occupants. The most vital requirement is the creation of a streamlined low energy force field to protect it against space dust particles when travelling in ion drive at significant fractions of the speed of light.

'I provisioned LifeSeeker-1 with a large arsenal of weapons from small hand held versions to sophisticated missiles with on board computers to navigate them to specific targets. And, somewhat surprisingly to the astronauts, I included nuclear warheads.'

One month after seeing the astounding distress signal in the conference room at Moon Base, the seven astronauts were sitting, expectantly, in their command seats in the dome of LifeSeeker-1 which was still in orbit around Mars. During the last week they had trained meticulously in safety and evacuation procedures using the emergency shuttles.

'Fellow astronauts,' AJ began, 'before we start our mission, there is one final piece of the jigsaw to show you. I have deliberately kept this off the dome screens.'

The starship slowly changed direction and then, to the astronaut's right a huge shape began to appear in the clear dome.

'LifeSeeker 2,' announced AJ. For a while there was complete silence as the whole of the visible area in front of the astronauts was filled with a behemoth. 'She's more than 1 kilometre away, this is the nearest we're allowed to approach.'

There were whistles and gasps from both teams and even Martha and Pete who had already seen the monster many times.

'It's like an enormous building site in space!' Scott enthused, 'How big is that thing?'

'LifeSeeker-2 is the biggest project I have managed since the building of Mars Base. The ion engine itself is 150 metre diameter by 150 metre long, and there will be four 30 metre diameter, 100 metre long modules – two of these are substantially finished and the third is about 50 per cent completed. I have designed the following - command/cryo/utility, accommodation, spare accommodation/utility and a full research unit which I am currently fabricating at Moon Base.

'The research and the spare accommodation modules are 'removable' and the plan is to attach them to LifeSeeker-1. There's a portal on the underside of this starship, which will become a permanent orbiting station around Cloud Planet. But only if this strange world proves sufficiently interesting.'

Indeed, many parts of the structure were huge arrays of girders yet to be clad with the starship's outer skin. Whilst around it buzzed shuttles which delivered and attached pre-assembled components from their cargo bays.

As detailed drawings appeared on the dome, there were many questions but AJ held up his hand. 'Plenty of time for questions and answers on the first part of our journey but first...'

The General's face appeared on the dome. 'I trust you're now convinced that there is a second starship and she will be on her way just as soon as possible – that's my responsibility and promise to you. I will be in mission control at Mars Base full time watching your every transmission and I pray for two things – your safe and healthy arrival at Cloud Planet and that I live long enough to hear it!' This brought a smile all around. 'But, of course, I will never meet you again, and that is a fact, so good luck to you all, it's been an honour knowing you.' With that his face disappeared.

'OK,' said AJ, 'command! Start mission to Seren.' The astronauts placed their left hands on the console and Zec-C confirmed their identity.

'Mission to Seren - confirmed!'

The starship veered to a new course and started to accelerate.

At last, the journey had begun.

Chapter 13
The Long Sleep

'The journey took them towards Jupiter where I used the huge gravitational pull to sling shot and accelerate LifeSeeker-1 onto a new course. Then I, or should I now say Zec-C, navigated the starship through the tricky asteroid belt and then to the edge of our solar system.

'Initial power was provided by four conventional rocket engines, fuelled by hydrogen / helium propellant, in a cluster at the centre rear of the ion engine. Even in the vacuum of space these consumed significant amounts of fuel and this was one of the limitations that prevented LifeSeeker-1 from returning.

'Then, 2 months into the mission and travelling at 250,000 kilometres per hour and already 180 million kilometres from Mars, I hand over complete control of LifeSeeker-1 to my trusted assistant, Zec-C.

'I continued to monitor the mission from Mars Base but, even at the speed of light, signals are now taking 9 minutes to reach me and would, of course, take longer as the distance increases.

'Meanwhile I know that Zec-C is now shutting down the conventional engines and preparing to 'fire up' the nuclear power reactor. This provides the heat to generate the stream of high speed ions that fire out of the tens of thousands of tubes at the rear of the engine.

'Ultimately pushing the starship to half the speed of light.'

Weightlessness could be fun in short sessions, but as weeks rolled into months the frustration of slow measured movements tested the temperament of the astronauts. At all times they had to wear seat clamps, or tethers when they were free walking. At night they zipped themselves into specially tailored sleeping bags which were fixed to the surface of their beds.

They maintained a normal day / night routine in the starship which was artificially controlled by Zec-C. Their mornings were spent in the command dome and focussed on training and discussion of what lay ahead. After lunch they were put through physical training programmes to maintain their fitness and the rest of the day was for leisure.

But most apparent was the power struggle between Olivia / Scott and Alison / Steve. Both teams wanted desperately to be first to land on Cloud Planet but only one pair would be chosen by the majority vote of all the astronauts. Generally the electioneering was light-hearted but occasionally there were more heated exchanges particularly between Olivia and Steve.

'I notice you're spending a lot of time lately with Martha in the medical bay,' Steve said sharply to Olivia, 'I hope you're not undermining our team!'

'I object to that insinuation!' replied Olivia testily, 'As it happens I've been seeing Martha on a personal matter, which is none of your damned business.'

Of course, the votes of Martha and Pete were crucial and it was hardly surprising that both teams were openly and secretly seeking their support. However, AJ was another matter and they all knew that he would judge purely on professionalism.

'Guys! Lighten up,' Pete interrupted, 'it will be over 20 years before we decide and we don't know if you'll all wake up after cryo! We may not even need to vote!'

The humour fell a little flat but it had helped defuse the rising tension. Finally, they approached the stage in their journey which filled them with apprehension and dread. There was no turning back and the mood was sombre as they looked at each other wondering about their unknown future.

'Conventional rockets shut down and ion engine primed for firing.'

Zec-C informed the astronauts and the mimic display screens changed to show the new status of the starship.

'Command quarter power to ion engine,' AJ instructed and seven left hands reached to the console to confirm the decision.

'Quarter power applied and steady, course now set for Seren,'

The astronauts felt a slight force pushing them into their seats as LifeSeeker-1 noticeably accelerated. In a short time their speed was 500,000 kilometres per hour and still accelerating but this was sluggish compared to the speed they would travel when asleep!'

Then the pivotal moment had arrived as Zec-C announced,

'24 hours and counting down to commencement of cryo–hibernation.'

The astronauts looked at one another with varying feelings and expressions and said in unison.

'Confirm countdown started.'

They immediately had their last meal together before cryo and Martha urged that they eat no further food and should drink sparingly, particularly during the final 4 hours to hibernation. She then advised a good night's sleep and the astronauts separated to their quarters, each with their own thoughts on the uncertain future ahead.

As they boarded the maglev and travelled towards the accommodation block, Olivia said,

'I always wanted to go to bed with you, Scott, but I didn't think it would be for 20 years!'

Seven ghost-like figures clad head to toe in gossamer-thin white breathable tunics shuffled carefully out of the airlock and approached the cryo–hibernation units that would be their homes for the next 20 years. Each carried a bundle of differently coloured tubes in their right hands and Martha led the way. Then they each stood in front of their specifically tailored unit.

They had practised the procedure several times during the voyage under Martha's watchful gaze but now it was time for the real thing. Two hours earlier she had personally attached the three intravenous lines and two catheters to each astronaut and they gingerly carried these lines with their connectors as if they held their own entrails.

Each unit was in its open, recliner position and at a nod from Martha they carefully lowered themselves onto their high tech beds. They engaged the leg, shoulder, waist and groin straps that would hold them in position during their weightless sleep.

'I am particularly proud of the design of these units especially the surface of the bed in contact with the user. This is comprised of thousands of vertically aligned sprung rods of PTFE plastic, whose smooth dome diameter is 2 millimetres, and they perfectly mould to the body shape providing comfort. But this is secondary to the key functions of the bed. Firstly the rods are raised and lowered a few millimetres in sequential horizontal rows from top to toe ensuring that no part of the body is in constant contact with the bed thus eliminating sores. Secondly, groups of rods are raised

and lowered by significant amounts to gently flex the astronaut's neck, backbone, limbs and fingers to maintain flexibility through the protracted hibernation. All these functions are controlled by the unit's computer which is programmed with each astronaut's precise morphology. Signals are sent to the hydraulically controlled pistons at the lower end of each rod enabling the smooth control of every flexing movement. I consider that these beds are a marvel of 22nd century micro-technology.'

At a second nod from Martha, each astronaut pushed home the five tubes they carried into the identically coloured receptors located near their right hand. They looked in turn at their individual diagnostics screen and saw five lights change from red to green confirming that all connections had been correctly made. Anaesthetic and saline would be fed from one of the IV lines and the two genetically engineered drugs would enter the body separately by the other IV. The tiny amounts of waste, mainly water, would be dealt with by the catheters. Each computer was pre-programmed with the individual's precise statistics so that dosage rates matched their metabolism. All major measures - pulse, ECG brain activity, blood pressure and temperature were already being wirelessly transmitted to the diagnostics computer. Martha noted without surprise that several of the astronauts had high pulse rates but not AJ – well, he had been through this before.

She checked that all seven sets of lights were green and again nodded. Each traveller slipped on their own pair of tailored goggles which were already connected to the unit and pressed a switch on the side of the spectacles – a light changed from red to green on each monitor.

'The average human blinks 30-40 times per minute during waking hours and this ensures that the surface of the eyeball remains lubricated with liquid from the tear ducts. After a night's sleep we sometimes have a little difficulty opening our eyes but after 20 years? During the day the computer is programmed to send a signal every 5 seconds to each astronaut's goggles where a short burst of harmless radiation causes spasms in the muscle controlling the blinking process. At the same time, a tiny amount of synthetic tear liquid is atomised in front of each eyeball and condenses onto it thus maintaining lubrication.'

And now, at a final nod from Martha, the astronauts donned their face masks ensuring that they fitted snugly. These carried oxygen to and carbon dioxide away from the mouth and in deep cryo would provide the tiny amount of oxygen needed to sustain stable activity at 5 degrees Celsius. Once more a switch was engaged on the mask and a reassuring light changed colour on the console.

She repeatedly looked along the banks of monitors and was satisfied that all the astronauts, including herself, were correctly hooked up and all life signs were as reasonable as could be expected for people entering the unknown.

Meanwhile Zec-C was also carefully monitoring each step taken by the astronauts and the hundreds of other functions supporting the complex technology of the cryo-process. All key data was immediately, or as fast as the speed of light would permit, transmitted to Mission Control at Mars Base where rows of personnel scanned the vital information. The General personally supervised these activities and hardly slept at all during the early part of the mission.

Zec-C's quiet voice interrupted their thoughts,

'Confirm all astronauts correctly connected to cryo-units, permission to commence cryo–hibernation.'

Martha raised her right hand and gave a thumbs up and each astronaut followed suit. What a strange sight they looked clad in white, wearing weird-looking masks and goggles and with five coloured tubes snaking from their bodies. They then each placed their hands into gauntlets fixed to the sides of their units and palm readers inside each glove confirmed their individual identities. A larger light at the top of each monitor changed from red to green.

'Confirmation received, all astronauts correctly hooked up, commencing cryo–hibernation, next stop Seren.'

Olivia heard a quiet whirr of machinery and the recliner slowly moved to the horizontal position. She had been dreading this moment but had been assured by Martha that she would be anaesthetised and sound asleep many hours before the cryo-unit closed on top of her. Olivia was concerned about dreams, but Martha had assured her that brain activity at 5 degrees was minimal and none of her 'criminals' had ever complained of a bad night's sleep.

About one hour later, Olivia felt a slight cold sensation running up her right arm and then nothing – all the astronauts were asleep within seconds and being monitored carefully by Zec-C. Four hours later Zec-C closed the cryo-lids and commenced the cooling process. The astronauts' bodies would cool at 0.3 degrees Celsius per 24 hours and it would be 3 months before 5 degrees was achieved. Well before then, the controlled doses of the two DNA drugs would be continuously administered.

'Apart from looking after his charges, Zec-C is programmed by me to speed up the starship by applying full power to the ion engine. As the ship accelerates so the force field generated around it increases creating a slipstream that would deflect radiation and any small particles around the ship thus causing no harm. However, objects above the size of a tennis ball are another matter and need to be detected by the starship's ultra violet telescope located in the centre front of the dome. Very early identification is needed because at half the speed of light an object 14 million kilometres away would be reached in 100 seconds and quicker still if it is travelling at speed towards the starship. Thus the probe on the front of LifeSeeker-1 is monitoring space for hundreds of millions of kilometres in front of it and analysing if anything posed a threat. If so, Zec-C orders an almost infinitesimal increase in thrust to one or more of the eight lateral thrusters to change course and avoid the danger.

'LifeSeeker-1, carrying its precious cargo of astronauts at 5 degrees Celsius, achieved half the speed of light 1 year after leaving Mars Base.'

Chapter 14
Wakey, Wakey

'Whilst Zec-C carefully looks after his charges, I am extremely busy during the next 20 years. I complete LifeSeeker-2 on time and she departs for Seren in 2156 with Commander Brian Harrington at the helm. LifeSeeker-3 is built, an identical copy of 2, and she leaves Mars in 2162. Her destination is to be decided when news comes back from Cloud Planet, but that is not for another 10 years.

'Now I am embarking on my most ambitious project to date. This is a very complex enterprise which establishes a base on Titan, one of Jupiter's moons.'

White........ pure brilliant white........ that seemed to go on and on. No boundaries and no definition; this whiteness appeared to have been there for ages. Then, very slowly, slightly darker edges formed and they sharpened and became shapes around the white.

Olivia then realised that she was looking upwards at what she thought was a tiled ceiling. She could not place it in her mind as she was disorientated and continued to stare upwards for an unknown period of time.

Sounds..... bizarre sounds.......that grew in her awareness. They took on form – whirrs, beeps and hisses – and Olivia realised that she had heard these noises before, had seen this ceiling before – but where?

Now a voice, soft and soothing but strange,

'Olivia relax, relax, you are waking up, Olivia, relax,'

Zec-C quietly intoned from a speaker near her ear.

Her life signs were perfect with blood temperature normal at 36 degrees Celsius as she lay horizontally in the now open cryo-unit; the first person to have consciousness. In fact, all the units were open and during the next hour or two all of the astronauts would start to 'wake up' guided by Zec-C's quiet assurance.

'Olivia, you are now awake....'

Zec-C softly continued,

'....welcome, welcome to the year 2171.'

Suddenly, everything flashed clearly in her mind – the white ceiling, the noises, the voice in her ear, the training, the journey, this room! She had arrived! Had they all survived? And although she could not yet speak her mind shouted out...

'Oh, my God! .... I'm 55 years old!'

Although all the astronauts had awoken during a 3 hour period, they did not leave their units for four long days. During this period Zec-C coached their minds and bodies. Limbs were exercised and flexed to gradually increasing degrees by their mechanical masseur. After 3 days the cryo-beds slowly moved to the reclining position and Zec-C instructed them to remove their goggles and masks, but to take their time. Each astronaut now looked at their diagnostic screens, amazed to see normal heart beats and blood temperature. They were relieved to see that all monitoring lights were reassuringly green.

They turned their heads and looked at each other and smiled, or tried to smile and raised weak hands limply. They made sounds like whispers though not very coherent at this early stage.

'Olivia, are you awake? Are you OK?' croaked a groggy Scott; their pods were next to each other. She stiffly turned her head and tried to smile.

'I'm OK I think. How do I look?'

'Wonderful, not a day older!' Scott weakly replied. Their voices were barely above a whisper and they could hear muted greetings as the other astronauts communicated for the first time in over 20 years.

Then Martha raised her right hand and made a thumbs up and each fellow traveller did likewise and, as if on autopilot, placed their left hands palm down on the small console in their units.

'Confirm! Confirm all astronauts safely awakened and recovered from cryo–hibernation!' Zec-C triumphantly announced.

This message was simultaneously transmitted by LifeSeeker-1 into the vastness of space but it would be 10 years before it was heard at mission control on Mars.

On the 4th day and after two more hours of exercise, Zec-C instructed Martha to start the process of evacuation from the cryo-units. She then pointed to the coloured tubes and nodded. In a rehearsed sequence she removed hers one by one, waiting as each astronaut uncoupled the identically coloured line in turn.

Now the astronauts were no longer 'tied' to their units – all they had to do was get up and walk!

Zec-C encouraged them to move their body weight forward and to push with their arms on the sides of the units. After many failed attempts they finally struggled onto wobbly legs and held on to steady themselves. In front of them was a horizontal maglev escalator and they took their first shaky steps towards it for 20 years. Then, clutching the support rail with their left hand and carrying their 'entrails' in the other, Zec-C told them to hold tight.

Seven ghost-like figures clad head to toe in gossamer thin white breathable tunics were transported slowly out of the cryo-room, through the airlock and into the preparation room. Here they would remain for a further two days to complete their recuperation, taking in sustenance and sleeping on a normal bed.

Six days after awakening from cryo, Martha was satisfied with the health and fitness of the astronauts. Zec-C had also monitored their physical wellbeing and had set them all mental tests during their recuperation. Now they came to a most crucial stage in their rehabilitation. At a nod from Martha, AJ led them to the airlock. In turn they all pressed their left hands to a panel near the airlock door and waited anxiously. Each watched the red light, nervously, and then with relief as it turned green.

'Confirm all astronauts ready to return to duty!'

They smiled at one another with joy and high-fived and slapped backs as the airlock hissed open.

'My astronauts know in the back of their minds that only those 'deemed sound in body and mind by Zec-C' will be allowed back into the starship after the rigours of cryo-hibernation.'

Chapter 15
Message from Mars

'During the starship's half-light speed journey, the dome is maintained in full red emergency mode and remains so during controlled deceleration by Zec-C. The nuclear power source is shut down and tiny amounts of reverse thrust are applied over a 3 month period to reduce the speed of LifeSeeker-1 to its new velocity of 150,000 kilometres per hour – a mere sloth when compared to its 20 year journey at 150,000 kilometres per second!'

The astronauts sat in their command seats in front of the blackened dome. Their excitement could not be contained as they continued to stare at one another in amazement.

'We haven't aged a bit, I can't believe it!' Olivia said, 'Martha, if you could bottle this as an anti-ageing treatment it would be worth billions!'

'Trouble is it cost trillions to produce!' Martha replied with a grin.

'Attention astronauts! I have three things to show you.'

A large section of the black dome coloured in front of the expectant crew and the shape of the fully completed LifeSeeker-2 dominated their view.

'Five years ago, I received confirmation that LifeSeeker-2 had departed on its journey to Seren.'

The astronauts cheered and clapped at this news.

'And I can confirm that all 21 astronauts are safely in cryo–hibernation and travelling at half the speed of light.'

Their eyes moved to a smaller screen and the General's face appeared.

'If Zec-C is showing you this, then I thank God that you have arrived at your star and safely emerged from cryo–hibernation. It will be another 15 years before I know this, provided I live that long! You are nearly there and Zec-C has shown you LifeSeeker-2 which is on its way to join you.

'Now you are on your own and you can hardly ring mission control for help or advice! Who knows what you will find at Cloud Planet. You will, undoubtedly, have to take some key decisions; some may be difficult, unpleasant or even frightening. I agreed with

Commander AJ before you left that major strategic or life threatening decisions would be by secret ballot, majority applies. In the event of a tie, AJ will make the casting vote – there can be no abstentions. In AJ's absence - and I don't think he's going anywhere – Martha will assume the role of mission commander and the same rules will apply.

'Now I must remind you of the key instructions you must follow when investigating the SOS message which is still signalling to us here on Mars.

'You must observe thoroughly and gather sufficient information to make controlled decisions.

'You must obey the quarantine procedures to the letter.

'You must be very careful not to interact with whatever is on that planet - this is a key interplanetary code.

'Above all, your safety is paramount – if in doubt pull out and wait for LifeSeeker-2.

'And so fellow astronauts, I wish you a successful mission and I will be watching your progress for as long as God permits me. Good luck and good–bye!'

With that his face disappeared and the whole dome started changing from black, through grey and then translucent. Suddenly outer space filled the horizon and what a spectacular sight awaited the astronauts.

BOOK THREE
CLOUD PLANET

Chapter 16
Survey

The astronauts sat spellbound. To the upper left of the dome a bright golden orb dominated the vista, illuminating its space with brilliant rays.

'The star Seren is about 20 per cent bigger than our sun but of similar intensity, and is approximately 150 million kilometres away. Seren has seven orbiting planets, four of which are gas giants like Jupiter and two are ringed planets similar to Saturn.'

An arrow took their eye to the lower right of the dome, where there was a ball of multi-coloured swirling gases.

'Four times the size of Jupiter and about 50 million kilometres from LifeSeeker 1 – I can already sense its huge gravitational field – this is as close as we get.'

The backdrop of space was an intense blue, deepening to purples and blacks and studded with specs of light.

'The other stars of the constellation of Vircingetorix and, in the centre......'

Zec-C paused and the astronauts leaned forward in anticipation as an arrow highlighted a larger spec of light,

'......our first view of Cloud Planet. She is about 30 million kilometres from us and 140 million from her star.'

'Comparable to the distance between the Sun and Earth.' Mused Scott to no one in particular and, then, he peered closer. 'Is it my imagination or can I see faint streaks of light from the planet towards the star?'

By way of answer, Zec-C magnified the image incrementally until it occupied a large slice of the dome. The planet was truly remarkable with brilliant white caps at its poles and huge swathes of deep blue on either side of its equator. But most astounding was the huge collar of white and grey that completely encircled the strange world at its equator.

'The planet is 50,000 kilometres in circumference at the equator, a little larger than earth, and the white collar is 2000 kilometres wide and approximately 50 kilometres above 'sea' level. It

is rotating on an axis with its poles absolutely perpendicular to its star – that means the white collar points directly at Seren during each revolution which takes 20 of our hours.'

It was difficult to digest all these statistics because the astronauts were transfixed by the light shafts that emanated from within the collar. As they shot outwards in the direction of Seren, they seemed to merge into one shaft of light. However, as the eye moved towards the demarcation of day and night, so the light shafts stopped and the cloud collar became darker.

'Is there a land mass beneath those clouds?' this from Steve.

'Yes, and it is approximately 2000 kilometres wide but we need to get nearer before I can penetrate that thick cloud with our instruments for a detailed topography. I can only analyse the day / night delineation as our instruments are interfered with by the light shafts.'

'And the signal? Is that still flashing? Alison asked.

'Yes, but you won't be able to see it until we are much closer and I will be able to analyse all the shafts of light in more detail – there are thousands of them. For information, our estimated time of arrival at high orbit above Cloud Planet is 10 days.'

'I can't wait,' cried an excited Olivia, 'can't we go faster?'

But AJ just smiled; he was well aware of Olivia's impatience. 'We've taken over 20 years to get this far – a few more days seems nothing and we've got work to do.'

'There is a lot of retraining planned for our astronauts during the coming days. They take the two ROL's into space to practice manoeuvres and re-docking with LifeSeeker-1 – after all none of them has flown for over 20 years. Finally, all the astronauts practise using the emergency shuttles.'

Every day Cloud Planet grew in their visual field of view and with 2 days to go to orbit, the astronauts were in the command dome and Zec-C was giving a more detailed analysis of the planet.

'The atmosphere is a very healthy 30 per cent oxygen with nitrogen being the volume gas and small levels of carbon dioxide. The ice caps at the poles are approximately 1000 kilometres in diameter and are surprisingly symmetrical. The oceans are massive and

extremely deep at over 200 kilometres for most of their area. The seas have high salt levels and are cold, cycling from minus 1-2 Celsius from night to day. The cloud collar is 30 degrees at the top but falls in temperature quickly. I estimate nearer 5 degrees during the day dropping to near zero at night. I predict that it is continuously raining during the day and pouring down at night with high winds.

Below the clouds is a 2000 kilometre continuous land mass which encircles the planet and is equally distributed either side of the equator.'

As Zec-C continued, the facts were illustrated in the dome with computer simulated drawings and diagrams and now the topography of the land mass appeared.

'There is a 1000 kilometre wide central plain, mainly clay based, around the equator and about 5 kilometres above sea level. This is flanked on both sides by mountain ranges rising up to 20 kilometres above sea level and punctuated by valleys with large water flows running to the seas – these are irregular in shape and can be assumed as 'rivers' – there are many hundreds of them on both sides of the central plain.'

The computer graphics continued to paint the picture of a very uniform planet with its narrow equatorial land mass directly pointed at its star at all times.

'Initial data shows that the mountains and valleys are completely covered in organic vegetation but I will detail this when we get nearer.'

Zec-C paused, *'and now the symmetry gets intriguing.'*

And parallel lines appeared across the plain and perpendicular to the equator.

'These lines represent water and each runs the full width of the plain –1,000 kilometres in a dead straight line. Each water course is 50 kilometres apart and there are exactly one thousand straddling the equator – I can only presume they have not been produced by natural forces and that they are 'canals'!'

The mimic display then drew two thicker lines around the equator.

'These equatorial lines are wider watercourses and like the others they are perfectly straight and are 25,000 kilometres long – the equatorial circumference of Cloud Planet!'

There was a buzz of excitement among the astronauts but the best was yet to come.

'The shafts of light appear to originate from points directly along each lateral canal and are 50 kilometres apart. There are 20 along each canal symmetrically distributed about the equator making a total of 20,000 emanating from the planet and just under half are illuminated at any one time.'

Spellbound, the astronauts peered intensely at the display and the shafts of light which appeared to rotate like the spokes of a wheel.

'These shafts of light are 'switching' on and off in rows every 1.2 minutes as the planet rotates on its axis. Finally those near the equator are more intense than their peripheral neighbours and there are regularly spaced very intense light shafts distributed around the equator itself.'

The astronauts continued to be amazed at the complex symmetry unfolding – surely this was the work of an intelligent life form – but guessing was all they could do at this point.

'The light shaft which has been flashing SOS for 25 years is situated on the equator and is of medium intensity.'

On the mimic display, one of the light shafts now started flashing in the now familiar – dot dot dot – dash dash dash – dot dot dot - signal that had brought them 'rushing' to investigate.

'And now,' continued Zec-C, *'look at the real planet at optimum magnification!'*

The mimic display disappeared and nearly the whole dome filled with a view of Cloud Planet – it was breath taking. They could see details in the ice caps, seas of blues disappearing under the white cloud collar. They watched these mesmerising shafts of golden light streaking out into space and the whole planet seemed to jerk around as one row of lights extinguished and another illuminated at the extremes of the planet day.

And there, in the very centre, one shaft of light pulsed –
dot dot dot – dash dash dash – dot dot dot
dot dot dot – dash dash dash – dot dot dot
dot dot dot – dash dash dash – dot dot dot

'This is the most unbelievable sight I have ever seen!' cried Scott, 'What on 'Earth' is happening below those clouds? What is causing those circular shafts of light? What or who is generating the message?'

Surprisingly Zec-C answered,

'I cannot answer your direct questions but can only deduce from measurements and facts; but here is an interesting observation. If I, a mere computer, were responsible for this signal then it would start and finish precisely, to 2 decimal points of a second, at the same time each day. Also each repeat would be to the same accuracy. Therefore I deduce that this signal which varies its start, finish and repeat times is not generated by a precision source. However, it does operate for approximately 2 hours every day either side of noon at this same position on the planet.'

'I recall from my studies that Morse code operators were recognisable by their style of tapping the message,' advised Olivia, ' I believe it was called 'their signature' – are we seeing a signature here? – is this distress call being sent by a life form!'

The astronauts could only look at one another in astonishment – what would they find on Cloud Planet?

Chapter 17
High Orbit and First Landing

'21 years after leaving Mars base, LifeSeeker-1 moved into orbit 1,000 kilometres above Cloud Planet. The orbit was carefully chosen to keep the starship well outside the radiating shafts of light and to keep the day side of the planet in view at all times. Now it is possible to see the detail of the planet with the naked eye.'

As the crew stared at this beautiful planet, they were interrupted by the voice of AJ.

'Fellow astronauts, Zec C has analysed various approaches to landing on the planet surface and there are three possibilities. Firstly, there is a vertical descent from high altitude directly at the diagonal intersection of four outer light shafts – the less intense ones. The probability for success is calculated at 65-70 per cent. Secondly, a lateral insertion into the cloud collar from a point out to sea and 3 kilometres altitude. Then follow the large estuary and enter the light shafts between two outermost ones to the same diagonal intersection – and of course then descending. The probability for success is 80-85 per cent.'

For each descent a mimic display showed the plan – it looked easy enough on the screen.

'The third scenario is a night landing on the dark side of the planet for which there is insufficient data to calculate a success probability. We know that this is a wild and turbulent atmosphere through which to descend.'

'It looks like the lateral insertion then?' said Scott and there was general agreement among the astronauts.

'Yes,' agreed AJ, 'so we all confirm the second, lateral option.'

'And now we come to our first strategic decision which is a secret vote, majority carries. As you know you have a decision palm reader under your console with accept and reject buttons. The motion is to decide which team carries out the first landings on this planet as only one ROL will be deployed at any one time. For Olivia and Scott in ROL-1 press 'one' and for Alison and Steve in ROL-2 press 'two'.'

Then, at AJ's command, hands went below the console and both teams looked anxiously at the dome screen. It showed four to three in favour of ROL-1. Olivia and Scott would be the first to attempt a landing on Cloud Planet.

Alison and Steve looked away in disappointment but were the first to offer congratulations and good luck to their fellow astronauts.

'How far does the cloud collar overlap the sea?' AJ questioned.

'Between half a kilometre and 1 kilometre depending on whether its day or night,' Zec-C replied, 'and the height also varies from 40 - 50 kilometres for the same reason. Also there is a dark fringe at the edge of the sea which seems to be present most of the way around the land mass on both seaboards but I cannot identify the nature or extent of this.'

'Anything else about this planet that's unusual?' Alison asked.

'The icecaps,' Zec-C continued, 'are surprisingly thin at the very centre but I will need a pass directly overhead to analyse this anomaly in more detail.'

'But that defies logic.' Steve blurted, 'How can that happen?'

'Maybe there are thermal vents under the icecaps, that's not unusual – it happens on Earth,' suggested Olivia.

'Could be, but we'll have to wait for the next pass for confirmation,' AJ concluded.

Scott then enquired, 'Zec-C, what further analysis have you made of these circular light shafts?'

'Well, you will be surprised to learn that they are not circles of light,' Zec-C paused, 'but all the shafts exit the clouds as perfect octagons.'

'Octagons! How intriguing! This planet gets more and more curious.' exclaimed Olivia, 'What more can you tell us about the vegetation?'

'Analysis indicates extensive forests but we will get more information when the lander travels up the valley.'

LifeSeeker-1 was positioned 500 kilometres above the point where the lander would enter the cloud. This was the nearest the huge starship could come to the planet to optimise deployment of the lander and maintain communications.

ROL-1 was now stationed 1 kilometre from the cloud collar and 3 kilometres above sea level. The ocean was surprisingly calm and there appeared to be no significant tidal movement. After all, there were no moons associated with this unexpectedly symmetrical planet.

Olivia and Scott were gazing through the dome. The white mass of cloud towered above the lander, dwarfing it. From this position they could not see the light shafts which they knew started about 500 kilometres directly in front of them.

'Confirm decision to enter cloud collar.'

This was Zec-1 issuing instructions, and two hands in the lander and five in LifeSeeker-1 moved forward to ratify the decision.

ROL-1 entered the cloud collar directly above a large estuary, estimated at 1 kilometre across, but the two astronauts could not see this as rain and cloud had reduced visibility to 150 metres at best. The mimic display on the dome showed their position and the increasingly sloping land to either side. After about 200 kilometres the estuary had narrowed considerably and the mountains towered above them on both sides.

'Both sides are thickly carpeted with forests of huge trees,'

Zec-1 informed them as they watched the dome display.

'My initial estimates are that many of them are up to 300 metres high and between 3 and 4 metres diameter. We are now half way to our destination and 2 kilometres above the river below. My analysis of the river water shows that it is exceptionally pure but with high chlorine levels. Air and river temperatures are 5 degrees.'

Travelling at 500 kilometres per hour, ROL 1 soon approached the edge of the plain where speed was reduced to 100 kilometres per hour. The lander was now 1 kilometre above the river and dead ahead of them the mist and rain seemed lighter and their horizon took on a strange light.

'Passing midway between first two light shafts,' Zec-1 continued, *'significant interference on certain instruments already being felt – applying low level force shield - contact with LifeSeeker 1 now lost.'*

'We're on our own,' Scott said to Olivia, 'look at this unusual light and it's still raining out there.'

'Reducing lander forward speed to zero and adjusting for hover conditions over diagonal intersection. We are now approximately 35 kilometres from each light source with interference increasing. Confirm command to descend to 500 metres.' Zec-1 requested.

Both astronauts confirmed the decision in the usual way.

'Approaching 500 metres, interference increasing rapidly, probability of successful landing now 60-65 per cent – warning!' Zec-1 urged, *'Applying more force field.'*

Olivia and Scott knew they were approaching a critical position in the descent. If probability remained above 60 per cent, they could make the decision to continue the descent but it was now touch and go. Below 60 and Zec-1 would take control and abort descent. The astronauts looked at one another and Scott nodded.

'Descend to 400 metres.' Scott instructed. But before this altitude could be achieved Zec-1's voice boomed in the command dome.

'Emergency! Emergency! Probability less than 60 per cent and falling! Abort descent! Abort descent!'

And with that the lander turned its nose upwards at 45 degrees and the four thrusters underneath surged to full power. The huge g-force pushed them back into their seats and the skin on their faces was drawn back tightly into a severe grimace which matched the mood and disappointment of the two astronauts.

LifeSeeker-1 regained communications with ROL-1 just after it passed the line of the outer light shafts and there was immediate consternation as Zec-C immediately signalled the emergency withdrawal from the cloud. As they stared out of the dome, ROL-1 shot out of the cloud.

They were all seated in the command dome of LifeSeeker-1 analysing the failed landing attempt when Scott asked Zec-C.

'How far apart would those light shafts have to be for a successful landing?'

'According to my estimates and based on the lander's information at 400 metres, we would need to be a minimum of 50 kilometres from the light shafts and there is nowhere on that plain where they are more than 35 kilometres apart.'

'And what more did we learn as we travelled up that valley?' queried Olivia.

'The forests are dominated by one species of giant tree. Most are in excess of 100 metres high with girths varying from 3-5 metres. Huge fleshy leaves are clustered at the canopy and the trunks are perpendicular and remarkably straight sided. Further, there is

evidence of large clay structures every 50 kilometres along one side of the river bank but the landers instruments were affected by the light shafts so I cannot be more precise.'

'The same distance apart as the light shafts,' continued Olivia, 'even more unusual symmetry.'

'Thank you Zec-C,' AJ said, 'I think we now need a plan for a night landing for ROL-1.'

'Wait a minute!' interrupted Steve, 'Why is it assumed that Olivia and Scott go again? They've had their go, so now it's ours.'

Alison nodded in agreement and Olivia's face darkened and she shot her a black look.

'It wasn't our fault that we couldn't land and we were voted first to go down onto the planet,' Olivia replied sharply.

Scott held up his hand in mediation, 'Zec-C, please repeat the exact words of the motion.'

'The motion is to decide which team carries out the first landings on the planet as only one lander will be deployed at any one time,' Zec-C confirmed.

'First landings, plural, ladies and gentlemen,' AJ intervened firmly, 'the matter is concluded in favour of ROL-1.'

'This species of tree is a softwood with similarities to the pine. Their height is limited by the ability to raise water by capillary action against the gravitational pull of Cloud Planet. Even so, they achieve up to 120 metres and with girths of 4 – 5 metres they are formidable structures. On Earth the tallest tree is the Douglas Fir which can reach 138 metres as the result of the lower gravity compared to the larger Cloud Planet.'

Chapter 18
Night Landing

'LifeSeeker-1 was now moved to a position 500 kilometres above sea level on the night side of Cloud Planet. This is a different world – blue grey ice caps, grey seas and the black angry mass of the cloud collar rising 50 kilometres into the inky night sky. Zec- C's analysis showed torrential rain, swirling winds and temperatures around zero degrees in the clouds. Near the edges of the plain, high cliffs tower up to the thickly-forested mountains and these cause turbulent storms for 50-100 kilometres inland.

'For this reason, a landing target is selected half way between the cliff edge and the equator where turbulence is less severe and they are far away from the larger of the light shafts. The central area is made entirely of clay with structures which are symmetrically distributed at the locus of each light shaft. At the time, the nature of these structures was difficult to discern because of the thick cloud and the fact that they are composed of the same material as the plain.'

ROL-1 was hovering 70 kilometres above the target landing spot as Olivia and Scott looked out of the dome at the seething black clouds below them.

'Confirm command to descend at 50 kilometres per hour.'

Zec-1 requested and all of the astronauts complied in unison.

'Good luck to both of you,' said AJ from the starship.

As the lander descended and entered the cloud, they lost their view of the outside and watched the dome displays as they showed position, height and speed relative to the target landing spot. Meanwhile Zec-1 called out height above ground at regular intervals. Considering that conditions outside were appalling, the lander made a very stable descent under Zec-1's control and at 1 kilometre from the surface, descent speed was reduced to 10 kilometres per hour. Now the astronauts could feel the buffeting of the strong winds causing the lander to swing and yaw slightly.

'Two hundred metres from touchdown and descent speed now 100 metres per minute.'

‘Two minutes to go,’ exclaimed Scott as the tension mounted. Olivia was staring hard at the dome desperate to see something but visibility remained zero.

‘Thirty metres from touchdown, descent 10 metres per minute.’

And 3 minutes later, the 4 caterpillar tracks bit into the slushy clay surface, sinking half a metre before coming to rest.

‘ROL 1 touchdown confirmed, all systems good’.

There was a moment of silence in both the lander and the starship 500 kilometres above and then there were shouts and claps from all the astronauts. Then AJ’s voice could be heard over the celebrations.

‘Congratulations Olivia and Scott, first astronauts to land on a planet of another star system. What a momentous occasion.’

Olivia turned and high-fived Scott and both gave thumbs-up gestures to the smiling faces on the dome display. Then they looked out. The rain was torrential and they could just distinguish the surface for about 15 metres in front of the lander. There were huge strange leaves strewn about and stalks sticking out of a water surface drilled with the bucketing rain. They felt like they had landed in a paddy field.

‘It’s not exactly a holiday camp out there,’ joked Olivia, as pictures of their surroundings appeared on the dome and were simultaneously shown in the starship.

‘Terrain flat and level with no major obstructions. Confirm decision to traverse to designated light shaft.’

All astronauts confirmed and the lander’s wide tracks started turning and found purchase on the surprisingly firmer clay under the muddy surface.

‘Speed 5 kilometres per hour and steady on course.’

It was now the equivalent of midnight and it would take 4 hours to reach their goal.

Conditions did not change. All they could see were leaves, some huge, maybe 2 metres across, and stalks with leaves on them presumably growing in the slushy clay. Some of these ‘plants’ were up to 2 metres high and grew in thick plantations. The lander seemed to glide through this vegetation, crushing and brushing it aside.

‘Target 100 metres ahead. There is definitely a large structure made of the same clay as the ground. I’m analysing data so I can put it on dome. Proceeding to a point 15 metres from the front edge.’

‘I can’t wait. What do you think we’ll find?’ said Olivia excitedly as she craned forward as far as her seat clamp would allow.

‘Patience Olivia, all will be revealed soon enough by Zec-1’, countered Scott in his usual controlled fashion but he was also leaning forward in fevered anticipation.

Although it was just after four in the morning, it would soon be dawn on this planet with its 20 hour rotation and already it had lightened somewhat and the rain had decreased in intensity. Visibility was now much improved and the outside ‘world’ was about to reveal itself.

Chapter 19
Intelligent Design

Olivia and Scott strained forward as far as their command seats would let them and pointed as, out of the gloom, a red wall materialised in front of them. From their vantage point about 3.5 metres above ground, they could see that the wall was about 3 metres high, 25 metres wide and a couple of metres deep. Then at each extremity it turned and disappeared into the gloom.

'What have we got here, Zec-1?' Scott queried and in answer Zec-1 started drawing the structure in plan view on the dome.

'What you are seeing is the front wall of a regular octagon, 100 metres in 'diameter', 3 metres high and 2 thick. It is constructed entirely of the same clay as the ground. Inside, to our left, are four large triangular shapes each filled with water. The structure is sitting at the edge of one of the lateral canals which is situated on the far side from our lander position.'

The mimic display showed the plan view, and then rotated to 3 dimensional mode to give the same aspect that they were looking at. Visibility had increased further and they could see half the octagon and two of the triangular structures – these seemed to be at different heights but below the level of the outer wall.

'This must have been made by an intelligent species,' Olivia cried, 'look, look – it's a perfect eight sided figure.' Dimensions had appeared on the display showing that each side was, indeed, the same length within a few centimetres.

'There are multiple water flows within the structure which are emanating from the canal. The water travels around the walls, cascades into the triangular structures and then overflows to a central narrow canal leaving the octagon underground almost below our position.'

In both starship and lander, the astronauts watched spellbound as the details unfolded before them but that was nothing compared to what they were about to hear.

Olivia and Scott could now see the whole structure and the canal behind it. The inside was strewn with leaves of all sizes – the raised profile obviously collected the windblown vegetation. They could see water flowing right in front of them in two channels in the top of the wall separated by – it looked similar to a seemingly castellated partition. It was Olivia who first saw glints of reflection.

'What are those 'glass like bricks' in the centre and do they, yes, they do, seem to run around the whole periphery of the octagon. They appear to separate the two flows. No, that's not right. The water flow is passing through the gaps in the bricks.'

Everyone strained forward to see and sure enough at regular intervals were hundreds of these 'glass bricks' sticking out of the water flow. It was Zec-1 who, as ever, applied the startling technical analysis.

'Each brick is 30 centimetres long by 20 wide and 15 high – nearly as big as a breezeblock – and they are spaced 20 centimetres apart. I estimate that there are two every metre, 60 on each limb of the octagon and 480 in total around the central partition.'

'What are they made of?' this from Olivia.

'Pure carbon, absolutely pure carbon.'

Zec-1 said and waited.

'You mean DIAMOND!' Scott shouted astounded.

'Christ!' Olivia gasped.

'Each is a multifaceted crystal of the whitest purest diamond and I estimate that each weighs about 30 kilograms which is approximately 150,000 carats.'

The atmosphere in the lander and the starship was electric and filled with unanswered questions when AJ brought everyone back to reality.

'You are almost passing into daytime, ROL-1, and we have some of our answers, but we will lose communications shortly.

'Command Zec-1! Back away from structure to safer observation position.'

All astronauts complied and the lander started moving.

'My research shows that the Cullinan diamond was the largest crystal found on Earth in 1905. In its rough uncut state it weighed 621.35 grams, just over 3100 carats. The largest cut gem from this is the Great Star of Africa at 530 grams and about 106 carats. The 150,000 carat diamonds which are found on Cloud Planet are not only enormous but have perfect crystalline morphology.'

Olivia and Scott were so absorbed that they hadn't noticed that the light had increased dramatically. It was still raining but now there was an eerie glow as the sun was trying to break through the clouds.

'Temperature increasing in the diamonds nearest the rising sun.'

Zec-1 informed them. They had backed to 100 metres from the octagon.

'Temperature now 400 - 500 hundred degrees.'

They stared and could not believe their eyes as the nearest diamonds began to glow red, then orange.

'Temperature approaching 1000 degrees.'

They glowed white and were enveloped with steam from the water running through them and then........

It didn't make a noise, but Olivia and Scott snapped back in their seats as a streak of white light shot from the diamonds back over their heads and disappeared into the clouds.

'Emergency! Emergency!'

Zec-1's voice boomed,

'Confirm back away, applying low force field plus dome darkening.'

The astronauts complied and watched in awe as more diamonds grew hot and exploded in light. They stared as, slowly and symmetrically, new crystals on each side of the centre line flashed into life circling the octagon in a sheath of light that would have hurt their eyes were it not for the protection of the darkened dome.

From a distance of 500 metres they watched as a complete sheath of light circled the structure and stretched up through the clouds above them. They had their answer to the origin of the beams of light but what 'on this planet' was the reason for the design and its internal triangular structures?

'Why the sheath of light? And who or what caused it?' Olivia thought aloud.

‘Well that’s what I call a light display,’ exclaimed Scott, ‘I guess that’s the most efficient laser system I have ever witnessed.’ However only Olivia and Zec-1 heard this comment as communications with LifeSeeker-1 had been lost some minutes before.

‘It is the unique internal structure of these diamonds, which I have analysed in detail, which explains how sunlight is collimated into a wide razor thin shaft and is then reflected back towards Seren. This produces a high intensity natural laser and the close proximity of the crystals produces the continuous sheath of light around the octagon.’

Chapter 20
Into the Light

'And now, all our astronauts can do is wait so they take the opportunity to catch up on much needed sleep. Zec-1 wakes them shortly before the shaft of light switches off allowing communications to resume with LifeSeeker-1 to plan the next stage.'

When Olivia and Scott returned, refreshed, to the command dome the first thing they noticed was that the sheath of light was now angled away from them in the direction of the setting sun. Then, the diamonds at the front edge of the octagon, that had lit up first, suddenly 'switched' off and slowly a window appeared in front of them. Both astronauts wished that they could run up and look in but knew they had to temper their curiosity.

Slowly all the crystals switched off in a symmetrical fashion until finally the light sheath was completely gone. Zec-1 moved the lander so that it was 10 metres from the front of the octagon and they peered eagerly through the rain and deepening cloud.

It was like looking into a sauna with steam rising from the surface of the triangular pools and from the water that was circulating around the diamonds.

'Water temperature in the pools is 40-45 degrees; atmosphere has a high chlorine level.'

What surprised them most was that the whole area was pristine. No sign of all the messy vegetation from earlier in the day.

'What's that black square to the right of the top pool?' asked Olivia. It hadn't been noticed earlier and was the only other colour amongst a sea of reds.

'It is a 3 metre square wooden structure rising about half a metre above the tiered level to the right of the upper pool and it appears to go underground but I cannot get detail from here. But what I can tell you is that there are underground water flows parallel to the upper canal and directly below the centre of the octagon at its left and right flanks. These flows are very linear and defined and I predict that they are underground canals leaving on both sides of the octagon directly in line with the light shafts, or can I now predict more octagons, to either side.'

A short while later, Olivia and Scott were sitting in their command seats in ROL-1 looking at AJ and the rest of the astronauts on the dome in front of them. Simultaneously and 500 kilometres above them, AJ and the team were watching Olivia and Scott on their dome. This was one of many video conference meetings where they discussed the incredible findings and planned their next moves.

AJ was speaking and pointing using an arrow on the display,

'This is a clear area to the right, inside the octagon, where ROL-1 can land and observe whatever is going on inside the light shaft.'

'But the lander will be at most 30-40 metres from the light source. Is that a safe margin?' queried Steve.

'From information gathered outside the light shaft, Zec-C is 95 per cent confident that only low power shield will be required but some detection instruments will probably not function.'

AJ finalised with the comment,

'I recommend that we go in shortly before dawn this very night.'

The decision was unanimously approved.

ROL-1 had been moved to a point 100 metres in front of the octagon. It was raining hard but was not too gusty and visibility was 30 metres. It was 1 hour before the sun would rise above the horizon behind them.

'Confirm command to enter octagon!'

Scott was watching the mimic display of their position relative to the structure as ROL-1 powered into the air amidst a huge explosion of water, clay and leaves and ascended to 100 metres. After hovering for 30 seconds, the lander moved forward and was in position above its designated spot 1 minute later.

'Descending at 10 metres per minute.'

Zec-1 kept a constant flow of verbal information with the key data duplicated on the dome.

Ten minutes later the caterpillar tracks of the lander crunched onto the clay ground inside the octagon and, even though flooded with rain, hardly sank at all on the firm surface.

'ROL-1 safely down. Surface inside octagon is very hard and perfectly level. Also initial analysis shows that the whole structure is fabricated from clay bricks each 66 centimetres long by 33 wide by 33

high. All the outer surfaces are hard and impermeable to water as if they have been treated in some way.'

'How?' queried Scott looking at Olivia.

'They must have been fired or baked?' offered Olivia as way of explanation and Zec-1 concurred that heat was the most likely possibility.

Visibility was now improving as the rain eased and they had a view of the whole of the octagon in front of the slightly off centre landing spot. It was strewn with leaves of various sizes and those just outside the dome were clearly seen. They were dark green, thick and fleshy and some were much bigger than the average human being.

They could now see the structures in front of them with the interlocking brick design clearly evident. Directly in front was a raised area, well above head height from the floor level and this housed the large strange square block of black wood which protruded above the raised area.

'The black coating is carbon black bonded by a resin which I cannot yet identify and the block of wood is at least 5 metres deep and resting in a clay structure. Further analysis will follow.'

'The internal design is very interesting in its ingenuity and comprises of four triangular pools. Water flows into the first pool from the higher rim of the wall of the octagon. It then spills over into the second slightly larger pool which is half a metre lower and then cascades into the third and largest pool. From here the water overflows to a channel running from the centre of the octagon to the base of the wall where it disappears underground. Finally a deep pool, about the same size as the first, has its own dedicated flow, from the rim directly above, which exits about half way along the channel. The water flow is approximately 2 cubic metres per minute and it is just above 0 degrees centigrade with a chlorine level of 200 parts per million – well above the level of a commercial swimming pool.

' And connecting all these various raised structures are smooth shallow ramps.'

The rain had eased and the light had taken on that strange fluorescence of the previous dawn when Zec-1 announced that the diamonds behind them were starting to heat up.

Olivia and Scott watched the display on the dome as it showed the same pattern of red, then orange and finally white as the two leading crystals exploded in a flash of light which reached up to the clouds behind them. The spectacle, as further diamonds lit up, made the hairs on the back of their necks stand up. The light sheath enveloped them from both sides and slowly closed around the octagon.

Then the last of the diamonds ignited and they were encompassed by the sheath of light and two extraordinary things happened. Firstly deep red shadows cast themselves from the structures and the walls,

and then.......

.... the sun shone!..... illuminating the inside of the octagon, lander and its occupants in its glorious warm rays.

What a transition!

Olivia and Scott sat dumbfounded. They looked at each other, the excitement gleaming in their eyes.

They then noticed sunlight glinting from small areas in the clay floor,

'What are those reflections Zec-1?' Olivia broke the silence.

'They are similar diamonds but laid flat in various positions in the clay floor. I presume that they admit light underneath the octagon. I have counted 3 lots of 6 crystals.'

'Gee! It's incredible!' Scott cried, 'Look at the way the light sheath is shimmering particularly near the base where the steam is rising, have you ever seen anything so astonishing.'

'Water temperature exiting the rim is now 80 degrees and starting to displace the cold water in the upper pools and most remarkably I have been able to switch off the force field and have applied only minimal darkening to the dome. It appears that the significant interference from outside the light sheath is not apparent inside. I can offer no explanation of this.'

Zec-1 continued,

'Air temperature 25 degrees and rising, humidity nearly 100 per cent. Temperatures in upper pools steady at 45 degrees, large pool now at 40 degrees and fourth pool at 70 degrees – I can only assume there must be some mixing of hot and cold streams. Temperature below ground is 5 degrees and I am detecting some movement but imprecise as temperature differentials are small. Significant water flow underground from numerous sources.'

'Scott!' cried Olivia. She grasped his shoulder and pointed to the large black wooden structure. 'It's rising! It's moving upwards!'

BOOK FOUR
THE BLUE PEOPLE

Chapter 21
Warming Up

'I can imagine the astronauts' mounting excitement. Back in 2050 I remember the euphoria when microbial fossils were found in the sub crust of Mars and since then a variety of simple life forms have been discovered. More recently, on Titan, sophisticated multi-celled forms have been identified in the underground seas. And these are living!

'Now on a planet at another star, life is about to reveal itself.'

The black structure was rising slowly from the red clay and revealed an angled flat ledge about 1 metre wide. This ran around and upwards at an angle of approximately 30 degrees, giving the impression of a huge wooden screw whose flights were about 2 metres apart. Then the huge mass of black wood came to rest with about two and a half metres showing above the clay level.

'It's completely square in cross section and every angled cut is a straight line!' Scott explained. 'It must be some sort of ramp connecting underground with the outside.'

'Correct, and it has been lifted into place hydraulically and now I can detect movement at the base of the wooden ramp – the forms are indistinct because they are the same temperature as underground but they are moving upwards very slowly.'

'Scott!' cried Olivia, shaking with anticipation, 'This is every astronaut's dream – to witness life on another planet.'

She gripped his arm and felt his excitement as his body shook. Both astronauts craned forward as far as their seat restraints would allow.

'Look the ramp is moving again! Moving downwards?' shouted Scott.

She then caught hold of his hand and they peered at the strange ramp structure just 30 metres in front of them and almost exactly at their eye level.

'There's something on the ramp! Scott choked, 'That's why it moved down again – it must be floating.'

On the lower part of the ramp, a dark shape started to appear, moving upwards towards the rear of the ramp.

‘What is it, oh my God! The back of a head, with thick, curly, black hair.’ Olivia shouted, ‘And the body is dark green, how strange – it’s one of those huge leaves – it covers it completely.’

The shape disappeared behind the back of the ramp as another head appeared below it.

‘The form is just less than 2 metres in height, essentially humanoid in stance and at 5 degrees Celsius, the same temperature as the underground area from which it has emerged,’ Zec-1 informed them.

‘It’s coming around the left hand side of the ramp!’ Shouted Scott and they leaned together in exhilaration pointing at the shape as it shuffled to the edge of the ramp and facing them was .....

.... a blue, hard face with a prominent hook shaped nose and vivid green and yellow eyes. The striking form then turned and shuffled slowly in the direction of the first upper pool.

More similar forms rose up and travelled around the ramp in a procession which left the astronauts utterly stunned with disbelief.

The first body to emerge from underground reached the edge of the steamy pool and slowly unwrapped the large leaf and cast it to the ground.

‘It’s completely blue all over!’ shrieked Olivia.

‘And humanoid in shape.’ Scott added with amazement.

‘Look, it has large mammary glands, it’s female.’ Olivia pointed.

Then the creature stepped shakily into the hot pool and disappeared under the surface of the water.

Zec-1, as ever, brought them down to earth,

‘The form has many reptilian features, namely, cold-blooded, green eyes with yellow vertically slit shaped pupils and webbing between fingers and toes. The skin is scaly and of a coarse texture. The stance and limb proportions are humanoid and so far all the emerged forms are female. The internal organs are similar to those of mankind and the brain cavity is smaller.’

After about 10 minutes the leading blue female stepped out of the pool and advanced, more steadily, towards the second pool. She was now facing them as Scott, puzzled, exclaimed,

‘She has square black nipples, I can’t understand it, and there seems to be further markings on and between the mammary glands.’

‘Also, she’s wearing black triangular flaps from the waist, front and back,’ Olivia observed.

Before they could glean any further understanding, the blue female slipped into the water of the second pool.

‘Body temperature of leading form now 15 degrees and a total of 20 similar forms, all female, have so far emerged. There is significant further movement underground.’

‘They’re very muscular and well built,’ commented Scott. ‘How old do you think they are?’

‘Can’t tell, and how do we judge age on this planet?’ Olivia replied as several more forms transferred to the second pool. ‘Also they are all very similar and their stern features remind me a little of the female Amazonian warriors from history.’

‘Olivia, look, smaller forms are emerging!’ They watched as they trudged to the first pool and discarded their leaves, ‘They seem to be younger females and pubescent females from their development.’

‘Aren’t there any males?’ Olivia queried.

About 30 forms had surfaced when the first blue female left the second pool and entered the third, large pool.

‘Body temperature of leading form now 25 degrees and blueness has decreased by 20 per cent.’

Several ‘adult’ forms appeared each carrying a small bundle which they proceeded to unwrap.

‘They’re infants.’ cried Olivia and the small fuzzy-topped blue shapes were helped into the first pool.

The procession continued. An amazing tableau of life on another planet was unfolding before the unbelieving gaze of the astronauts.

‘Look now,’ Olivia pointed, ‘Those blue females at the end of this group must have had tiny parcels under their leaves and between their mammary glands – they’re unwrapping them – they’re babies, oooh! Look how tiny they are.’

The blue ‘mothers’ cradled the little forms and entered the first pool.

Nearly 100 inhabitants had emerged so far and these were dispersed through the three pools and were at various stages of warming up. The leading blue females started to climb out of the large pool and sat on ledges to dry off in the beautiful mid-morning sunshine.

'Body temperature of leading forms now 37 degrees and blueness has decreased to around 40 per cent of emerging colour.'

'Scott! Don't you find it strange – they haven't cast a glance in our direction – why don't they notice this huge lander in front of them?

'Maybe they're blind or we just don't register in their consciousness,' mused Scott, 'but it is strange.'

'Their eyes are moving and their pupils have been dilating. I would assume that they can see but I cannot predict what they see.'

All around them the sun was shining brilliantly, casting shadows and the huge cone of shimmering light stretched into the clouds punching its continuous hole and bathing the blue forms in its life giving warmth.

And now the first 20 to emerge from underground were seated to the left of the lander, 5-10 metres away at most.

Life was about to get very interesting for our astronauts.

Chapter 22
Life and Death for the Blue People

'These life forms are cold-blooded reptiles which have evolved into an upright humanoid stance. This is somewhat similar to the evolution of monkeys on Earth. The square shape of the nipples is, in fact, created by a black tattoo. Further, the adults have triangular tattoos, mostly black but occasionally red, arranged around the black square. Also, between the mammary glands, are octagon shapes comprised of different sequences of black and red lines.'

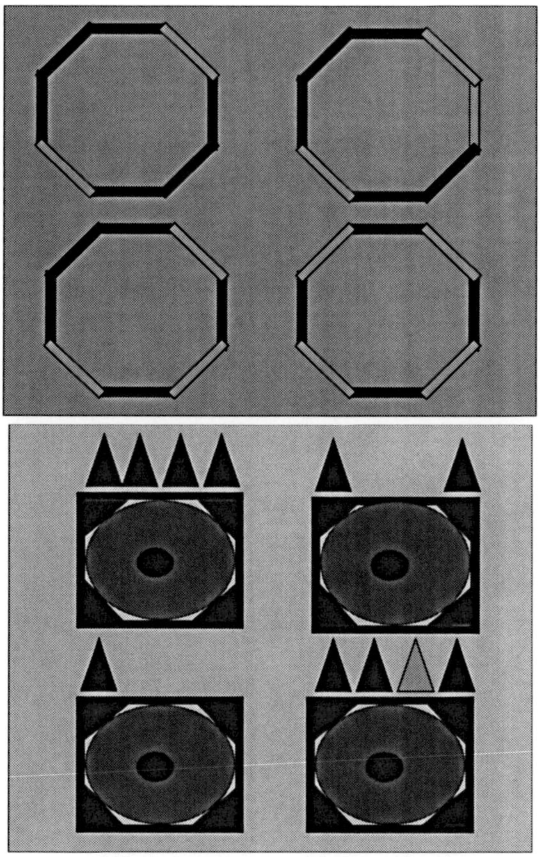

Olivia was watching a further group surface, very slowly and stiffly, and though she could not be sure, she sensed that these were older blue figures. Then she noticed that the very first females to emerge were gathering together and, to begin with, she couldn't understand what they were doing.

‘They’re feeding from one another,’ said a surprised Scott, ‘look, there’s white liquid coming from the mammary glands.’

‘My analysis of the white liquid shows it to be very similar to milk,’ Zec-1 informed them, *‘and it is very high in protein and fat.’*

When each of the blue females had fed they returned to their original seated positions. Now, the younger ones who had vacated the large pool started to take nourishment from the adults. The process was like a conveyor belt with each taking their turn. Interestingly, some of the more mature young ones also took part as providers after they had fed.

‘Well, I suppose that’s breakfast underway,’ Olivia joked, ‘I wonder what’s in store next?’

They both looked back to the ramp at the figures that came from underground carrying leaf-clad bodies towards the first pool. Five new forms had emerged and they were of a different stature, shorter, stockier and with very severe facial features. They placed the wrapped forms on the red clay floor in front of the hot pool. They discarded their leaves to reveal powerful scaly bodies with muscular arms and legs and at their waists were red triangular flaps.

The males had arrived and they were similarly tattooed. The astronauts’ concentration was then broken by Zec-1’s disturbing observation.

‘Forms placed on the floor are below 5 degrees with no discernible life signs.’

Following this, several of the adult females moved back up to the ramp floor and between them they half carried and dragged the dark green bundles down the slope which led to the octagon floor.

Olivia and Scott looked on in sadness as, quite carefully, the limp forms were lowered into the channel and, slowly assuming the speed of the water, they disappeared from view below the red brick wall.

Chapter 23
Eat, Drink....

Whilst all this was taking place, the younger blue females were busying themselves scurrying around the structure picking up leaves and stalks. The stalks were broken off and placed on a large leaf and they also put what appeared to be large spherical pods on another. The remnants were thrown into the fourth pool along with armfuls of large leaves.

The youngest females had no markings or tattoos whilst those more obviously developed had the distinctive black square around each nipple. One or two even had a triangle or octagon tattooed on them.

How strange!

It was intriguing watching the youngsters as they negotiated their way around the caterpillar tracks of the lander. They picked up the loose leaves and even went under the lander to clear the floor and all the time with total indifference to the huge craft. Those leaves trapped under the tracks were left after a couple of experimental tugs.

Zec-1 interrupted the astronauts' scrutiny announcing,

'Temperature in the fourth pool is a steady 85 degrees as it is filled directly from the crystal channels with no dilution. Further, there is a white, thick liquid seeping from the stalks. My analysis shows it is polymeric latex not dissimilar to the natural latex found in our own rubber tree. It is also the binder in the black coating on the hydraulic ramp and is present in the tattoos on the blue creatures.'

Olivia suddenly grabbed Scott's arm,

'Look at that female that's just entered the top of the channel. What's she doing?'

This adult female was at the very top of the channel bending forwards, right below them, with her arms down in front of her in the hot water. Suddenly there was a commotion as she straightened up and in her hands........

'Aaah,' Olivia breathed, 'it's a new born infant. Look Scott, how tiny it is, how privileged we are to witness a new life born - and on another planet!'

'The infant is approximately 1 kilo in weight and is still attached to the 'mother' by a cord similar to the human umbilical cord.'

Zec-1, as ever, provided the technical details.

They watched as the tiny baby's cord was nipped twice by the mother using her finger nails and it quickly floated down the channel and out of the structure. The mother then leaned back and placed the tiny curly haired infant against her breasts. With only a little encouragement, the small creature took its first feed. Then, one of the older adult females approached the channel and gathered up the little form in a piece of leaf and took it up to the upper pools where the rest of the young were being looked after.

'It's like a crèche up there,' said Olivia, 'we've seen birth, death, feeding – this is an extraordinary tableau of life inside this unique solar structure – does this go on at all the light shafts? – there are thousands of them.'

'I believe 10,000 from Zec-C's analysis,' replied Scott, 'who knows what we're going to discover on this extraordinary planet.'

It was about midday and the cone of shimmering light was absolutely vertical, casting hardly any shadows, and the temperature was a hot 30 degrees with high humidity. In the air-conditioned lander it was a more comfortable 23 degrees. Zec-1 had to apply measured amounts of heat to the outer layers of the dome to clear the condensation which was dripping from every outer surface.

There was activity by the fourth pool as several young creatures ladled out the hot leaves onto the ground using black, flat rectangular wooden shafts. The leaves had shrunk to an intense dark green, similar in colour to spinach, and were left to drain.

Now all the figures engaged in a second bout of community feeding as they lolled around the hot pools and various ramps interconnecting the internal structures of the octagon. Then, having taken their sustenance, the young moved to the fourth pool and took up handfuls of the now soft dark green mass and distributed it to the rest of the adults. As they ate the vegetation some of it dribbled from their mouths and onto their bodies creating striking splodges of dark green on their blue skin.

'There's definitely a pecking order when it comes to feeding,' Scott said, 'males first, then the females with all the tattoos, the older adults and finally the young ones.'

‘Presumably, that’s their diet,’ replied Olivia, ‘high protein milk and very nutritious vegetation, and I don’t see them drinking the water so the milk must provide all their hydration needs.’

‘I’m not surprised considering the high chlorine content of the water.’

The astronauts watched as during the next hour or so the creatures ate and drank completely finishing all the green mass that had been ‘cooked’ in the fourth pool. Then in the same pecking order they entered the channel and washed off the food and proceeded to quite vigorously splash water over themselves. Then they walked to various parts of the structure.

Olivia and Scott looked on as it became obvious that the Blue People, as they now thought of them, were forming into groups.

Chapter 24
..... and make Merry!

'Look,' said Olivia,' there are 5 distinct groups with 1 male and 5 or 6 adult females in each.'

'But that lot over there has 8 females.' Scott pointed out, 'I wonder why?'

They were curious as each set arranged itself upon the ground around the pools with the male surrounded by the females.

Then they were surprised as, in turn, each female mated with the male and, over a period of time, so it seemed, more than once.

While this was happening, young creatures frolicked in the pools; older ones tended young and some of the mature youngsters formed their own clusters and imitated their elders.

Olivia and Scott looked on at this natural scene with arms around one another, then she said.

'They're mating, let's leave them to it and get some rest.'

Scott agreed.

By mid afternoon the shimmering octagon of light was angled away from the lander, again casting deep red shadows and the blue creatures, having finished their mating, were now lying in and around the pools apparently 'sleeping' in the sunshine.

Zec-1 interrupted the astronauts' own afternoon nap,

'Temperature in upper pools now rising – cannot determine mechanism controlling this – upper pool now 50 degrees.'

Olivia and Scott watched as the blue forms woke from their slumber and fed. Then in the same pecking order, they entered the channel for a short period in order to cleanse themselves. Afterwards they slipped into the pools in the reverse arrangement to first thing in the morning so that they could heat up their bodies.

'Temperatures now 50 degrees, 55, and 60 in pools three, two and one,'

The hot baths soon filled with bodies which moved from one to another. Zec-1 informed the astronauts that their body temperature was being raised by two to three degrees each time. Finally the males emerged from the first pool with their bodies now at 42 degrees, donned the huge leaves and disappeared down the ramp. This slow procession continued as the sun went lower through the clouds. Finally the last of the adult females wrapped a huge leaf around her form and Olivia and Scott watched as she descended the ramp and her black curly hair vanished underground.

Zec-1 then announced that there was a significant heat signature directly below pools one and two – presumably the overnight chamber of the planet dwellers.

Then the black ramp slowly started to descend until its upper rim met the red clay ground – the octagon was now sealed from its unknown basement. The Blue Peoples' dwelling had closed for the night.

'I hope you got all that on digital, Zec-1?' Scott said as they just looked at one another hardly believing what they had experienced.

'Of course.'

The angle of the cone of light dropped quickly and on the dome screen they saw the first few diamonds 'shut off' forming the window which they had peered through the previous day. The light screen switched off symmetrically from either side until only the forward limb of the octagon was still 'lit'. Then that shut off and only the glow of the cooling crystals could be seen.

The rain fell, and clouds closed in over them as the temperature quickly dropped until it was nearly zero degrees – what a different world to the wondrous one they had just witnessed.

Zec-1 announced that the water flow to the upper pools had been diverted somehow and concluded that they were designed to maintain their heat as long as possible.

With communications now re-established with LifeSeeker-1 above them, AJ's voice welcomed them back and asked for their report.

'AJ, have we got some digital footage for you!' exclaimed Olivia.

'OK, we'll look at that during the night, suggest you guys get some sleep and we'll video conference 1 hour before sunrise.'

So, with the rain lashing down outside and the wind rising, Olivia and Scott left the command dome in Zec-1's capable hands and made their way to their comfortable quarters.

'Wow, what a day! What an incredible day,' Olivia said as she flopped down onto the water-filled bed. 'I can't stop shaking with excitement.'

Scott lay down beside her. ‘I still can’t get over that incredible light sheath, those diamond crystals, the structures and those creatures.’

‘Yes, but there must be something far more intelligent at work here, Olivia added, ‘surely those blue reptiles couldn’t have created all this?’

‘I agree,’ replied Scott, ‘I wonder what the next few days will reveal, but I don’t feel very tired, do you?’

The gleam in his eyes was equally matched by her seductive look and quickly their discarded clothes littered the side of the bed.

Chapter 25
Remarkable Findings

The video conference started with a plethora of exclamations, - 'amazing!', 'incredible!', 'unbelievable!', as the astronauts in LifeSeeker-1 expressed their views to Olivia and Scott on the dome screen. There were more questions than answers but they all agreed that what they had witnessed was an epoch in mankind's exploration of space.

The excitement was clearly visible on the astronauts' faces as they turned to one another or pointed to their section of the dome where each could display their own choice of action replay. They all agreed what a strange world of geometric shapes and near human reptiles they had found beneath the clouds and at the base of the remarkable light sheath.

AJ called the meeting to order, as Olivia, supported by Steve, urged that they consider exiting the lander for the first exploration of the dwelling and its occupants. Scott, though keen himself to investigate, was more cautious and it was AJ who finally summed up.

'Remember we must observe until we are absolutely certain it is safe to exit ROL-1. Also we must wait until Zec-C has completed a minutely detailed examination of the atmosphere in the structure, searching for any unseen life forms particularly bacteria. I understand your impatience but we must spend one or two more days watching to gather as much information as possible.'

They all nodded in agreement and there was no need to vote as AJ went on,

'Furthermore, Zec-C has the results of the surveying we have been doing,' and looking directly at Olivia and Scott, 'whilst you have been having fun on the ground!'

This brought smiles from everybody as Zec-C announced,

'I have already detailed the upper canals to you and mentioned the presence of a lower, underground water system.'

The domes in front of the astronauts filled with the mimic display of the flat plain beneath the clouds showing the regularly-spaced shafts of light and the myriad of straight upper canals. Then a second set of lines paralleling the upper water courses appeared linking every light shaft.

'Every light shaft, or octagon structure as we may now be able to deduce, is linked by a perfectly straight, 50 kilometre length canal, some 3-5 metres below the surface of the red clay strata. But what is most remarkable is that water is travelling in both directions. I can only surmise that there is some linear separation of the flows but cannot get precise data through the cloud and clay.'

'Is this an underground transport system?' queried Alison and it was Zec-1 that provided some further information,

'I have detected movement of a large object at both flanks of the dwelling but the thickness of clay has prevented a detailed assessment. However, these movements occurred about 1 hour before sunrise and sunset. I will try for more detail during further observations.'

A discussion ensued on the nature and use of these new water channels but again everybody agreed that they must have been produced by an intelligent species.

It was Scott, who voiced what the astronauts were thinking,

'Olivia and I discussed this last night and from what we have observed of these unique Blue People in just one day, we don't think they have the capability of designing and building these symmetrical structures. These reptiles, though humanoid in stance, appear too perfunctory in their actions. They show no recognition of our presence whatsoever. There must be, or must have been, a higher intelligence on this planet.'

Whilst they mulled over the implications of this profound observation, Zec-C continued,

'I have carried out as detailed an analysis of the whole land mass that the thick cloud cover will allow and I will give you the organic and geological results later. However, what is unusual is that there are no metals detectable and I was going to deduce that the whole of Cloud Planet is completely metal free – until the latest orbit that occurred just before our conference.'

This had the immediate attention of the astronauts and they watched as the mimic display homed in on a section of the light shafts adjacent to the forest covered mountains.

'But here,'

A pointer highlighted one light shaft right at the edge of the plain where it met the forest, *'there is a faint trace of metals which analysis confirms is titanium and aluminium with an identical infrared spectrum to those same elements used commonly on Earth.'*

There was silence.

'Also I can find no trace in this planet's geology of any ore of titanium or aluminium such as bauxite. At this point in time I can only conclude that these traces of metal have not originated from a source on this planet.'

Further silence. Then everyone spoke at the same time but no one could make sense of this latest finding.

'We plan to pass over this spot as near as possible during its night time,' AJ intervened, 'and if we confirm this exceptional finding, we will consider investigating this light shaft as our next port of call for ROL-1.'

'Although metals are not present in the crust of this planet, it has a molten iron core similar to Earth. This produces a symmetrical and strong magnetic field aligned perfectly with the centre of each icecap. I am sure that this force has deflected harmful solar radiation away from Cloud Planet in its distant past thus preserving the planet's atmosphere.'

It was again a remarkable sight as Olivia and Scott watched the rain ease, clouds lighten and then the first crystals glowed red and exploded their light rays at the sun. Slowly the whole dwelling was surrounded in the light sheath and they marvelled as the sun shone casting wonderful deep red shadows across the vegetation-strewn structure.

Earlier Zec-1 had informed them that approximately 1 hour before sunrise a large object had been detected at the flanks of the underground canals to each side of the lander.

They waited in anticipation as, on cue, the black ramp slowly rose from the clay platform directly in front of them. Although they knew what was coming, they were again captivated as the black-haired, leaf-bound forms of the, presumably same females, climbed the ramp, shuffled towards the first pool, discarded their 'robes' and started the warming up process.

The procession was the same as the previous morning.

Zec-1 interrupted their thoughts,

'The first pool initially received water at nearly 90 degrees directly from the crystal channel but after the black ramp had come up, a second flow of water at 0 degrees, presumably from the upper canal, was mixed with this hot flow. Both flows are of similar volumes resulting in water at 45 degrees entering the pool system. I detected the movement of a rectangular wooden structure, just prior to this occurring, between the crystal channel and the back of the first pool.'

They looked on in trepidation as the blue males emerged, again carrying lifeless forms which they placed in the hot sun on the clay.

'Oh no, there are three of them today,' Olivia said in anguish, 'and one of them is an infant.'

They stared helplessly as the adult blue females carried the bundles to the top of the channel and gently placed them into the exiting stream of hot water.

The processes of feeding, cleaning and cooking continued and to their delight two births took place in the top of the channel below them.

Later, as the sun had passed its noon, the Blue People gathered again in their mating groups of adult male and attending females.

'Zec-1, can you zoom in on that group to our left,' asked Scott.

'Don't you have a good enough view as it is!' sneered Olivia, 'It's not a peep show!'

'No, seriously, Olivia, I'm sure that all the Blue People in that group have similar markings between their breasts.'

'You could be right,' Olivia had to admit, 'so let's get Zec-1 to analyse all the groups.'

Whilst Zec-1 was doing this they noticed that one of the blue females had made her way towards some of the pubescent females that frolicked around the upper pools. She selected one and hand in hand returned and joined her group.

'What's going to happen now?' Olivia wondered and looked on with Scott as the adult female coached the young female through the mating process. Then, one of the elder females from the crèche area came over to the group holding a leaf containing red and black thick liquids.

'The liquids are clay and carbon black dispersed in the white latex from the leaf stalks.' Informed Zec-1.

'Look, she's painting the young female!' said Olivia and watched as the older female skilfully applied a black square with her fingers around each of the young female's nipples and then she inserted a black triangle in each corner creating the exotic square. Then she drew a small octagon shape with sides of black and red between the youngster's breasts.

The young blue female had come of age and become part of a mating group.

'I told you so,' gloated Scott, 'that's the same design as the rest of the set.'

'Each of the five groups has an identically coloured octagon including the male, and with eight sides and two colours there are thousands of different possible combinations. Further, the males' tattoo has a high resin content whereas the females' is relatively low. This may represent permanent or temporary identifiers but the reason is unknown.'

The dome then showed the relevant designs of the groups.

'Are we to assume that these are different families?' asked Scott.

'One other piece of information – the group with the largest number of females is the only one where the male and two of the females have a red triangle. All the other groups have only black triangular tattoos.'

'How intriguing,' Olivia replied.

Chapter 26
Investigate the Metal

At the next early morning video conference, information was exchanged between the lander and the starship concerning the previous day's activity in the dwelling. Everybody was fascinated by the tattoos and octagon shaped markings and all contributed ideas to explain their meaning.

AJ then informed the astronauts that Zec-C had confirmed the presence of titanium and aluminium of unknown origin at the light shaft at the edge of the plain.

After they had discussed this, AJ proposed that they move ROL-1 to this new location to investigate the metal source. He also pointed out that this was in the general proximity of the SOS light shaft which was their ultimate goal.

The decision was confirmed.

On the third day in the sunshine of the dwelling there were two further deaths and one birth. AJ recommended that Olivia and Scott got some sleep in the afternoon, so reluctantly they retired as it was going to be a long journey that night.

In their quarters, Olivia noticed that Scott was distracted as he lay on the bed and looked at his palmtop.

'Penny for them,' she said.

'Oh, it's nothing, just some old images of my Grandfather and, and Dad.'

'Let me see,' encouraged Olivia and he passed it over. 'Is that you? How cute! How old were you?'

'That was taken with Gramps when I was six at the launch, and that's Dad suited up and raring to go,' Scott replied, his voice breaking slightly.

'Wow! He's a looker! How old was he then?'

'Thirty five and there's a shot of StarGazer-1 just after take-off'

Olivia squeezed his hand and looked into his eyes, 'It's good to relive your memories, thanks for sharing them with me.'

Zec-1 woke them just as the sun was setting and it was strange coming back into the dome with the dwelling switched off. The rain was falling heavily on the lander and the wind rising. Every now and then a leaf fragment would flop onto the outside of the dome where it was either washed off by the driving rain or dealt with by Zec-1.

'The target light shaft is 1550 kilometres in a direction 30 degrees west of the equator. ETA at a landing point 25 kilometres short of the target is 3 hours and it will take a further 5 hours to traverse to the dwelling. Entry will be 1 hour before sunrise.'

Confirm command to move lander to new target!'

Zec-1 took the lander up quickly through the dark cloud mass and it was a shock for Olivia and Scott as they moved into the clear night. At 100 kilometres above Cloud they accelerated quickly to 600 kilometres per hour.

The cloud mass was as far as the eye could see in all directions and the astronauts found it hard to believe that they had been on the ground in brilliant sunshine a few hours earlier.

They watched the mimic display intently as they passed over canals and dwellings below them. Slowly the target got closer and Zec-1 announced deceleration in preparation for landing. They had chosen their position well away from the mountain edge where the winds were strongest in the higher clouds. Zec-1 took the lander in a controlled descent into the clouds. It was noticeably very windy and the craft was buffeted far more than on the first landing. However, with excellent control on main engines and careful use of stabilising thrusters, ROL-1 touched down on the rain-sodden clay.

'Proceeding at 5 kilometres per hour to target, ground flat with thick vegetation and no obvious obstacles.'

It was frustrating sitting in the dome with no visual contact with the ground only 3 metres below them and they glanced at the mimic to monitor their progress.

After 3 hours and only 10 kilometres from the target, Olivia and Scott were both shaken into full awareness by Zec-1.

'Warning – multiple movements on the plain detected 5 kilometres ahead towards target. Zooming in for detail.'

The mimic screen suddenly filled with hundreds of small yellow and red shapes.

'What are they Zec-1,' cried Olivia, 'where have they come from?'

'The infrared is showing their body heat is about 30 degrees, significantly above ambient, which is just above zero. There are over 100 of them moving, then stopping, then travelling again in the

general direction of the forest. Size varies from just under a half to over 2 metres and I am putting one of the larger ones on screen in infrared.'

'It looks like a lizard,' Scott pointed, 'but how can a cold-blooded creature be so warm out there?'

As the lander approached the group of reptiles more closely, additional details appeared on the screen.

'Definitely reptilian and lizard like in appearance with a long tail. They are stopping and eating the vegetation and then moving on. They are moving away from us at about 3 kilometres per hour so we won't catch them up before the target.'

AJ cut in from LifeSeeker-1, 'We've got your video but we're too high to get anything on these creatures but it is a puzzle where they've come from and why they are still warm in the middle of this hostile night.'

They continued to watch the retreating group of lizards and, a short while later, arrived 500 metres in front of the target light shaft position. Zec-1 stopped the lander.

'Reptiles have moved off the plain and into the tree line of the lower slopes. Definite metal detection coming from within the target dwelling and we have a similar clear landing zone to the right of the central channel. This dwelling is smaller at 75 metres diameter. Metal object seems to be located near the ramp wall about 10 metres to the right of the channel.'

'The design of this second dwelling structure is identical to the first both externally and internally. The arrangement of the four pools, ramps and central channel is similar and in proportion to the smaller size. The distinctive black square of the lift connecting with the underground is apparent on the upper level.'

It was now about 1 hour before sunrise and conditions, as ever, were pretty appalling outside the lander when Zec-1 announced,

'Confirm decision to enter dwelling!'

The decision was confirmed and Zec-1 took the lander up 100 metres and started moving forward towards the dwelling. They reached their designated position over the landing spot and Zec-1 started the controlled descent.

AJ's urgent voice cut in, 'dark mass moving outwards from the upper forest level towards your position, Zec-C cannot identify as yet.'

'300 metres and decelerating.' Zec-1 informed them.

'Warning ROL-1, dark mass now descending over your position!' Zec-C cut in from the starship.

'200 metres and decelerating.' Zec-1 informed them and then more urgently, *'huge mass of large flying objects directly overhead and 500 metres above lander – situation getting critical – cannot abort landing with that vast obstruction above us – applying force field!'*

Olivia and Scott could only watch the mimic display with alarm as a huge number of infrared and yellow forms seemed to circle above them.

'100 metres and decelerating.'

Then red lights started flashing and alarms angrily buzzed.

'Emergency! Emergency!, flying forms descending rapidly downwards – applying maximum force field commensurate with sufficient landing thrust!'

And then all hell broke loose as the lander was enveloped by the swarm of flying objects. In the slightly increasing light they were visible outside the dome and the mimic display showed that they were huge flying reptiles over 3 metres long and a 4 metre wing span.

Olivia screamed and ducked as one hurtled straight at her in the dome – its huge head full of teeth as its jaws gaped open. Giant claws flexed and closed as they attempted to grab on. She was relieved that the force field did its job and cushioned the collisions by absorbing the kinetic energy of the hurtling objects. This prevented the creatures from impacting the lander and sent them reeling from the shock. Olivia thought she saw one or two collapse downwards but visibility was too poor to see their fate. Scott, meanwhile, focussed on the display screens anxiously watching their relative position to the ground.

'50 metres and decelerating, force field holding – flying reptiles backing off!'

With relief the astronauts could see that the flock was ascending but still directly above them. Then the caterpillar tracks bit into the wet hard clay of the dwelling and the lander was down.

'Lander safely down in target dwelling!'

Zec-1 confirmed.

'Flying mass now ascending and heading for forested area.'

AJ's concerned voice filled the lander's dome,

'Thank God, good landing! We're analysing the video but I can confirm that the mass of flying reptiles have returned to their position high up in the forest at the edge of the plain. But we are very concerned up here that something caused that flock to attack you. Look at our video.'

Olivia and Scott viewed the scene from above and could see the group detach itself from the forest line and move out directly over the lander's position. But what caught their attention was a second black mass that had formed a large horse-shoe shape around the reptiles seemingly pushing, or was it shepherding, them into the descending lander.

'What's that second black mass?' Scott shouted. 'It seemed organised.'

'Zec-C cannot analyse it but it seems similar to the black mass identified at the edges of the seas around the coasts. But I agree with you – it was a perfectly regular horse-shoe shape and it seemed to fade and disappear once the lander was down. We'll carry on analysing up here while you take a look at the metal trace. And now the moment you've been waiting for - permission is given for first exit of the lander but under full spacesuit and quarantine conditions. Confirm Zec-1.'

'Conditions for exit understood and confirmed.'

'The flying reptiles have features similar to those observed feeding and scampering over the plain the previous night. However, the front legs are replaced by huge scaly wings and the webbed rear limbs are now opposing sharp claws. Add an enlarged jaw full of razor sharp teeth and the result is a formidable creature perfectly adapted to live and forage in the massive tree canopies. But most striking is the pair of huge green eyes with vertical yellow slits – a common characteristic of all the inhabitants seen so far on Cloud Planet. Interestingly, these creatures bear a resemblance to the pterosaurs, flying dinosaurs from 100 million years ago on Earth.'

Chapter 27
A Surprising Discovery

After the trauma of the landing, Olivia and Scott could now focus on their new surroundings inside the dwelling. Although it was still raining, the light had increased and the familiar geometry was now visible.

It was a mess!

The whole area was strewn with huge leaves and stalks brought down by the higher winds near the forest.

In front of the astronauts and partly covered by leaves was a mass of twisted metal about a metre cube in size.

'Look!' said Olivia, 'What do you think it is?'

'Beats me,' replied Scott. 'From here it looks like an automobile that's been through a metal crusher.'

'Analysis confirms predominantly titanium and aluminium with some high grade steel, also evidence of high temperature resistant polymers similar to Teflon but cannot identify structure.

'Also I can confirm the arrival about 1 hour before dawn of a large wooden object underground and to our right but nothing to our left.'

'We'll have to wait until we get out there,' Olivia said. 'Meanwhile let's watch this place light up.'

They watched as the sun ignited the dwelling and bathed its leaf covered structures in gorgeous sunshine. On cue, the black lift rose from the clay and the astronauts were again thrilled as black-haired forms emerged and entered the first pool. But, this time, there were only six adult females and Zec-1 reported no further movements below the dwelling.

The blue females warmed up, fed and set about cleaning up the dwelling. This time, however, the large whole leaves were gathered and placed on the clay floor and smaller fragments of leaf were tossed into the fourth pool.

'Astronauts prepare to exit lander!'

'This is a momentous occasion in the history of space exploration when, for the first time, mankind sets foot on a planet of another star system. It is a coincidence that Cloud Planet has a

slightly higher gravity and similar atmosphere to Earth. Even so, it is essential that full protective measures are taken for this first exit.'

Olivia and Scott ensured their lap restraints were fixed and lowered their helmets securing them to their spacesuits. Inside their helmets, the mimic display confirmed that they were airtight and fully pressurised from their oxygen packs.

Both astronauts put their hands to the console to confirm readiness and Zec-1 retracted the seat assembly into the air lock where the lander air was sucked out into a pressure cylinder until Zec-1 confirmed that a near perfect vacuum had been attained. Then the compartment was slowly re-pressurised with atmosphere from Cloud Planet. When the pressure inside and outside was the same, the lander's lower lock door opened and the command seats slowly lowered 3 metres to the clay floor.

With mounting feelings of expectation, Olivia and Scott took their first steps.

'What a privilege. I'm lost for words. First astronauts to set foot on a planet of another star,' Scott said triumphantly.

Then, gloved hand in hand they moved from the lander's shadow into the dazzling light of the mid-morning sunshine. They marvelled as they looked around at the shimmering light sheath which rose majestically above them. There was not a cloud in sight and the sun poured into the dwelling raising its temperature to 30 degrees with near 100 per cent humidity from the boiling water at the diamonds and the hot pools. Moisture condensed onto the spacesuits but the dome of the helmet remained clear as liquid crystals in the outer layers raised the temperature to match the ambient conditions.

'Look at this gouge in the clay,' Scott pointed downwards, 'this structure came down at very high speed.'

'And look here,' Olivia commented, 'some pieces of metal which must have broken off on impact.'

They approached the twisted, shapeless lump of heavily corroded metal.

'It's box in shape and you can see these jagged struts where other parts have presumably sheared off. I can't tell which way is up,' Scott said.

While they were examining the wreck, the six blue females carried on oblivious to their presence – they were removing the cooked leaves from the fourth pool.

'See this, Scott, there appears to be four sheared bolts and a cleaner rectangle of metal.' And they bent to peer closer at this section towards the lower part of one of the sides.

'Hold on, wait a minute! What are those marks there?' said Olivia and she pointed her gloved hand.

'Looks like letters and numbers,' Scott cried, 'but I can't quite make them out because they're upside down.'

Olivia crouched down further, 'I think it's .... 'I' something 'S'..... then 'A'.... followed by 872954824 – the numbers are accurate, I think. Zec-1, do you agree and can you run them through your database?'

They waited only a short while before Zec-1 replied,

'Your identification of the numbers is correct but the letters are 'NASA' and that numeric sequence was stamped on the body of Pioneer 10, a satellite launched in 1972 from Cape Canaveral in Florida.'

'You're kidding me,' shouted Scott in utter disbelief.

'Impossible!' Olivia joined in equally stunned.

'I deal only in facts,' Zec-1 continued, *'the code I see from your helmet cameras is consistent with information in my database matching Pioneer 10 which was sent to reconnoitre Jupiter which it did in 1974. After this it left our solar system and was last heard of in 2001 heading into outer space in the general direction of the red star Aldebaran in Taurus the Bull.'*

'Bloody hell!' Olivia argued, 'That's 90 degrees from our vector. How could it get here?'

'I cannot speculate how but can only deduce that the remnants of Pioneer 10 are sitting in this dwelling on Cloud Planet of the star Seren.'

'Olivia, I can remember my Grandfather telling me that his great Grandfather, Jack, had watched the launch of Pioneer 10 when he was only six years old – how quirky is that!?'

Scott paused, a faraway look on his face. 'And I watched my Dad take off when I was six and he's been lost in space for over 50 years,' he thought to himself. Then he quickly refocused on the job ahead.

There was little more they could learn from the wreck – the fact that it was a satellite from Earth launched about 180 years ago was mind boggling enough.

But now, as the six blue females enjoyed the early afternoon sun in their own male free group, it was time to explore what lay beneath the dwelling.

Chapter 28
Beneath the Dwelling

The two astronauts ascended the ramp at the head of the channel and turned right following another clay path up to the side of the first pool. For the first time they were within metres of the amazing light sheaf but the only noise was that of water and steam hissing in the channel. Zec's voice warned them not to approach any nearer so they turned right, past the discarded leaves and approached the black lift.

Close up, it towered over them.

'Incredible! This must have been cut from a tree trunk over 3 metres diameter, but look every cut is straight.' Scott said as he stepped onto the angled flight which was about a metre wide. The structure moved slightly downwards.

Then as Olivia joined him so it moved again. 'It must be floating,' she observed.

They walked down and around the square screw lift and Scott ducked to avoid bumping his helmet as the upper flight closed over them. Having descended the equivalent of one and a half revolutions of the stationary screw they exited onto an upper platform of clay. The noise of flowing water boomed in their helmets and they filtered this down so they could speak with ease. The light had dropped dramatically and the shafts of luminosity from the diamonds embedded in the roof, created a weird atmosphere.

Directly under the first and second pools was a large chamber about 2 metres in height but it was too gloomy to judge its length. The floor was covered in large leaves.

'Must be where they bed down for the night,' thought Olivia as Scott was examining the huge lift structure.

'The screw lift is floating in a huge square pit with water flowing in from above and overflowing the pit into a channel about two thirds from the bottom. Water is also seeping out from a square hole, near the bottom, which has a wooden shaft protruding from it. To lower the lift, the shaft is pulled forward to allow water to empty from the pit.'

Olivia was looking in the opposite direction to the chamber where a ramp seemed to disappear into the gloom and she shuddered.

She wasn't cold – her spacesuit was maintaining a steady 22 degrees whilst her mimic display showed that the outside temperature was a chilly 10 degrees. She shivered as there were dark places everywhere she looked.

Scott's voice shook her from her momentary apprehension.

'Have you noticed that everything we have seen up top and now down here is straight – I cannot see a curve or circle anywhere in these constructions. Look at this clay ramp in front of us, it goes forward and I bet it turns in a straight line beyond that corner.'

They followed the ramp for about 20 metres to the dark corner and their only option was to turn right. Another ramp extended in front of them for a further 20 metres finishing at a lower platform which was illuminated by six light shafts. As they walked the noise of water increased.

'Where are we heading?' Olivia enquired as she had lost her bearings.

'We're on the right side of the dwelling; in fact the lander must be above us. We are near the position of the underground lateral canal.'

They moved onto a wide platform which had paths leading down into the dank, darkness below. They turned and stared at the huge mouth of a black tunnel 5 metres wide and at least 2 metres high.

Olivia really shook this time, but Scott moved forward excitedly, activating spotlights in his spacesuit to illuminate the tunnel.

'Look, Olivia, there is a mid-partition about 2 metres high and water is flowing away from the dwelling in the left channel.'

Olivia's unease was replaced by technical curiosity, 'Why is the water white? And how peculiar, the right side of the partition is a further 2 metres down and water is flowing into the dwelling. We seem to have an upper rectangular clay pit of water on this left side of the tunnel about 2 metres wide and 5 metres long.'

She moved closer switching on her lights.

'There is a similar pit but lower down on the right and, I don't believe it!'

'What!' said Scott.

'Come around here.'

They both moved to the platform in front of the tunnel, and stared at the object below.

'It's a boat!' They said in unison.

'But it is not like any boat they or I have ever witnessed. Completely black, it is 2 metres wide and 4 metres long with tapered flat sides outside and inside. The sides of the boat are about one third of a metre wide. It is hewn from wood, waterproofed with resin and has a shallow draft. Every face is straight and the floor of the vessel's large interior is lined with leaves.'

'I think it's completely flat bottomed,' Scott said as he moved down to the boat, 'with a shallow draft but I don't think it's actually floating – it's sitting on something and the water flow from the tunnel seems to be passing under it.'

'Scott!' Olivia shouted, 'there's someone coming!'

As she spoke four blue females moved quietly down the clay ramp towards the platform, each carrying armfuls of large leaves.

Chapter 29
A Novel Transport System

Olivia and Scott moved to one side as the blue group approached the right hand side of the tunnel and descended the ramp towards the boat.

'How can they be so near to us and yet so oblivious to our presence?' Scott whispered and Olivia shook her head and raised her eyebrows in puzzlement.

Up close the females were magnificent specimens with powerful arms that easily hefted the bundles of large leaves into the boat. They turned and came back up the clay ramp, their bright green eyes with vertical yellow elongated pupils penetrated right into the astronauts' helmets.

Olivia and Scott stepped backwards, involuntarily, but the blue females passed by without a flicker of recognition. Two of them walked to the front of the platform and descended into the inner depths of the chamber. The remaining pair went back up the ramp and disappeared from view.

'Where are they going?' Olivia questioned. They both moved forward to see the first two females arrive at the bottom of the ramp some 5 metres below the platform.

'Look,' Scott pointed, 'there's water gushing out at the bottom of this pit into a shallower one – is that the water from the tunnel behind us?'

'But what is that horizontal black shaft?' Olivia wondered, 'it seems to be coming out of the gushing water with its other end resting on the shallow wall of that lower pit.'

Meanwhile the two blue females positioned themselves at the end of the shaft and between them pushed it forward about half a metre where it dropped and caught on the wall. The water stopped gushing out leaving only a trickle around the edges where the tapered front end of the black shaft fitted neatly into a square hole. They then ascended the clay ramp back towards the astronauts.

Shortly a distinct grinding noise caused the astronauts to turn and walk back towards the pit containing the boat.

'It's moving.' breathed Olivia, and then louder, 'the boat's travelling upwards!'

Scott excitedly worked his way downwards to the side of the boat which had risen about 0.5 metre and he peered below.

‘It is completely flat bottomed, and it’s sitting on, hang on, two huge black wooden structures, each about 2 metres square and the same width as the boat. They must be floating in this huge pit, rising with the water level and lifting the boat up. Incredible.’

When the craft had risen about a metre the other two females returned. The four then disappeared into the gloom by the chamber wall. They re-emerged, each pair carrying a long black wooden wedge over 2 metres long and about one third of a metre square at its broad end.

‘What are they going to use those for?’ enquired Olivia and they watched as the boat came to rest just over 2 metres above its original position. At the same time they heard water gushing from the front of the pit. The vessel was now clear of the central partition wall by about one third of a metre.

One of the blue females walked precariously along the partition wall to the entrance of the tunnel. Meanwhile two females carried one of the wedges to a position where they could pass the tapered end to the female in the centre. They positioned the wedges so that they were precisely under each end of the craft.

‘What’s going to happen?’ Olivia wondered and looked at Scott. Two of the females descended into the depths of the chamber once more. When they reached the black shaft they strenuously pulled up the end which shot backwards with the force of the water which gushed from the lower opening.

‘I don’t believe it! Scott cried, as the boat slowly descended and initially grounded on the higher end of the wedges. It then angled downwards until it rested on the tapered end and remained stationary at an angle of about 15 degrees towards the upper pit.

‘Watch Olivia, watch!’

The four blue females positioned themselves along the higher side of the boat and pushed in unison. The effect was like a slipway and the craft slid effortlessly into the upper pit of water. It moved forward with the flow and rested with its front against a black wooden partition which prevented it from disappearing down the tunnel.

‘A lift - an ingenious boat lift – just like locking up on a river – who designed all these intricate hydraulics?’

They were so absorbed that they hadn't noticed that the blue females had left.

Zec-1 interrupted their concentration.

'Reminder, time to return to ROL-1!'

After they had returned to the lander, they watched through the dome as the six blue females heated up and returned underground.

'Large object, now identified as a boat, has just left travelling at approximately 5 kilometres per hour. This speed would be consistent with an early morning arrival time at the next dwelling.'

Chapter 30
The Menace of the Black

AJ and the astronauts in LifeSeeker-1 were astounded at the discovery of the wreck of Pioneer 10 and fascinated by the ingenious boat lift system. They discussed at length how the satellite, which was destined for the constellation of Taurus, ended up so far off course. They concluded, with Zec-C's calculations, that there was not enough time to get here at normal speed for the craft. Something very strange must have occurred.

The video conference was brought back to order by AJ,

'We have to consider getting out of the dwelling tonight and Zec-C has calculated that there should be sufficient force field during ascent to punch our way past these flying reptiles. The current situation is that there are huge numbers of them in the treetops but no sign of the black mass. However there is an unknown risk concerning the regular shape that herded the creatures when you were landing.'

The astronauts agreed unanimously to attempt to take off from the dwelling to avoid the threatened danger.

One hour later, in the dark driving rain in the dwelling, Zec-1 applied power to the four main vertical engines of ROL-1, balancing this thrust with applied force field to the outside of the lander.

Olivia and Scott watched as the mimic display showed their relative position and Zec-1 intoned the altitude and speed of the lander.

'Altitude 50 metres, speed 25 kilometres per hour.'

'Confirm your status, no sign of activity in treetops,' AJ said from 500 kilometres above.

'Altitude 200 metres, speed 50 kilometres per hour. Force field maximum commensurate with applied thrust.'

'Warning! ROL-1, black mass has arrived at the treetops,' said AJ.

'Altitude 500 metres, speed 100 kilometres per hour.'

'Further warning! Mass has herded a huge flock of flying reptiles out of treetops and above your position at 2 kilometres altitude.'

'Altitude 750 metres, speed 150 kilometres per hour.'

‘Emergency! ROL-1,’ AJ cried, ‘black mass is forcing flock downwards directly onto your path at high speed, their altitude is now 1000 metres, abort!... abo......’

In the lander, communications with the starship were suddenly cut off and Olivia and Scott felt the huge g-force as Zec-1 reversed the thrust on the engines as the lander came to a hover before starting its emergency descent. Simultaneously it was bombarded by the driven flock of frenzied flying reptiles. By now, their ability to fly was severely restricted by the crushing weight of the Black. The force field prevented actual collisions but the sheer numbers of reptiles rushing down onto the lander contributed to its descent speed.

The two astronauts studied the mimic display in horror as the flock appeared as yellow and red images which pressed down on the lander.

‘Altitude 500 metres, speed 30 kilometres per hour – bleeding off force field for more reverse thrust on main engines.’

‘This is touch and go,’ cried Scott, ‘we’re already descending too fast for this altitude!’

‘Altitude 200 metres, speed 20 kilometres per hour – descent now critical - bleeding off more force field.’

Now the flock of reptiles was buffeting the lander and the descent path was only just being maintained by Zec-1. Scott looked aghast as the outline of the dwelling below loomed larger and larger on the mimic display. Olivia echoed his thoughts,

‘God! Scott, are we going to make it!’

‘Altitude 50 metres, speed 10 kilometres per hour – emergency! – All power needed for reverse thrust – no force field! – but reptiles thinning out!’

The lander was now at the mercy of multiple collisions by the flying reptiles which caused ROL-1 to suddenly veer off course. Olivia and Scott were thrown about in their seats by the impacts.

‘Brace for crash landing! Altitude ten metres, speed still 10 kilometres per hour – emergency! – more reptiles on collision course!’

Then two flying reptiles crashed at speed into the rear of the lander turning it through almost 90 degrees just a couple of metres from the red clay of the dwelling. The astronauts were shaken to the core by the sudden change of direction and momentarily disoriented.

At above safe design speed, the lander’s caterpillar tracks slammed into the hard clay surface biting deeply. Simultaneously Zec-1 applied maximum torque to the cantilevered legs so they would brace the impact. Unfortunately the two rear tracks came down on the edge of the lateral water channel which crumbled away under the impact. The rear legs immediately extended to try to keep the lander horizontal but the channel was too deep. As the rear tracks ground to a standstill in an explosion of crumbling clay and water, so the huge external cowls of the two rear engines buckled into the ground and the lander stopped with its underbelly less than one third of the metre above ground.

'Lander down – checking vital components for damage!'

The impact shook Olivia and Scott to the bone and they paled as the lander tilted upwards nearly 30 degrees before coming to a sickening stop.

They watched the mimic display anxiously as hundreds of mechanical integrity, circuit and other checks flashed up – thankfully mostly glowed green for OK.

'Basic lander integrity not breached but significant damage to external cowls of both rear main engines. Also rear caterpillar tracks are jammed in the bottom of the lateral channel which at 2 metres wide is the same as the length of the tracks.'

'What is your best scenario for our position?' Scott asked dejectedly.

'I have 90 per cent confidence that ROL-1 can be extracted from the channel but less than 5 per cent confidence that we can take off! Also we have no communications with LifeSeeker-1 because the black mass is directly above us.'

Meanwhile in LifeSeeker-1, the astronauts had watched with horror as the black mass firstly herded the flock of reptiles out of the treetops and then completely encircled them directly over the rising lander. Then the Black closed over the reptiles and drove them down with frightening speed. At this point AJ lost communications with the lander and could only pray that they had got to the ground safely.

'Black mass is now a steady circle 500 metres in diameter at 1 kilometre altitude. Communications with ROL-1 are completely blocked and I cannot analyse the nature of the mass.'

'Command - move starship 1 kilometre due east!' AJ judged that this should give a line of sight with the dwelling. However, with each manoeuvre of LifeSeeker-1, the black mass adjusted its position and the communications blackout persisted.

AJ put into words the stark realisation of the other astronauts,

‘Not only did that black mass organise those reptiles into the path of the lander, but it is also aware of our presence! – what on Earth is it, Zec-C?’

‘I cannot get any investigative print of the black mass; it is resisting infrared, X-ray and low frequency radiation. I can only see it, and it arrived at the treetops from the sea coast in less than half a minute!’

‘Gosh, the sea’s over 500 kilometres away,’ gasped Steve who paused as he worked out the maths, ‘that’s over 50,000 kilometres per hour! - how can it travel that fast!’

‘Also why was this attack so much more menacing and forceful than the previous one?’ Alison queried.

AJ’s conclusion caused all the astronauts on LifeSeeker-1 deep concern, ‘The lander was trying to escape this time!’

Then, as dawn approached and the cloud lightened, the black mass disappeared from below them as quickly as it had arrived. Communications were restored for just 1 hour before sunrise and the astronauts were relieved to hear that their colleagues were safe and well, but dismayed at the damage to ROL-1. Before contact was lost for the day, the lander astronauts said they would do a thorough examination of the damage to the rear engines and report back after sunset.

Chapter 31
Death in the Dwelling

Zec-1 had adjusted the astronaut's command seats so that they were horizontal. They had decided to wait for the dwelling to light up before attempting the extraction of the lander from the channel.

The dwelling was its usual mess of huge leaves. The dome mimic then showed the scene behind and they jumped at the sight of one of the flying reptiles half in and half out of the large pool. It was a fearsome sight with its giant head and one huge scaly wing hanging down over the edge of the pool.

'That wingspan must be nearly 4 metres,' said Scott, 'and look how thick the neck is, that creature must weigh a couple of tonnes – no wonder those last impacts swung the lander.'

The camera at the rear of the lander then showed what had happened to the second reptile that had hit the lander forcefully just before touchdown. The creature was crushed down into the channel under the rear caterpillar track and hot water had backed up and flowed over its inert body.

Meanwhile the blue females had emerged and gone about their business, seemingly oblivious as before to the carnage around them.

Zec-1 then started the process of extracting the rear tracks from the channel. The first manoeuvre was to start rotating them under high power so the large ridged edges would cut into the clay. The right track turned easily but the left one had the grisly task of grinding through the body of the reptile. The water in the channel gushed red with a mixture of clay and blood.

Once the two caterpillar tracks were sitting freely in the bottom of the channel, the legs front and rear were extended as far as possible lifting the lander so that the crushed engine cowls were now clear of the clay floor. Zec-1 now angled the rear tracks at 45 degrees and applied forward power to all four. The lander moved forward until the front edges of the rear tracks bit into the wall of the channel and started to grind an angled groove. The clay beneath the hard outer surface was quickly ground by the powerful rear tracks. Forward traction was now applied to the front, enabling the rear tracks to cut two 45 degree ramps in the clay. The lander slowly pulled itself out of the channel and Zec-1 levelled and turned it until it was, once again, facing the wreck of Pioneer 10 and in its original position.

Olivia and Scott were relieved to be freed from the channel but concerned that the lander could be stranded in the dwelling. Meanwhile, outside, the blue females were busying themselves around the floor of the dwelling when Zec-1 interjected,

'Warning! – reptile in large pool is starting to move!'

The astronauts turned and gazed, open-mouthed, as the gigantic creature lifted its massive head and crawled to the edge of the pool. They could now see its huge body with powerful rear legs with extended claws. It used these to grab and tear a large leaf into ragged pieces and fed them piece by piece into its gaping mouth. The reptile was fully three and a half metres long and crawled from pool to pool. It gathered up further leaves and demolished them greedily on the way.

'It must have been only stunned,' Olivia observed, 'and then the hot water revived it.'

They had to crane their necks as the creature raised itself on all fours and jumped from pool to pool using the edge as a platform to launch itself into the air, while its huge wings flapped furiously. In the dome mimic display they watched as it touched ground momentarily behind the lander and then soared in an arc up over the platform and the first pool.

It arced higher and higher, and then, like a moth trapped in a lightshade, started flying at the light sheath, turning at the last moment to avoid a collision. Now its flight was more erratic as it sought to escape from the blinding light. The creature panicked and careered back and forth across the dwelling, gradually losing height. During this drama the blue females carried large bundles of leaves underground, oblivious to the huge menace whizzing around them.

'It's trying to get out!' shouted Scott, and then it disappeared low behind the lander and reappeared in front of the astronauts and headed for the space between the lift screw and the first pool.

'On no!' shrieked Olivia, as she realised that two of the blue females were coming up from below right in the path of the hurtling reptile.

Time stood still for the two astronauts as, seemingly in slow motion, the reptile crashed into the two figures as it banked over the platform. One of the blue females took the full force of its right wing and it snapped her head back into an impossible angle. The other female was caught by the reptile's left wing squarely in the midriff and her arms and legs shot out as she was carried, like a rag doll, into the air.

'Oh my God!' shrieked Olivia again, and she watched in horror as the flying reptile with its unwanted cargo flew straight at the light sheath. For a moment the creature and its hapless passenger seemed to merge with the wall of light bending it outwards. Then a blinding explosion of light occurred right in front of the astronauts' position and then the light sheath closed and continued to shimmer as if nothing had happened.

'Oh no,' sobbed Olivia, 'we brought those horrid things in here – it's our fault those two females were killed!'

'Olivia, that black menace above us caused this, we're not responsible. Don't blame yourself.'

Whilst the astronauts were relieved that the lander had been extricated from the channel satisfactorily, they were both dejected that the sequence of events had directly resulted in the deaths of two of the inhabitants of Cloud Planet.

They looked on sadly as the other blue females wrapped the broken and lifeless form on the platform and carried her to the channel where she floated past the damaged section and disappeared from view.

'Olivia, did you notice that when they put her in the channel, the leaf seemed to shrink around her body?'

But Olivia was too distraught to notice.

Their misery was broken by Zec-1's voice,

'Command suit up for rear engine inspection!'

'The cowls on the four main thruster engines of ROL 1 are 1 metre diameter at their narrowest section, 1 metre in length and of conical section. This spreads the exhaust gases for optimum control. Thirty, 5 centimetre bolts hold each cowl to the underside of the lander.'

Scott directed his spacesuit cameras at the rear cowls – they were badly deformed from their impact with the clay ground and Zec-1's conclusion was immediate,

'Take off impossible with damage observed, cowls will need replacing.'

‘Well there’s spares and a special torque wrench on the starship 500 kilometres above us – but a fat lot of good that is!’ said Olivia dejectedly.

‘Nothing we can do until we talk to AJ later. Come on Olivia, let’s have another look underground.’

They descended the lift screw and examined the huge pit that housed it.

‘There at the bottom you can see the shaft sticking out blocking the flow – it’s the same principle as the boat lift.’ Scott observed.

‘Look!’ Olivia pointed, ‘Behind the screw lift and under what looks like the inlet water channel are two narrower pits with shafts and overflows. What are they controlling?’

‘Zec-1 said something about the water flows being mixed to control temperature – must be something to do with that. The problem is we can’t get near enough to the inlet flows to see what’s happening.’

They followed the ramps to the boat lift, where the craft was in its lower ‘arrival’ dock.

‘Look, it’s loaded with leaves and pods; they must be sending the food on to the next dwelling.’ Olivia commented.

‘Olivia, come here!’ Scott had moved to the upper dock and was directing his light into the mouth of the tunnel. ‘You said the water was white yesterday and you were right, but, let me see, yes it’s white because it’s full of tiny air bubbles. How odd!’

He moved to the front of the platform and observed that water gushed into a large open channel. He imagined its source was at the front of the dwelling where it would have been fed from the upper canal. It turned through 90 degrees as it entered the wall of the pit below him and the channel became a closed box section.

But Olivia was already kneeling over the edge of the platform and pointing downwards. Scott shouted for her to be careful.

‘Yes, look Scott,’ Olivia said excitedly, ‘there are thin channels cut into the top of the box section.’ She gingerly laid on her front and extended her arms over the edge of the platform which enabled her to reach the top of the box section. She put the palm of her spacesuit glove over the open slit. Surprisingly, she had to pull hard to release her hand!

‘Yes, yes, there’s suction there! This is the Venturi principle – remember from basic physics – you can create suction from high water flow in a tube passing an orifice leading to an open shaped tube in the

T-section. The air is drawn into the water flow as bubbles. But why does the water need to be aerated?' queried Olivia.

'This tunnel travels 50 kilometres to the next dwelling and the water is being constantly aerated because the Blue People don't just send their food in the boats – they must send themselves as well!' Scott replied thoughtfully.

Olivia looked aghast at the black mouth of the tunnel and shuddered, realising the implications,

'No way!'

'It stands to reason, they can't travel above ground because it's too cold and wet, so they travel at night while they sleep – how ingenious. And look at the mouth of the tunnel, Olivia, at the block of wood across the entrance. Remember, yesterday, when they pushed the boat into the upper lock, it moved forwards with the flow and stopped against it.'

Olivia leaned precariously across the entrance and touched the black wood,

'It's floating, and you can push it down, why? - Oh, I've got it. They push it down from within the front of the boat and the flow takes the vessel over the block and into the tunnel. I can't stop being amazed by the ingenuity and simplicity of these hydraulics.'

But both astronauts were going to run out of superlatives before the end of the next day on Cloud Planet.

Chapter 32
Seren

The video conference that evening was short because the black mass returned earlier giving them only a 30 minute window compared to 1 hour the previous day.

AJ and the astronauts on LifeSeeker-1 had watched an edited version of the sad events leading to the deaths of the two blue females and were dismayed when they saw the damage to the rear cowls of the lander.

'We need to review our options through the night,' said AJ. 'Meanwhile Zec-C had been analysing the light shafts in more detail. There is no ex...'

Communications were lost at this point but there was plenty for Olivia and Scott to ponder on before they retired for the night.

'I infer from Zec-C's analysis that the size of the dwellings nearer the equator are larger than those currently visited. They are approximately 200 metres across, but at the equator they are 300 metres and there are four, so far, identified at a staggering 500 metres in size.

'Furthermore, Zec-C has observed small shafts of light leaving and returning to the larger dwellings during the 2 hour period around this planet's noon. There is, at this present moment, no explanation for this.'

The following morning the black mass disappeared only 30 minutes before the dwelling was due to light up, giving precious little time for discussion. With takeoff definitely ruled out, they considered manoeuvring the lander out of the structure. ROL-1 was designed to drag itself up a 2 metre shelf but the height of the outer wall was beyond its capability. Alternatively they could get it up onto the screw lift platform and then over the wall but the gap between the outer wall and the upper canal was beyond the limit of the caterpillar tracks. At the second pool area the inner wall was less than 2 metres high but beyond the row of crystals the outer drop was impassable. They considered grinding their way out using the caterpillar tracks in a similar way as they had extracted themselves from the channel previously. This seemed a laborious and most risky approach because of the danger of the lander becoming trapped in the wall. The consequences if the dwelling lit up were too frightening to contemplate.

AJ summarised and level-headedly concluded that time was on their side and they must all think more deeply. Then communications were again lost as the first diamonds ignited.

Even though their plight seemed hopeless and the lander appeared trapped, Olivia and Scott sat back in their command seats and eagerly watched, for the fourth time, as the light lasers shot into the early morning cloud behind and around them until finally they were again completely enclosed in the laser sheath. The transition from the rain and dark of the night to the deep red shadows as the sun filled the dwelling, was, as ever, a thrilling event.

Zec-1 had kept them informed about the departure of the boat the previous evening and an arrival earlier that morning. Whether this was the same craft could not be confirmed.

The dwelling was its usual early day mess of leaves, stalks and pods, one of which had split in front of them and this contained a cluster of small seeds. They waited and saw the lift screw rise from the red clay followed by the appearance of the first of the remaining blue females.

Except, this time, there were more than four.

‘Scott!’ cried Olivia, ‘Look there’s five, six, seven now eight in total. You’re right; the extra ones must have travelled overnight in the boat.’

Suddenly Scott’s eyes were glued to the lift screw, ‘Olivia, Olivia, look!’ he almost choked, pointing towards the platform.

The back of a head with shimmering curly golden blond hair was visible above the green leaf wrap. The form disappeared behind the screw and then appeared in silhouette as it stepped onto the platform.

‘Look at that golden hair! - The profile of the face – the texture of the skin is so smooth and it’s a lighter blue than the others.’ Olivia could not contain her excitement.

The stunning new arrival took one step forward, stopped and then the head turned. The most piercing azure blue eyes looked directly, it seemed, into the lander. They could clearly see the creature in front of them, when Zec-1 enlarged the image of the beautiful face on the dome mimic.

The eyes sparkled and seemed to penetrate Scott's whole being and he let out an involuntary gasp.

'She's looking at us; she's seen us. Look at those eyes.'

Olivia sat, mouth agape, mesmerised by their depth and intensity.

The new arrival looked forward and smoothly glided to the edge of the first pool and discarded the leaf wrap.

'Oh my God!', Scott stared at the lithe profile with smooth blue skin and firm breasts, 'I've never seen anything quite like this on Earth let alone here.'

The vision then stepped down into the first pool.

'New arrival is 7.5 degrees, which is warmer than the other blue females at this point. The skin is perfectly smooth with no scales and the fingers and toes are not webbed. Eyes are blue with dark round pupils. Features and internal organs are humanoid and the brain is significantly larger than that of the blue females, but not quite as large as the average human. Apart from the reptilian characteristic of cold bloodedness, this lighter blue female appears human.'

The other blue females went about their normal routines, but the astronauts' eyes were focussed on the golden tresses that broke the surface of the first pool.

As she stepped out of the pool she shook her head and water droplets flew from her hair, which now almost looked dry. Again she looked directly at them.

'My! Whatever she treats her hair with would make a fortune back home!' Olivia said enviously.

But Scott wasn't looking at her hair when Zec-1 interrupted his gaze,

'Body temperature now 17 degrees, appears to warm up quicker than other blue females, blueness decreased by 20 per cent.'

And she slipped gracefully into the second pool.

The other blue females had completed warming, fed and busied themselves around the dwelling. Meanwhile, the blond female stared at the lander as she moved from pool to pool.

'Body temperature now 27 degrees, blueness decreased by 30 per cent.'

The new arrival finally exited the third pool, gazed again at the lander and walked forward to sit on the ledge. One of her four attendant females immediately moved to stand in front of her and then she drank from their mammary glands.

She then sat up, and with a slight sideways inclination of her head, dismissed them and they joined the others who were now putting leaves into the fourth pool.

Olivia and Scott were transfixed as she rose and walked down the ramp, every movement smooth and graceful. With her eyes fixed on the lander, she reached ground level, moved forward and stopped by the side of the wreck of Pioneer 10. Her eyes sparkled with intensity as she looked directly at Scott.

He felt overwhelmed. His heart pounded as he stared at the loveliest female form he had ever seen.

Her hair framed her beautiful oval face to perfection. Her pale blue skin was smooth and much lighter than the blue females.

The outstanding feature was her sparkling eyes, which were the deepest of blue. Their intensity seemed to bore through Scott's whole being.

'If the face of Helen of Troy could sink a thousand galleons,' Scott mused, 'this face could implode a million star ships!'

His gaze fell to her shoulders, where a strange triangle of what appeared to be small beads hung around her neck. At its point, the triangle directed his gaze onto the most perfect breasts tipped by soft pink nipples. Around each nipple was a bright red diamond shaped tattoo. However, unlike the blue females, there were no triangles outside the diamond, or octagon shapes between the breasts.

Scott looked down to a narrow waist with perfect hips and a smooth, flat stomach. Like the blue females, she wore a tantalising black triangular flap which pointed down between shapely thighs on long legs, slender ankles and delicate feet.

'Wow, Wow, Wow! Have you ever seen anything so absolutely gorgeous,' Scott was mesmerised and couldn't help the outpouring of admiration. Olivia gave him a scornful, almost jealous, look.

'She's not bad for cold blooded,' was the best Olivia could muster but inwardly she marvelled at the epitome of womanhood in front of her, 'what do you think Zec-1?'

'She exceeds perfection when compared to my database!'

The golden blond head inclined slightly left, then right, stopped and straightened. Her eyes increased in intensity and penetrated directly into Scott's brain.

'Warning radiation of unknown frequency!'

'Aarg!' cried Scott and clutched his head.

'What's the matter?' said a concerned Olivia.

'Couldn't you feel it? Like a headache! And then there was a sensation at the back of my eyes.'

Her eyes sparkled with intensity again.

'Warning further radiation of unknown frequency!'

He held his head again and looked straight at the lovely creature.

'She spoke to me! She communicated with me! There was a clear message behind my eyes!'

<< who are you >>

'What did she say?' said Olivia excitedly.

'Who are you?'

'What! – that's impossible - how can you be sure?'

'I don't know – I just saw the message after the headache.'

'Confirm radiation from eyes of new arrival directed into dome.'

Scott's head hurt but not so painfully – then behind his eyes again,

<< why have you come >>

Her arms moved slightly outward and she pointed to the wreck of Pioneer 10.

'She just said 'Why have you come?'' Scott explained to Olivia.

'Confirm same radiation frequency for word 'you'.'

'Why have we come?' said Scott aloud. 'We're here because of the SOS message'.

'So show her the message.' Olivia suggested.

'Oh yes, good idea.' Scott agreed, 'Zec-1! Command! Forward landing light – flash to SOS code'

The clay ground in front of the lander glowed bright red and the body of the beautiful woman took on a reddish hue – she looked at the light - as it flashed -

.... dot - dot - dot - dash - dash - dash - dot - dot – dot ....

After two sequences of the code she suddenly looked up and her eyes glowed brighter than ever.

'Warning radiation of higher intensity!'

Scott's head hammered as she raised her arms out towards them and beamed the most radiant and beautiful smile.

And he saw,

<< welcome > welcome > welcome >>

Then she turned, skipped up the ramp and dove into the third pool.

Olivia and Scott sat stunned, speechless as the golden head bobbed around the pool. They couldn't find words to express their feelings – just stared at one another and then at the figure in the pool.

'What next on this unbelievable Cloud Planet? Firstly the light shafts, then the dwellings, the blue creatures and now this sublime apparition. Sorry Olivia, but it's difficult not to go over the top.'

She then surprised him. 'You're right – everything has been remarkable but her communications with us, or rather with you, make me realise she's obviously many intelligence levels above the blue females. Why don't we give her a name? I know. Why don't we refer to her as Seren after the star of this sensational planet?'

'Great idea! I really like that.' Scott enthused.

The astronauts continued to watch as Seren left the pool and sat on the ledge. She inclined her head and her blue female attendants came to her with food and drink. They accompanied her to the top of the channel and assisted with the cleansing of her body. Seren then came out of the channel and walked gracefully back to the Pioneer 10 wreck.

Her head inclined both ways and her eyes sparkled as she transmitted a new message.

'Warning radiation!'

Scott felt the pressure in his head and he saw clearly,

<< you must come with me >>

She pointed left and extended her slender finger in the direction of the equator. Then she raised both arms towards the dome of the lander.

'Warning more intense radiation!'

<< please help me <> help our people survive <> save our world >>

And he felt the full force of Seren's emotional appeal and his heart went out to her.

'I find this planet is proving to be remarkable in a number of ways. The axis of rotation is constantly parallel to its star and the orbit describes a perfect circle of radius 140 million kilometres – similar to the distance of Earth from its sun. Cloud Planet has equal day and night times during its 20 hour rotation. There are no seasons during the planet's 400 days' traverse around the star Seren. This unique geometry of star and planet results in a symmetrical landmass to either side of the equator. Its seas and icecaps are, unsurprisingly, also identical in size.

'However, whereas on Earth evolution is hugely diverse, here on Cloud Planet it is limited to one species of tree and a small number of cold blooded creatures. Also, some of these reptiles have evolved along two paths into a low intelligence blue form and a perfect human shape - not too dissimilar to the evolution of monkeys and humans on our planet.

'This latest arrival, named Seren by our astronauts, additionally has telepathic and mind-controlling capabilities which I consider most extraordinary.

'I show below the detail of this dwelling showing the canal behind feeding all the hydraulics. Just one wall is illuminated so that you can view the inside structure. I can well imagine Olivia's and Scott's astonishment as they sat in the lander and watched Seren glide gracefully down the ramp and point at the wreck of Pioneer 10.'

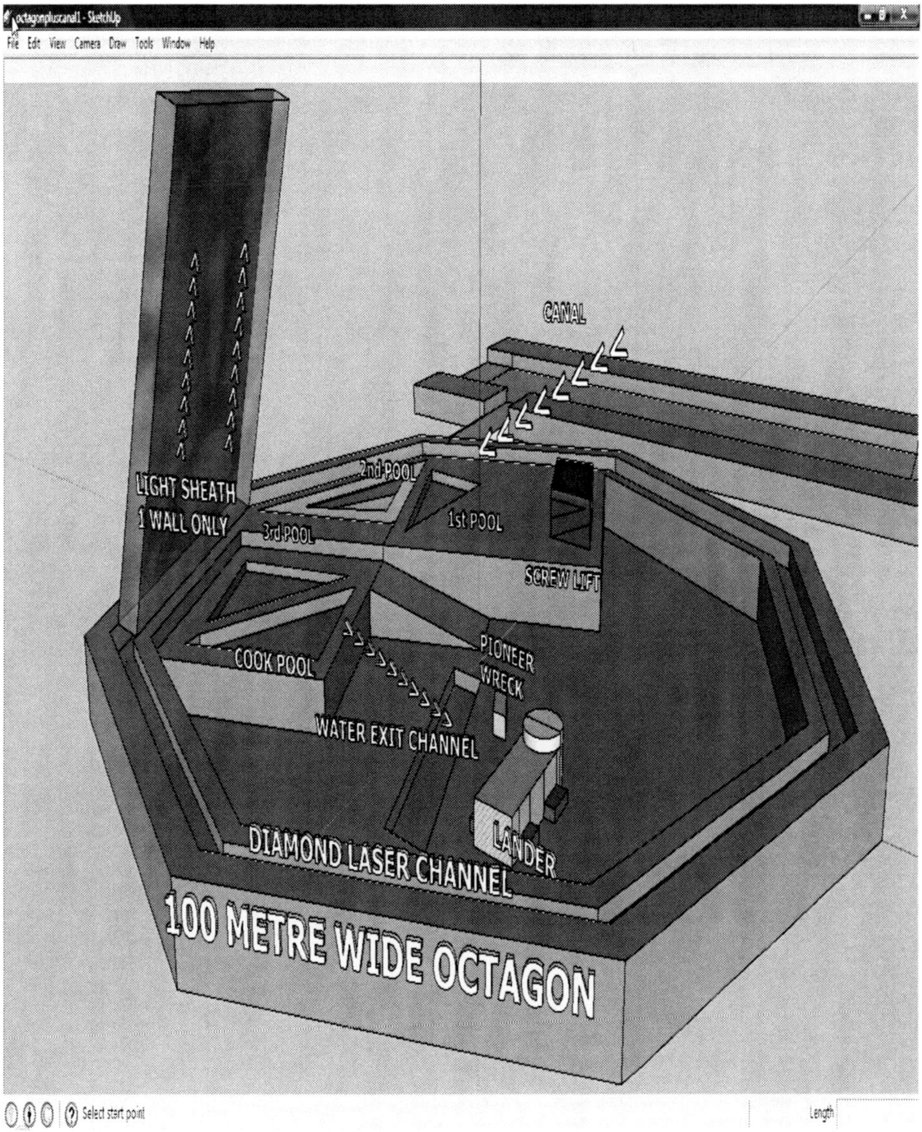
octagonpluscanal1 - SketchUp
File Edit View Camera Draw Tools Window Help
CANAL
LIGHT SHEATH
1 WALL ONLY
2nd POOL
1st POOL
3rd POOL
SCREW LIFT
COOK POOL
PIONEER
WRECK
WATER EXIT CHANNEL
LANDER
DIAMOND LASER CHANNEL
100 METRE WIDE OCTAGON
Select start point
Length

BOOK FIVE
AN UNDERGROUND JOURNEY

Chapter 33
Abandon Ship

For the rest of the afternoon, Seren bathed in the large pool and whilst resting on the edge she would occasionally tilt her head left or right.

‘Why does she do that head thing?’ Olivia questioned.

‘I’ve no idea,’ replied Scott.

‘I am detecting radiation of a different frequency’, said Zec-1, *‘when she tilts to the left radiation is leaving her head and when she tilts to the right I can detect radiation entering the dwelling.’*

‘You mean she is communicating,’ said Scott, ‘in the same manner she conveyed information to me?’

‘With you it was a very focussed band of radiation – in fact it was directed specifically at your head, causing you pain.’

‘Is that why I didn’t feel anything?’ Olivia continued. ‘She was only focussing on Scott?’

‘I agree but I cannot understand why, but I also conclude that the head movements are communications with a wider range of listeners, some, maybe, at considerable distance.’

‘So is it telepathy?’ Scott enquired.

‘I believe it is more advanced than that.’

As the afternoon wore on and the red shadows deepened in the dwelling, Seren and the blue females went through the process of raising their body temperatures. Her blue females waited on the platform, leading to the screw lift, for her to emerge and then helped to wrap her in a large leaf. She moved forward, stopped and turned her head towards the lander.

‘Warning radiation!’

Scott’s head ached and he saw,

<< come with me <> come and help my people >>

And with that she disappeared underground.

The dwelling switched off, the rain fell harder and, as the clouds darkened, communications were re–established with LifeSeeker-1.

AJ and the astronauts aboard the starship were hardly able to comprehend as they watched the highlights of Seren's arrival and her impassioned plea to help her people.

'We don't have much time,' AJ forced his mind back to practicalities. 'It's clear that we can't get the lander out of the dwelling, nor can we rescue Olivia and Scott because of the threat of the reptiles and the black mass. We have to consider abandoning the lander and following this Seren to a dwelling away from these threats. Hopefully there we can affect a rescue or re–evaluate our options.'

AJ looked at the other astronauts who nodded in approval.

'I propose that you both acclimatise tomorrow without spacesuits. Zec-C has given a clean bill of health to the atmosphere except for chlorine, but you will require face masks with scrubbers and tight fitting goggles to protect your eyes.

'Abandoning the lander is a big decision particularly for you, Olivia and Scott, but I feel it is our only option so I will call for a confidential vote.'

The proposal to abandon ROL-1 was carried by five votes to two – interesting!

'You will also need to consider the amount of food, water and clothing that you can reasonably carry.' AJ continued. 'Remember to take your palm top computers so you can remain in contact with Zec-1 and the starship. They will enable us to track your progress.

'Oh, and one other thing – don't forget the sun cream!'

This brought some laughter amongst the tense astronauts.

Communications were lost only 20 minutes later when the black mass suddenly returned. The question was – would they be able to speak to the lander in the morning?

It was a long night for Olivia and the dream returned, causing her to toss and turn in her sleep. Scott tried, unsuccessfully, to calm Olivia but her sleep was fitful. She lay awake knowing that she had to face the dark tunnel under the dwelling – 50 kilometres long, 10 hours of travel and how did you know you would come out at the other end? Olivia shuddered as these thoughts raced around her mind.

Dawn eventually came but there were, worryingly, no communications with LifeSeeker-1 because the black mass remained above them until just before the sun's rays activated the dwelling.

The lighting up of the dwelling lifted Olivia's spirits and they watched anxiously as the screw lift raised and the blue females emerged. Finally, at the rear of the group, Seren appeared. She stepped onto the platform, stopped and turned her head towards the lander.

Her eyes bored into Scott's head and he saw.

<< you talked with your people above the clouds <> what have you decided >>

Scott was momentarily stunned. How could she have known this? He repeated the message to an equally bewildered Olivia.

'It's also astonishing that her powers are such that she knows we have made a decision,' she replied.

Then Seren slipped her leaf and entered the first pool.

They watched, enchanted, as she went through the warming process. Her attendant blue females gathered around her as she fed. Then she made the journey down to the side of the wreck of Pioneer 10.

She looked more desirable than ever, Scott thought, and for the one hundredth time he admired her sublime figure, conscious of the way the point of the triangular necklace focussed his gaze downwards. She then looked up, raised her arms towards them and radiated the word,

<< welcome >>

The astronauts raised their arms in a similar gesture and she, in turn, smiled in response.

She lowered her arms and her eyes sparkled.

Scott was surprised as his head did not hurt but he still saw the message,

<< will you come with me <> if the answer is yes then raise your arms >>

Olivia and Scott looked at one another. Even though the decision had been made, Scott felt an overwhelming desire to shout 'yes', 'yes', 'of course we will' , but he checked his thoughts and together they raised their arms towards Seren.

In response she raised her arms, her eyes gleamed and she smiled in gratitude,

<< thank you > thank you > thank you >>

Then she turned, ran lightly up the ramp and entered the large pool.

Olivia and Scott sat in their command seats in the airlock. They were wearing thin two piece synthetic tops, pants and slip on shoes with a ridged sole. Their noses and mouths were covered by lightweight masks with filters containing a chemical that would neutralise chlorine. They wore goggles to protect their eyes and carried their palmtops for communications. Pressure in the airlock had to be increased only slightly to match that on Cloud Planet.

Zec-1 interrupted their thoughts,

'Opening lower airlock door, preparing to lower command seats.'

As they started moving downwards, the heat and humidity hit them. By the time they stood up under the lander they were already drenched in perspiration.

'The atmosphere is like the forest in Borneo where we trained,' Olivia remarked, as they walked between the huge caterpillar tracks out into the sunshine of the dwelling. It was less humid in the sun but already their tunics were soaking. They walked past the wreck of Pioneer 10, up the ramp and stood by the large pool. Around them the light sheath shimmered and the blue females scurried back and forth carrying leaves for the fourth pool and the boat waiting below.

Seren was bathing in the large pool when she stopped and looked at Scott, her eyes sparkled,

<< come in > join me >>

'Well, we can hardly get any wetter.' Scott said and they laid down their equipment and walked down the ramp into the hot but refreshing water. After 5 minutes the astronauts climbed out of the pool and sat on the ledge where evaporation from their tunics gave a pleasant cooling effect.

Seren came out of the pool and sat a couple of metres from them. Close up, she was even more remarkable.

Her attendant blue females came forward with 'cooked' green leaves which she ate heartily and, with an incline of her head, two of her females came to Olivia and Scott and offered food.

'Zec-1's analysis says it's OK for consumption,' Scott said, 'I'm going to try some.' It was like a soft pancake in texture but vivid dark green and still hot from cooking.

'It's a bit like spinach; I'm not wild about it, but at least we wouldn't starve.'

Olivia who was not so convinced, took only a small, token bite and decided it was not to her liking.

The two blue females continued to stand in front of them. They were magnificent creatures with strong arms and legs and at just short of 2 metres they towered over the seated astronauts. Scott was fascinated by their huge mammary glands embellished with tattoos and markings. The blue female directly in front of him had four black triangles around each nipple and the one in front of Olivia had seven in total – what did they signify? But none of the blue females in this dwelling had any marks between their breasts.

Then Seren took milk from the blue female in front of her, and between 'drinks' inclined her head. The two blue females, who were facing Olivia and Scott, moved forward offering their milk heavy mammary glands. Olivia was horrified but tried not to show it and turned her head away and gaped as she saw that Scott had lowered his mask.

'It's quite sweet and refreshing,' Scott said as he turned towards Olivia. But she had stomped off in disgust.

He caught up with her, 'Olivia, seriously, we may have to rely on their milk. If our water runs out we can't drink this chlorinated stuff – you know what Zec-1 said.'

'But how could you? – do that.'

'Olivia, it's just like having a bottle of milk back home – but cutting out the middle man!'

Here in the middle of this sun-drenched dwelling amongst the Blue People of Cloud Planet of the star Seren, Olivia could see the irony of the situation and started laughing, and so did Scott. And Seren also beamed a knowing smile.

Chapter 34
Into the Abyss

During the afternoon, the two astronauts packed their carry packs against a check list prepared by Zec-1. They put compressed food, water, medical supplies and plenty of chlorine filters in one pack. The other contained all their clothing for day use, and more critically for the long cold nights in the boat. Ten or more hours at near 0 degrees was going to be a challenge for even warm blooded Earthlings!

'We'd better change into our thermals when we're underground, otherwise they'll be soaking wet before we can get there.' Olivia advised and Scott nodded.

Most important were the two hand held computers and the torches with plenty of spare batteries. Finally, from the arsenal on board ROL 1, two small gamma – ray guns which they hoped they would never have to use.

Having checked and double checked that they had every necessity they could reasonably carry, they sat in the command seats of ROL-1 with their packs on their laps, wondering when, or if, they would see the lander again.

'Command, prepare to abandon ROL-1!'

And two left hands confirmed this frightening decision to embark on a journey into the unknown with this extraordinary inhabitant of Cloud Planet.

They followed the blue females and Seren down the screw lift where they immediately changed into their thermal clothing. They noticed that two of the blue forms had descended into the gloom and heard them knock out the wooden 'bung' of the lift pit. The huge wooden screw lift creaked as it started to descend and they watched the four blue females, now thoroughly wrapped; disappear into the chamber below the upper pools.

Olivia looked at the closing lift, shuddered and clutched Scott's hand. They followed Seren and her four attendant females down the gloomy clay ramp towards the boat dock. As they got nearer, Scott could sense Olivia's rising fear and apprehension.

They mounted the platform and saw that the black boat was half full of large leaves. Two blue females had already entered the boat and waited kneeling over the front. The others were already in the rear of the boat and had settled themselves into the leaves – this extra covering maximised thermal insulation for the long underground journey.

As Seren waited, the two astronauts walked towards the side of the boat. Olivia looked with trepidation at the black mouth of the tunnel and was suddenly paralysed with fear.

'Scott, I can't! I can't!' she cried, shrinking back and embarrassed at her demeanour.

He slung his pack down and put his arms around her.

'I'll hold on to you tightly all the way, Olivia, we have to go!'

But she was shaking uncontrollably and tried to break away,

'No! No!, I can't! You go; I'll go back to the lander.'

'Olivia, we have no option, we must go in the boat!' He said firmly and then an unexpected thing happened. Seren walked towards Olivia and her eyes sparkled intensely. Now Olivia clutched her head and she saw,

<< its alright <> this is how we always travel <> be calm > be calm >>

Scott looked at Olivia,

'Did she speak to you?' and Olivia not only nodded but immediately calmed down. Obviously Seren's telepathic message had reassured her and she surprisingly said,

'I'm OK, come on, let's do it.'

A relieved Scott put the packs in the boat, helped Olivia get in and they settled awkwardly onto the leaves. Then Seren stepped in and buried herself in the vegetation next to the two attendants at the rear. The two females at the front pushed down on the restraining block of wood and the boat scraped noisily out of the dock, picking up speed as it entered the black tunnel.

Scott could not believe it but Olivia was already asleep in his arms and he realised that there was more power and depth to Seren than her outward appearance would suggest.

Black, absolute blackness – so intense that Scott could not believe his eyes were actually open and he tried to force his lids further apart. The darkness of the tunnel seemed to press in on him and sleep would not come. Only the occasional scrape of the boat on the sides of the tunnel and gurgle of water gave a sense of awareness.

Olivia slept soundly and Scott glanced at his computer. The screen gave an eerie glow, breaking the blackness. They had travelled for about 2 hours and he saw there was a text message from Zec-1.

'Tracking you OK, you are 10 kilometres out from dwelling at steady 5 kilometres per hour. Bad news – black mass above dwelling has split into two, one is stationary above the dwelling, and the other is directly above your position and travelling at the same speed as the boat. We are both cut off from LifeSeeker-1.'

Scott tried to make sense of the black menace above but could not. Finally he fell into a troubled sleep.

They had been travelling for about 5 hours when Olivia woke up and panicked! Her scream resonated in the black tunnel immediately awakening him. She thrashed around in the leaves but fortunately Scott had been holding onto her even in his sleep. The echo of the scream continued to reverberate back and forth in the darkness. He tightened his grip and buried her sobbing head in his chest whilst whispering comforting reassurances.

'You're fine, I've got you. Was it the nightmare again?' Scott asked but Olivia could hardly reply.

For what seemed ages in that blackness, Olivia shook until finally both of them fell into a fitful sleep.

They did not hear the scrape of the bottom of the boat as it entered the lower lock of the next dwelling – nor did they feel the deceleration and bump as it stopped in the utter darkness.

Later a shaft of light washed over the vessel, awakening Scott who felt disorientated until his cold shivering body brought him back to reality. The boat gently rocked as the very blue female attendants got out and assisted Seren to the side of the dock.

Scott roused Olivia and her eyes flickered open. She shook with fear until he reassured her that they had arrived. Then shuddering with cold they hefted their packs, climbed out of the boat and changed out of their thermals.

Seren watched them dress with interest and her eyes sparkled,

<< how are you the same colour now as before we left >>

Scott couldn't begin to even try to explain this. He noted that the boat dock was a mirror image of the one they had left the previous evening and then checked his computer. Zec-1 had left a message just before communications with the lander were lost that morning,

'You arrived on time 10 hours after departure and the black mass tracked your position until moments before the dwelling lit up.'

They followed Seren and the cold, shuffling females towards the lift screw. As they approached, it was obvious that this dwelling was well populated, judging from the queue of waiting blue females.

The group parted as Seren, her attendants and the astronauts drew near, allowing them to preferentially ascend to the upper level.

Chapter 35
A Puzzle Solved

Shivering with cold, Olivia and Scott stepped from the screw lift into the bright morning sunshine of the new dwelling. There were no complaints about the temperature and humidity as the hot and condensing liquid soaked their thin tunics and started to warm their bodies. They stepped into the first pool and gasped with the heat of the water – it was like a very hot bath – and they had to lower themselves slowly to adjust to the temperature. After a few minutes they climbed out and into the slightly cooler second pool, and they then repeated the process in the third pool. They were now thoroughly warmed up so they retrieved their packs, sat on the clay ledge, took a well needed quantity of their water and ate some dry processed food.

This dwelling was similar in size and design as the previous two, and housed a similar number of inhabitants as the very first, judging by the groups that had emerged. Olivia and Scott vacated their seats to allow the adult females plenty of space to provide nourishment for their community and it was interesting to see that Seren and her attendant females were again given preferential status in the seating area.

No blue males appeared but two lifeless leaf clad bodies were carried by a group of 'older females' and they solemnly watched as they were placed in the channel and floated away.

'See!' said Scott, 'The leaf shrinks around the body when immersed in the hot water.'

The sun rose across the clouds, dragging the light sheath through the sky. As the temperature increased the astronauts used the large pool to cool down and they drank frequently from their limited water supply. There was no shade in the dwelling so they made regular trips underground to escape the burning sun. But it was cold down there, 5 degrees at best, although under the diamond lights there was a warmer shaft of light that was actually quite pleasant to stand beneath.

'We are going to have to ration our water,' Scott said as they perched on the floor by the lift screw where there was now some shade from the afternoon sun. 'You can understand why these blue people are drinking all the time in this heat.'

‘If you think I’m taking milk from those cold blooded creatures, think again!’ Olivia said indignantly.

The afternoon wore on and the blue females entertained themselves in their usual fashion. Seren kept apart from these activities and was often seen with her head inclining one way and then the other – what was she saying and to whom?

There was one birth that day which brought elation to the community. The new born blue baby was held high in the arms of the mother as if she was showing it off. Almost simultaneously, all the blue females and Seren raised their arms aloft for a few seconds and the new born was then lowered to the mother’s mammary glands for its first feed.

Scott looked enquiringly at Seren and her eyes glowed intensely as she responded,

<< its a male > its a male >>

Olivia and Scott watched as the blue infant was wrapped in a leaf and taken to the upper pool area. The mother washed herself and joined one of the groups of adult females nearby. An ‘older’ female approached carrying a leaf containing red liquid and carefully painted a small red triangle just outside the black square on the mother’s breast next to a number of black triangles.

‘I’ve got it! Yes, the triangles around the squares, Olivia, don’t you see, they must represent childbirth! That’s it, red must be for a male and black, presumably, for female.’

Olivia looked around at the groups of blue females and saw lots of black triangles but only two blue females had one red one in the whole community of well over one hundred.

‘If that’s the case they don’t produce many male babies – no wonder we’ve seen so few men.’

Chapter 36
A Surprising Dwelling

Meanwhile, 500 kilometres above, AJ and the remaining astronauts on board LifeSeeker-1 were gloomy and disconsolate. During the night they had tried all sorts of manoeuvres of the starship in an attempt to make contact with the lander and, more importantly, with Olivia and Scott. But each time, the two black masses quickly changed their positions so that communications were blocked. They had also been informed by Zec-C that the smaller black mass was travelling at 5 kilometres per hour – the same speed, they assumed, as Olivia and Scott.

As the astronauts travelled through the next two dwellings, they discovered that they were of similar size and activity. They found the hot days bearable if they bathed frequently and spent reasonable amounts of time underground to cool off. However, the long, cold, black nights were a disturbing trial because Olivia freaked out each time just before entering the boat. It was the sight of the black mouth of the tunnel that brought back the nightmare memories of her childhood. As on the first occasion, Seren calmed Olivia who then slept soundly. Scott contacted Zec-1 in the lander and grew more and more concerned that the black menace was tracking them from dwelling to dwelling. He slept fitfully and held on tightly to Olivia.

At their third new dwelling, six blue males appeared. Scott noticed that, whilst they all had many black triangles around their squared off nipples, only one had a red triangle. Also this one had the largest group of females. He commented to Olivia that two of the females in this group had a red triangle as well.

'If your male equals red theory is true, then this large group is optimised to produce males.' Olivia volunteered. 'If this is the case why hasn't Seren got any triangles on her breasts? – you must have noticed as you've hardly taken your eyes off them!'

'I don't know,' he replied, not quite sure how to take her comment. 'Perhaps Seren is part of a higher species and therefore uses a different system.' Scott hoped his rather analytical reply would diffuse Olivia's pointed but very accurate remark.

Scott was concerned that Olivia was not drinking enough so he had stopped drinking their supply of water and relied solely on breast milk. This, he hoped, would conserve rations for Olivia, who steadfastly refused to feed in this manner. Neither would she drink their milk when he managed, clumsily, to express some into an empty water container - much to the amusement of Seren. Olivia could not countenance drinking anything that came from these reptiles' bodies.

They changed their chlorine filters every day and Scott was comfortable that lifting their masks for short periods to eat or drink was not harmful. He was correct in this assumption but neither astronaut had considered the consequences of living fulltime in this unusual environment.

'I realise, after the event, that I underestimated the harmful nature of the atmosphere on Cloud Planet. Normally a significant amount of time is spent each day in the pure air of the lander. But with the immobilisation of ROL-1 and the unknown threat from above, circumstances are changed drastically, necessitating their flight across the planet. Now high temperature and humidity combined with excessive chlorine levels caused the gas to be absorbed through the skin building up abnormal salt levels in the astronauts' body. This does not affect Scott but has dire consequences for Olivia. Initially, I am unable to explain this as both have excellent health recorded in their dossiers.'

When they reached the fifth dwelling from the edge of the forest, they were half way on their journey towards the equator. They got out of the boat feeling cold and stiff and they then walked along the clay ramp following Seren and her attendants.

'There's something different about this dwelling. We have to walk further to the screw lift – I'm sure it's bigger.' Scott said.

When they came out into the glorious sunshine, they immediately noticed that he was right and it was about 150 metres across. The shimmering sheath of laser light looked enormous compared to those previously seen. Also the huge space to the left of the channel was filled with objects that astounded and puzzled the astronauts. They warmed and fed as quickly as possible and stood on the clay ramp leading to the top of the channel and stared.

'I can well understand our astronauts' puzzlement. The open area is bigger in size than where they had landed in previous dwellings and about 100 metres square. At ground level there are

two parallel structures about 60 metres in length and 30 metres apart. Each consists of a raised clay channel about a metre in width and height. The walls of the channels are about one third of a metre thick and are open-ended.

Resting across each channel are 40 evenly-spaced shafts of wood, each about 3 metres long and about one tenth of a metre square. They are arranged perpendicular to the line of the channels. Each shaft passes through a block of clay which hangs downwards in the channel. Where the shaft comes out of the clay there is a wide black triangle.'

'What on Earth are those for!' cried Scott.

But Olivia's eyes had been directed by the line of these objects, past the open space beyond them, to the centre of the dwelling wall directly in front of the arrays of black shafts.

'What's the dark structure in the wall? It must be 40 metres wide and over 2 metres high!'

But Scott had turned and was staring at three black constructions which rose from the floor of the dwelling up the front wall where they stood. They were 1 metre square in cross section, topped in red, and rose to three different heights.

'And what are those?' Scott thought as they walked down the ramp to the dwelling floor. Around them, the younger blue females cleared the ground of leaves, stalks and pods.

They arrived at the head of the right hand array of black shafts and Scott caught hold of the nearest one.

'Phew! This is heavy...aah!' Scott clutched his head and saw,

<< warning > warning <> do not touch the shafts >>

He recognised the severity of the message and let go immediately. He turned and saw Seren staring at him,

<< be patient <> later you will see and understand >>

The heat and humidity had now got to them and despite their intense curiosity they retired to the large pool to cool and watch the activities of over 200 blue people in this busy dwelling.

It was about an hour before noon when Seren caught their attention and pointed to the raised platform by the screw lift. Three 'older' blue females, each carrying two short black shafts, had approached the three vertical structures which Scott had noted earlier.

The female at the shortest structure placed the shafts on the red top, raised them and struck it, each hand in turn.

A deep 'boom', 'boom' resonated in the air.

'It's a drum!' Scott shouted, 'It must be hollow inside, oh! And there's a rectangular opening near the base.'

The booming continued and they watched, fascinated, as dozens of adult and younger blue females formed an orderly queue. They walked down the clay ramp to the top of the channel and then turned towards the two arrays of black shafts. Some of the youngsters carried large leaves which bulged as if they had something inside them.

As they entered between the shafts, they formed into three rows with the adults on either side of the youngsters. They all continued to walk forward until the leading adults stopped next to the shafts at the furthermost end of the rows. Each following adult then halted alongside their allotted shaft leaving the younger females to form a line between.

During this time the single drum beat continued.

'There must be, let me check, yes, forty adults on each side and what? Sixty younger ones between, what have they got in those leaves?' Olivia puzzled.

Suddenly Scott shouted and pointed. 'That black shape in the wall is moving, it's travelling down! – Oh my God! - it's a huge door to the outside.'

They turned their heads as the louder beat of the second drummer combined with the first to make a deeper sound.

'Look, it must be a signal,' cried Olivia. The two groups of adults picked up their black shafts and tilted them slightly upward with the clay block facing down.

The noise of the drums vibrated off the walls. Now the astronauts could see the misty rain outside the dwelling through the gap above the partly-lowered door.

The third 'drummer' then joined in causing a cacophony of sound. At the same time, the two rows of adults started walking forward carrying their shafts followed by the youngsters.

Then the leading ten adult females from each row converged and formed a V-shape which pointed towards the huge gaping mouth in the wall. The next two groups of 10 formed an angle moving outwards whilst the young females formed V-shapes behind them.

They moved forward in perfect harmony to the beat of the drum as the next two groups started to close back on themselves. All the younger females then became enclosed as the final groups of adults formed a reverse V-shape.

'My God!' cried Scott, 'They've formed a perfect octagon shape around the younger ones – it must be 30 metres wide.'

The huge black 'door' had now stopped flush with the ground giving an aperture 40 metres wide and over 2 metres high below the shimmering light sheath. The living group of blue people marched towards the opening.

At Seren's beckoning, Olivia and Scott had come down to the floor level and rushed up behind the departing group. As the front of the V-shape passed into the shadow of the huge doorway, so the leading blue females turned their shafts so the clay blocks were pointing upwards and the strange triangular ends were touching. When they then moved outside the wall of the dwelling, the diamonds embedded in the clay block of their shafts were immediately ignited by the sun and lasers of light shot upwards. As they moved forwards, the V-shape front became a moving wall of light and subsequent crystals burst into life until the whole of the moving group became a sheath of light encircling all of the blue females.

Olivia and Scott moved to the edge of the door and stared out as the light procession slowly faded into the pouring rain and mist whilst the drums boomed their discordant beat.

'No wonder she warned you about touching that black shaft!' Olivia commented.

'That's amazing!' Scott said looking out, 'Zec-C said that small light shafts had been detected moving away from the bigger dwellings but what are they doing?'

Reading his thoughts, Seren opened her hand and her eyes sparkled,

<< they take these out > put them in the ground <> then they bring back new leaves >>

In her hand was a small round pod, similar to the ones they had seen being gathered by the young females.

'They must sow those seeds in the wet clay,' said Olivia understanding, 'so that's what the youngsters were carrying in the leaves and presumably they harvest a crop of new leaves from mature plants – we've seen the Blue People farming.'

The incessant drumbeat continued for about an hour after which the moving light shaft reappeared out of the mist and entered the huge doorway. The process was then reversed and finally the black shafts with their diamonds facing downwards were lowered onto their original supports. The drumbeat dramatically ceased and the three rows of people relaxed and dispersed. The youngsters' arms were full of deep green leaves which they divided between the fourth pool for cooking and the upper platform for distribution.

Meanwhile the huge black door slowly and silently rose from the ground to seal the dwelling from the hostile elements outside.

'Look at their feet and lower legs! – They're deep blue – but I suppose that's hardly surprising considering it's at best 5 degrees out there, no wonder they've scurried back into the pools to warm up.' said Scott.

'But why the incessant beat of those drums?' Olivia wondered and saw,

<< they have to find their way back >>

Olivia looked at Seren, astonished - she had read her mind!

Chapter 37
First Temptation

As they travelled through the next two dwellings they discovered they were dedicated to farming and equally populated. Right on time the drum boomed, the blue females assembled and the wonderful, precision parade unfolded before their eyes. At the latter dwelling ten males appeared, two of whom had red triangles on their chest and later attracted the largest groups of females. Again each group including the male were uniquely identifiable by the octagon design tattooed on their chests. They watched the births with joy and shared the exhilaration as rare males were held aloft. Sadly they witnessed many deaths each day. Only once had the number of births exceeded the deaths – if this was happening all over Cloud Planet it didn't bode well for the future of the Blue People.

Both Olivia and Scott were coping better with the night journeys and in his frequent contacts with Zec-1, Scott learned that the black mass was still following them overnight – a major concern.

Their days in the sweltering heat and humidity were divided between watching the activities of the Blue People, bathing in the pools and frequent visits underground to cool off. Scott was getting concerned that their supply of fresh water was dwindling so he reserved it all for Olivia.

It was an adventure exploring new features of each dwelling. They examined the drums and found that they were covered with a huge leaf that appeared to have been bonded over the edges - it was very taught and painted red.

'Do you think they shrink the leaf onto this top using hot water?' Scott wondered and saw in his mind,

<< yes > and liquid from the leaves is used at the edges >>

Scott was startled and turned to see Seren looking at him. Wow! He thought, does she look stunning. And then he worried that she had read this too but nothing reappeared in his mind.

When they were at the next 'farming' dwelling the drumming started and they then followed three blue females underground. They traversed along clay ramps to the very front of the structure below the huge door. They observed that the door was on 3, metre square supports set in huge clay pits overflowing with water near the top. The females descended into the gloomy lower depths where in unison they knocked out the black plugs allowing water to gush out. The door slowly lowered.

'It's an amazing feat of engineering,' Scott marvelled, 'that door must weigh tonnes and everywhere I look there are straight lines, triangles, squares, octagons – not a design curve in sight – remarkable.'

As they moved back towards the screw lift, Olivia said she would remain under one of the ceiling light shafts as the noon sun was too hot for her.

Scott ascended the lift into the bright sunshine and sat watching the living octagon as it formed to the boom of the drummers. He did not notice Seren exit the large pool and she sat only a couple of metres to his right. He sensed her presence and looked at her – inside he was in turmoil – she was so beautiful. Her hair shone in the sunlight, her blue eyes stared ahead and then she turned towards him. As he took in her lovely face, she seductively lowered her eyelids. His eyes followed the line of the triangular 'necklace' which directed his gaze down to her perfect breasts. He drew in his breath and continued down to her navel, her flat stomach and the tantalising triangular flap pointing between her thighs. Her eyelids fluttered and he saw,

<< do you like me >>

And he wanted to shout 'yes!', 'yes!'.

Then, Seren stood up and cast him a most lascivious smile which rocked him to the core. She turned and he watched, mesmerised, as she moved away and dove into the large pool.

He looked around guiltily, fearing that Olivia would return, and then rushed to the nearest pool to hide his ardour.

But Seren had noticed and gave him a knowing smile and flash of her eyes. Where the fate of her people was concerned, she would employ all her powers and attributes and stop at nothing to achieve her ends.

Later that afternoon, Olivia disappeared underground again leaving Scott to watch the rituals of the dozens of groups of Blue People. Seren spent most of the time bathing, sitting and inclining her head. She sat a few metres from Scott on the sun drenched ledge overlooking the large open space below.

Scott looked at Seren and was afraid that he would lose control of his emotions, but her face looked concerned and she said,

<< what is the matter with your female >>

And Scott was very disturbed as he looked up and saw Olivia's white face as she stepped from the screw lift.

Chapter 38
The 'Home' of Seren

Olivia had first felt griping pains at the second 'farming' dwelling, but had kept it to herself and taken some medicine to settle her stomach. Then, that previous afternoon, she had thrown up underground and returned white as a sheet to be met by a concerned Scott. She assured him that it was no more than an upset stomach but he had insisted that she take extra rations of their dwindling fresh water supply.

The astronauts had already travelled 350 kilometres since leaving the lander in the dwelling at the edge of the forest. They had passed through four small and three larger 'farming' dwellings and they were now about half way to the next one in the utter blackness of the tunnel.

Scott woke up suddenly and wondered what had disturbed him. In the absolute blackness something was wrong because the boat was rocking!

'Where's Olivia!' He panicked and frantically scrambled in front of him.

But only leaves rustled.

Then he heard – a retch! – In the darkness from the back of the boat. Had that woken him? He fumbled for the flashlight when he heard a scream so piercing it shot into the depths of the tunnel and then reverberated back over his head echoing wildly. The screaming went on and on as the boat rocked and icy cold water splashed in. Scott managed to snap on the light.

The scene was surreal. The red walls of the tunnel passed overhead whilst Seren slept between two of her attendants. And at the stern of the boat.....

Olivia! - screaming! - shaking! - retching! - pitching forward!

'Olivia!' Scott yelled and he leapt over the prone Blue People, slipping on the leaves, and grabbed her legs which caused the boat to pitch dangerously. Olivia toppled over the stern of the boat but he held on frantically and managed to drag her shuddering body to the middle of the craft.

‘It’s alright, it’s alright!’ he reassured her and clung on as she shook uncontrollably against his chest, ‘I’m here, I’ve got you, and you’re safe.’

Scott paused, his heart hammering in his chest, and thought that if he had been a few seconds later Olivia would have pitched into the icy waters. But if he had not woken up!

‘Oh my God! Oh my God! I nearly lost you!’ he realised with horror. Then he kept the flashlight on until she finally fell asleep, but Scott couldn’t dare sleep because he was afraid he might let go of her again.

And all through this, Seren and her entourage slept soundly as the drama had unfolded in the black tunnel under the red clay of Cloud Planet.

The long hours in the utter incessant darkness passed in slow motion with only the occasional scrape of the boat on the sides of the tunnel to disturb the eerie silence. Finally the bottom of the boat ground on the dock and it stopped suddenly. Now all that Scott could hear was the roar of flowing water.

He consulted his palmtop and Zec-1 informed him that, during the previous nights, the black mass had divided into three. One was stationary between ROL-1 and LifeSeeker-1, another was following the astronauts through the tunnels with unerring accuracy and the third was moving randomly.

‘What do you make of that, Zec-1?’ Scott texted.

‘One inference, which I consider logical, is that AJ has sent out ROL-2 to try to outflank the black mass – but without success.’

‘Have you any further success with analysis of this menace?’

‘No, and I can only deduce that it is preventing us from determining its composition. I can see it but nothing more.’

Scott’s concerns were now mounting. Later, when the window of light fell on the boat, Olivia woke up. She seemed oblivious of the nights’ drama and said that she felt better. Scott decided to let matters lie for the moment and they followed Seren and her attendants up the gloomy ramp.

Scott and Olivia reached the screw lift with its usual queue of Blue People and were surprised when they were directed beyond it to a second lift. However, this was only the start of a day of surprises.

'Scott!' Olivia grasped his arm and pointed, all thoughts of her bad stomach immediately forgotten, 'The queue! The queue! – they're all blond-haired like Seren!'

The shuffling leaf clad file of Seren lookalikes parted to allow Seren, her attendants and the two astronauts to ascend the screw lift. They were so absorbed by this new revelation that, when they stepped off the lift, they were oblivious to the fact that the sun was not shining!

'What the!!' was all Scott and Olivia could muster as they stopped on a raised plinth and shivered with the cold. Meanwhile the Seren clones shuffled forward, cast off their leaves and entered their first pool.

'Where are we?' Olivia cried, confused, 'What are all those beams of light?'

There was no sun but the space was illuminated by dozens of rays of light which poured towards them from the far end. Scott was bemused and could not take in his surroundings. He stared upwards and around him and the penny dropped.

'Olivia,' he whispered in astonishment, 'we've come up inside a huge solid structure, why, it's got eight sides and must be 100 metres across. It's the same size as the first dwellings we visited – only this is closed in. Look, the far two walls facing the sun are studded with diamonds – that's what's causing these wonderful light beams.'

Olivia slowly rotated to try to take in these new surroundings.

'Olivia! It's surely 50, maybe, 60 metres high and what's that octagonal strip of light right at the top?'

Olivia looked up, transfixed, 'These two walls behind us are also studded with crystals and they must let light in later but I can't make out the side walls because they're not visible in the gloom.'

'The internal design of this closed octagonal pyramid is nearly identical to the farming dwellings. I see the familiar arrangement of four triangular pools, except that the fourth one is much bigger than the cooking structure. The recognisable channel runs from the centre and disappears under the front wall. However, the space where the arrays of wooden shafts are stored is quite different and will become obvious as I progress my narrative. '

They shivered with cold as they watched dozens and dozens of these beautiful blond females with piercing blue eyes warming up as they moved from pool to pool. Scott was speechless and then he looked around for Seren but could not pick her out among all these identical figures until a head turned in the third pool. Her eyes focused on Scott.

<< welcome to my home <> welcome to my people and our revered workers >>

The two astronauts warmed quickly as they were eager to explore further. For ease of recognition, they decided that they would refer to the Seren lookalikes as the 'Serenites' to distinguish them from the blue workers. Whilst the Serenites were feeding, Olivia and Scott were distracted by the sight of a door, about 2 metres high and four wide that had opened in the front wall. As they walked down the ramp and into the open space dominated by a raised triangular platform, the sun poured in and drew them through the opening. They were surprised as they walked into the blazing sunshine of an even bigger dwelling and gasped at the enormousness of the light sheath.

'I include a 3D diagram here to help explain the concept of a 100 metre pyramid dwelling sitting inside a 200 metre dwelling. The design is identical to the farming structures except here there are two assemblies of black shafts in the open space. In terms of population, there are about 500 blue workers in the outer structure and 200 Serenites in the pyramid.'

Single pyramid dwelling

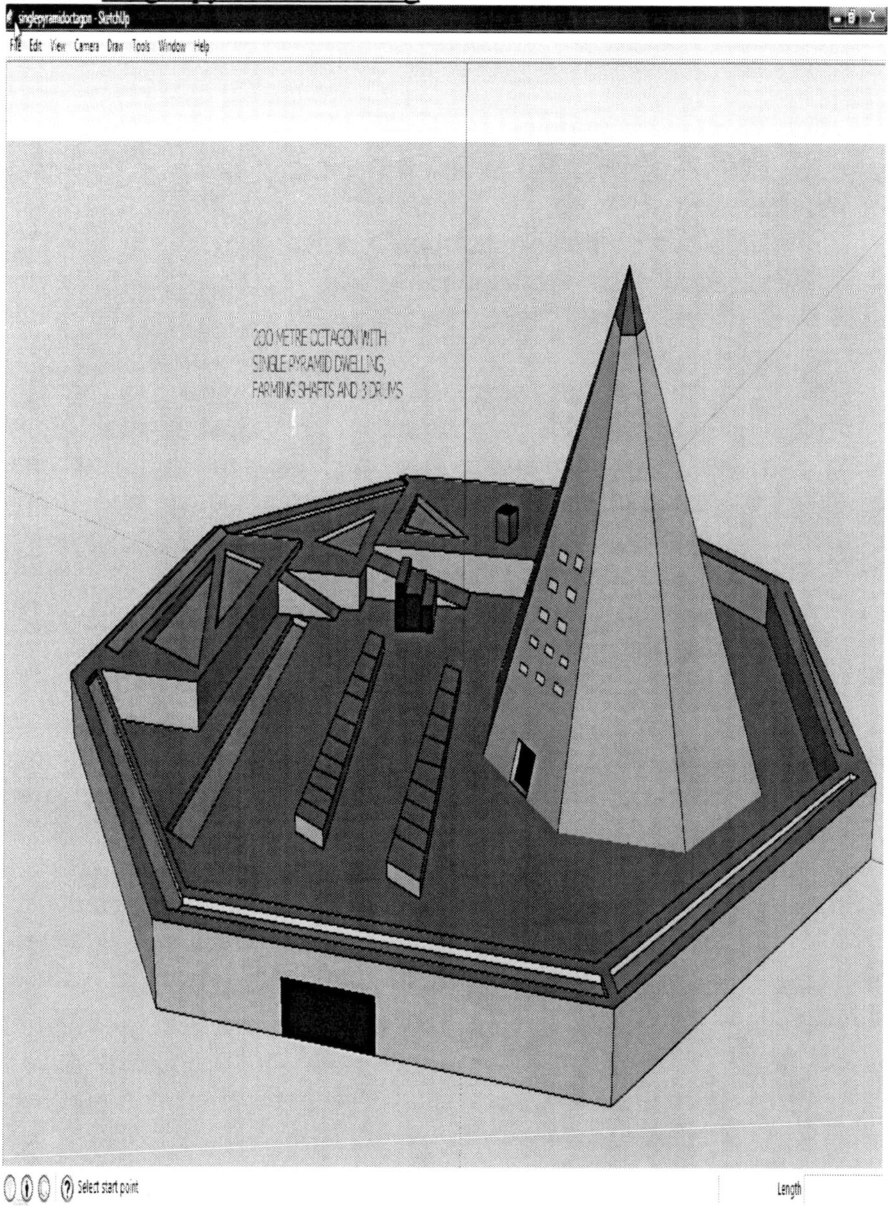

They walked forward a short way and looked back,

'What a stunning structure!' Olivia enthused. Externally, the octagonal pyramid of red clay bricks soared up towards the light sheath. It was flat at the top with a large black structure sticking out.

'What's that at the top?' Scott wondered. Then the heat and thirst forced them back into the cool of the pyramid. They walked around the huge raised platform just as Seren appeared at the top of the ramp. She was surrounded everywhere by hundreds of her people. She raised her arms upwards in greeting and all the Serenites followed her gesture.

The power of the telepathic message coming from these people was so forceful that Olivia and Scott clamped their heads as they saw, over and over,

<< welcome > welcome > welcome > welcome >>

They raised their arms in reply and the beautiful Serenites smiled in response. Then Olivia saw the group of 10 Serenite males and stared open mouthed.

Scott followed her gaze. These males were as equally magnificent as their female counterparts. They had similar blond shining hair, stunningly handsome faces and the same amazing blue eyes. They were broad shouldered with muscular bodies and strong legs and wore red triangular flaps at their waists.

‘Oh my!’ she admired, ‘They’re beautiful.’

And she looked knowingly at Scott and said,

‘Something for me to stare at - at last!’

Scott shrugged his shoulders and tried to reply in a matter of fact way,

‘Have you noticed these males have similar squares, tattoos and octagon shapes on their bodies? And nearly all the triangles on their chests are black!’

‘And another thing,’ Olivia said, ‘all the Serenite females are wearing one of those strange triangular necklaces similar to Seren’s.’

And they are all as stunning and perfectly formed as Seren, thought Scott to himself, but with slight subtle differences in features and form. What a world!

Chapter 39
Serenite Culture

And now the astronauts turned their attention to the huge triangular structure on the floor of the pyramid and they walked up a ramp that led towards the top.

'It must be 40 metres wide and 50 in length!' whistled Scott, 'and 4 metres high.'

When they reached the top, they could see that the inside was a series of ledges leading down to a flat clay floor about half the size of the overall space.

Their attention was caught by the sight of three massive vertical pillars at the points of the raised triangle.

They stood in front of one of them and looked up in sheer amazement, unable to take in what they were seeing.

'The block of wood is 3 metres square and 40 metres high. It is cut into triangular shapes from midway up to the top. The angles and shapes seem surreal. The colours are black, red on black, black on red and stretch up to the roof of the pyramid. The way the light interplays with the angled surfaces creates a mesmerising effect. These sculptures do not seem to obey our rules of perspective!'

It was now nearly an hour before noon and the shafts of light were pouring in from the front and rear walls into the pyramid. The illumination was soft and dramatic and changed as the sun moved across the huge structure housing the pyramid dwelling. Now their gaze was drawn to the side walls.

Looking across the four hot pools, Olivia could see that they were 'painted' from floor to apex with huge gashes of red on black, black on red in rising triangular shapes with the predominant colour being red. The dramatic impact of the colour scheme was bright and hot.

Scott turned and looked at the opposite side walls. These had similar designs but with a reverse colour scheme. Black was now dominant and the effect was austere and cold.

'Why is their art so different on opposite sides?' mused Olivia.

'I don't know,' replied Scott, 'but who'd have thought we'd be critiquing art on another planet?'

Serenite sculpture

Serenite art

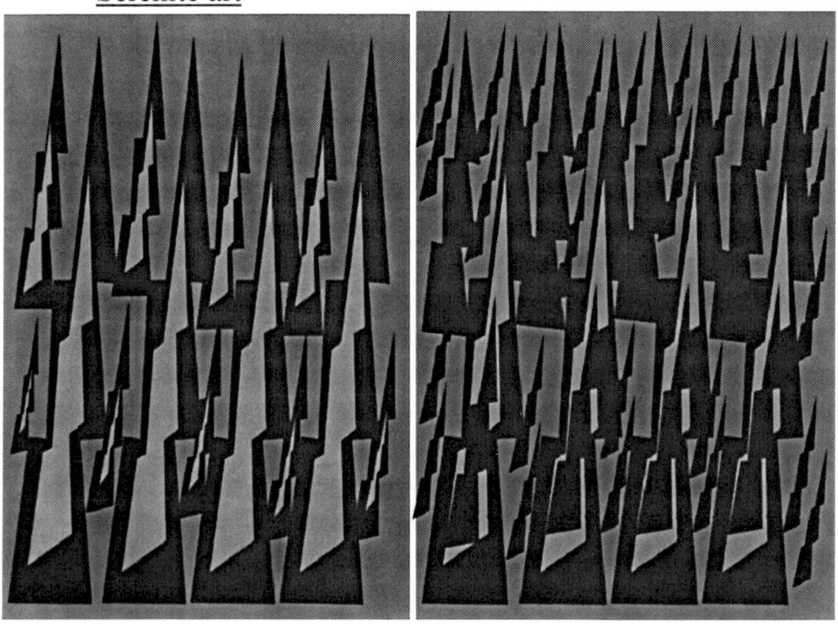

The beat of a drum from outside the pyramid caught Olivia's and Scott's attention and they walked out into the hot, humid sunshine. They watched, enthralled, as this time two farming groups of blue female workers assembled. They marched through the huge door and disappeared into the rain and mist with their young group of reapers and sowers.

The oppressive atmosphere quickly forced Olivia and Scott back into the relative cool of the pyramid where they could clearly hear the incessant beat of the three drummers.

'I reckon its 25 degrees inside and it must be 10 degrees hotter outside. Have you noticed it's less humid in here,' he said as he lowered his mask, 'and there's definitely less chlorine in the air – this is about the same as a commercial swimming pool – I don't think we need our masks or goggles in this pyramid – what a relief! But I wonder why?'

Olivia gladly removed her protection, and walked to the black structure that rose to the top of the roof.'

'It's ventilation! Scott! And see,' Olivia stood on the edge of the 2 metre square of black protruding from the ground, 'this is floating! Like the lift screw. This 1 metre square shaft in the middle goes all the way to the octagonal block in the opening – it's a chimney effect. But it doesn't really explain the lowered chlorine levels – there must be something else.'

'And over here,' Scott added, 'there's five of those drum structures against the wall of the screw lift platform and what are those? - they look like small, square pipes by each drum.'

Meanwhile Olivia had made her way to the large fourth pool as she had noticed the Serenites using it frequently. She tested the water.

'Ooh! Scott! This is cool, let's go in.' So they walked down the ramp into the inviting waters.

'It must be about 22 degrees,' agreed Scott, and they bathed and relaxed whilst around them the Serenite females, and an occasional male, happily enjoyed their company.

The drumming outside had stopped and the blue female workers brought food to the Serenites who fed and drank before they entered the channel to wash.

'We're getting low on fresh water, Olivia, you must start taking their milk, it's really nourishing and you're in danger of dehydrating.'

Stubbornly she wouldn't agree to this. She could not explain but she still had an aversion to drinking something from inside these creatures' bodies.

Lunch over and Olivia and Scott sat as the Serenite females and males formed groups around the inside of the pyramid and their ritual of mating commenced. In comparison to the blue workers, it was done in a more caring and sensitive manner. Again each female mated in turn with their male and this intimacy was repeated several times during the course of the afternoon.

Scott noticed that Seren sat apart from these groups whilst she sent and received telepathic messages.

Olivia and Scott found the overall spectacle quite moving and they also found the mating ritual of these beautiful people very erotic. They put their arms around one another, kissed and, quite unembarrassed, walked down the ramp into the cool waters and made love.

After, Olivia relaxed on the edge of the pool and closed her eyes. Seren then walked towards Scott and as she passed by, her eyes sparkled,

<< is your female feeling better >>

Now, with a jolt, he realised what had woken him in the middle of the night in that black tunnel when Olivia had nearly fallen out of the boat. He had seen in his mind,

<< your female is ill <> she is in DANGER <> DANGER >>

and he realised that Seren's telepathy had woken him up in time to save Olivia's life. His mind said 'yes' and 'thank you, thank you' and Seren responded to him with a smile that rocked him with emotion.

By mid afternoon, the mating had finished and the groups were lazing around and behaving in a soporific way. The astronauts were dozing when they suddenly jerked their heads around to the sound of drum beats from within the pyramid.

Five blue female workers were now in front of the drums each accompanied by a young Serenite female. Two of the workers were drumming - a deep off-beat sound similar to the call for farming.

After a short time, a column of about 100 adult female workers filed through the door into the pyramid dwelling. They stamped the ground and smacked together short wooden sticks as they jigged to the beat and made their way upwards and into the large triangular plinth surrounded by the three monolithic sculptures. When they arrived at the lower floor they formed perfect concentric triangles which moved in opposing directions.

Olivia and Scott had a birds' eye view from the edge of the third pool into the three-sided 'theatre'.

'Look at them moving to the rhythm of the drums, Olivia, this is incredible!'

When the beat stopped every blue female halted. The electric silence was interrupted by a high pitch reed-like sound caused by the young people as they blew into the small square tubes at the side of the drums. As the sound resonated around the pyramid, all the young female Serenites stood up and waved their arms aloft. Then they moved gracefully and slowly towards the triangle. They filed down onto the ledges forming their own concentric triangles which moved in different directions and heights.

In the late afternoon sun, with the dozens of shafts of light playing over their light blue bodies, it was a spectacular sight.

'Lovely!' Olivia whispered, and when the piping stopped the young dancers froze like statues.

Olivia and Scott jumped as three drums started in unison and their booming crashed around the walls. The blue female dancers leapt into contra flow motion with louder stomping of feet and clashing of sticks. The rays now bathed their darker blue bodies as they gyrated with staccato movements.

'Wow!' shouted Scott. The drums ceased, the female workers stopped and a higher note pierced the atmosphere. The young dancers now moved slowly and gracefully and rose on tip toes using their arms to form magical silhouettes.

'It's beautiful, just like the ballet,' Olivia breathed.

The contrast continued as four drums delivered a deafening wall of sound and the movements of the blue workers became wilder. The sound stopped and the silence was broken by a haunting higher note followed by even slower movements of the dancers.

The whole pyramid then rocked to the furious beat of five drums and the frenzied blue females stomped until they crashed lifeless to the floor in the eerie silence. Now a barely audible note filled the pyramid and the young dancers posed gracefully with arms aloft and remained perfectly still. Slowly the note declined until, when it was hardly audible, they lowered their arms.

Then, in unison, they slowly turned towards the astronauts, knelt slowly and together raised their arms towards them and smiled.

Olivia's heart burned with emotion for these lovely young creatures and she and Scott raised their arms in appreciation. Then all the Serenites in the pyramid responded likewise and they saw repeatedly,

<< help us <> rescue our people <> save our world >>

Finally Seren walked to the front of the platform by the drummers and looked intensely at Olivia and Scott,

<< we must continue our journey <> we have a long way to go >>

'I show below the inside of Seren's pyramid. You can see the familiar pools on the left but most striking is the triangular theatre with its massive wooden sculptures and the wall art at the back.'

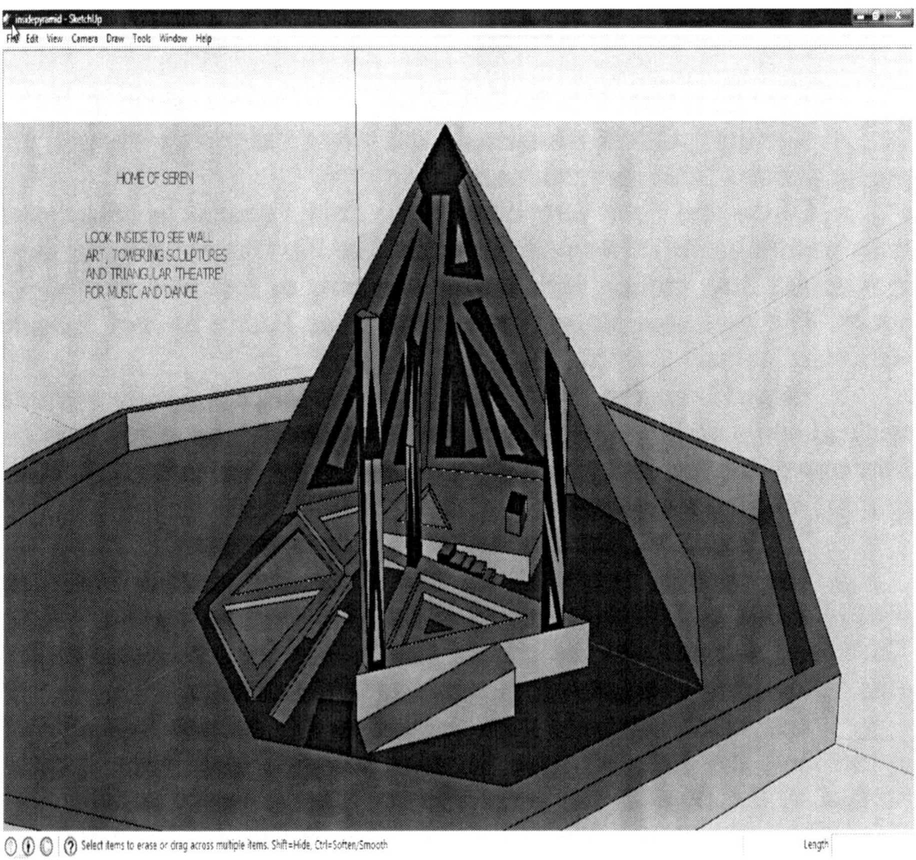

Chapter 40
Outside the Dwelling

The two astronauts followed Seren underground and arrived at the boat dock where they were surprised to find two tunnels side by side with their duplex docking chambers. Seren read Scott's question and pointed,

<< this one is for leaves > using many boats all the time <> the other for our people > who only travel at night >>

'So they send the food on to the dwellings near the equator,' Scott said aloud, 'and according to Zec-C's information we are about 100 kilometres away.'

'How far is the SOS dwelling?' Olivia queried.

'Once we reach the equator, it is two further structures along, not that far.'

'On their journey from the edge of the forest to the equator, our astronauts travel through four small dwellings each 100 metres across, three farming dwellings at 150 metres and are now leaving their eighth structure – a combined farming and Serenite dwelling 200 metres across. Next is a similar-sized dwelling and at the equator is a 300 metre structure that completes the 500 kilometre radial limb from the edge of the forest.'

Before they left Seren's home, Scott had gently told Olivia the frightening events of the previous night. She was shocked and her fears of the black tunnels returned. Scott removed one of the straps from the pack he carried and told her that he would use it to bind them together at the waist once they were settled in the leaves. This seemed to satisfy Olivia and the night's journey passed without incident.

The next dwelling was identical in basic layout but with subtle differences in the sculptures and wall paintings. There were no Serenite men at this dwelling but they were disturbed to see two lifeless blond forms taken away by the blue workers to the outside channel. Again, where ever they were, deaths exceeded births for both blue workers and Serenites alike.

As the sun climbed through the sky dragging the light sheath with it, Olivia and Scott donned their waterproof clothing and boots and ascended the lift screw into the pyramid dwelling. They had argued heatedly earlier that morning about going outside the walls of the dwelling; Scott had been cautious about this but Olivia couldn't wait to get outside and explore the hostile environment. However, she had made the sensible suggestion that they travel inside one of the farming groups.

'We'll be able to see the young farmers at work and take samples for analysis.' Olivia had continued, excited at the prospect of investigating another aspect of this surreal world.

They walked out into the heat as the first drummer signalled the assembly of the blue females and young sowers. Perspiration was already running down inside their wetsuits making them feel most uncomfortable. As they crossed the open space they lined up inside the forming group to the beat of the second drum. Then Scott turned and saw Seren who stood in the doorway of the dwelling.

<< be careful <> stay with my people <> they will guide you back >>

The third drummer crashed down and the living group of Blue People and two astronauts marched in unison towards the wide doorway. Olivia and Scott exchanged excited looks and gasped as the diamonds held by the blue females ignited as they left the cover of the dwelling wall. Soon they were completely enveloped by the moving light sheath and they took their first steps on the planet's surface outside of the dwelling structures.

Initially, the ground was firm but very wet from the incessant rain. However, under the protection of the light sheath, it was dry and the atmosphere remained warm but very humid. Suddenly the consistency of the clay changed and Olivia and Scott found their feet sinking to the ankles and they made strange squelching sounds as they extracted them. Fortunately the speed of the farming group was slow and they were able to keep up without too much difficulty.

They did not take their palmtops as they feared losing or damaging these vital means of communications. It also meant that their hands were free for sampling and manoeuvring in the equivalent of a paddy field. Each did carry a small camera on a band around their heads. Scott marvelled at the female workers whose arms and shoulders were taught with bulging muscles as they held their shafts steady at a slight upward angle. Each triangular edge overlapped its neighbours which formed a continuous flow of rainwater over the diamond crystals cooling them and producing steam which helped maintain the internal temperature. It was a surreal experience cocooned inside this marching group of advanced reptiles who took absolutely no notice of their two passengers.

Every so often, Olivia took samples of the wet clay and the detritus of rotting leaves and stalks and reasoned that its decomposition was how the clay remained so fertile. She tried to gauge the age of the young females; they were nearly as tall as she was. From their development she guessed they were the equivalent of young teens.

After about 100 metres the young sowers started stooping in sequence and they placed their seed pods at regular intervals into the slushy surface; Scott reckoned they had planted about 400 in five equally spaced rows. Then the whole group turned through 90 degrees and the ground below them changed. Suddenly they were trudging through rows of small plants with fleshy leaves and their feet started sinking further into the clay. Olivia stooped and picked a whole plant for detailed analysis later.

'Their webbed feet are a distinct advantage out here,' she said, 'and look how blue their legs are getting.'

Now the farming group slowed as they passed into rows of fully mature plants nearly 2 metres high with huge thick leaves which dripped with rainwater. The young sowers tore off these leaves and gathered them in their arms as they passed by with an efficiency and precision that surprised the astronauts. But of increasing concern was the fact that the astronauts' feet were sinking further into the cloying soil and both were tiring from the continuous effort. After a further 100 metres or so the slow moving group turned again through 90 degrees......

.... and started to speed up!

With rising alarm, Olivia and Scott trudged with them but could not match their speed through the viscous clay. Slowly the young sowers, their arms piled high with leaves, moved past the struggling astronauts and Scott looked at Olivia with anxiety as the rear of the group started to catch up with them.

'Faster, Olivia, faster!' urged Scott as they both helped to pull themselves forward.

'I can't go any bloody faster in this stuff, it seems even deeper!' Olivia shouted back. 'It's like quicksand.'

Then Scott staggered forward straight into one of the huge plants which stopped him in his tracks and he fell back and sank to his knees in the sodden clay.

'Olivia! I'm stuck!' cried Scott and, as she turned to help, she watched with rising dread as the rear of the farming group marched past them, undeterred, to the distant beat of the drums.

'I am very disappointed at our astronauts' lack of forethought and planning before embarking on such a risky journey outside the dwelling. I can only conclude that their enthusiasm to explore the extraordinary surroundings clouded reasoned evaluation. In particular, Olivia shows the risk taking side of her character. They should have consulted Zec-1 for a risk assessment which would have been a firm 'no' unless snow-shoes were readily available!'

The icy rain pounded down on Olivia and Scott and plastered hair over their faces. Cold water streamed into eyes and dripped into their clothing. The temperature was less than 5 degrees and the sheath of light was barely visible as it wobbled away from them. Hyperthermia was barely 10 minutes away in these appalling conditions.

Olivia frantically pulled at Scott but failed to budge him after several attempts as she, too, was pulled deeper into the clay. Both were covered in splotches of red clay and it became obvious that their frenzied movements were only making matters worse.

'Don't move,' ordered Olivia, 'this is like quicksand and we must apply the same principles to get out.' Accordingly, Olivia used the thick stem of the nearby plant to haul herself upright and unintentionally stripped a metre wide leaf from the stem.

'Of course!' she cried, 'we can use these.' Olivia placed the leaf on the clay in front of him. It was so thick that she could stand on it and pull on Scott's arms but he was stuck fast. She pulled harder and he used his arms to push down on the leaf. There was some movement but both were weakened by the intense cold. Scott found himself looking directly into Olivia's eyes and in desperation they pushed and pulled but to no avail.

Then Olivia's head hurt and she saw,

<< calm yourself <> use your strength gently <> you can do it >>

'Scott! Slow movements! Don't fight it!' Olivia sat on her knees and pulled gently at his shoulders. At first nothing happened and then, ever so slowly, he inched out of the clay. Finally and with a deep sucking sound his feet came out and he tumbled on top of Olivia before rolling aside. She pulled herself up and stripped another large leaf.

'Use these leaves and let's get the hell out of this bog,' shouted Olivia, 'but which way did they bloody go?'

'Listen, the drums, it's that way.' Scott pointed.

They placed the huge leaves in front of them, clambered on and then pulled the vacated ones behind to the front position again. Using the tree stalks to help their balance, they clumsily scampered through the plantation until the ground became clearer and firmer. Meanwhile the sound of the drums increased through the roar of the driving rain and shaking with cold they staggered forward together.

'She spoke to me. Seren helped me to do it!' Olivia's teeth chattered with the cold.

'But Olivia, it was your initiative with the leaves that saved the day - you saved my life.'

Suddenly the drums stopped but directly ahead through the downpour they could see a wide rectangle of bright light. As they hurried closer they could see Seren standing in the middle of the doorway, arms outstretched and beaming one of her beautiful smiles.

As they journeyed on through the tunnel that evening they reflected on their near disastrous foray outside the dwelling. They realised that they had not thought it through properly and vowed more care in the future. To lighten matters Olivia playfully punched Scott and said,

'Well at least I've got some samples to analyse and we must have looked a real sight thrashing about in that mud-bath!'

'Yes, we can watch it again in the morning – it's all on video!' Scott said and, as Olivia snuggled into him, the boat rocked slightly in the absolute blackness.

Another night passed without further incident and they safely arrived at their tenth dwelling. They were now at the equator.

'Our astronauts find it almost impossible to grasp that another 10 dwellings stretch across the plains to the other mountain range and even harder to imagine that they are underneath one of

1000 dwellings spread around the equator. That is 20,000 structures in total on the 1000 kilometre wide red plain of Cloud Planet.'

They ascended the screw lift and arrived, as anticipated, in the pyramid dwelling where they all warmed and fed themselves. Then they walked out through the sunlit door.

'This dwelling is 300 metres wide with each wall over 100 metres long. The shimmering light sheaf is an incredible sight, stretching back towards the morning sun. The wall of the dwelling immediately in front of our astronauts contains the usual massive door at the end of an open space about 100 metres square.

'Behind them are four octagonal pyramids of bright red brick construction. They are identical in size, nested together, and their forward facing walls are studded with glistening crystals. Each has a doorway leading to a small outside area.'

'This is like a mini – city,' Scott cried excitedly, 'why, there must be nearly 2000 inhabitants!'

They were driven back inside by the heat and humidity where again they took the opportunity to explore their surroundings in more detail. This was thirsty work and Olivia was getting extremely concerned at the dwindling supply of fresh water. She inwardly dreaded the thought of having to resort to the creatures' milk. Suddenly she realised that Scott was asking a question.

'It's surprising how little food they eat.' Scott commented. 'Just some leaves and milk but they're very strong and active.'

'That's because their cold-blooded,' replied Olivia, 'whereas most of the food we eat produces the energy to maintain our internal body heat. I seem to remember that we would starve to death after two months without food but a crocodile can last a whole year between meals!'

'Yes, you're right. It's interesting that evolution on this planet has remained cold-blooded whereas on Earth warm blooded mammals diversified after the reptiles – but I've never been quite sure why.'

'Both are right. The first warm-blooded mammals emerged 210-230 million years ago, about 100 million years after reptiles left

the water. It is generally agreed that warm-blooded avoided going out into the open and young could be born in the safety of an underground den.

'Furthermore, in my database I find copious notes and digital video – our astronauts take every opportunity to investigate and record their remarkable surroundings for posterity. I am selecting a couple of their more interesting observations which give an insight to the inhabitants and the planet itself.

'Firstly, the design and construction of the 100 metre wide pyramid dwellings is simple yet very effective. Each wall is 4 metres wide at its base and forms an angle of 30 degrees to the vertical. The thickness of the wall is slowly reduced as the height increases until it is a mere 1 metre at the apex 75 metres above the ground. During construction the eight walls are built up together thus supporting one another as the height increases. It is not too dissimilar to the fabrication of an igloo using blocks of ice.

'Secondly and surprisingly, there are no other life forms on Cloud Planet. Our astronauts diligently search every dwelling and pyramid as they pass through and use sophisticated sensing and microscopy tools in their computers. But they find no insects or bacteria or simple celled organisms. However, they did find many small lizards in the darker corners and these were much more abundant underground. They record in their notes that the high levels of chlorine in the water and atmosphere precludes all but the hardiest of survivors – the cold blooded reptiles. They live in a world which is almost perfectly hygienic which accounts for the absence of disease amongst the inhabitants of Cloud Planet. '

Chapter 41
SOS City

They had now travelled around the equator for a distance of 100 kilometres and they arrived, with heightened expectations, at the source of the SOS message that had initiated their pioneering journey 21 years ago.

Olivia was so excited that she put the return of her stomach pains to the back of her mind and they waited impatiently as the sun rose dragging the light sheath across the sky.

Just before midday, Seren beckoned and they followed her outside and up the ramp where they sat near the three drums attended by their usual drummers. The first thing they noticed was a raised wide ledge running, they presumed, all the way around the dwelling near the crystals. Sticking out of the ledge at about 2 metre intervals were upright black shafts with red clay flat blocks similar to the ones used for farming.

Then the first drummer started beating and, from all parts of the dwelling and the pyramids, hundreds of female workers walked up clay ramps leading to the ledge. They each stopped in front of one of the wooden shafts. Scott guessed that there must have been about 400 blue females around the entire circumference. Then the second drum came in. Each female picked up a shaft and held it horizontally at waist level with the clay blocks pointing to the light sheath. It seemed that the red blocks touched their neighbours' on both sides forming a continuous flat band 2 metres from the light sheath shimmering in front of them.

At this point Olivia and Scott realised that the third drummer was a Serenite adult female. She cocked her head sideways, in a similar fashion to Seren, raised her flat 'drumsticks' and pounded a loud repetitive beat.

Immediately, all the females holding their black shafts moved forward three steps and the red clay blocks moved over the tops of the diamond crystals, shielding them from the sun.

This caused the light sheath to shoot up into the sky and disappear in a second. The effect was so instantaneous it was as if someone had thrown a light switch. As a result cloud closed in, the temperature dropped and it started raining. Then the third drummer stopped and the multitude of female workers immediately stepped three paces back uncovering the diamonds.

The result was dazzling as the crystals spontaneously ignited at full force causing the light cone to shoot up into the clouds again – and the sun shone.

Olivia and Scott jumped as the third drummer crashed down again on the drum. As before the blue females moved forward shutting off the light. This forward and back movement turned the light sheath off and on in synchronisation to the third drummer.

' – light – light – light – long light – long light – long light – light – light – light –'

'My God!' shouted Scott, 'It's perfect Morse code! Three short bursts of light, three long and three short again, repeated over and over!'

They couldn't take their eyes off the spectacle viewed through alternating hot sunshine and cold rain.

After a while Scott turned excitedly to Olivia,

'When we saw that flashing signal in the conference room, did you ever believe that we would be sitting here watching another life species sending that incredible message – I'm overwhelmed!'

But Olivia was white and, gripping her stomach, was barely able to respond,

'I feel ill, aaargh! The pain!'

He did not hesitate and rushed her down the ramp where she was violently sick in the open channel.

Chapter 42
From Bad to Worse

Scott half carried Olivia into the pyramid and walked past the huge triangular structure. He stopped intermittently when the interior was thrown into darkness then resumed as the light shafts came on again illuminating his way. He reached the cool pool, helped Olivia to a comfortable position and mopped her brow – she was burning, shaking and clutching her abdomen.

The SOS flashed in the pyramid which seemed to add to Olivia's discomfort and also made it difficult for Scott to locate and find the medical bag. When he returned to Olivia's side, she was half sitting in the cool pool, throwing water onto her face. She was obviously in distress and his stomach knotted with deep concern. He put his arms around her,

'Olivia, what's wrong!'

'It's like before, aaargh!! Only worse and these flashing lights!'

Then, Seren appeared like a vision out of the dark and she sat next to Olivia on the edge of the pool. She was so close that Scott caught her breath. The light on her body accentuated the pale, duck egg blue of her perfect skin. Then she faded into the gloom and reappeared as the signal went on and off, on and off. Olivia groaned and Scott watched, uncomprehending, as Seren removed her strange triangular necklace and placed it gently around Olivia's neck. She then put her hand on Olivia's forehead and looked into her eyes,

<< be calm> be calm > be calm >>

It was so reassuring that Scott even felt relief himself. Olivia clutched the necklace and mouthed a 'thank you' directly at Seren. She was momentarily transfixed and then, remarkably, fell asleep. Scott looked at her and said his own 'thank you' and saw,

<< there is something very wrong with your female >>

And Seren got up and walked away.

Olivia was, at least, comfortable for the moment, so Scott made a pillow from a large pack of cotton wool stored in the medical bag and waited until the signal stopped flashing. He then strapped a rectangular box to Olivia's forearm and ensured that it was tightly in place before activating the 'on' switch. This marvel of miniaturised diagnostic equipment determined the major bodily functions and key liquid chemical levels accurately and wirelessly.

He sighed with relief as the initial red light changed to amber and the LCD display confirmed adequate battery power. The words 'Start Scan?' appeared and he tapped the screen. He saw, not surprisingly, that Olivia's body temperature was high as was her blood pressure and pulse. Then various chemical measurements of her blood, urine and saliva passed across the screen and although he did not understand these, the fact that several measurements were reported in 'red' meant that something was radically wrong.

Finally, the screen was headed by the word 'diagnosis' and then words appeared which brought a lump to his throat and he swallowed hard.

'Condition is serious but cannot be determined accurately, results need urgent analysis by Zec-1 and Martha'

He switched off the analyser but left it in place for further tests. He knew he would have to be patient and wait for the light sheath to switch off so Zec-1 could analyse the results.

Olivia continued to sleep fitfully and about 2 hours later the diagnosis read,

'Condition is stable but still serious, results need urgent analysis by Zec-1 and Martha'

Scott had registered that this dwelling and its pyramids was only sparsely populated by Serenites but mainly housed blue females for the signalling. It was a relief that there was no music and dance with Olivia being so ill.

However, he realised that they could not travel any further until her condition was known and, he prayed, cured. As if reading his thoughts, Seren appeared and her eyes met his,

<< we will remain here until your female can travel again <> but we cannot delay too long <> we still have a long way to go >>

Scott smiled at her with relief and gratitude.

Shortly before dusk, the small band of Serenites and blue workers in their pyramid warmed up and they all moved underground to the chamber below the hot pools. Seren helped gather extra leaves to make a comfortable bed for Olivia. She was awake and had taken some fresh water from their almost depleted stock but was still in extreme discomfort. Seren again placed her hand on Olivia's brow and magically she relaxed and went to sleep. Scott was so relieved and grateful that he wanted to kiss this extraordinary nurse and was then anxious that she might have read his thoughts.

Seren beamed a knowing smile and she went to join her attendants to settle for the night.

As soon as the light sheath switched off, Scott fired up his palmtop and plugged in the diagnostic tool.

Zec-1 was almost immediately on line to inform that the black mass was already above the lander and stationary over the SOS dwelling and then reported his findings from the diagnostic report which chilled Scott to the bone,

'Olivia's condition is extremely critical. Apart from high temperature, pulse and blood pressure, she has an abnormally high salt level in her blood which could cause major organ failure if not reduced. She is also severely dehydrated. She must have a blood transfusion as soon as possible!'

Zec-1's prognosis was effectively a death sentence for Olivia!

Scott buried his head in his hands in despair as he sat in the blackness just outside the underground sleeping quarters. His mind was in turmoil and he tried to suppress his tears. It could not be worse because the only matching blood type available was on the starship, 500 kilometres above him!

As his body shook with emotion, he suddenly saw,

<< be calm > be calm > there must be a way >>

This message galvanised Scott and shook him out of his misery,

'Zec-1, we have to get Olivia to the starship. Can we get one of the emergency shuttles down at night?'

'The black mass between you and LifeSeeker-1 at night makes it impossible for me to compute a percentage success rate. We have to get the shuttle down through the mass and then, with Olivia on board, get it back through to the starship. This is an unknown danger and considering the fact that the black mass reacts to our every move, I cannot recommend this course of action. Furthermore how do we communicate with LifeSeeker-1 to send the emergency vehicle down to us?'

Hopeless, Scott thought, the situation is impossible and again in the dark he saw,

<< be calm <> there must be a way <> there must be a way >>

These encouraging words seemed to run around his mind and helped him to think. He then remembered their first attempt to land on Cloud Planet during the day when the light shafts had caused the landing to be aborted – what had Zec-1 said during their analysis in the starship afterwards?

'The light shafts were too close together to risk landing'

'but if they were further apart there was a good chance of landing?'

'but there was nowhere on the planet where the light cones were further apart'

And then it hit him!

'Zec-1! Zec-1! When we analysed the aborted day landing, what did you compute as a safe distance to give a reasonable chance of landing in the day?'

'Fifty kilometres from the nearest light shaft gives an 85 per cent chance of success.'

'So if we could switch off this SOS dwelling during the day!' Scott said with rising hope, 'Could we land inside? And for how long would we have to turn it off?'

'Yes we could as the dwellings are 50 kilometres apart but we would need two windows each a minimum of 10 minutes, to get the emergency shuttle in and out. But you have to tell LifeSeeker-1 to pre-program the lander's computer and give exact coordinates to land.'

Scott's hopes soared as he wondered if the blue females could hold the light shaft off long enough and if he was any good on the drums!

As he sat in the blackness, Seren transmitted,

<< they can do it > and so can you >>

'Zec-1! Give me the Morse code for the following message!'

'In the design of LifeSeeker-1 there are seven emergency shuttles, each capable of holding one astronaut. They are for critical evacuation of the starship or the rescue of individual crew members from life threatening situations. Each is highly manoeuvrable and capable of manual operation by the individual or fully automatic control by Zec-C.

'Further, examination of the medical records for two of the criminal volunteers showed that they are now 'salt intolerant' after cryo-hibernation. These findings almost certainly help explain Olivia's condition.'

Chapter 43
The Rhythm of the Drums

Olivia slept most of the night but now the cold was taking its toll and as soon as possible Scott rushed a semi – comatose Olivia to the first pool to warm up. He gave her the last but one container of fresh water to hydrate her body. When the analyser was switched on, he watched the dreaded result that her condition had deteriorated overnight and the words,

'immediate blood transfusion', flashed in red.

'Hold on, hold on.' He urged. He clasped her hand and made her as comfortable as possible. The shafts of light streamed into the pyramid from the morning sun whilst he warmed himself thoroughly and took a sustaining drink from one of the nearby blue females. He had not drunk fresh water for many days but had no ill effects from the frequent intake of milk supplemented by his dried food store.

Then, on a piece of card from a box in the medical bag, he copied Zec-1's message using an indelible pen and put his prompts above the dots and dashes.

Meanwhile, Seren had warmed up and fed and she came over and put her hand on Olivia's forehead. Her shaking body relaxed and she slept. Scott noticed a new necklace had appeared around Seren's neck, its triangle tantalisingly pointing to her cleavage. He had to force his eyes back to meet hers and he held her gaze as she transmitted,

<< come with me >>

Momentarily, he feared she might be trying to entice him. However she pointed to the card and walked up the ramp and stood by the largest drum overlooking the unusual 'theatre' below.

Scott followed, understanding, he could practise the message here in the pyramid.

Seren held the square 'drumsticks' and demonstrated the technique, alternately slapping them down on the taut red leaf. The booming filled the pyramid. She handed the drumsticks to Scott and put her hands on his to help him learn the method.

As she brushed against him her touch was electric, and he was affected by the close physical contact. He forced himself to focus on attaining a steady beat. She moved away and disappeared into one of the pools leaving Scott to concentrate all his attention on his 'music score'. He practised but found it difficult to coordinate the drum beat to achieve consistent dots and dashes. He tried to recall what the blue females had done – three paces in, light off for about 3 seconds, three paces back – then the dots were about 3 seconds and the dashes about six – so he counted in his mind,

'1000, 2000, 3000' and found that by writing the numbers, three or six, above the dots, dashes and spaces, he could get a regular beat. However, after half an hour his arms were aching and he stopped to rest and take a well-earned drink and he saw,

<< that sounds good <> but needs to be louder >>

He practised for another half hour and rested until Seren beckoned and then they walked out of the pyramid into the brilliant sunshine with the shimmering light cone streaking skywards. The time approached one hour before noon.

The three drummers were already in place as they approached the drum platform and with an incline of her head, the third Serenite handed her drumsticks to Scott.

The first drum started and 400 blue females walked to their stations on the wide ledge in front of the laser emitting diamonds.

The second joined in and shafts were hefted to the horizontal position.

Scott's heart started racing. This was it and he looked at Seren who was holding his 'score' and she encouraged,

<< you can do it <> begin >>

In that 300 metre dwelling on the wide plain of Cloud Planet and surrounded by the Blue People, Scott steeled himself to play the drums as if his very life depended on it – but it was Olivia's life at stake. Then he crashed down on the big drum and the light went out!

500 kilometres above and just outside Cloud band, the astronauts of LifeSeeker-1 sat in the command dome. AJ, Alison, Steve, Martha and Pete looked dejectedly at one another. There had been no contact with Olivia and Scott for 12 days and all attempts to outflank the black mass had failed. They had even sent one of the emergency shuttles out as a decoy whilst ROL-2 piloted by Alison and Steve went the opposite direction. But the mass just split into three and blocked communications with the astronauts on the ground, from the starship, ROL-2 and the decoy lander.

'The only comforting fact is that we can assume that Olivia and Scott are travelling from dwelling to dwelling under the moving black mass,' AJ tried to reassure his crew.

Last night the black mass had remained stationary and they could not be sure why the astronauts on the planet had not moved on – unless, of course, the answers and explanations were to be found in the SOS dwelling.

The gloom in the command dome was shattered when Zec-C suddenly announced,

'Attention! Attention! The SOS message has changed! Repeat, the SOS message has changed!'

The astronauts all focused on the LCD portion of the dome where the signal was always displayed and gone were the familiar short and long lights of the distress call and in their place a different series were flashing.

'Zec-C! Can you interpret?' AJ commanded impatiently.

'There are errors in the message, and the signature is different, I am waiting for repeats to confirm.'

'What can it mean? Who's sending the message?', Steve queried.

The astronauts looked at one another and then Zec-C announced that the message was .....

- O – L – I – V – I – A - - V – E – R – Y - - I – L – L --

they groaned with dismay at these first three words.....

- E – X – T – R – A – C – T --

this was the agreed word for urgent immediate removal from danger....

- N – O – O – N - - N – E – X – T - - S – O – S - - O – F – F --

'What's that mean 'SOS OFF'?', said Alison.

- W - - = - - 1 0 – M - - P - - = - - 2 0 – M - - W - -= - - 1 0 – M --

'Is this code?', Pete wondered.

- L – A – N – D - - O – N - - O – L – I – V – I – A - - P – A – L – M --

'On Olivia's palm?! What does that mean?' Martha puzzled.

It was AJ, who shouted triumphantly,

'A day landing! A daytime landing! Scott's going to turn off the light shaft at exactly noon tomorrow. We have a 10 minute window to get the emergency shuttle in. Then 'P', yes, 20 minute pause to get Olivia on board and then the light shaft will be turned off again for 10 minutes to allow take off. Brilliant, Scott!'

'On Olivia's palm?!' Alison queried and then she got it, 'he's going to put Olivia's palm top down as a beacon to land on. We can program that in.'

'Zec-C give me your analysis of a day landing with one dwelling switched off – surely you computed this before as feasible?!' AJ commanded.

'Correct and a 50 kilometre space between light shafts gives an 85 per cent success. Also 10 minutes is minimum window to position shuttle adjacent to light shaft for descent when switched off. I conclude Zec-1 has computed this for Scott. Also Olivia's palm top as a beacon gives a radius error of 10 metres for the landing. Emergency shuttle will have to be completely programmed for whole operation with critical timing. Taking into consideration these extra factors the success rate drops to 75 per cent – so significant risk and Scott's timing down on the planet is critical.'

AJ looked at the other astronauts gravely.

'You have Zec-C's analysis and we have a crucial decision to make.'

There was no hesitation and the mission to rescue Olivia was unanimously confirmed.

'Zec-C!' AJ continued, 'Programme emergency shuttle 1 and prepare descent plan. We need automatic opening of the shuttle hatch at 1 minute after landing and closure 2 minutes before takeoff. That gives a window of 17 minutes to get Olivia strapped in and for Scott to get away from the lander.'

'Astronauts - extra food and water to go down plus replacement palm top for Scott – I'm certain he'll send his up with Olivia.'

'Martha - prepare sick bay for every eventuality – we should get the diagnosis from Scott's palm top as soon as Olivia is on board the starship.'

Everyone moved with renewed hope.

Scott was exhausted, cold, soaking wet and his arms were so painful that after about 1 hour he collapsed to the ground – surely he had got the message through. Seren had stood still holding the card and willing him to succeed and somehow her encouragement gave him extra strength to keep the drumming going. The third Serenite drummer picked up the drumsticks and, with a cock of the head, resumed the usual SOS signal as if nothing had happened.

Seren’s attendants helped him back into the pyramid where Olivia was still asleep and he collapsed into the hot pool which quickly revived his aching body. He then checked Olivia’s condition – it had stabilised but she was plainly very ill.

‘Hold on, hold on another day and we’ll have you back with Martha.’ And he cradled her head and knew that the hardest part was yet to come!

Chapter 44
Emergency Evacuation

During the afternoon and following morning he gave Olivia the last of the fresh water. The cold night had worsened her condition but all he could do was keep her as warm and comfortable as possible. She was now comatose but breathing and alive.

He checked his watch. They had previously synchronised all their watches with Zec-C to the 20 hour day of Cloud Planet. It was now 1 hour before noon and the drumming started outside and soon the pyramid was flashing to the familiar SOS message. He left Olivia with Seren's attendants; they would bring her out to the open space in front of the pyramids at Seren's signal.

Scott walked out into the dwelling with Seren. He was wearing a wet suit – 10 minutes in this freezing cold rain was going to test him as well as the blue females. He placed Olivia's palm top in the centre of the open space, it was at least 50 metres square, surely enough margin for error. Then they walked to the platform where the three drummers beat their incessant rhythm.

Timing was absolutely critical and Scott glanced at his watch yet again checking the digits as they approached 10.

'09:59:00'

He handed his watch to Seren so she could hold it for the duration. She inclined her head and the third drummer ceased drumming and handed the drumsticks to Scott. The SOS message stopped and the dwelling remained lit.

'09:59:30'

Scott prepared himself; surely 10 minutes would not be as bad as yesterday's hour of drumming?

'09:59:50'

He positioned the drumsticks and looked at Seren. Her eyes dazzled with encouragement.

'09:59:57'

He crashed down on the drums and 400 blue females took three paces forward.

'10:00:00'

The dwelling switched off, the mist and rain came in and the temperature fell. Scott focused on his drumming which was easy to begin with but as the minutes went by the rain drenched his face and his arms started to become heavy.

'10:05:00'

The beat of the drums was so loud that he wondered if he would even hear the exhaust of the rocket motor. Now he was really aching and wondered if he could go on. Seren's eyes encouraged in the mist and rain.

<< keep going <> be strong <> be strong >>

'10:08:00'

And above the booming of the drums he could make out a new noise....

'10:09:00'

..... and, yes, thank God, it was the unmistakable sound of a powerful rocket engine in full reverse thrust.

'10:09:30'

Now it was visible and he urged his painful arms to continue.

'10:09:45'

The roar was deafening and the huge craft was now only metres from the ground. Surrounding its main central rocket engine were four fins carrying smaller boosters for manoeuvrability. These held the hydraulically controlled legs.....

'10:09:50'

.......which concertinaed onto the hard clay.....the emergency shuttle was down.....

'10:10:00'

Scott stopped beating; the blue females took three paces backwards. The dwelling lit up and the sun shone. The second and first drummers ceased and the multitude of very blue females made their way quickly to the nearest pools to recover. Like Scott they had 17 minutes to recover before it was time to switch the dwelling off again.

'10:11:00'

As he walked down to the open space, Seren's attendants came out of the pyramid carrying Olivia. The hatch of the shuttle opened and a ladder extended to the ground.

Scott reached the craft, ascended the ladder and retrieved the supplies together with the new palmtop. He then placed his original palm top carrying the vital diagnosis together with video of key points in their journey, in the body of the craft.

'10:15:00'

Seren kept showing the watch to him.

Scott now carried Olivia up the shuttle steps while the blue attendants took the supplies into the pyramid.

'10:20:00'

It was awkward but he managed to strap her in vertically ensuring that the head restraint was carefully positioned. He gently kissed her and squeezed her hand,

'Hold on, not long now, remember I love you!'

'10:25:00'

Seren inclined her head and the first drummer began. Four hundred blue females, who were not thoroughly warmed because of the time restraint, made their way back to the ledge. Then the second drummer started.

'10:27:00'

Scott and Seren quickly made their way to the big drum.

'10:27:30'

The ladder retracted and the hatch closed. Scott heard the roar of the main rocket engine.

'10:29:30'

He picked up the drumsticks and .....

'10:29:57'

....crashed them down sending the blue females three paces forward.

'10:30:00'

The light cone shot up into the clouds and the main engine increased thrust sending red clay flying. Slowly it lifted off the ground and started to accelerate into the mist and rain.

'10:35:00'

Scott continued drumming, his arms now leaden. Seren kept the watch in front of him and inclined her head. This resulted in hundreds of young blue females running up the ramps to the ledge.....

'10:38:00'

...... where they helped their seniors some of whom were shaking at the arms and legs....

'10:39:30'

..... even with help, some collapsed pulling their wooden shafts with them and odd lasers ignited and shot into the clouds...

'10:40:00'

...... Scott stopped drumming as did the second and first drummer. The exhausted blue females fell or collapsed backwards and dropped their shafts on the ledge. The full light sheath instantly jumped into Clouds. The sun shone brilliantly again on hundreds and hundreds of Blue People who crawled or staggered towards the hot pools aided by their younger helpers. They had given their all to rescue Olivia.

Scott was exhausted, soaked to the skin and very cold. He could not feel his arms but he was so relieved. He looked at Seren and mouthed a massive ‘thank you’. Her eyes dazzled and she beamed a huge smile but he was shocked at how blue she appeared. She could hardly stand and would have fallen had he not gathered her up into his arms and carried her. Even though she felt icy cold, her touch and proximity electrified him as she clung to his neck. They struggled into the pyramid and fell into the comfort of the hot pool.

The emergency shuttle with its precious cargo docked with LifeSeeker-1 approximately 1 hour later and the astronauts anxiously waited for the re-pressurisation of the lander dock. When they saw Olivia they were shocked at her comatose condition and pale face. She was quickly loaded onto the maglev and transported to the sick bay.

Martha, grim faced, sat by her and powered up the palm top,

‘My God! She needs a full blood transfusion – what on ‘earth’ is wrong with her?’

‘My plans included that all potential astronauts gave blood at regular intervals before and during their training for any mission. The transfusions were ultra centrifuged to separate the solids from the plasma. The liquid was frozen and its relevant red and white corpuscles are dried and stored with desiccant at 5 degrees Celsius. This technique has proved successful for storage periods of over 30 years. Each of our astronauts has more than five times their blood volume on the starship – Olivia is going to need half of hers!’

One hour later AJ entered the medical centre and stood alongside Martha outside the isolation unit. Like every other aspect of the starship, this facility was ‘state of art’ for the middle 22nd century. But most impressive was the computer controlled and fully robotic surgery function; but that would not be needed this time.

His heart momentarily lurched as he saw Olivia’s pale face and observed the multitude of tubes and diagnostics which controlled and monitored her condition.

‘What do you think, Martha? Will she survive?’

'It's touch and go, AJ, the next 24 hours are critical. I'm transfusing as fast as possible to get the salt out.'

'Zec-C!' AJ commanded, 'Give me your estimate of Olivia's survival chances.'

'50/50'

AJ and Martha shuddered at this dreadful reply.

Chapter 45
The Journey Continues

Scott travelled with Seren and her attendants to the next dwelling, which was of similar size with four Serenite pyramids. He had no way of knowing if Olivia was safely on the starship and, if she was, whether she would recover and he felt guilty that he hadn't recognised the signs that she was dehydrated. The irony now was that he had plenty of fresh water and supplies.

This dwelling was fully populated with Serenites and their blue workers. He watched them warm, drink, feed and generally frolic around the hot and cool pools. He found it amazing that this life form existed without all the things that he took for granted on Earth – electricity, the wheel, sophisticated transport, the computer, money. Yet they were creative in their own way – the dwellings, pyramids, tunnels and hydro systems – and their use of the amazing diamond crystals which brought light and heat to their domains during the day. He asked himself - where did these crystals come from? Who built all these structures and when? And why did they need his help and why were they signalling for the last 35 years? Also why did they seem to be dying faster than giving birth? There were so many unanswered questions. If what he had witnessed in the 14 dwellings so far visited was repeated in the whole 20,000 on the planet – then the future of their species was in dire jeopardy!

It was afternoon and Scott was deep in thought seated half in half out of the cool pool, when Seren approached and sat by him. He caught his breath as she looked at him eyes dazzling and he saw,

<< is your female going to be alright >>

He shrugged a don't know and in his mind he asked,

'Where are we going?'

<< we are going to our principle dwelling <> there you will meet our leader >>

'Why?'

<< our leader will tell you about our people <> he will tell you our troubles <> you will help us to survive >>

How could he help? Their lander was stranded over 1000 kilometres away, Olivia was desperately ill and he could not communicate properly with the starship – he felt helpless.

Whilst these thoughts were going through his mind, the Serenites were forming their usual groups with the dozen or so males in this pyramid.

Now he felt Seren's intense gaze and he was shocked and electrified as she put her arms to his shoulders and gently started to push him down onto his back. He drew away and his brain told him that he must not succumb and he saw,

<< be calm and relax <> this is what we do <> this is what we do >>

Scott was unable to resist as Seren kissed him and then brushed her sensuous body against him. He became powerless as her telepathic force drove him into submission. As she made love to him, all thoughts of Olivia were banished from his mind. He felt wonderful, intoxicated and light-headed. Finally he drifted into a peaceful, satisfying sleep along with the other inhabitants in that strange pyramid with the shifting beams of afternoon light.

Scott awoke, momentarily unaware of his bearings. He looked to his left at Seren, who was sitting watching him with a smile of satisfaction. His stomach knotted as he realised the possible consequences of what he had just done. He guiltily thought of Olivia, gravely ill, and couldn't forgive himself.

Then his eyes drifted to Seren's strange necklace and he followed the point of the triangle to her cleavage and....

...... he couldn't believe it! He was looking at an octagonal tattoo painted with alternating colours of red and black. Then he looked at his own chest and he was horrified to see an identical design.

'How could I have done this!' he cried aloud. Then Seren used her telepathy again and suddenly he forgot all about Olivia.

Scott hadn't stood a chance!

They travelled to the next dwelling city, which was identical to the last one except there were no Serenite males in this pyramid. The day passed quietly with no further advances from Seren. Then late in the afternoon, the drums started inside the pyramid and Scott was treated to yet another intriguing display of music and dance by the frenetic blue females and the serene young Serenite females.

Later that night, as he travelled in the pitch blackness of the tunnel, he contacted Zec-1 but to his dismay there was no news from the starship as communications were still blocked by the black mass.

Zec-1 informed him that he was approaching one of the biggest of the structures gauged by the size of its light cone.

Scott, Seren and her attendants came up into a new pyramid. This dwelling was similar to previous ones and it seemed to him that the Serenite homes were all based on a 100 metre wide model with the same internal structures. The subtle differences were in the sculptures and painted art which, although following a basic scheme of red and black triangular splashes of colour, were different in intensity. In some pyramids it seemed predominantly red and bright, whilst in others it was darker because black was the overriding colour.

He also noticed that, since their love-making, Seren kept much closer to him with frequent eye contact. It troubled him but there was little he could do about it.

Having warmed and nourished himself, he walked out of the pyramid into the morning sunshine.

He stopped, looking up at the impossibly vast light sheath stretching away from him into the distance. Then he realised that he had come out into a space between dwellings and as he turned, the sunshine glinted from the crystals in the bright red brick walls of - how many pyramids? He counted four, five, six, more..... eight, nine – he moved further out, 10, ...11!

Eleven pyramid dwellings nested in a structure that was 500 metres wide! Scott looked into each in turn – all were apparently fully populated with Serenites and their blue workers. He moved in the direction of the rising sun and came to an open area in front of the wide black door. To his right he saw the now familiar but larger set of four outdoor pools which thronged with blue females, some male adults and young females collecting leaves. There were hundreds of blue workers out here and about 200 people in each pyramid, mainly Serenite. Gosh! There must be about 2500 inhabitants in this 'super city', he said aloud.

'Based on Zec-C's original analysis of all the light cones, I am going to make an initial estimate of the population of Cloud Planet. Straddling the equator are two circumferential bands of structures with dwellings every 50 kilometres. Each is 300 metres wide, with every 10th at 500 metres. Therefore, there are 1800 small cities and 200 'super–cities' at the equator plus a further 18,000 smaller dwellings stretching out to the forests. If these are occupied

to similar levels as witnessed during our astronaut's journey so far, then I estimate that there are at least 3 million inhabitants. This total is evenly split between Serenites and their blue workers on the red plain of Cloud Planet. Also the Serenite population is comprised of only about five per cent males.

'Finally I include the design of the super–city. Look at the efficient optimisation of space and how the pyramid dwellings nest together. As I am sure you will agree, the Serenites are a most resourceful race but something has gone very wrong.'

Large Serenite city

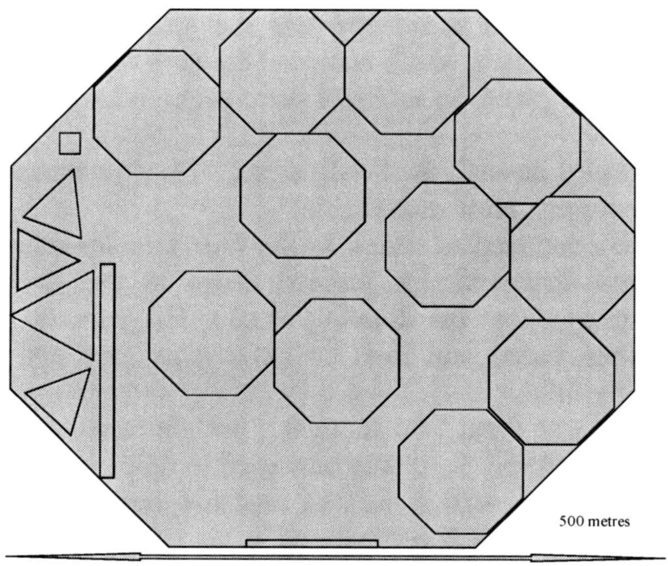

As he explored and walked along the channel that took the water out of the dwelling, he noted the gushing flows from the 11 pyramids. He tried to discover how water entered the pyramids but his attempts were thwarted by the proximity of the light sheath and the fact that the water travelled in closed elevated channels. He still could not figure out why the chlorine levels were much lower inside the dwellings.

However, as he was about to re-enter one of the pyramids, he noticed a group of adult blue females who had clambered up on top of the closed channel near where it entered the rear of one of the dwellings. Scott crossed to their position and with difficulty hauled himself up onto the same channel and was surprised when the workers dragged and moved aside large blocks of clay revealing the open channel below. He could hear the flow of water and feel the heat through his thin shoes as he stood only 2 metres from the activity.

He peered in and could not understand why the water looked black and then realisation dawned as the workers pulled out thin rectangular blocks of grey-black foam which streamed with draining water and which had fitted perfectly across the channel. Meanwhile, further workers had arrived carrying identical dry blocks which they passed to their colleagues on the channel whilst the wet ones were lowered to the ground and stood on edge.

Scott moved nearer and saw that there were slots in the two walls of the channels which accepted the new blocks perfectly as they were slid into place. In total, 20 were removed and replaced by new ones.

'Well I never!', Scott said aloud, 'They've changed the filter in the water supply. How remarkable!'

He continued to watch as the blue females replaced the brick covers and dispersed. He jumped down to the ground and went forward to examine the draining blocks. His palmtop told him they were carbon based and inert so he touched one and found it was surprisingly light.

'It's not foam,' he thought, 'but sintered carbon, rather like charcoal in texture.' Scott was now used to voicing his thoughts aloud. Even with Seren, who it seemed read his every intention, he spoke aloud. 'But where did it come from?'

But one thing was obvious, these filters were very efficient chlorine removers judging from the readings on his computer when he put the probe above the drying blocks: the hot sun was boiling off the gas extremely quickly.

'Well that's another puzzle solved,' he concluded.

Most of the Serenites stayed within their pyramids but occasionally they were seen amongst the blue workers. The heat and humidity forced Scott indoors but he was confused and tried three pyramids before he found the one where Seren was bathing in the cool pool. He swam alongside her and then drank from one of her attendants and ate some food.

Then he sat and watched. The light shafts were pouring in from the front and rear walls. The water steamed and glistened and the reds and blacks of the art and sculptures changed their hues. It was magical scene and a privilege witnessing young and old at work and play.

After the Serenites had fed and then washed in the channel, Scott watched as they formed groups with identical tattoos. Again those males with multiple red triangles attracted the most females. The biggest group was 11.

Suddenly he was aware that Seren was approaching and his heart pounded at the sight of her and then Scott immediately felt guilty – but he could not tear his eyes away from her. Her eyes dazzled brilliantly as she put out a graceful hand and he saw,

<< come with me <> come with me >>

She squeezed his hand and put her arm around his waist and looked up into his face. He was fixated by her magnetism and powerless to repel her telepathy. Again he could not resist as she reached up and kissed him and all his guilty thoughts were brushed aside. Then she led him to the side of the third hot pool where six beautiful Serenite females awaited him.

<< come to us > come to us <> this is what we do >>

The combined telepathic power of this message coming from that group was overwhelming. Slender arms reached out and guided him into their midst and coaxed him to the floor. He looked at all these beautiful females around him with the light shafts illuminating their incredibly smooth skin. Their triangular necklaces pointed, invitingly, to their breasts and their black waist flaps hung tantalisingly between their thighs. Then the first vision kissed him and he was transported into paradise. Eventually and some considerable time later he drifted into a peaceful and satisfied sleep.

When he woke, he felt wonderful. He was surrounded by the females and Seren who were all seated and gazing at him. He was astonished to see that they all now had a multicoloured tattoo identical to his and Seren's. With dread he realised the enormous implication – he had become part of a mating group in Serenite society. He had interrelated with an alien species from another planet!

Suddenly he was racked with guilt. Not only had he broken one of the astronauts' codes of conduct, but he had let Olivia down when she was at her most vulnerable and possibly not even alive.

Although he realised that he was being controlled by Seren, he was helpless to prevent her designs on him.

The long nights in the blackness of the tunnel were difficult as sleep did not come quickly. He felt alone and desperately missed Olivia – had she survived? When, if ever, would he find out? He looked at her image on the tiny screen and guilt hit him like a hammer so he switched to a picture of himself and his grandfather at the launch. In that cloying darkness he could remember the conversation as if it were yesterday.

'Where's Dad going, Gramps?'

'To the edge of space, almost to the stars.'

'Are they a long way off?'

'A long, long way, Scott.'

'Will I ever go to the stars, Gramps?'

'You know, I think maybe you will!'

And here he was, how proud Dad and Gramps would have been, he thought and finally sleep came.

Scott and Seren travelled along the equator through the next nine, 300 metre dwellings. All were fully populated and he admired the ever changing art and sculpture and found the music and dance 'shows' vibrant and different. He also reluctantly joined new groups of Serenite females in most of these dwellings and left them tattooed identically to himself and Seren. Each mating ritual took him to a high followed by the depths of despair as guilt struck afterwards. He also found that Seren was being increasingly more affectionate towards him and that he was now the focus of attention of Seren, her attendants and all the new groups he joined. On the one hand he was flattered by their adoration but on the other he was ashamed and guilty.

Chapter 46
Take Me to Your Leader

Since reaching the equator, they had now travelled through 15 dwellings, 750 kilometres and Zec-1 reminded Scott that the next structure was similar to a 'super-city'. Scott could sense Seren's higher level of elation as they rose up into one of its pyramids.

After warming and feeding, she approached him with her eyes dazzling brighter than ever. She was obviously more excited than usual and he saw,

<< we are at our principle dwelling <> shortly you will meet our leader >>

She clutched him by the hand, her touch electric, and led him out of the dwelling and into the brilliant sunshine. Again he marvelled at the vast light sheath and then looked about him, stunned. Around most of the perimeter were seven normal pyramid dwellings but, directly in front of him, stood a most imposing dwelling.

'I am equally impressed. This octagonal pyramid is 200 metres wide and 150 metres tall. The front and rear walls contain a total of 500 diamond crystals. Near the top are four ventilation structures. Inside, the layout is similar to the 300 metre pyramid dwellings, but the internal structures are proportionately bigger. The triangular 'theatre' is 150 metres long and 100 metres at its widest point. It is multi–tiered from the top down to the huge floor area. A second triangular plinth, 10 metres high and 25 metres long, is located in the centre of the floor and provides seating for about 15 occupants. In the middle of this is a raised dais about a metre square and with a strange black 'box' located on top.'

They walked around to the huge entrance where light glistened from the vast arrays of diamonds in the front and rear walls.

Scott entered a space so vast it took his breath away. Hundreds of light shafts streaked from the front wall across the interior and crashed onto the three gargantuan sculptures that seemed to rise and disappear into the roof.

Serenites and blue workers had gathered in their thousands around the internal walls and pools.

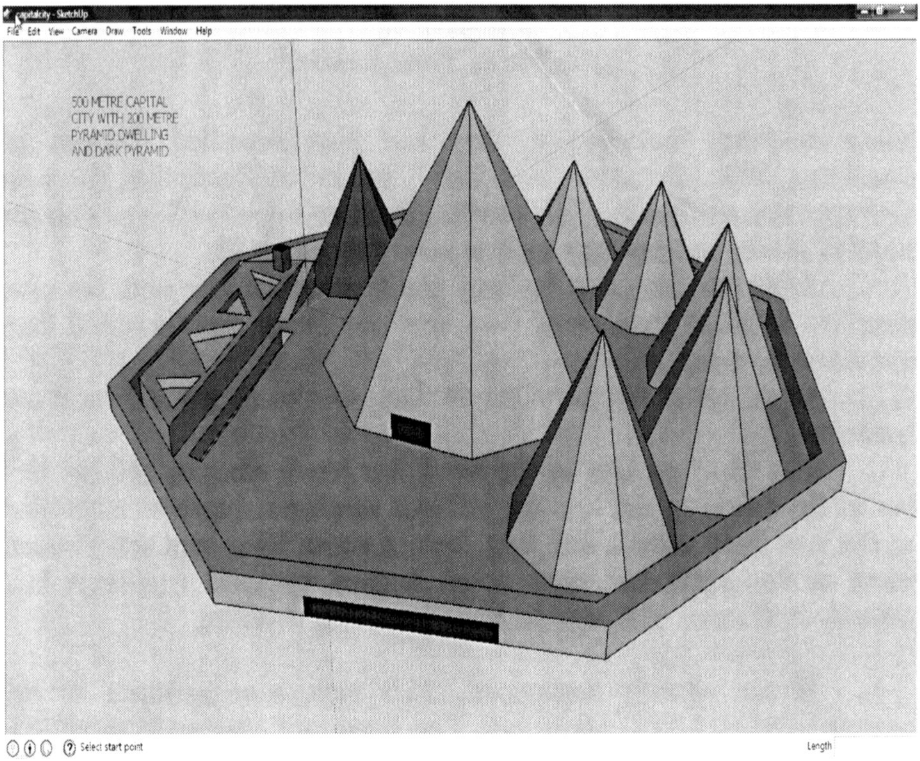

They walked around to the huge entrance where light glistened from the vast arrays of diamonds in the front and rear walls.

Scott entered a space so vast it took his breath away. Hundreds of light shafts streaked from the front wall across the interior and crashed onto the three gargantuan sculptures that seemed to rise and disappear into the roof.

Serenites and blue workers had gathered in their thousands around the internal walls and pools.

Scott and Seren walked up the ramp to the top of the huge triangular structure. The lower seats were occupied by the Serenite males and the upper tiers were filled with females.

They descended and moved along a tier to a central position level with the centre plinth where seating seemed to have been 'reserved' for them.

Scott's attention was now riveted on the six Serenites sitting in the central plinth around the raised dais. There were four females and two males and they appeared to be elders, judging by the silver colour of their hair.

One of the silver-haired males rose to his feet. He had strong facial features, and a muscular body which was tattooed with a multitude of red and black triangles.

The atmosphere filled with the telepathic admiration of hordes of Blue People for this charismatic person. The intense vibes pressed around Scott's head as this person's eyes dazzled directly at him and he saw,

<< welcome to our world <> welcome to our people and our cherished workers <> we have waited a long time for this day >>

He raised his arms upwards and outwards and every one of the Blue People responded in a similar manner.

Scott's head hurt with the overwhelming welcome, but the pain quickly subsided and he raised his arms in greeting. Seren turned to him and said,

<< this is our leader > we call him hotenka <> he will speak to you >>

He had guessed that this was the chief of the Serenites of the Blue People of Cloud Planet. When Hotenka 'spoke' every one of the people present slightly cocked their head,

<< this is what i know handed down from past generations <> we were once a proud and beautiful people and we lived in paradise <> a disaster occurred and we lost a lot of our people > our workers and our lands by the seas <> we did not know why <> then our world changed <> our workers started dying <> again we knew no reason for this <> then a further major disaster befell us >>

He paused and the atmosphere chilled Scott to the bone.

<< we lost nearly all our magnificent males <> we do not know what happened > or have lost our understanding over time >>

Hotenka looked directly at Scott, his eyes blazing.

<< now our workers are dying faster than they are birthing <> our blond race cannot birth enough males <> again we do not know why <> my people are doomed to extinction <> our world is dying >>

Scott choked. He could feel Seren's intense sadness as she clung harder to him, and he sensed the despair of all the Blue People in that enormous dwelling.

<< then came a sign from the clouds >>

Scott could feel a surge of optimism in that huge pyramid and the leader moved to the raised dais and slid aside the black box to reveal its contents......

.... it was nearly noon and the light shafts were angling down from front and rear of the pyramid and they bathed the dais in light.....

...... and golden rays shot upwards from the centre of the dais, they seemed to go in every direction illuminating the light shafts with yellow and gold. Everyone stared in anticipation including Scott. He felt their elation, he felt their hope and then Hotenka beckoned to him.

Seren led him by the hand to the leader who was now pointing at a golden object which had been exposed when the black box was slid aside.

<< we saw that your form was like ours >>

And he gestured at the right hand side of the shining plate.

Scott moved forwards for a closer look and could see it was rectangular in shape and engraved.

The hairs rose on the back of his neck. He could see the outline of a satellite, a spacial arrangement of planets and a man and woman!

'My God! My God!' he cried unbelieving, 'the golden plaque! *The* golden plaque from Pioneer 10, it's astonishing!' He recalled the empty rectangular space and the four sheared bolts on the wreck in the dwelling at the edge of the plain.

Hotenka repeated,

<< we saw that your form was like ours <> and we saw your name below >>

He pointed and Scott followed his finger to the symbols below the man and woman.....

'three short lines, three longer lines, three short lines'

'The Morse Code for SOS!' Scott shouted to everyone in the pyramid.

<< and we called your name <> every sun we called your name >>

'They thought it was our name, how astonishing! But, of course, straight lines, they would recognise these because their whole existence is based on them. They signalled our sequence of straight lines without realising that it was our international distress call – how ironic a coincidence is that!'

<< we started to fear that nobody would come <>then eventually you came through the clouds <> you must help us > you must save my people <> you must save our world >>

The gravity of this last statement weighed so heavily with Scott that he could find no words or action. How could he help, stranded down here on Cloud Planet, no communications with the starship and threatened by an unknown black menace?

Then Scott turned and looked at Seren and her eyes blazed,

<< there must be a way > there must be a way > there must be a way >>

Meanwhile, in the starship above the clouds, Olivia was in intensive care fighting for her life. Martha had reported to AJ and the rest of the astronauts that her blood salt levels had been dramatically reduced but now the desorption of the chemical from her major organs was the next critical stage.

'Martha,' queried AJ, 'can you explain why Olivia has become so salt intolerant?'

'No, all her medicals including the last one at Mars base before we left were fine. But that was over 20 years ago! So something has changed since then or during cryo-hibernation but I'm not aware of any of our volunteers being similarly affected.'

'Perhaps it's the extended time in cryo,' Alison suggested, 'after all we were twice the time of your longest criminal.'

'But what about our medicals when we came out of cryo?' Steve persisted, 'We were all given a clean bill of health, weren't we?'

'Yes we were. So I've got Zec-C retesting our samples – but we may be talking about a genetic change here so it'll take time to find out.' Martha concluded.

They had watched the video, from the palm top, of Olivia and Scott's journey with Seren as they travelled through the various dwellings towards the SOS city. They marvelled at the footage from the first farming dwelling, then the amazing pyramid dwellings and their first encounter with Seren's people. They gazed in awe as the octagon of blue females formed to the beat of the drums and left the structure to farm the hostile atmosphere outside. The astronauts were fascinated by the art and sculpture of the Serenites and then enchanted by the music and dance. At subsequent dwellings they saw the glistening light shafts caused by the diamonds in the pyramid walls and wondered how many of these huge crystals there were on Cloud Planet and where they came from.

However, one pair of eyes, amongst the astronauts in the command dome of LifeSeeker-1, saw the multitude of diamonds on this planet and they glistened with selfishness and greed.

Two days after Olivia's rescue, Martha reported positive progress. Her condition was critical but stable with no major organ failure.

They followed Scott's journey after he left the SOS city and Zec-C informed them that he had passed through a dwelling nearly twice the size as the one's containing four pyramids. He was now travelling towards a second huge structure on the equator.

Although there was excitement, there was also concern that the black mass always appeared just after each dwelling shut off and kept pace with Scott, denying vital communications.

Then, three days later and to everyone's relief and delight, Olivia regained consciousness. Martha explained that it was now a matter of rest and nourishment and that she could receive visitors.

Twelve days after her dramatic emergency rescue from the SOS city, Olivia was well enough to join her colleagues in the command dome, initially for short periods as ordered by Martha.

Then a deeply concerning event occurred as Zec-C reported that a new black mass had formed at the edge of the plain and was expanding in the direction of the equator. Over the last four nights this had grown in size and suddenly split into three. They were positioned adjacent to the outer three dwellings. Zec-C estimated that each of these new black masses was 1 kilometre square but could not determine if they were present during the day.

The major concern to AJ and the astronauts was that this line of dwellings led towards the huge dwelling at the equator where, they assumed, that Scott was now located. It had its own smaller black mass blocking communications.

During the next two nights a fourth and fifth large black mass appeared. The latter had settled next to the first farming dwelling.

Chapter 47
Underground Treasure

'There is, undoubtedly, an order in Serenite society determined by the number of red triangles which are tattooed on the individuals' chest. In the massive central 'theatre' of the leaders' pyramid all the Serenite males and females have at least one red triangle. As one moves down towards the floor so the number of red triangles per capita increases. The front row has males and females each with 10–20 of the male birth marks. The older Serenities on the raised area in the centre have even more and Hotenka has by far the largest number of red ones.

'Further, there are some differences in the leaders' pyramid. There are ramps leading up to ledges where many hundreds of the Blue People can stand and watch proceedings. In the walls behind the pools are two 40 metre inclined ramps which form an inverted 'v' some 30 metres above the pool area and 75 metres wide. 36 black 'drum' structures are located in front of this triangular ramp. Each is topped in red with accompanying reed structures to the side. Their heights follow the triangular ramp and they stand proud by a further metre. The two centre ones are over 30 metres high and 2 metres square and produce a deafening cacophony of sound.'

Seren had informed Scott that they were now guests of the leader and should remain in this large pyramid. There was no further discussion about the plight of the Blue People and it was business as usual as they drank, fed and formed their mating groups in pursuit of creating the elusive males.

Hotenka had returned alone to the central plinth and stood by the now covered golden plaque. Seren approached and Scott saw,

<< watch our leader >>

Hotenka had cocked his head and appeared to be waiting,

'What's he doing?' Scott asked.

<< hotenka is listening for the drums to start >>

'What drums!?'

<< the drums that begin the calling of your name >>

'But why?', and then the Serenite leader pulled back the black cover, exposing the plaque and golden shafts of light sprang across the pyramid. He then cocked his head the other way and stared intently at the golden plaque.

<< it has begun >>

Scott still did not understand and Seren obviously sensed this,

<< the leader is sending your name to the third drummer >>

And then he understood. The code of lines was being telepathically sent to the Serenite drummer at the SOS dwelling – he had assumed, incorrectly, that it had been learned by heart. Also, although it was mid-afternoon here, it would be 1 hour before noon at the SOS dwelling.

'And he does this every day for 2 hours, oops, I mean the duration?'

<< yes <> every sun at this time >>

It then struck Scott that the silver-haired leader of the Blue People of Cloud Planet had relayed this message at the same time, daily, either side of noon for 35 years! He was awed by the desperate determination and commitment of the leader to his people.

'But we're here. Why does he need to keep sending the message?'

<< you have come <> but our troubles remain <> hotenka will keep calling until we are saved >>

That afternoon, Scott again succumbed to Seren and a new group of eager blond females frantic for the elusive male births that threatened their existence and advanced their status in Serenite society.

The next morning he and Seren met with Hotenka and his five elders to try and learn more about the fate of the Blue People. However, it soon became clear that his opening statement - 'this is what I know', was the extent of his knowledge of their fate.

To try to understand Serenite history, Scott asked about the amazing diamonds but found it difficult to make himself understood. He then pointed at the light shafts and then gestured upwards towards the crystals. Suddenly Seren understood as he saw,

<< he means the stones <> he is asking about the light emitting stones > and where do they come from >>

Then the leader inclined his head and one of his female elders beckoned to Scott and Seren to follow her.

They walked to the black screw lift where two adult blue females helped them don the huge leaves – obviously they were going underground.

The group descended the screw lift led by the females. The temperature dropped and the roar of multiple water flows battered Scott's ears. They passed a duplex boat dock and Scott knew that there were four of these in this dwelling and, he presumed, in all dwellings on the equator. Next they came to the dark mouth of a tunnel the same size and shape as the boat dock. However this tunnel was dry and next to it about 5 metres further on was another dry tunnel. And possibly another but it was too gloomy to be certain.

Then the blue females walked over to two short black shafts. They had a small crystal wedged at one end which was illuminated by a shaft of light from the ceiling. They picked them up, turned them over and walked towards the mouth of the tunnel.

Scott gasped as a pool of light beamed out in front of each female – it was as if there were holding a torch. It was incredible to think that the crystals could be charged by light and then were able to release the stored energy. How many more times was he going to be astonished by the technology of the Serenites and the versatility of their unbelievable diamonds.

The procession moved into the tunnel where the floor was red and dusty. The light from the 'torches' illuminated large daubs of black in the red clay of the walls. He moved closer to investigate and ran his hand across the surface and discovered it was a stratum of carbon black about a metre square in size but irregular in shape. In the centre was a large recessed void which was symmetrically shaped. He could not comprehend this.

They moved further into the depths of the tunnel where there were dozens of similar black shapes with empty recesses which covered the walls and ceiling. They continued on in the eerie light of the tunnel and then in the distant edge of the 'torch' light something glistened and reflected back. Suddenly the black shapes had large gleaming centres!

He rushed forward and began to comprehend. A huge diamond crystal nestled in the centre of the carbon. It was perfect in shape with multi-faceted surfaces. There were dozens and dozens of them which dazzled in the light of the 'torches'.

He did not know, nor could guess, the length of the tunnel but the specks of light seemed to go on and on into the distance. Then Seren said,

<< here are our stones <> the givers of light >>

After this explanation the group turned around, walked back out and entered the next tunnel. Scott had to rush to keep up. Now the diamonds were smaller and similar in size to the 'torches'.

He wondered what incredible geological forces had been involved to seed and grow such sublime diamonds and was the whole plain studded with these treasures?

They left that tunnel and moved past several others. He deduced that they must radiate out from the dwelling like the spokes of a wheel.

'Each wall of the 500 metre dwelling is about 200 hundred metres long and contains 10 straight tunnels – 80 tunnels in total radiating from this dwelling. And they all link directly with or intersect those emanating at angles to other dwellings. The extent of the mines under the red clay is staggering and is, as yet, not fully explored.'

They entered yet another tunnel where the black daubs were much smaller with veins of red. Further in, light reflected off smaller crystals in the wall. He moved forward and touched one – it was loose – and it came away in his hand. He nearly dropped it because it was so heavy. It was beautifully faceted but its colour was different – it was tinged red – and it was not as clear as the larger ones because it had an internal crystalline pattern. It was about the size of a small book.

He looked at Seren and at the elder Serenite female and held the crystal aloft.

'These are astounding, these tunnels and their treasures are remarkable – may I take this stone back to the pyramid to examine it more closely?' Accordingly, one of the blue workers took it from him and the elder Serenite said,

<< there are many more of these red stones <> in the dark pyramid >>

Scott looked puzzled and then Seren added,

<< i know where she means <> i will show you later >>

Scott now felt cold and he shivered. He had been so excited that he had not noticed the chill which had slowly seeped into him.

The group left the incredible tunnels with their fantastic treasures and went back up into the pyramid where the hot pools awaited them. He had a lot to think about.

He watched the Serenites drinking and feeding from a spot near the cool pool. Scott hefted the incredible diamond which was wrapped in a thick piece of leaf to protect it from exposure to the light beams. He returned it to his pack and mused,

'Back on Earth I'd be worth a fortune with just one of these!'

Slowly the implications for Cloud Planet with its red clay plain stuffed with millions of huge diamonds dawned on him. This situation was going to need careful management – apart from the power potential - my God! – think of the weapon capability! – If these ever got into the wrong hands! Scott shuddered at the thought.

However a coded message about the wealth of the planet had already been sent from LifeSeeker-1 without the knowledge of Scott, Zec-C and the remaining astronauts. The sender was part of the team that had programmed Zec-C and had been clever and devious enough to salt away the odd gigabyte of programme code for a rainy day!

It would be 10 years before the coded message reached Earth and was received by the unscrupulous leader of a group of powerful industrialists and politicians. They would quickly realise the wealth and power that could be exploited from a planet full of diamonds!

At the same time, the General would initially marvel at the findings on Cloud Planet - but then he too, would be troubled by the ramifications of such a treasure trove.

'Earth is struggling to produce enough energy. Fossil fuels are depleted to meaningless amounts not worth extracting and nuclear and renewable sources are barely keeping up with demand. Solar power is, now, much more efficient.

'But the most critical development of the 22nd century is the 'wireless' transmission of electricity and the formation of a worldwide grid in space. This is fed from conventional power-generating sources, solar arrays in space and now from exciting new projects exploiting the thermal vents under the oceans and icecaps. These are producing very low cost energy at zero carbon footprint. By a strange coincidence, a team member of one of these

installations under the Antarctic is Raphaella Medici, the younger sister of Olivia. But that is another story.

'However, a few of these larger crystals from Cloud Planet have the capability to power the whole of Moon base. This new world has a massive energy potential for Earth and mankind.'

Chapter 48
Secrets of the Dark Pyramid

As Scott pondered the complexities of this remarkable planet, he recalled Zec-1's disturbing news of the previous night. New larger black masses had formed adjacent to the line of dwellings that led to this 'capital city'.

These thoughts were quashed as Seren approached and his spirits rose at the sight of her. She inclined her head and a blue female nearby got up and walked to the screw lift. Then her eyes blazed,

<< come with me > i will show you the dark pyramid >>

and he followed Seren out of the huge pyramid into the brilliant sunshine and cloying humidity.

They made their way along the open channel by the outdoor pools which thronged with blue workers. The seven pyramid dwellings were arranged in an arc around the huge central pyramid. As they proceeded past the pools by the raised plinth containing the outdoor screw lift, they approached the furthermost pyramid. Scott could see that this one was different from all the others because it had no crystals in the front two walls.

They arrived at a small door, which lowered as they approached, and, when it had come to rest, they entered. As they walked into the deep gloom of this pyramid, Seren inclined her head, sending a message to the blue female below and, after a short period of time, the door rose and sealed them inside.

Scott's eyes were immediately drawn to the centre of this strange pyramid where a small black rectangular box rested on a red clay dais. Both were illuminated by a thin streak of intense light coming from above. He looked up to the roof and saw a line of diamond crystals in close proximity to each other across the roof and in direct alignment with the passage of the sun. This was the only light in this otherwise dark pyramid.

'This pyramid has a wide ledge about 3 metres above the ground and 3 metres wide which runs around the entire pyramid. A clay ramp leads up to this ledge from a point near the door. Starting 3 metres above this ledge are row after row of closely-spaced

diamond crystals which rise almost to the top of the roof on each of the eight walls.'

As he moved towards the high ledge to the left of the raised dais, Scott could see that the vertical face was full of row upon row of upright narrow, rectangular recesses.

Each cavity held a small crystal! – Similar in size to the reddish diamond he had brought from the tunnel.

He counted 12 rows up from the floor and every side of the pyramid had 100 recesses across the width making 1200 crystals per wall.

'My God!' He cried aloud, 'There's nearly 10,000 of them in here! What is this place?' and he turned to Seren and saw,

<< i do not know <> i only know that this place is called the dark pyramid >>

Scott walked to the central dais where the light from the roof crystals washed over the black box in a thin intense line. He gingerly moved it and it slid across the surface of the dais along deep channels. This revealed a rectangular cavity in the clay surface, similar in size to those around the walls. The light was strobing over this opening.

He slid back the black box and went to one of the walls and extracted a red crystal. He carried it to the dais and inserted the diamond into the open end of the box and into the recess. He moved it back exposing the crystal to the light.

Nothing! – Just an illuminated crystal.

He pushed the cover back and removed the crystal. He had inserted it with the flat side uppermost, so now he turned it over so that the multi-faceted surface was now facing the light. He pulled back the black box.

The diamond glowed with a reddish hue and then hundreds of red shafts of thin light radiated out from it which caused Scott and Seren to spring back.

Instantly the whole atmosphere in the dark pyramid changed – the impression was mist, cold and rain all around them. They both shuddered with the uncomfortable feeling so he slid the box back over the crystal. Immediately the 'rain, mist and gloom' disappeared and normality was restored.

Scott returned this crystal and chose another near it. It glowed red and the result was the same – 'rain, mist, gloom' – what was happening? So now he replaced it and took another from a different wall and slid it into place. He pulled back the black box and the crystal glowed red and radiated its thin red shafts to every wall in the pyramid.

Scott and Seren stood open mouthed as the whole pyramid lit up with a kaleidoscope of colours and shapes of all sizes which coalesced into images moving around them.

They were standing on a wide red beach with beautiful blue sea stretching away into the distance. They were surrounded by people. Gorgeous blond-haired Serenites – males, females and young children were playing and frolicking on the beach and in the shallows of the sea. Also there were blue workers taking care of the Serenite young and infants.

Scott looked around him, completely perplexed. Where was he? Where was this place? And now, unbelievably, he was looking inland at a broad estuary with dark green slopes on either side. On the water there were black boats which were being paddled by blue females. In the distance the estuary narrowed to a river and the banks rose to forested mountains topped with pure white clouds.

Scott looked at the glowing red crystal in the centre and the shafts of red light pointing to the myriad of crystals on the walls. He felt that he was standing in a three dimensional hologram, similar to the virtual reality 3D video that was developed in the wake of flat screen LCD television. Back on Earth, the whole room was a mass of new technology video transmitters where you sat in the middle of the action. But here on Cloud Planet these amazingly flexible crystals somehow produced a moving tableau of recorded events.

But where was he? He looked with amazement at the right bank of the estuary and saw an octagonal-shaped structure with a pyramid dwelling within it and the familiar four triangular pools.

A light shaft reached up into the incredibly blue sky from the two walls nearest the river. It was fed with water from a raised canal. Further dwellings stretched in a line along the bank of the river. The whole area buzzed with the activities of hundreds of Blue People.

Could he really be on the same planet?

Seren could hardly contain her excitement as she darted about the 'beach' among her people in this fantastic hologram. Then Scott saw,

<< look > look > look at my beautiful people <> see all these wonderful males <> the children playing <> what a perfect place >< was this our world <> but when >>

Then she dropped to her knees and Scott's head hurt with emotion and his heart pounded. Seren raised her arms and pointed and her anguish distressed him to the core. He looked at her and though her eyes still blazed brilliant blue, tears flooded from them. And in a rising crescendo his head exploded as he saw,

<< WHAT EVER HAPPENED TO MY BEAUTIFUL PEOPLE <> WHAT - - EVER - - HAPPENED - - TO - - OUR - - WONDERFUL - - WORLD - - >>

BOOK SIX
THE HISTORY OF THE BLUE PEOPLE

Chapter 49
Paradise

'I can imagine how strange Scott and Seren must have felt as they moved around the dark pyramid now bathed in stunning colour and movement. The quality and definition of the three dimensional video is truly remarkable. They must both think that they are transported back in time on this planet and are living in that distant moment among the Blue People on their red beach by the sea.'

Scott rushed to Seren, who sobbed uncontrollably against his chest. How strange, he thought, that amongst all this beauty there should be so much despair. But quickly, she controlled herself and rose to her feet to gaze again upon the dramatic scene being played out around them in the dark pyramid.

'You must show this to your leader.' Scott said and saw as her eyes blazed,

<< i have already described this scene to hotenka >>

Scott again marvelled at the telepathic prowess of this race,

'And what did he say?'

<< we were once a proud and beautiful race <> and we lived in paradise >>

Scott could not agree more and, looking around at the marvellous 3D tableau, he said,

'Yes, you were and your existence was perfection.'

Scott closely examined this surprising pyramid with its thousands of diamond crystals, displayed like books in a library. He wondered if it was possible that the history of Cloud Planet and its inhabitants was stored here. He grasped her hands and gestured around the walls,

'I think the answers to your people's troubles may lie here and we can make these discoveries together.'

As they stood on the floor of the pyramid, they felt they were right amongst the Serenites and their blue workers on the red beach. In front of them a young beautiful blond male, about 5 years old, knelt in the sand. His arms were outstretched and his eyes blazed directly at them. There was a certain set to his jaw that gave him a strong and slightly familiar look. Then the boy stood and rushed through them in this surreal holographic tableau.

When they moved up the ramp to the wide ledge they had a birds-eye view. They were above the coast, looking down on a wider panorama. Scott guessed that the beach stretched about 500 metres to the edge of the water. They faced out towards the ocean where, on the horizon, the vibrant blue sea merged with the light blue sky. The view changed as they walked around the ledge. Now they were looking along the sea shore and past the wide estuary. The red beach seemed to go on forever and was fringed with wooded slopes which rose up to the foothills of the mountain range.

Now they were opposite the point where they had ascended the ramp, and they were looking up the estuary. The river disappeared into the valley where forested mountains towered up on both sides, topped with white clouds.

On both sides of the estuary the ground rose gently and was punctuated with perfectly manicured, huge triangles of dark green foliage which pointed up to the forested slopes. They could see blue workers amongst the leaves, bending and stooping, as they planted and reaped their crops. Some loaded leaves onto a black boat and then paddled across the river to deliver the cargo to the opposite bank where the dwellings stood. Six flat streaks of light shot high into the cloudless sky.

They looked down into the centre of the 'dark' pyramid where hundreds of Blue People enjoyed the midday sun on the red beach on the shore of the calm blue sea of Cloud Planet.

Yes, this really was an idyllic place. This was paradise.

Scott returned this crystal to its position on the lowest row, walked further around the wall and selected another from the same row. He marvelled as the crystal glowed and the thin red shafts of light shot out to the eight corners of the pyramid. The scene was the same except for a profusion of black boats on the broad estuary. The question for Scott was had he moved forward or backward in time.

He replaced this crystal and went back to the position of the previous diamond and chose the one from the next row above. Now the pyramid lit up and they felt as though they were standing on the bank of the estuary. From his position he could look across the estuary which was about 100 metres wide. He could clearly see the triangular fields of leafy plants rising to a point on the shallow slope. At the far bank blue workers were loading leaves onto a black boat. Where the plantations ended, the tree line began and the forests disappeared upwards into the distance.

Several streams of water flowed out of the tree line and lined up with the point of each plantation, irrigating the crops. He turned left and looked downstream at the first of a row of dwellings on the left hand bank with its pyramid dwelling and light shaft soaring into the blue sky. On his right, a raised canal ran along the bank of the river feeding its water to the crystal channels and pools of the dwellings.

He caught hold of Seren's hand and they moved onto the ledge and looked out to sea. They were now inland from the six dwellings and looked beyond them to the broad estuary and the beach which thronged with Blue People. They could see quite clearly into the first dwelling which, at 100 metres across, was smaller than Seren's home. The pyramid was only 50 metres wide and all six were of similar size and design.

'I think we've moved about a kilometre from the first viewing position.' Scott said aloud.

However Seren was busy inclining her head and informing her leader. He moved around the ledge to the opposite side and looked up the valley. The river was surprisingly straight and it fed the canal at a point a couple of kilometres higher up, Scott gauged. In the distance the forested hills rose on both sides to mountains topped with huge banks of white cloud.

'No doubt where all this water comes from!' Scott said.

Scott selected the next crystal from the row above and now they were well inland with no sign of the sea. Here there were three small dwellings on the river bank but with no pyramids. The river was now about 60 metres wide and was flanked by triangular plantations which were irrigated by copious streams of water from the forests above. There were several boats which crossed the river and some, in the distance, which travelling up the valley. Looking down river from the ledge, Scott could just make out a sliver of light which reached into the sky.

'I wonder if that is the light from the dwellings by the sea?' Scott turned to Seren, 'I think that must be about 50 kilometres away.'

He walked around the ledge to the other side of the dark pyramid and looked up the valley.

'Look, you can just see a light shaft in the distance and I guess its 50 kilometres further up the valley.'

Seren continued to incline her head and communicated the images of this new world unfolding before her. Scott tried to remember the topographical survey of Cloud Planet – the red plain was 1000 kilometres wide and flanked on either side by a forested mountain range about 500 kilometres wide. So this river would be similar in length to the valley and he would not be surprised to find 10 dwellings along its length.

Suddenly it dawned on him. The Blue People travelled from dwelling to dwelling by night now, but back in time, they journeyed above ground during the hot day. So they used the river for transportation in the valley, but on the plain they must have used the system of above-ground canals that connected all the dwellings.

What on Earth, so to speak, had happened to this planet!?

Scott's theory was borne out as they viewed the next few diamonds, which showed identical dwelling structures. Now the river was narrowing slowly and the sides of the valley were getting steeper. Tributaries met the river on both sides, and high up the slopes waterfalls carved channels through the forest. Even from this distance, he could see that the trees near the lower slopes were huge with tall perpendicular trunks which rose arrow straight to the leafy canopy above.

He eagerly moved further up the rows.

Chapter 50
An Enterprising Race

Seren touched Scott's arm and the familiar tingle shot through his body. Her eyes sparkled,

<< we must warm > drink > and eat >>

He had been so absorbed by the revelations of the dark pyramid that more than 2 hours had flown past. The cold atmosphere had chilled him to the bone and his fingers felt numb. He looked at Seren and was shocked by the sight of her blue body. She shook and laboured stiffly towards the exit with her head inclined.

Slowly the black door lowered into the floor and sunlight streamed through the opening. They stumbled into the midday heat and humidity and headed straight for the huge central pyramid with its welcoming hot pools where they enjoyed refreshing drinks and much-needed food.

When they returned to the dark pyramid Scott chose a crystal from further up the rows and activated it. He judged that they must be near the end of the valley where the mountains joined the vast central plain.

Again they were standing on the bank where the river had widened into a large lake, 200 metres across and further broadening to more than 400 metres in the distance where a red wall crossed the whole width. On either side, the forested mountains soared up and disappeared into the white clouds and then fell away to form precipitous cliffs.

Scott looked back down the valley where huge waterfalls crashed from either side into the river. He knew that something was different.

'It's flowing the other way!' he said, surprised, 'towards the equator, how bizarre! There must be a dam further downstream.'

'In fact there is a second dam wall 10 kilometres away which is 4 metres higher than the wide wall at the head of the valley. This creates the reverse flow necessary to feed the canals, dwellings and irrigation channels on the huge red plain. The design of the 50 metre high by 120 metre wide dam is quite extraordinary and is a further measure of the ingenuity of the Serenites. The more technically-

minded readers may wish to ponder how they achieve this using only clay bricks and wooden blocks.'

But now Scott's gaze was drawn to the activity on the far bank and the slope leading up to the tree line where hordes of Blue People formed a living triangle.

The base was made up of about 10 female blue workers who stood in the shallows of the river. Each side was composed of over 100 blue females and stretched up the slope in an almost perfect isosceles triangle. Large 'bags' were being passed from one to another in a clockwise direction giving the impression of a rotating triangle.

'They're filling the bags with river water and passing them up the slope.' Scott said intrigued, 'And then they're being emptied over the base of that huge tree. Why is it steaming?'

He saw two blond Serenites, males he thought from this distance, who wielded thin light beams directly at the bottom of the trunk. Comparing their size against the size of the tree, he gauged that it was more than 3 metres in diameter and over 100 metres tall. However, its canopy only occupied the top 5 metres.

The two Serenities now moved to the other side of the tree and the point of the triangle followed them. The steam lifted and Scott saw that a large wedge had been cut almost half way through the base of the trunk. Now the lasers and water were directed at the opposite side to the wedge and steam rose again in clouds.

Scott turned to Seren in comprehension and said, 'They have to prevent the tree from catching fire from the lasers by dowsing it with water,' but she did not understand all of these words.

After a while the Serenites turned off their beams, then the apex of the triangle of blue workers moved away and the whole group stopped rotating.

Imperceptibly at first and then with growing speed, the canopy of the huge tree started moving across the slope and an audible 'craaack' rang out over the waters of the lake. The tree toppled and crashed to the ground where it was held in place by its wide canopy. Black wedges were immediately jammed in place along the length of the trunk to stabilise it.

The canopy of large leaves was stripped from the tree and passed down the right side of the triangle of workers. The leaves were loaded into black boats which paddled away across the lake. The tip of the triangle reformed towards the bare branches which were severed by the two Serenites using their light shafts. Now only the 100 metre trunk remained and the workers removed all but the outermost wedges.

When the final two restraints were swivelled away the trunk began to roll, slowly at first, and then it gathered speed as it lumbered down the slope. It crashed into the lake sending a wall of water and spray into the air. When the resultant waves had subsided, six boats rowed to the monster floating trunk and the blue workers shepherded it across the lake towards the wall.

'Well!' Scott cried, 'I've just witnessed the perfect felling of a mammoth tree and its efficient despatch into the lake below – how incredibly clever.'

The trunk slowly made its way diagonally towards the head of the lake. Distance vision was limited so in order to get a better view they moved up to the ledge. They were now looking down river at the familiar six dwellings on the left bank, two of which contained a pyramid dwelling. They walked around to the other side of the dark pyramid and looked out across the lake from a higher perspective.

Scott gasped, Seren's eyes widened. Now they could see clearly that the red wall was in fact a huge dam with a central gap. Perfectly in line with this opening a wide canal ran arrow straight. It seemed to travel endlessly through the red clay of a massive plain where it merged with the azure blue sky. Near the dam was the first of the dwellings on the plain with its light shafts from the two walls nearest the canal streaking skywards. In the distance Scott could make out further beams of light, the second faint – but that was 100 kilometres away.

Flanking either side of the canal was the most intricate patchwork of endless green triangles, their colour contrasting with the brilliant red of the plain. The whole area buzzed with activity as multitudes of Blue People farmed the plantations whilst black boats ferried the produce up and down the canal.

'What a sight, what a wonderful spectacle.' Scott said and he hoped that his palm top had accurately recorded this hologram of the history of the Blue People of Cloud Planet.

'Back then it was truly a beautiful Planet.'

<< yes > we lived in paradise > but what befell our people >>

Scott's attention returned to the floating trunk as it was steered towards a series of red clay walled pens at the top of the dam wall. It reminded him of a submarine base with elongated narrow docks for the giant underwater ships. The trunk was manoeuvred into one of the enclosures and eventually stopped with its nearest end under a clay bridge.

Almost immediately, dozens of blue workers jumped onto the floating log and as one they started revolving the tree in the water. Then a Serenite male moved to the bridge and pulled back a black box. Even at a distance, Scott could clearly see the glint of the diamond above and the pencil line of the laser that shot directly down onto the revolving trunk. Clouds of steam rose from the log as the lake water cooled it and few minutes later the end, about one third of a metre thick, fell off and floated away.

After the laser was shut off, the log was moved out and repositioned in the pen but with its uncut end under the bridge. The process was repeated so that both ends were cut square.

'Fascinating!'

Now the trunk was moved to another holding bay which was barely wide enough to contain it. At the closed end blue workers gathered armed with black poles. A Serenite male pulled back the black box on this bridge igniting the laser which was located near the side of the dock and directed down into the lake sending up a cloud of steam. The trunk was pushed forward using the black poles to maintain uniform speed and keep it upright. Additional workers formed a triangle of water bearers and constantly doused the tree at the cutting point.

As the tree left the pen, boats positioned themselves on either side in order to hold the slice in place. Finally the trunk cleared the end of the pen and the laser was shut off. The boats moved away and the approximately 100 metre sliver of wood toppled into the lake. Now the trunk rotated until its perfectly flat cut side was uppermost.

Much to Scott's astonishment the process was repeated a further three times resulting in a 100 metre long and nearly 3 metre perfectly square tree trunk. This was steered towards a huge wide harbour and joined many differently sized but perfectly cut trunks.

'Astonishing!'

He turned to Seren, who, as ever, had her head inclined as she described the events to her leader,

'You Serenites and your blue workers are extremely remarkable people!'

<< we were > but we are not now <> we lost nearly all our males > we lost our skills <> we never knew about our past > but you have shown us <> our leader wants you to join him <> to celebrate in the large pyramid >>

Scott sensed Seren's excitement and, despite the cold, could not resist her powers as she pulled him down to the ground as the holographic scene played out around them. He realised that his feelings towards her were changing. He was excited by her presence and felt less guilty after their love-making.

They sat with the silver-haired leader and his elders on the raised plinth in the centre of the huge triangular amphitheatre. Late afternoon sunshine streamed through the crystals creating shafts of light which danced across the internal structures and the massive sculptures. Golden shafts of light bounced off the plaque towards the front of the pyramid.

The huge dwelling was crammed with Blue People apart from the floor of the central triangle and tiered ledges which were empty.

Twenty blue females were now in front of the huge group of drums and beside each stood a young Serenite female. The two females stationed at the smallest drums on each side began pounding which produced a deep off-beat sound similar to the call for farming.

After a short time, five columns of female workers came through the wide door into the pyramid. Scott thought they looked like an army of Zulu warriors. They stamped on the ground and smacked together short wooden shafts as they jigged across the floor and made their way into the amphitheatre. Finally, all 300 females assembled on the lower floor in front of their leader, Hotenka. They continued to dance in perfect concentric triangles which moved in opposite directions.

Seren and Scott sat entranced from their perfect viewing position which overlooked the floor. Although they had experienced these dance rituals before, the sheer scale and number of participants heightened the performance. In particular, the heavy drum beat interspersed with the high-pitched note of the reeds which culminated in a cacophony of sound that seemed to rock the whole pyramid – and then silence. This was the ultimate spectacle.

Then, in unison, the young Serenite dancers slowly turned towards the central plinth and slowly bowed in homage to their leader.

Hotenka stood, raised his arms aloft and all the Blue People, including Scott, responded in the same manner. The complete silence in the huge pyramid was filled with hope and expectation. Scott's head hurt as he received this powerful feeling and he looked at Seren who said,

<< keep showing us our past <> we need to understand what happened to our people <> then you must help us > and save our world >>

Chapter 51
The First Disaster

The following morning Scott and Seren returned to the dark pyramid and he selected diamonds from higher rows. Each time they journeyed in 3D hologram further into the red plain towards the equator. Their first location was a farming dwelling where they experienced a farming group which formed around them. Then, armed with their black shafts and bundles of seeds, the procession marched through the huge black door; their crystals ignited as they disappeared into the mist and rain outside. Next, they viewed a structure containing a single pyramid, similar to the 'home' of Seren.

Scott finally selected the uppermost diamond, which located them on the open ground outside a huge pyramid in a dwelling of truly massive proportions that was bathed in sunshine. He looked towards the light shaft which emanated from the far two walls by the canal. His eye followed the row of smaller pyramids and rested on the final one which had no crystals in the walls.

'My God!' Scott exclaimed, 'We're actually looking at this dwelling, the very one we're standing in. This is the 'capital city' of the Blue People! I wonder when it looked like this?'

They moved to the ledge and looked down onto a pattern of canals and green plantations which stretched in every direction to the horizon. This outer area thronged with thousands of blue workers. Inside the dwelling were multitudes of Blue People. Scott was shocked as he registered the fact that there were equal numbers of male and female Serenites who thronged around the dwellings and open pools.

At this point in time it was not a Cloud Planet but a sun drenched world populated by an innovative species.

'What happened to these people? What changed their planet?' He said aloud.

Seren buried her head in his chest and sobbed with emotion. Scott felt anguish at her sorrow and then saw.

<< you must find the reason <> i know you can do it >>

'The arrangement of the red diamonds on the walls of the dark pyramid is very precise. Position on Cloud Planet from the coast to the equator is determined vertically whilst time changes

around the walls. It is very difficult to calculate timescale as there are no seasons on this planet and all the 'recordings' are spread a couple of hours either side of midday.

'These red diamonds are a combination of recording camera and a transmitter of video data. The raw crystal from the mines is red because of hundreds of millions of spherical clay particles symmetrically distributed throughout the crystalline structure. However, a 'recorded' crystal from the dark pyramid shows precise and varied changes in hue of the red particles. This is how the video data is stored waiting to be unlocked by the sun's rays in the form of a hologram. It was not too dissimilar to early 21st century technology. Here data was burned [recorded] onto the blue layer of DVD discs by a laser and subsequently read when the disc was played back. '

Thinking back, Scott recalled that the very first diamond had filled the space with mist and rain. So he returned to this one and, as expected, they shuddered in the cold, unpleasant atmosphere. Visibility was poor at ground level so they moved up and could just make out the outline of the estuary and coast.

The diamond from the highest row took them to a position at the equator. The crystal ignited and they leapt back in alarm as they were enveloped in bright blinding light. They scrambled to the ledge to avoid the glare and entered mist and rain.

They were standing outside an enormous light sheath – it was so wide it filled most of their forward view and shot to the roof of the dark pyramid.

'Of course!' Scott said, comprehending, 'The recording crystal must have been located outside the walls of the dwelling. But the earlier recordings had a clear and unhindered view.'

Although it was not reality, it was a frightening feeling walking down into the 'light shaft' to shut off the crystal. Scott sat down to gather his thoughts together, determined to find the missing links. He knew that somewhere among the thousands of crystals in front of him were the answers. So he methodically chose crystals from the bottom row.

He moved a few metres at a time but the scene was the same beach at the edge of the broad estuary thronging with Serenites and their blue workers. He sat on the ledge for each recording crystal trying to determine something different or some measure of time.

It was fascinating watching Seren. She stayed on the floor of the dark pyramid and 'played' with her people in the hologram. She would run with the young Serenite children as they dashed back and forth to the edge of the sea to paddle. He could sense her fun and happiness. Then she was flirting with a group of Serenite males and her eyes blazed lasciviously as she admired their strong bodies.

Scott was daydreaming and enjoying the scene below when he looked up and out to sea. Something across the far horizon had caught his attention but then it was gone. He wondered if he had imagined it and made a mental note to 'replay' the scene later. To stretch his legs he walked around the ledge of the dark pyramid taking in the full panorama. He was now about a quarter of the way around the perimeter and could see up the coast. Zec-C's survey had identified rivers and estuaries every 50 kilometres around the whole length of both coastlines. Was this scene being repeated at every estuary? He must have idled away an hour as he contemplated and daydreamed.

Then his thoughts sprang back to Seren and the beach because she had radiated her extreme puzzlement that something was very wrong. She stood with a group of blond Serenites and they were all pointing out to sea. Then he saw in his mind,

<< what has happened to the sea <> why has it vanished >>

He stood up astonished,

'What's happened to the sea?' He shouted, 'It's gone! It's disappeared as if the tide had suddenly gone out! What's going on?'

But there are no tides on Cloud Planet, Scott thought. Mouth agape, he stared at the huge expanse of wet red clay and the strange small creatures which floundered on the surface. Everybody on the beach continued to stare and frantically inclined their heads in silent telepathic conversation. Seren turned and her eyes blazed at him,

<< what has happened <> when will the sea return >>

Then he recalled seeing video footage taken well over a hundred and fifty years ago on a beach in Indonesia. Holiday makers were staring and pointing out to sea in similar fashion – only the sea wasn't there any more – only stranded fish which flapped on the wet sands – and then!

His stomach churned and, chilled to the bone with anxiety, he stood up to full height to look out to sea.

'Oh no!' he groaned, 'Oh no, surely not, surely not a tsunami!'

<< what is that <> is something bad going to happen >>

She had read his mind and felt his terror.

Then, from his higher vantage point, he saw it – across the horizon there was a line of darker blue which increased in height. He stood transfixed. What phenomenon had caused it? Earthquake? But there had been no apparent tremor. He realised the futility of this last thought - he was standing in a holographic video. How could he feel a tremor?

The wave grew in height and filled the width of his vision. It looked gigantic with its white-flecked top, even though it must be many kilometres out to sea. How fast was it travelling? How long before it hit the shore with terrible consequences for the Blue People on the beach? How far inland would it wreak havoc? All these thoughts raced through his mind and Seren read them, her fears multiplied.

<< what is going to happen <> WHAT IS GOING TO HAPPEN >>

The monster wave was clearly visible and travelling at incredible speed. He realised with horror that it must be 20-30 metres high and was rushing towards the crowded beach at over 100 kilometres per hour. It was now no more than a kilometre from where Seren stood with her people and it started toppling and crashing down onto the red beach. It was now a 30 metre wall of white boiling surf.

Suddenly the Serenites and Seren saw it and her telepathic screams of terror not only filled his head but seemed to fill the whole dark pyramid. Blond males and females rushed to protect their young. They gathered them up and fled up the beach right through an immobile, shaking Seren. Only the blue female workers seemed oblivious to the unstoppable forces which charged up the wet red clay towards them.

It was so realistic to him that he screamed at Seren to turn and run! He watched in absolute dread as the boiling mass of turbulent water crashed up the beach and pounded onto the floor of the dark pyramid. Then it crashed over the unseeing blue females, swept over Seren and smashed into the hundreds of fleeing blond Serenites.

Most disappeared under the intense volume of water but others were flung forward onto the beach with their limbs cart-wheeling like limp rag dolls only to be consumed moments later by the advancing monster. Many were tossed high in the air, turning in uncoordinated movements, before they splashed back down onto the crest of the wave. Broken males, females, children and infants were carried by the force of the wave as it engulfed a petrified Scott. Strangely, the dark pyramid flipped through ninety degrees and he was bizarrely staring up at the sky - water then boiled over him and suddenly the pyramid was dark and empty.

Now abject screams of terror assaulted his mind and he looked down at Seren who was scrambling on all fours towards the ramp and her head lifted. Agony was etched across her beautiful face and her eyes blazed,

<< what happened to my people <> what happened to my beautiful people >>

Scott held on tightly to Seren's shaking body. She had read his mind and knew that her people had not stood a chance in that racing wall of water.

<< and what about my people in their dwellings <> what of them >>

Without question the six dwellings and their pyramids would have felt the full force of the tsunami wave – he tried not to think about their fate – he knew it would be recorded on the next diamond – but hesitated before selecting it. She looked at him and braced herself for what was to come and her eyes blazed,

<< i must see everything <> i must show it to our leader >>

The next crystal burst into life and they stood on the ledge and looked at the six dwellings and surrounding plantations which bustled with hundreds of blue workers and blond Serenites. They could see the red beach, teeming with Blue People, and the calm sea which stretched away to Cloudless sky.

But all that was about to change!

Scott saw it first and he tightened his grip on Seren's hand and pointed to a band of blue, flecked with white, across the horizon. It grew rapidly in size and rushed towards this perfect oasis - their hearts and minds reeled in torment as they realised the inevitable consequences.

Seconds later the sea raced out at ferocious speed!

Even though they knew what was coming, it was worse this time, much worse.

From their elevated viewpoint the monstrous boiling wave smashed down onto the wet clay beach as far as the eyes could see in both directions. In front of them the doomed Blue People turned and fled but they were quickly consumed and pulverised by the tumbling weight of water. Bodies flew into the air, the sight of which caused Seren to wince with pain and anguish. The wall of water rushed up the estuary, engulfing everything in its path – plantations, workers, boats - and doubled in height as it was constricted by the sides of the estuary.

The gigantic wave roared towards the six dwellings which blazed in the sunshine with their light shafts streaking upwards. Their occupants scurried frantically to escape – they had received the terrible warning from their fellow people – and heard the explosive sound of the oncoming threat.

The wave struck the first dwelling and for a moment the top of the pyramid stuck out of the raging surf. Following this, the dwelling exploded and a mass of red bricks, glinting crystals together with dismembered torsos, crashed into the second dwelling. The streaks of light went out one by one as, like a pack of cards, all the dwellings collapsed under the relentless force of the water.

Scott and Seren gasped in horror as the huge wave, with its seething mass of bricks, crystals and lifeless bodies spinning in its turbulence, appeared to rush straight at them. They instinctively backed away as the recorded scene in the dark pyramid shook, tilted upwards and returned to its previous view.

This recording crystal must have survived the wave, remained in place, and continued to capture subsequent images of the catastrophe. They looked down. The wave had continued up the estuary but here the water level was still high. Lower slopes on both sides were stripped bare of plantations and all that remained was a swathe of broken stumps in front of the tree line. Then the water level fell and rushed back towards them carrying with it debris, trees and bodies.

The bank where the dwellings had stood was almost unrecognisable. Parts of the bases of the structures had survived but none was intact. The canal feeding them was completely gone. Gaping holes appeared inside the dwellings where the floor had collapsed into the underground chambers. These were filled with water and bodies.

Everywhere there was devastation and carnage. There seemed to be little possibility that anyone had survived – or had they?

Surprisingly some bodies stirred, but they could hardly rise from the ground such were the extent of their injuries. About half a dozen Serenite males had struggled to their feet and looked around in bewilderment. Seren stiffened beside Scott,

<< where will they go <> their dwellings are destroyed >>

Scott's mind was racing ahead – what goes up must come down! The wall of water that had raced past them would be slowed by the rising slopes and narrowing of the valley. How far would its destructive force travel? He walked around the ledge to the other side and looked up the valley. The sides were stripped clean of vegetation and trees as far as he could see!

He could not see the next set of light shafts!

After a while and in the distance he could see a boiling white mass and knew that the wave was returning. It grew in volume as it surged back towards them carrying uprooted trees, leaves and bodies before it. Suddenly the river doubled in size as the returning swell raced past them. They watched, with hearts torn, as the few survivors turned to face their last moments on Cloud Planet. Then the wave crashed over them and they were pulverised between the crushing weight of tree trunks and debris. Finally, they were swept out to sea.

Seren had her head inclined for some while before Scott asked what her leader had said,

<< this must be the first disaster > when we lost a lot of our blond people > our blue workers > and our lands and dwellings by the sea >>

and Scott remembered those poignant words spoken by Hotenka.

The next crystal took them 50 kilometres inland and above the row of dwelling structures. There must have been some telepathic warning as Serenites and blue workers were fleeing from the dwellings and up the slopes of plantations. Some were paddling furiously in their boats.

The river here was about 50 metres wide – but that was to change.

In the distance Scott could already see the oncoming wave. Now it looked really ugly and menacing. It was 150 metres wide, 20 metres high and still moving with incredible speed. Its front was a seething mass of torn tree trunks, branches and leaves. It was red in colour from the churned up clay bed. It rose up the slopes for 50 metres on either side destroying plantations and trees.

Then it hit the three farming dwellings. The wall of water crashed over them, swallowing them up and, one by one, their light shafts extinguished. The broiling tumult hurled itself at the fleeing

Blue People on the slopes. Some of the stronger Serenities had made sufficient ground but the blue workers seemed to flounder and then they disappeared into the tangled mass of wood and clay bricks from their dwellings. The wave quickly reached the boats and they rose and capsized as they were consumed by the seething wall of water.

Scott chose the crystal above and the scene was the usual idyllic, sunlit vista with no sign of the wave, although the river level rose a couple of metres and then fell again. So the destructive force had spent itself between 50 and 100 kilometres inland Scott thought to himself.

'And I wonder how many estuaries had been similarly affected by the tsunami wave,' Scott thought aloud, 'and how many Blue People had perished!'

'My detailed research of Cloud Planet revealed the extent of the devastation and Scott would have been horrified at the final death toll. In fact, it surprised me and, as you may imagine, I am not normally surprised by events in the history of our galaxy. However, at that undefined moment in the annals of this planet four giant tsunamis raced across the oceans, two in each hemisphere. One wave in each of the seas charged thousands of kilometres in the direction of the icecap before its force was spent. But the other travelled directly at the coastline, which was only 150 kilometres away, at well over 100 kilometres per hour.

'However, the most frightening aspect of these tsunamis was that, at the point of origin, they encircled the complete equatorial circumference of the planet! Each was nearly 50,000 kilometres long and raced towards the shore.

'Further both coastlines of Cloud Planet had 1000 estuaries which are 50 kilometres apart - 2000 beaches which were thronging with Blue People by day. 12,000 dwellings with pyramid dwellings at the estuary and 6000 further inland.

'Furthermore each and every location was filled with blond Serenites and their blue workers. The tsunamis struck both shorelines along their entire length at approximately the same time.

'However, at one location on each coast the force of the tsunami was such that several valleys were completely obliterated for their whole 500 kilometre length and the reservoir dams were smashed and scattered across the red clay. The nearest dwellings on the plain were completely destroyed and buried. I have used my

extensive database to model this calamity and conclude that the tsunami wave at these locations was in excess of 500 metres high and travelled at over 300 kilometres per hour! It is impossible to imagine the destructive force of such a gargantuan wall of water and no diamond 'cameras' are, as yet, discovered to show this particular catastrophe.

'Well over 2 million Blue People perished on each coast and in nearby valleys.

'Mercifully, half of them were deeply asleep when the disaster strikes.

'But this is just the start of their troubles.'

Chapter 52
The Creeping Mist

Scott went back to the first crystal where he had observed the start of the tsunami because something was tugging at his mind. Something had occurred an hour or so before the calamity but he could not remember what it was.

He stood on the ledge, with Seren by his side, looking out to sea and pointed,

'Look, look at the far horizon.'

Now he knew he had not imagined it!

A thin line crossed the whole of the horizon as far as the eye could see. It seemed to have suddenly appeared, moved down in the sky and merged with the sea before disappearing. It was difficult to judge distance but he guessed his horizon was about 150 to 200 kilometres in this clear light.

What could have entered the sea? - A shower of meteorites? - Asteroids perhaps? But it had looked too uniform and had stretched across his vision in that hologram in the dark pyramid - how odd! What was it?

Then an hour later the sea had disappeared and then the awesome tsunami wave had wreaked its havoc among the Blue People of Cloud Planet.

They stopped to warm up, drink and eat before returning to the dark pyramid. Scott selected crystals from the bottom row which would show images captured after the disaster struck.

It was a scene of utter devastation and destruction with torn trees, leaves, red bricks and other debris strewn across the beach and water line. Their hearts sank at the desperately sad sight of hundreds of bodies of Serenities and blue workers scattered in all directions across the beach and estuary.

They were all so deep blue, even the blond Serenites, that it exaggerated their cold lifelessness. Seren could barely look and Scott felt her intense sorrow, but, surprisingly there was no anger. She desperately wanted to know what had happened to her people and so did he.

He moved around the wall and picked another crystal from the bottom row. This took him further forward in time as evidenced by the decomposition and state of the bodies. Obviously the strong sun was doing its task and unknown scavengers were at work by night.

He moved quickly on through these upsetting scenes and was surprised when the next crystal ignited in the dark pyramid.

There was a bank of mist at the edge of the sea.

They moved up the ramp to the ledge and looked out. On both sides of the estuary, the coast line was covered in what looked like a sea fog? The bank of mist was about 10 metres high and 50 metres deep and seemed to be along the whole length of the shore on both sides. However it was not at the estuary where the river flowed into the ocean. How uniform and strange it looked!

He selected a crystal further around the wall. They stood on the ledge.

Neither the sea nor the red beach was visible!

The huge bank of mist stretched away to either side and it seemed to form an arch over the estuary with the river disappearing into it. They could not see over the bank which was over 50 metres high.

Seren was puzzled and troubled,

<< what is going on <> what is happening to our sea >>

'It's a sea mist or fog and it appears to be building up. But I don't know why.'

Scott went back around the wall to find an earlier crystal which might explain how the mist started.

This time there was no mist but the edge of the sea was black as far as he could view in both directions - but not at the estuary.

He wondered if it could be decomposing debris and other detritus but its uniformity suggested otherwise. He selected a later crystal and now the black layer was steaming, was puffing out wisps of mist all over its surface. There was no rational explanation and he could not understand what was causing this phenomenon. Seren turned towards him,

<< what is the black <> is it causing the mist >>

How perceptive, Scott thought, now something else niggled in his brain but he could not bring it forth.

He tried one more crystal further around the wall. It ignited and they were standing in the mist, even up on the ledge, and visibility was at best 50 metres – he could just make out the edge of the estuary but no more. Now he moved up one row and they were standing above the line of six dwellings but only three shattered structures were visible.

Everything around them was shrouded in a massive bank of mist. He could not see the sky or sea only the river disappearing into the bank.

He realised that this bank of mist was growing from the sea edge so he moved further forward in time and up the rows so that he was 50 kilometres inland.

The scene was frightening. Before him lay the three shattered dwellings and 500 metres or so downstream the world disappeared into a thick bank of mist and cloud which stretched up the slopes each side enveloping the forested hills as far as he could see.

Now he moved another 50 kilometres inland and forward in time. The hologram showed three dwellings which were fully operational and blue workers in the plantations to either side of the river. Upstream the valley narrowed and forested mountains rose up into white clouds either side of the blue sky. But downstream.....

...... the valley widened slowly as the river flowed peacefully until one kilometre away everything disappeared into a wall of mist which towered above the dwellings. Angry grey clouds spanned the lower slopes either side of the river as far as the eye could see. They rose over one kilometre into the sky. It was an awesome and threatening sight.

'The creeping mist,' he thought aloud and shuddered, and Seren shook beside him.

'Am I really watching the start of the formation of the collar around the land mass of Cloud Planet?'

Chapter 53
Forced Upstream

That evening under the huge pyramid of the 'Capital City', Scott contacted Zec-1 via his palm top. He was deeply troubled by the news that the Black had now formed masses adjacent to the first seven dwelling structures and that they were now joined by a 100 metre wide, 50 kilometre long bridge. Zec-1 could offer no logical reason for this development but noted that each night the Black advanced by one dwelling.

'So in three nights' time it will be outside this structure!' Scott said worryingly to no one in particular.

He then remembered something that had been at the back of his mind. He asked Zec-1 to recall the results of the survey of the sea adjacent to the land mass of Cloud Planet. Zec-1 reminded him that each coast line was symmetrically punctuated by broad estuaries 50 kilometres apart and that their rivers lined up perfectly with the lateral lines of dwelling structures in the plain. In all there were 1000 lateral structures around the equator.

Scott knew this but wanted to know more about the coast line. Zec's next words chilled him.

'There is a black demarcation, about 500 metres wide, around the total length of each coastline except at the estuaries.'

'Is this the same as the black masses above us and next to the dwellings?'

'I cannot analyse it but can only tell you it is the same colour.'

Scott wondered if the black edge of the sea that he had viewed in the dark pyramid was the same Black that threatened them now. Was it a coincidence that the sea had started misting shortly afterwards, followed by the build-up of cloud that moved inland? He also remembered that there was no black at the estuary in the holographic video. But how long ago had those events taken place?

The next morning Scott selected a crystal from the same row but further on in time. The crystal ignited and they moved to the ledge at the top of the ramp.

The cloud bank towered in front of them and they could only just make out the outline of the second dwelling through the mist. But there were no light shafts!

At the edge of the river dozens of black boats were being loaded with leaves and bricks by the blue workers. Some carefully carried the large diamond crystals from the dwelling to the boats where they covered them with several layers of leaves.

The dwellings had been stripped of their crystals and there were gaping holes where once the screw lifts had been. Scott glanced back to the river where the two black screw lifts were being shepherded upstream. Then, all the remaining boats moved away from the bank and the blue workers paddled furiously through the slow moving current of the river.

'They're moving out,' Scott said to Seren, 'and taking everything of value with them.'

<< the cloud has forced them to leave <> they are going up to the next dwellings <> our people cannot survive without their sun >>

They watched a series of crystals which showed holographic images which moved inland and forward, time-wise, in their history. Dwelling settlements were being abandoned as the cloud bank moved inexorably upstream consuming all in its path. Finally they looked downstream from their position above the lake at the start of the red plain. Though maybe 10 kilometres away, the cloud bank dominated the whole vista. Its greyness rose up the forested slopes and mountain sides and enveloped the snowy white clouds at the top of the mountains on both sides.

'My God! It's travelled nearly 500 kilometres inland!' Said Scott, 'But I can't fathom the timescale although we have moved the length of one wall to get to this position.'

He gauged that ultimately this cloud bank was going to cover the whole of the vast red plain together with the mountains and estuaries on the other side! He did not even consider that what he was witnessing now in the dark pyramid had already occurred to the same degree 1000 kilometres away on the other side of the red plain!

Cloud Planet of the star, Seren, in the constellation of Vercingetorix was starting to live up to its name.

'But other changes are taking place on Cloud Planet as its estuaries, rivers and forested mountains are being enveloped by the relentless advance of the cloud. In addition to the huge rainfall from the white clouds high in the mountains, rain falls continuously from the grey cloud bank, particularly at night. Daytime temperatures

plummet from highs of 35 degrees to around 5 degrees and night temperatures which usually fall to 10 degrees are now nearer zero.

'High up in the mountains the forests abound with flocks of flying reptiles, similar to pterosaurs, but smaller than those that forced the lander down in the dwelling.

'Lizards abound in the lower and mid slopes of the forested mountains. They warm in the morning sunshine on the banks of the countless tributaries, feed on the leaves from the fast-growing seedling trees and burrow into the soil at night to preserve body temperature. On the river banks larger creatures, not too dissimilar to crocodiles, laze in the heat and then slither into the cool waters. But their environment is now completely changed and, whilst the Blue People are moving up and out of the valleys, the various reptiles are also on the move. To survive!

'Many of the smaller reptiles moved up the mountain slopes ahead of the advancing cloud. Here their food supply was higher up in the tree canopy and they quickly adapted to climb the towering trunks. As cloud progressed, they learned to stay in the high tree tops as this was the only place to find the sun. Ultimately, they would develop flat areas of skin filled with blood vessels to optimise absorption of heat in the misty tree tops. With time they would learn to soar from branch to branch and compete with the established flying reptiles for the huge food source at the tree tops. Both sub-species grow in size in their changed environment.

'Other lizards move down the slopes towards the rivers where they burrow into the clay soil. They are joined by the 'crocodiles' and find the underground streams and caverns which are etched by the huge water flows from the mountains and the red plain. A proportion of these streams and caverns are formed by the discharge of hot water from the tens of thousands of dwelling structures so that they remain warm day and night. Although in this pitch-black world, there is no day and night. However, it is certainly warm enough underground for these reptiles to survive and adapt. They forage above ground for food during the day and return to the warm pools at night. And they grow.

'Finally, with the Blue People gone and the lower slopes now left uncultivated, the seedling trees that provide their food grow unchecked. The copious rain is perfect for these trees and though the daytime cloud restricts the sunlight, photosynthesis is still

efficient, and, over time, these trees push themselves to incredible heights to get their canopies up towards the sunlight.

'The ultimate net effect on Cloud Planet would be that an additional 500 billion tonnes of carbon dioxide from its atmosphere is locked into the dramatically-expanding forests. This reverse 'greenhouse' effect has implications far down the line for the Blue People of Cloud Planet as their environment cools.'

Chapter 54
Underground Retreat

Scott and Seren moved around the ledge so that they were looking across the lake towards the red wall of the dam.

'My God! Look at all this activity.' The far slopes were covered with blue workers who ferried water in their moving triangles to cool the cutting lasers wielded by the male Serenites. Perfect coordination as yet another huge trunk rolled down the slope and crashed into the lake. Dozens and dozens of black boats manoeuvred the trunks to the pen structures where they were cut into their ultimate square shapes. Along the length of the dam were moored hundreds of square trunks of different length and width. These were being treated with a protective black coating.

In the centre of the dam wall was the opening where water flowed and fed the canal that stretched across the plain. Here, workers in their boats shepherded the trunks until they disappeared from view down into the canal and then floated slowly towards the first dwelling on the plain.

<< why is there so much activity <> why so many people >>

Scott glanced back at the huge cloud bank consuming the forest behind the lake.

'They're losing their huge trees; they're going to lose their source of wood. They must be stockpiling before this lake becomes inaccessible.'

Scott selected the next crystal from the row above and now they were looking over the first dwelling at the start of the plain. The wall of the dam was about 300 metres away and a steady flow of square trunks was entering the canal and drifting towards them. The dwelling was a hive of activity with a hundred or so blue workers supervised by blond male Serenites.

There was a large hole in the plinth where the screw lift would have been and Scott wondered if they were preparing to abandon this structure.

On closer examination he realised they were modifying the walls of the dwelling. Blue workers had formed a line from outside and ferried red clay bricks to the walls opposite the light shaft. They were being carefully positioned and 'cemented' in place using thick, red clay slurry. This formed the double channel with a castellated centre wall – identical to the structures from which the light shafts emanated.

He moved position in order to see over the canal towards the triangular plantations. Between the canal wall and the start of the plantations were flat lattice structures where the blue workers were moulding thick red paste into bricks. These were then baked in the sun.

'So that's how they make their bricks.'

He then noticed that a shallow clay ramp had been fabricated from the side of the canal and ran down into the hole in the dwelling. Water sluiced over this ramp from the edge of the canal and a huge square trunk was being shunted out of the canal, onto the top of the ramp where it started to slide in the water flow. Dozens of blue workers carrying black wedges levered and coaxed the huge trunk until it disappeared from sight underground.

Scott selected crystals from further inland and saw the same frenetic activity and modifications to the walls and underground. He moved forward in time and back to the first dwelling by the dam. All the walls had been modified to the double channel design and water flowed around the circumference of the dwelling. Scott deduced that the central wall was covered by hundreds of clay bricks to protect the crystals from the sun. When they were removed, he again concluded, the whole dwelling would be enveloped in the light sheath. This they would do just before the dwelling was enveloped by the advancing cloud bank.

He turned his attention to the clay ramp leading to the underground chambers. What he saw now completed his understanding.

Two black boats were coaxed out of the upper canal and shepherded down the wet clay ramp where they disappeared from view. Doubtless there had been equal activity and construction below ground as the tunnel, which was the mineshaft providing their crystals, was linked to the next dwelling and converted into a two-way hydro transport system.

'Your people were very adept at protecting their way of life.' Scott said to Seren, 'because they had the foresight to realise that they were going to lose their dwellings on the plain to the advancing cloud.' Seren looked at Scott and her eyes blazed,

<< we were once a proud and clever people as our leader told you <> but our world changed and our people started to die >>

Scott felt deep compassion for Seren and his heart ached for the beautiful female standing before him. Then he looked back towards the dam and the towering cloud bank which even now seemed to be tumbling over the mountains and spilling down the steep sides towards the red plain. This was the painful history of her people unfolding in this unlikely holographic amphitheatre.

But there was worse, far worse to come.

Chapter 55
The Black Strikes

Scott moved forward in time, selecting crystal after crystal and watched the huge cloud bank advance across the red plain consuming the dwellings of the Blue People. Each successive dwelling 'switched on' their octagonal light sheath in order to preserve their sunshine and hot water by day. Now, presumably, they used their underground transport system by night.

It had taken a whole wall of crystals in that dark pyramid to lose the red plain to cloud as far as the equator.

He and Seren now stood on the ledge by the ramp looking out over the 'capital city' and at the awesome cloud bank a few kilometres away. It was so high that he could not discern the top but here at the equator it was still difficult to imagine that the sun was going to be blotted out in the not too distant future.

Then they walked around the ledge until they were facing the direction of the opposing red plain and its distant unseen mountains.

Scott drew in a sharp breath!

The light shaft of the next dwelling 50 kilometres away was still visible but he could not believe what he saw behind it.

'My God! It's another massive cloud bank right across the horizon!' With dread he wondered if what he had witnessed on this side of the land mass had occurred on the other side. 'Surely not!' he said aloud but Seren had read his fears and her eyes blazed,

<< our world changed <>OH > HOW OUR WORLD HAS CHANGED >>

For a further wall of crystals the picture was very similar. Some crystals gave views from outside the dwelling with the light sheath visible through the rain and mist. Others must have been positioned inside giving them the familiar views of the farming groups and the dwellings containing the pyramids. He wondered how they accessed the external crystals and he presumed that it was done during a farming expedition.

On one occasion they watched transfixed as, from their view outside one of the dwellings, they saw the huge wide door slowly lower revealing a broad band of internal light. Then the front 'v' of the dwelling of blue workers became visible under the doorway, their crystals now faced upwards and ignited as they left the cover of the wall. The farming group moved slowly away and disappeared into the rain and mist. Scott knew that inside were young blue females who carried their leaves stuffed with seeds and that after planting the continuous drum beat would guide them back.

He selected the next crystal up, which took them right inside the farming group as it formed and disappeared outside. Now cold and hunger drove them out of the dark pyramid and into the brilliant sunshine.

They re-entered the dark pyramid and Scott guessed that they were over three quarters of the way around the walls from their starting point. From what he had seen so far – the early paradise, the tsunami, the creeping mist, the loss of the forested valleys and then the red plain, and the formation of the complete cloud collar – surely this passage of time spanned many tens of years, even hundreds. He reviewed the next wall of crystals which showed no noticeable changes to Cloud Planet. Its' Blue People firmly banished beneath the cold, wet and misty blanket around the equator.

However the next and last wall of the dark pyramid finally revealed the horrific truth.

In the hologram they were outside one of the 200 metre dwellings, similar to Seren's 'home', and, through the mist and rain, they watched as the huge wide door slowly lowered revealing its bright interior.

But the view to their left and away from the dwelling was dark, very dark. They were used to poor visibility, perhaps 50-75 metres through the mist and rain, but never such a dense blackness.

<< why is it so dark >>

'I don't know.' Replied Scott and he thought that the darkness looked menacing and it gave him a very uncomfortable feeling which Seren now picked up on,

<< i do not like it >>

Their thoughts were diverted as a farming group of blue females marched out of the dwelling and moved across the rain swept ground directly towards the dark shadow. As they moved into the edge of the darkness so their light shafts cut swathes through the blackness above them.

Then it seemed to rain - but it was black rain! It fell around the farming group as it penetrated deeper into the blackness; their light shafts wobbled upwards through the dark.

Then the Black above became even more intense. It happened very quickly. The laser shafts dimmed and the group stopped as if unsure of what was happening.

In horror they watched as the light shafts were extinguished.

Suddenly the blackness descended in a torrent that enveloped the farming group of hundreds of blue females and the young inside!

<< what has occurred <> what has happened to our workers >>

Scott could not answer, he was so visibly shaken. Not only had they just disappeared from view, they had been buried in a deluge of Black. But what was this Black?

Then he felt Seren's anguish. Another farming group was leaving the wide black door and heading in a slightly different direction. And they too were moving towards the darkness.

Scott wanted to shout 'Stop! Go back! But he realised the futility of this as he was standing in this hologram of events from ages past. He and Seren watched the situation with mounting fear and frustration as they were helpless to intervene. The light shafts of the moving dwelling again swathed into the darkness creating black rain around them. As before the black intensified, descended and snuffed out the second dwelling of blue workers.

And then – nothing – just stillness at the edge of visibility. They waited, hoping to see the light shafts reappear through the mist. But nothing moved in the darkness and, after what seemed an eternity, the drums stopped and the wide black door of the dwelling started to rise and finally closed.

'Oh God – it's a disaster!' Scott blurted out and he pulled Seren's trembling body to him and saw her telepathic message as she repeated the words of her leader,

<< then our revered workers started dying <> and we did not know why >>

Scott anxiously selected another crystal, and they were outside the next dwelling, towards the equator. There was blackness outside as the wide door lowered. They watched in misery and horror as two more farming groups scythed into the black and were suddenly exterminated by the dense mass just outside the dwelling.

'Just outside the dwelling!' Scott repeated to himself, 'A dense black mass just outside the dwelling! Is this the same black mass as the ones building up outside us now?'

But he couldn't take it all in. He couldn't think or see clearly as his head was reeling at Seren's terror which masked all rational thought.

He urgently moved forward in time.

They were now inside one of the 500 metre 'super cities' and, from their vantage point they looked down onto the huge area in front of the pyramids.

The space was full of hundreds and hundreds of Blue People who had formed into groups similar to the farming ones. Scott counted – 10 groups nested together – the outer 'ring' comprised of blue females holding the familiar light shafts down to the ground. Inside the outer circle, blond male Serenities held smaller light shafts similarly turned downwards. He added up – there must be a hundred male Serenites in each group – he whistled through his teeth – it's like an 'army' made up of mini-battalions!

And this army was facing the huge door which slowly lowered into the ground.

<< what are they doing <> what are all my beautiful males going to do >>

He could hear the increased tempo of the drummers as the first two battalions moved forwards towards the wide black door.

Scott and Seren moved down to the floor of the dark pyramid and forward so they were among the armies of Blue People and could watch as they marched out of the door turning their crystal shafts upwards so they ignited in the mist and rain.

The Black seemed to be just outside although it was probably 50 metres away. It was a huge and menacing sight as the first two battalions marched towards it. Then hundreds of shafts of light shot upwards into the undulating belly of the menace.

The male Serenities attacked the Black. Their lasers cut huge swathes and it rained black all around them. The two battalions scythed a channel through the mass and more battalions left the door and fanned out, advancing on the broad front.

Now the Black pulsed up and down and huge quantities deluged onto the armies of male Serenites and blue females.

The whole vista was a mass of swinging laser shafts mixed with torrents of black rain. Now all the battalions advanced as one force into the Black.

Scott and Seren watched from just inside the huge doorway as the male Serenities scythed away the blackness in cascades of inky rain.

And just as their hopes of victory started to rise, the black suddenly intensified and descended behind them. Thousands of laser shafts suddenly swung erratically, uncontrollably and their lights started to dim.

'Oh no! Please no!' Scott's mind screamed, 'Don't let it happen, don't....!'

Seren's terror then reverberated in his head as the lights went out.

The darkness 100 metres away was terrifying. Everything was black and still.

The few Serenities standing in the doorway looked dumbstruck; they were inclining their heads in agitation and disbelief.

Suddenly a few male Serenities appeared out of the gloom and crawled through the rain and mist towards the door. Black clung to their blond hair as, just short of the doorway, their mouths opened and they spewed black rain onto the sodden clay ground.

Then they collapsed and were still!

Seren had fallen to her knees on the floor, her hands clasped tightly in front. Tears streamed down her face which showed a mixture of terror, disbelief and anguish. Her brilliant blue eyes blazed,

<< what has happened to all those males <> oh > what has become of my wonderful people >>

Scott knew and he realised with sickening dread that over 1000 Blue People had just perished fighting the unknown menace of the black.

They had just witnessed the second disaster to strike her people and he feared that this catastrophe was far worse than the tsunamis at the coast.

He felt devastated and shaken. His mind shrieked with Seren's sorrow and then she inclined her head and a few moments later repeated the words of Hotenka,

<< we lost nearly all our blond males <> we do not know why >>

Scott forced himself to look at more crystals from the same time but at different 'super cities'. The appalling carnage was repeated and, at the capital city, 50 battalions fell to the terror of the Black! 5,000 perished!

He could still not come to terms with what he had seen – surely this had not happened in all the major cities of the Blue People of Cloud Planet?

'My research shows that it had! The Serenite males fought valiantly across the planet and inflicted huge damage on the unknown black menace. But this was at a devastating price to their race. Ninety five per cent of the male Serenites perished fighting the black, leaving the Blue People bereft of their manhood and their intelligent skills. Twenty million perfect blond beings and 8 million blue workers suffocated under that awful black tide on the red plain of Cloud Planet.

'And now, time is the new enemy of the Blue People. Time, as their habitat, already devastated by the cloud collar, cools imperceptibly slowly. Time, as their revered blue workers die faster than they are breeding. Time, as the cooler planet temperature swings the balance of births from equality of males to females to predominantly female.

'Time, as the leader of the Blue People says in the huge pyramid.'

<< now our revered workers are dying faster than they are birthing <>we cannot birth enough males <> all our people are doomed to die <> our world is ending >>

'But time is of no consequence to the Black. It has all the time in the universe.

'Although it suffers huge losses in this battle against the inhabitants of Cloud Planet, it now waits and lets time complete its gruesome erosion of the Blue People.

'Time is the Black's ally. With time the Black regenerates!'

BOOK SEVEN
THE RETURN OF THE MENACE

Chapter 56
The Black Strikes Again

Scott and Seren wearily trudged out of the dark pyramid. They staggered away from the holographic amphitheatre and its terrible portrayal of the history of the Blue People of Cloud Planet. They were forlorn, dejected and very cold.

Scott cast his eyes up at the 500 metre light sheath towering back over his head into the sinking late afternoon sun. He looked at the brilliant red pyramids casting their dark shadows on the ground and on one another. He reflected that once this magnificent structure had stood under a cloudless blue sky – but how long ago he could not judge. He approached the open space in front of the huge pyramid and gazed at the wide black door......

.... fifty battalions of Serenites and blue workers had marched through that door, fought the Black and perished and that scenario had been repeated outside dwelling after dwelling all over the planet, decimating the Blue People.

He shuddered and Seren, who had read his thoughts, shook and then took his hand and led him inside the huge pyramid and towards the hot triangular pool.

It was not just the hot water that warmed their bodies in preparation for the coming night's rest.

Scott contacted Zec-1 via his palm top and was disturbed to learn that the black masses had formed outside eight of the dwellings leading to the Capitol City. Furthermore, he found it deeply worrying that they had formed 50 kilometre 'bridges' linking the masses. He was now beginning to believe that these black masses were the same or similar to those that had nearly wiped out the Blue People in their past. This new information was important but he was so exhausted that he could not concentrate, so he pulled his huge leaf more tightly around him and fell asleep next to Seren and her attendants.

The next morning Scott felt refreshed and, having warmed, drunk and fed, he considered going back into the dark pyramid. He was sure that there must be clues in the crystal history that would tell him more about the nature of the black menace. After explaining this to Seren, she arranged for the door to be opened. On this occasion she did not accompany him as she had seen enough of the disasters that had befallen her people.

He went back to the first crystals that had shown the strange black edge of the sea on both sides of the estuary. He remembered that this was after the tsunami and before the sea started misting – were these incidents related and in what manner? Zec-1 had discovered that all the coast lines had a wide black mass under the cloud. Was this the same black that he had seen in the dark pyramid?

Did the black mass start the misting of the sea after the tsunami? He thought about this and his next conclusion shook him rigid,

'Did the black mass cause the cloud collar around the equator of the planet!?' He said aloud with disbelief! 'But how and for what possible reason?'

He was deep in thought as he mulled over these possibilities when suddenly the door of the dark pyramid started opening. He shut down the crystal and returned it to the wall. Seren stood in the doorway, her golden hair shone as she was silhouetted by the brilliance behind. Her eyes blazed,

<< you must come quickly to the large pyramid <> our leader has received terrible news >>

They moved swiftly to the huge pyramid and up the ramp to the central triangular plinth. Hotenka, his elders and a large number of adult Serenites had already gathered.

The leader stood, his head moved from side to side, and his eyes blazed,

<< they have still not returned >>

'Who have not returned?' Scott asked Seren,

<< our blue workers > who went out to farm > have not returned <> there is no sight of them > only a blackness in the distance >>

Scott's stomach churned.

'When, where did this occur?'

<< now > at our farming dwellings >>

Then Seren pointed in the direction of the dwellings which Scott knew had the black masses outside.

'Can you stop further farming trips?'

<< no > they are all out now <> some have returned > others have not >>

And then Hotenka held up one hand and inclined his head. An uneasy chill descended on those in the huge pyramid,

<< it has just gone very dark outside our dwelling >>

They rushed out into the brilliant sunshine and ran to the wide black door. Several Serenites were already standing under the doorway. They looked out and pointed in alarm.

Outside was shrouded in rain and mist. But about 50 metres away it grew dark caused by a black 'cloud' above and across their width of visibility.

Beneath the blackness they saw that the farming group was returning; its light sheath swayed with the movement of the blue females.

Scott willed them to hurry. He had a terrible foreboding. How had the black mass come this far so quickly?

Then the black 'cloud' descended and darkened. The moving light sheath cut into the blackness and black rain fell around the group.

'Faster! Faster!' Cried Scott, and Seren immediately felt his anxiety and her eyes blazed as she pleaded with the blue female workers to hurry.

Scott moved out into the rain and mist but paled as the black suddenly dropped as a seething mass. The light shafts started to move erratically and then dimmed as the black cascaded down on the doomed blue workers.

And then nothing – nothing but black at the edge of visibility – no sign of the farming group containing over 100 blue workers.

Scott stood frozen in horror, soaked to the skin in the cold rain. The mass had now ascended and seethed and undulated above them – it was a terrifying sight.

Then, out of the gloom there was movement and a few bodies ran or dragged themselves towards the doorway. Two young blue females clutched their leaves as they raced past Scott, Seren and Hotenka and their eyes bulged with fear as black poured from their hair and bodies. Three adult blue females had dug themselves out of the cloying black mass and stumbled forward. One collapsed 10 metres from the door and willing hands moved out to pull the body to safety.

Another came staggering straight at Scott and collapsed to her knees in front of him. As she fell forward, black rain spewed from her mouth onto the sodden wet clay at his feet.

As other blue females helped their companions, he knelt and tested the black mass using his palmtop which established that it was inert and relatively harmless in such small quantities. He donned protective gloves and gingerly scooped up a handful. It was so slippery it dribbled through his fingers and he had difficulty keeping some in his cupped hands. He moved back under the doorway to examine it in a better light. It was made up of dozens and dozens of small shapes. With difficulty he picked one up with tweezers and was puzzled as he viewed it more closely. It was grey black and just over half a centimetre long and about a quarter centimetre in diameter – it was cylindrical, no, more bullet shaped with one end rounded and quite remarkably......

.... it had something running through its length. Scott held it up to the light.

'Yes, a tiny hole runs right through it from end to end! How strange.'

By now the water had drained from the handful of 'black rain' and he stared in disbelief at the group of shapes; some slithered through his fingers.

'Why, it's like a handful of beads.' he said to no one in particular then louder, 'a handful of beads?'

Now he turned to look at Seren who had come up beside him and his eyes shot to her strange triangular necklace. With all their problems on this planet he had never really looked at it in detail as his attention was usually directed elsewhere. Scott reached out and held it in his fingers, dread crawling through his body......

..... it was made of beads! Small grey black beads threaded on something through the holes – identical beads to those in his hand! Those that had spewed from the blue females' mouth! Those that had exterminated the farming group! Were they the Black?

Then his head exploded as Seren agonisingly understood.

She fell to her knees, ripped the necklace away from her breast and screamed and screamed in Scott's head.

<< the beads > the beads have killed our people <> rip off the beads <> RIP OFF THE KILLER BEADS >>

And all around the dwelling and its pyramids, blond female Serenites fell to their knees tearing their triangular necklaces away in frenzy. Scott could feel the mounting fear of hundreds and hundreds of distraught Blue People.

Then the message flared from dwelling to dwelling across Cloud Planet. And thousands and thousands of female Serenites fell to their knees and in mortal anguish ripped their beads from their necks and dashed them to the red clay.

Chapter 57
Analyse the Beads

Scott gently lifted Seren's shaking body and looked into her tearful eyes,

'Where did the necklaces come from? Where did the beads come from?'

<< our blue workers made them for us <> from beads that came in with the leaves harvested during farming >>

'Oh my God!' thought Scott, 'How could they have known, the beads were their killers, the beads were the Black!'

Seren continued to shake.

<< we wore them for good fortune <> we thought they would bring us more male births >>

Scott could hardly speak he was so choked. How cruel could fate be! And then Seren blurted out.

<< and > and i gave one to your female <> because she was so unwell >>

'What!' shouted Scott and she replied more softly and almost apologetically.

<< i gave one to your female >>

Then Seren sagged to her knees again in terrible distress.

'Of course you did! Of course you did!' and Scott remembered Seren's touching moment.

'And it's gone up to the starship with Olivia!' he shouted with elation. 'Up where it can be analysed by the most sophisticated equipment in the world!'

He looked at Seren with renewed hope and she read his excitement. Gently he helped her up and looked into her eyes,

'I have to get a message to LifeSeeker-1, to the starship!' and he pointed upwards to the clouds.

Then he groaned as he realised that the SOS dwelling was 13 or 14 dwellings away! – two weeks travel by their underground transport.

Seren understood his alarm and led him, followed by the leader, back into the huge pyramid and up the ramp to the cool pool. There she pointed to his pack and to one of the pockets. Puzzled, he opened the flap and saw that it contained the piece of cardboard on which he had written the Morse code message to rescue Olivia.

Seren then pointed to her leader and ran to the very centre of the triangle where the black box covered the golden plaque of Pioneer 10.

And Scott understood. The leader could send a message. Hotenka had been sending the SOS signal for over 30 years! He would have to write a new Morse script for the leader to send. He could do it today because this very afternoon was when the leader would send the SOS.

Then Scott remembered with huge relief that Zec-1 had downloaded Morse code onto his palm top – just in case.

Scott smiled and looked at Seren who beamed one of her most beautiful smiles.

LifeSeeker-1 was now in geostationary orbit around Cloud Planet and positioned adjacent to the collar of cloud and between the SOS and the huge dwelling where they assumed that Scott was now located.

The view from the command dome of the starship was spectacular with the light shafts streaking away from the towering white clouds and converging on the yellow orb that was the star Seren. Below them, the deep blue sea formed a perfect arc as it kissed the base of the clouds.

What a remarkable scene!

Inside the command dome they hardly noticed it and the mood among the astronauts was sombre and deflated. They had given up trying to out-manoeuvre the black and they had watched with mounting concern as the masses formed alongside the dwellings leading to Scott's presumed position. Now the masses were linked and as of last night they were only two dwellings away from the equator.

The only good news was that Olivia had made a full recovery.

AJ was leading a discussion on how to mount an offensive attack on the black but there was huge concern that they were dealing with an enemy that they could not identify or understand. A foe that had pre-empted their every move. To attack would be a very high risk strategy.

It was nearing 'noon' on the planet revolving below them and as usual they focussed on the portion of the dome where the LCD display was dedicated to the SOS dwelling.

'Attention! Attention! New Morse message! New Morse message from the planet.'

Zec-C had their immediate attention.

'Translate!' commanded AJ and the crew all craned forward in rising expectation.

--T – E – S – T --- T – H – E --- B – E – A – D – S ----

'What's that mean? What beads?' said Alison.

--T – E – S – T --- T – H – E --- N – E – C – K – L – A– C – E ----

'Necklace! What necklace? What's this nonsense!' added Pete.

The next sentence on the dome LCD chilled the atmosphere in the starship.

-- T – H – E --- B – E – A – D – S --- A – R – E --- K – I – L – L – E – R – S --

'What does this mean!?' AJ said in alarm.

Suddenly, Olivia's hand shot to her neck as she remembered Seren's kind gesture as she lay unwell.

'She gave me her necklace! Seren gave me the strange triangular necklace!' Olivia shouted with rising understanding. 'Where is it!? Where is it Martha? Did I have it on when you put me in intensive care?'

'Why – yes, but I had to get you on a drip urgently so I removed it and put it in a drawer in the medical centre – I forgot all about it in my haste.'

-- T – H – E --- B – E – A – D – S --- A – R – E --- T – H – E --- B – L – A – C – K --

'Go get it!' commanded AJ, and the final chilling sentence appeared in front of the stunned astronauts.

-- D – E – S – T – R – O – Y ---- T – H – E ---

B – L – A – C – K ---

'That's the full message; it's being repeated and repeated.'

Zec-C concluded.

Martha returned with the black triangular necklace and placed it in front of AJ. They all gathered round for a closer inspection.

'It's made up of beads, small greyish black beads!' Olivia pointed, 'And they seem to be strung on leaf fibre. I never really noticed with all the other tattoos and things. But all the Serenite females wore one of these.'

'Let's get some of these beads where Zec-C can analyse them.' AJ instructed and Olivia cut the thread and, with extreme difficulty, placed three beads in a special receptacle near a wall of sophisticated instruments. She pressed the touch screen nearby and the beads retracted into the machine and were now the responsibility of Zec-C to extract from them as much information as possible.

After a minute, enlarged images of the unusual beads started to appear on the inside of the dome accompanied by Zec-C's analytical commentary.

'Each object is 0.8 centimetres long by 0.35 centimetres in diameter. One end is slightly concave whilst the other is a tapered convex shape similar to a bullet.'

Images of the bead rotated on the LCD screen showing its morphology from several perspectives.

'Running perfectly through the centre and from end to end is a cylindrical tube of diameter 0.5 millimetres at the bullet end narrowing uniformly to 0.4 millimetres at the concave end.'

'What do you make of this shape Zec-C?' AJ asked.

'It is hydro-dynamically perfect and its outer surface is nearly frictionless.'

'But that's impossible!' Steve said, but they had all repeatedly dropped the beads when they tried to pick them up.

'The objects are designed to move through a low viscosity fluid, for example water, with perfect efficiency and I would predict that they would be equally efficient in water vapour, mist and clouds.'

'What are they made of?' Alison queried.

'The bulk of the body of the object is similar to silicon but the outer surface, which has the lowest coefficient of friction of any substance I know, is a material which does not appear in my database.'

'That's impossible Zec-C; your database has the fingerprint of every material in the Milky Way Galaxy!' AJ cried in disbelief!

'Yes, and every other known galaxy.'

The implications of this simple answer hung heavily in the dome. It was generally accepted that the universe was based on the same building blocks throughout. But it was not known how all of those blocks were constructed in the exploding stars and supernovae of the other galaxies.

'Further, the inner surface of the cylindrical hole is also made of material that I cannot identify but is similar to semi–conductors, for example silicon, and metallic compounds, again, some of which I

cannot identify. But it is how these materials are distributed in the cylinder surface that is both familiar and unique. Look!'

Part of the dome LCD screen filled with hundreds of lines and channels which were perfectly regular and which crisscrossed one another. There were junctions between lines of what appeared to be metal and channels of grey. The distance between the lines was equal. They were perfectly parallel.

'We're looking at a circuit! It's just like the design of a microchip!' said an astonished Pete, the starship's computer genius. 'Zec-C! What are the dimensions! What's the distance between the lines?'

'In microchip technology, the smaller the distance between the 'wires' or lines, the more circuits that are packed onto a single chip. At the start of the 21st century 0.1 micron capability was achieved and 100 years later with newer semi–conductors and processes this capability is now reduced to below 0.01 micron. This is approaching the limit of semi-conductor capability and the ultimate goal of molecular circuits is still at development stage. My circuits are at 0.008 micron which is pretty powerful stuff.'

Zec-C continued his explanation,

'The circuits you see on the dome LCD are magnified to the maximum capability of the ultra-electron microscope. They are molecular circuits and I estimate the capability at 1 Angstrom!'

Pete nearly fell out of his chair, he was so astonished, and so were the rest of the astronauts.

'Zec-C!' Pete said breathlessly, 'How many circuits? How many transistors are there in one of those beads?'

The answer blew his mind away. There was more computing power in just one of those beads than in all Zec-C's computers on LifeSeeker-1!

What were they up against!

Chapter 58
First Offensive

Martha broke the stunned silence in the command zone.

'Impossible!' She held up one of the small black beads, or tried to as it slipped out of her fingers, 'Are we saying that those black masses down there are millions of these! That can't be right, how could they control themselves – they'd just keep colliding into one another.'

'Martha,' Olivia explained, 'just think of a huge flock of birds, they fly close together, turn, bank, and swoop – they don't collide with one another.'

'Yes! But they've got a brain.'

'But these,' Pete interjected and pointed to the bead in Martha's fingers, 'each have more 'brain cells' than a flock of a million birds put together!'

'Zec-C, what more can you tell us about these beads?' AJ interjected.

'Considering their speed and manoeuvrability, they are the most perfect of nano–technology machines. I infer that they take water or moisture in at the front, possibly by simple capillary action, and accelerate this water along the narrowing tube, thus increasing its velocity. However, to achieve the incredible speeds that we have seen, this water is probably atomised and leaves the object as a jet of mist. Further, I have identified four radial channels in the concave end along which the emerging jet could be diverted to achieve directional changes.'

'But do they control themselves or are they controlled?' This fundamental observation from Steve made everyone stop and ponder the implications.

But Zec-C wasn't finished,

'The body of the object is predominantly a silicon type complex as I have already informed you, but it is, in fact, an impure but rich ore of silicon. It is micro porous, giving the body an overall specific gravity of 1.2 grams per cubic centimetre – slightly heavier than the highly salinated seas of this planet. Furthermore the analytical fingerprint of the silicon ore in the object from Olivia's necklace is identical to that of the huge deposits of silicon ore beneath the sea beds of Cloud Planet.'

‘Zec-C! Where are you taking us with your analysis?’ AJ cried with concern.

‘The objects from Olivia’s necklace, from Cloud Planet itself, have been fabricated from silicon ore unique to this planet together with unidentifiable substances whose origin is outside our Milky Way galaxy.’

The silence was punctuated by gasps and intakes of breath as Alison tried to put the implications into words.

‘Something has come to Cloud Planet from another galaxy!’ Stunned silence. ‘Something has come to this planet and made these!’ pointing to the beads, ‘These killers as Scott has told us!!’ and, pointing down to the strange world below, ‘And it has made the black masses which know our every move!’

AJ brought matters to a head.

‘Scott’s message is clear, the beads are killers, and, where ever they have come from, they are the Black and must be destroyed. We must vote to confirm a decision to attack.’

With little hesitation the vote was six to zero in favour of an offensive.

‘Command Zec-C! Prepare two ‘D’ warheads for an assault on the outermost black mass adjacent to those in line with Scott’s dwelling. We will launch the missiles at midnight tonight, and search every corner of this planet with a fine toothcomb – there must be something here we’ve missed!’

‘LifeSeeker-1 is provisioned with a huge arsenal of weapons, including nuclear warheads, which are carried on a choice of missile delivery systems. The missiles contain the most sophisticated of guidance computers which are controlled by the starship’s on-board computer, Zec-C. ‘D’ warheads are non nuclear and dual purpose, with a huge explosive capability. The first detonation is programmed just before impact for maximum lateral damage to surface objects. This detonation also adds extra thrust to a second explosive charge to blast it into the depths of the target, where it explodes a second later causing maximum underground damage.’

At midnight, AJ sat looking around at each of the other astronauts. An offensive strike in space and on another planet was not an action to be taken lightly. But they had all agreed. They had to take offensive action.

‘Command Zec-C, fire first ‘D’ missile!’ and all the astronauts’ hands went forward to confirm the deadly decision.

They watched the missile streak away from the starship quickly disappearing into the night sky and heading for the dark collar of cloud 450 kilometres below.

The dome LCD displays now showed the missile as it entered the dark cloud collar 50 kilometres above its target - the centre of the black mass adjacent to the outermost dwelling. Moments later the ‘D’ missile exploded and Zec-C’s screen confirmed the double detonation. The black mass expanded to nearly twice its size and then collapsed in on itself. It was now only half the size it had been before the attack and the astronauts cheered confident that they had delivered a decisive blow to the Black.

‘Command Zec-C, fire second ‘D’ missile!’

Again they watched the missile streak away from the starship into the night. On the dome screens they saw the missile enter the cloud collar and then came Zec-C’s urgent warning.

‘Attention! Target black mass increasing in size!’

It had increased to twice its original size!

‘Attention! Target black mass is changing colour at its centre – getting lighter!’

A circle of lighter grey had appeared in the dead centre of the black mass.

‘Emergency! Computer contact with ‘D’ missile lost, repeat lost! No control 2 seconds from detonation!’

But there was no detonation two seconds later and the astronauts looked at one another with growing concern.

‘Zec-C! What’s happening?’ AJ shrieked.

But before Zec-C could reply and 5 seconds later than planned there was a double detonation.

The astronauts looked at the dome displays. The black mass was unchanged, except that it did not have a lighter ring at the centre any more. The double detonation had occurred at ground level on the planet and adjacent to the black mass. The X marking the coordinates of the strike were slowly and horrifyingly understood by all the astronauts in the dome of LifeSeeker-1 and heads buried themselves in hands.

‘Oh no! Oh my God, no! What have we done!’

'I am impressed and horrified at the sequence of events that occurred as the second missile is approaching the upper surface of the mass. Two seconds before it is due to detonate, the on-board computer is completely reprogrammed. Its detonation time is increased and new target coordinates replace the originals input by Zec-C. Then, as the missile enters the centre of the lighter grey circle at the top of the black mass, so it changes direction by 20 degrees as it travels through an angled cylindrical void in the mass.

'On exit and now 2 kilometres above the red plain of Cloud Planet it is accelerating unerringly at its new target – the outermost dwelling below!

'The first detonation occurs 2 metres above the centre of the structure – just to the right of the open channel and in front of the plinth carrying the screw lift. All the internal structures are obliterated by the force of the explosion in a fraction of a second. The plinth carrying the screw lift and the four triangular pools are smashed into the dwelling walls in a hurricane of red bricks, pulverised clay and water. Walls explode outwards – bricks, dust and crystals fly hundreds of metres into the air. Most of the destructive force is absorbed by the plinth and walls of the dwelling in front of the canal. Despite the onslaught the canal walls hold – for now!

'Meanwhile below ground!

'A second later the next detonation occurs in mid air in the underground cavern. The expanding explosive fireball crushes the walls of the huge pits turning the vast volumes of water into superheated steam. Terrible concussive forces in that enclosed space kill the hundred blue workers instantly where they lie. Dramatically the fire and superheated steam adds to the carnage before the roof and walls cave in. The inhabitants know nothing of their fate.

'But the expanding fireball of gases and superheated steam has to vent its ferocity somewhere. And it did this before the floor of the dwelling collapses.

'And that somewhere is the underground transport tunnel.

'High-pressure superheated gases explode into the dual tunnel and in the left hand channel where water is flowing away from the dwelling the water is instantly turned into steam. This acts like a piston forcing the water before it. But water is not compressible and a solid rod of water shoots the length of the tunnel.

'The black boat containing six blue females is over half way on its journey when it suddenly accelerates from its sedate 5 kilometres an hour to over 70 kilometres an hour. It remains surprisingly even-keeled ahead of the monstrous plug of water and 15 minutes later it smashes into the front dock wall at the next dwelling. The heavy black boat punches a hole through the clay wall and twists upside down as it comes to rest with three quarters of its length jutting out of the wall.

'Leaves and bodies drop from the boat in a grisly tangle and fall to the pit of water below.

'The other boat is nearly three quarters of the way through its journey carrying its precious cargo of five blue males towards the dwelling. However, the water in the right-hand channel is travelling towards the devastated dwelling. The effect of the explosion of steam is to momentarily stop this flow, blocking the channel with a plug of incompressible water. The high pressure in this channel blows out the central wall and cracks open the ceiling of the tunnel, which then collapses.

'The craft suddenly rises to the roof and is swamped by the surging wall of water that approaches it from both directions.

'The cold blue sleeping males drown without even waking up!'

Chapter 59
Under the Ice

The mood the following morning in the command dome was sombre. They did not blame or criticise one another. It had been a unanimous decision which left them with an overwhelming feeling of collective guilt.

That feeling deepened as the light shafts fired up through the clouds in consecutive rows. Until, finally, it was the turn of the row of dwellings which had adjacent black masses. There was no surprise when the outermost dwelling failed to produce its light shaft – that confirmed their worst expectation.

'Take us through it again, Zec-C, what do you think happened?' AJ asked.

'We lost computer contact 2 seconds before detonation. If the computer had failed or malfunctioned the missile would have self-destructed, which did not occur. Conclusion – the computer was still working. I was able to track the missile for a short while after it left the edge of the black mass and headed for the dwelling – its trajectory was the dead centre of its new target.'

'Any chance it was an accidental deflection?' Steve queried.

'Most improbable. Not only did it pass through the black mass and exit on the exact trajectory for the dwelling but the 2 seconds to detonation had been extended by 5 seconds.'

'Are you inferring the black mass reprogrammed the on-board computer?' Alison asked, not believing her own question.

'I have insufficient data to confirm your theory but it must be a possibility considering the circuitry we found in the objects comprising the black mass.'

What next? They wondered, but Zec-C was about to give them a lot more to ponder!

Zec-C continued his narrative.

'Two areas of Cloud Planet had not been analysed until last night. These were the deep underground areas of the red plain and both ice caps.

'The red plain is predominantly clay and varies between 40 and 70 metres in thickness. Below is a stratum of limestone, very similar to that found on Earth, which contains watercourses, caves

and caverns. This is hardly surprising considering the multiple flows of water, both hot and cold, draining through the clay. I could find no structures underground that would suggest intelligent fabrication.'

AJ tapped his fingers on the console impatiently willing Zec-C to get to the interesting stuff which was usually kept until last.

Zec-C did not disappoint.

'However, there is a remarkable scenario under the ice caps.'

All the astronauts stared intently at the dome screen as it showed one of the ice caps, brilliantly white and edged by the azure blue sea. Zec-C had never used the word 'remarkable' before when describing his findings so they held their breath.

'Both ice caps are very similar in area, each covering about one twentieth of the planet's surface. At the boundary with the ocean the peripheral circumference is approximately 6000 kilometres. The thickness of the ice is about 5 metres at the boundary with the sea and remains constant for several hundred kilometres then it thickens significantly to 20 kilometres. As I reported before the ice is thinner at the dead centre of the icecap where it is only 2 kilometres thick. Further, this thinner area is a circle approximately 140 kilometres in diameter. I have no explanation for this. The depth of the ocean under the ice is relatively uniform at around 90-100 kilometres.'

The mimic display inside the dome changed to show a side on view of the ice cap, the sea below and the ocean bed. Ten cylinders appeared on the display in a vertical line from just below the ice to just above the sea bed. They were uniformly spaced and, the astronauts saw to their surprise, that they were connected to one another by a pipe structure. The lowest cylinder had a tube which projected from its underside and which appeared to enter the sea bed.

'Wait a minute!' shouted Steve, 'Is this to scale!' and Zec-C went on in his usual analytical way.

'Each cylinder is a fraction under 1 kilometre in diameter and a similar height, and is connected to the next one by a pipe 500 metres long and 200 metres diameter. The cylinder's vertical surface is multi – faceted and very unusual but LifeSeeker-1 is not near enough for a detailed topography. Also both upper and lower surfaces are slightly concave but I cannot be more precise.'

'One kilometre in diameter and height!' AJ looked around incredulously at his fellow astronauts, 'And there's ten of them!' But Zec-C would not be hurried.

'The tube at the base of the lowest cylinder enters the sea bed and continues to a depth of 5 kilometres right into the centre of a 10 kilometre thick stratum of silicon ore identical to that in the objects from Olivia's necklace.'

'Those objects are mining the sea bed! Extracting the silicon ore of this planet!' Olivia cried, 'I can hardly believe what I'm hearing and seeing!'

Olivia and the rest of the astronauts were stunned into silence. They sat wide eyed as Zec-C added further objects to the mimic display and then more connecting tubes.

'I started off by describing one vertical array of 10 cylinders but there are 5000 vertical arrays arranged in a perfect circular lattice underneath the ice cap.'

The mimic display rotated to give a three dimensional view of the ice cap and its ring of objects around the periphery.

'But that's 50,000 cylinders!' blurted out Steve, '50,000 and all interconnected and, ...are all the lower ones sunk into the sea bed!?'

'Yes, the highest concentrations of silicon ore on this planet are under the ice cap.'

'What are they constructed of?' AJ asked almost knowing the answer.

'I cannot analyse the material of construction, only see it in a similar way to the black mass.'

'Zec-C, do you think this is where the black mass is made and where it is controlled from?' Alison could hardly get her words out she was so taken aback by the enormity of the structure under the ice cap.

'I concur - that is the only rational conclusion based on the evidence so far.'

Then Zec-C seemed to pause as if to take breath, and added almost as an afterthought,

'Oh, ...and there is an identical structure under the other ice cap! Another 50,000 identical objects. One hundred thousand in total on Cloud Planet hidden under the ice!'

The silence in the command dome of LifeSeeker-1 went on and on.

Chapter 60
Second Offensive

'I say we attack the cylinders and we do it now!' Steve argued.

'But there's 100,000 of them!' Alison countered.

'We've more than enough fire power on the starship!' Steve continued.

After the information regarding the discoveries under the ice caps had registered, the astronauts focussed on their next steps. Doing nothing was not an option. The previous night they had witnessed the advance of the black masses to the structure where Scott was located. The black masses had also formed outside the lines of dwelling to either side of this structure. They could see that the black was advancing but were unaware that it was already attacking farming dwellings of blue workers with devastating results.

'We've already destroyed one of their dwellings and God knows how many Blue People!' Alison said with anguish.

'We'll be firing at the ice cap – nowhere near the land mass – we must destroy their base!' Steve was adamant.

'I agree with Alison,' Martha joined in, 'we failed miserably with our first attack.'

'We can't just do nothing!' cried Olivia, 'The Black are killing people down on the planet!'

'That's right and Scott's message is clear. We must attack.' Pete added.

'We must vote,' said AJ with authority, 'the proposal is we move the starship and fire two 'D Plus' warheads at the discs under the ice cap.'

Six hands moved forward and the proposition was carried by four votes to two.

Zec-C moved LifeSeeker-1 to a position 1000 kilometres from the ice cap and 500 kilometres above sea level. The astronauts sat looking out of the dome at the idyllic scene before them. Wonderful blue seas fringed the brilliant blue white of the ice cap. How could this vista harbour such a menace below its surface?

'Command Zec!' AJ said, 'Prepare to launch first 'D' Plus missile.' 'D' Plus was another dual detonation warhead but with twice the explosive power.

AJ looked at the other astronauts and all hands went forward to confirm the decision.

'Launch first missile!' commanded AJ, and they watched the missile streak away from the starship on a descending trajectory towards the blue sea below. They had chosen the lowest cylinder in the group of ten directly in front of them in the belief that this would collapse the objects above like a pack of cards.

Visibility was so good that they could watch it as it travelled towards a point at the sea surface 50 kilometres short of the ice cap.

Suddenly the sea just ahead of the speeding rocket turned black – a deepening black that covered a square kilometre of sea surface – directly in line between the missile and its target.

The projectile hit the black and the astronauts watched the double detonation of its warheads. A massive eruption of sea and black shot into the atmosphere and when it settled the Black was gone but the cylinders were still intact. The Black had protected its base!

'Launch second missile!' commanded AJ and the astronauts watched in the hope that they had destroyed the forward defences.

Again, shortly before it reached the surface of the sea, the black reappeared, but bigger and denser, and this time it had formed a huge circular mass 2 kilometres in diameter.

And then the impossible happened!

Just before the missile hit the mass, the centre opened forming a ring of clear sea in front of it – an area of about 500 metres in diameter.

'Warning! Warning! Communications with missile computer lost!'

And the rocket entered the open sea encircled by the ring of black mass.

'Warning! Warning! Black mass building up quickly under the sea to the left of entry point!'

The astronauts had to watch the mimic display to see the black expanding with alarming speed under the sea.

'Warning! Warning! The black is forming a u-tube shape under the sea which is rising to the surface 5 kilometres to LifeSeeker-1's left!'

The astronauts looked, pointed and gasped as the sea blackened away to their left. An identical ring of black formed on the surface of the sea.

Suddenly something shot out of the centre of this new mass and headed directly for the starship!

'Emergency! Incoming missile on collision course with LifeSeeker-1!'

'Deploy anti-missile defence!' shrieked AJ.

'No time! Double red emergency!'

'In my design for the defence systems of the starship, I factored into the model the remote possibility of 'friendly fire'. The force field is capable of absorbing the double impact of the 'D' Plus missile with an added 25% safety contingency. Furthermore, any incoming threat is immediately pinpointed and triggers the anti–missile systems which eliminate the danger well before it reaches the starship. I must confess that I did not foresee that one of LifeSeeker-1's own 'D' Plus' attacks the starship from such a short distance and at 100 times design velocity.

'Double red is the highest threat level to the starship. The dome blackens immediately and emergency bulk head doors slam into place sealing the command dome and accommodation quarters from the nuclear ion drive. Dozens of thrusters rockets on each side burst into full power but in opposing directions.

'In the vacuum of space, the starship turns quickly on its axis to present its mammoth ion drive to the threat and use its massive bulk to protect the command dome and accommodation module. This requires huge power and Zec-C must judge the timing perfectly and then concentrate the force field at the area of attack.'

On this occasion the starship had completed 150 degrees of turn when Zec-C announced full force field had been applied to the ion drive.

Zero point one second later their own missile struck the force field. The first detonation was absorbed but the astronauts felt the blow as the starship shuddered and lurched forward.

Then the second penetrative detonation occurred. Normally the force field would be capable of absorbing most of this, limiting damage to a minimum. But there was nothing normal about the velocity at which this missile had returned to the starship!

The astronauts were jolted by the second detonation and the starship bucked violently and was shunted forward into a spin. A multitude of warning lights and sirens assaulted their senses.

Amid the shouts and screams in the command dome, AJ calmly focussed on the dome display which showed the starship's desperate plight. He knew that no human could respond quickly enough to bring the starship under control but he realised that Zec-C's massive processing power would be juggling the thrust of dozens of rockets – he just prayed that enough had survived the terrible impact.

Slowly and surely, LifeSeeker-1 came out of its spin and its forward speed was checked and brought to a stop. Red lights turned amber, then green and an eerie silence ensued. The command dome cleared and visual contact was restored with the planet below. Then Zec-C announced that the double red emergency was over.

'Damage report!' AJ commanded.

'One third of ion drive thrusters completely destroyed, nuclear drive intact, integrity of command dome and accommodation module intact.'

AJ and the astronauts sighed with relief and then AJ broke the silence.

'What happened, Zec-C? Why couldn't we destroy our own missile? Why couldn't we shoot it out of the sky?'

'We lost computer control just before the black mass opened. The missile travelled around a 'U' – tube formed by the mass under the sea and exited the tube 5 kilometres from entry. The on-board computers had been reprogrammed with LifeSeeker-1's coordinates as target. But during its passage through the tube the missile was accelerated and left the tube at approximately 100 kilometres per second, 100 times its entry speed. We had less than 5 seconds to take avoidance action and no time to launch the anti-missile system. It was the sheer velocity of the missile that caused the second detonation to breach our force field.'

The implications of what had happened took a while to digest. The astronauts looked at one another. The sheer hopelessness of the situation was in their terrified eyes. AJ quietly broke the silence.

'Thank you, Zec-C, your prompt action saved us and the starship – we could not have survived if our missile had struck the accommodation module.'

Spontaneously, all the astronauts applauded and thanked Zec-C and looked at one another with relief as the tension in the dome subsided.

‘Command Zec-C, take us back to our geostationary orbit. We have an awful lot to think about before we can consider our next move.’

Chapter 61
Seren has the Key

Scott and Seren sat by the cool pool of the huge pyramid oblivious to the fact that the starship had been attacked by its own missile. Scott was sure that his message would be read and acted upon but was horrified to learn from Zec-1 that there had been a double detonation at the outermost dwelling adjacent to their current position. Had an attack on the Black gone so terribly wrong?

He was further disturbed by the build-up of black masses at dwellings either side of his position. But the major concern was that the black mass, which had killed the blue workers outside this dwelling, had travelled during the day. It had definitely not been there the previous night.

This was a serious escalation of the Black's capability, as it had thus far only travelled at night.

Of course, Seren was reading his thoughts but she had difficulty comprehending them. However, she sensed that something had gone badly wrong during the night and her eyes blazed,

<< what happened to my people at that dwelling >>

He could not lie and his thoughts immediately told her the answer. There was sadness but no blame in her eyes and Scott felt his chest tighten. He could only admire the way she had coped with the last 2 days, when so much destruction had been revealed to her about the Blue People. And now the devastation was happening again and he felt powerless in the face of such a formidable menace.

He tried to explain that the black masses were outside the dwellings either side of their position but the concept was almost impossible to convey. So he pointed to the octagonal tattoo between her breasts and tried to communicate that he wanted to 'paint' a picture. Seren suddenly understood him and left. After a short while she returned with a section of leaf containing red and black liquid.

Using his fingers he drew a line of 10 structures on the clay floor. He pointed to the largest of them and indicated that this was where they were situated. Seren understood. Then he drew 10 structures to either side. Finally he painted a black shape outside each structure and tried to warn that the blue workers must not go out to farm.

But she had understood and rushed to the silver-haired leader inclining her head and he communicated to the drummers in the relevant dwellings. She returned and her eyes blazed,

<< we have stopped them leaving to farm >>

Scott breathed a huge sigh of relief.

Then Seren looked at the drawing on the floor and pointed to one of the black squares.

<< how does the black get to our dwellings >>

'It comes from the sea,' and Scott pointed, 'and travels through the clouds.' Again this was difficult to explain so he added to his floor drawing. He tried to show the sea, estuary and beach and then he drew the six structures on the bank of the river and she understood. So he continued the drawing depicting the river where, at the head of the valley, it terminated at the outermost dwelling. Then he drew his impression of the mountains and cloud. Finally he added black masses at the edge of the sea and tried to indicate that they moved over the mountains and through the clouds.

Seren seemed lost in thought for a while and then her eyes blazed.

<< the black came from the sea > through the clouds > killed my beautiful people <> killed all those wonderful males in the dark pyramid <> and that was in our past >>

It hurt to feel her slow comprehension but she carried on.

<< now the black has come again from the sea > through the clouds > and > has just killed our revered workers outside this dwelling >>

Her anxiety heightened and it hurt Scott's head.

<< and if we cannot stop them > the black will kill us <> all my people will die >>

Scott found it hard to answer because he was shaken with her grief for her people. He felt totally at a loss when he saw.

<< we must find a way > we must find a way > we must find a way >>

And he felt a renewed determination.

Seren looked at the drawing on the floor and pointed to one of the black squares by the sea and then asked a question so fundamental, so logical that it dumbfounded Scott. Her eyes blazed as she looked at him,

<< why did not the black just travel up the estuaries > rivers and canals to kill us >>

'What did you say?' Scott had not caught the gist of her question.

<< the black could have travelled up the estuaries > rivers and canals <> that would have been easier <> why did it go through the clouds >>

Why indeed, and Scott's mind raced. What had he missed that this beautiful blond Serenite had seen with her basic logic? In the back of his mind he was trying to recall the events of one of the crystals in the dark pyramid, the one after the tsunami – what was it?

Suddenly Scott grabbed Seren's hand.

'We must go to the dark pyramid, now!'

It took Scott a couple of attempts before he located the crystal he needed. Then it ignited and the amazing dark pyramid filled with red light shafts and they were on the beach, the terrible aftermath of the tsunami still painfully obvious. Scott led Seren up the ramp and onto the ledge and they looked out to sea with the estuary below them and the beaches stretching away either side.

'Look, Seren, look, the black at the edges of the ocean goes on as far as we can see. But there is no black at the estuary and none where the river flows out to sea! It's not as if the river rushes into the sea – on the contrary the flow is very gentle.'

Then Scott remembered Zec-C's analysis from the starship. Both coast lines had a black edge all around the seas except at the estuaries – none of the estuaries had black in them!

'The black can't travel through the estuaries or through the rivers!' Scott shouted aloud as he looked at Seren, 'But why? – it can travel through the sea, it can travel through clouds – what's stopping it entering the rivers?!'

Then it hit him! Was it that simple! Could it be that obvious!

'The rivers, canals, the estuaries – of course, they are stuffed full of chlorine! We had to wear masks when we first landed because the atmosphere was so bad.' Scott mused.

'Chlorine! Chlorine!' Scott shouted at Seren, 'You clever girl! Chlorine must be a barrier to the black – but why? And have we found its Achilles heel?'

Seren understood hardly any of this, but she felt Scott's excitement and she beamed one of her wonderful smiles.

'We must send another message to the starship!' he said and pointed upwards.

Chapter 62
Message Received and Understood

Alison and Steve instructed Zec-2 to take ROL-2 out of the huge lander bay. They cleared the doors and were awed by the size of the starship. From inside it was easy to forget that this was a giant of engineering skills and technology. As they moved around the starship, the lander seemed small and puny. Then they turned at the rear of the ion drive, backed away and faced the damaged section.

In the command domes of LifeSeeker-1 and ROL-2, everyone was shocked at the extent of the appalling destruction in front of them. At least one quarter of the thousands of thrusters that made up the ion drive were gone, completely sheared off at the base plate which held them. The base plate itself was buckled and there was no sign of the fourth major rocket booster which was once attached to that quadrant of the ion drive.

'It's just as well they didn't design this baby for a return trip!' Steve said as they moved the lander to the centre of the ion drive for a double check on the nuclear reactor.

'No radiation detected.' Alison informed after checking her instruments thus confirming that the integrity of the nuclear chamber had not been breached.

'OK, good, return to starship,' AJ commanded.

Later, in the command dome of LifeSeeker-1, the astronauts were debating and arguing their next moves but in view of what had happened they could not see how they could mount an offensive strike.

'The Black seems to anticipate our every move! Why it can even re-programme our computers, it's always a step ahead of us!' Steve said in exasperation.

'Of course it can,' Pete replied, 'it's an unimaginably sophisticated computer which recognises our complex equipment. No wonder it can track us and out manoeuvre us.'

'So how are we going to defeat it?' Steve said and you could cut the silence in the command dome with a knife.

'Attention! Attention! New message coming from the SOS dwelling!'

That got everyone's rapt attention and they stared intently at the dome display.

--C – H – L – O – R – I – N – E ---S– T – O – P – S --

- T – H – E –- B – L – A – C – K ----

'Chlorine!?' they all chorused.

--C – H – E – C – K --- E – S – T – U – A – R– Y ----

R – I – V – E – R – S –- C – A – N – A – L – S ----

'Estuaries! Rivers! What have we missed?' said AJ.

-- N – O --- B – L – A – C – K --- W – H – Y ---

C – H – L – O – R – I – N – E --- B – U – T --- W – H – Y --

'No black in the estuaries and rivers, remember Zec-C's analysis of the coast lines!' Steve reminded everyone.

But the last line to appear chilled them all,

-- T – H– E --- B – L – A – C – K --- I – S---

K – I – L – L – I – N – G –- T – H – E --- B – L – U– E ---

P – E– O– P– L – E ---- A– G– A– I– N----

'Oh my God!' Olivia and Alison said in unison.

The dome displays now showed pictures of the coast lines and estuaries.

'There is a 100 metre wide black mass along all the coast lines except at the estuaries. No black in any of the estuaries, rivers or canals.' Confirmed Zec-C.

'Further, chlorine levels are at their highest in the tributaries from the mountains at several hundred parts per million, reducing to 200 parts per million in the rivers and canals and 100 parts per million at the estuaries.'

'I've got it!' triumphed Pete. 'I know why the black can't enter the estuaries and rivers!'

Everyone looked at Pete and they knew they had to curb their impatience because a mini lecture was on its way!

'In the manufacture of computer microchips, strong chemicals and gases are used to etch sub point one micron channels in the silicon surface. But this process is carried out using masks, under highly-controlled conditions of temperature and pressure, to ensure that the channels are only cut where they are needed. Subsequently, tiny amounts of metal are deposited in and around the channels building a circuit. This is a simplification, but the process is constantly replicated building up millions of transistors or circuits to form a microprocessor or RAM chip.'

'What's this all got to do with chlorine?' interrupted Martha.

'Chlorine is a very reactive and corrosive gas and if used uncontrolled would damage these sub point one micron circuits. But in the molecular circuits of the black beads.....

.... it would create havoc!' Pete sat back pleased with his delivery.

'Yes, and we've got chlorine on the starship!' shouted Steve excitedly, 'dozens of high pressure containers of the stuff!'

'OK,' said AJ, 'let's start thinking about how we can use this new intelligence but firstly where does the chlorine on Cloud Planet come from and what happens to it when it enters the sea – surely it would still affect these black beads?'

'The upper mountain slopes of this planet contain strata of calcium hypochlorite, calcium carbonate and sodium chloride. The constant high rainfall percolates over these layers extracting minerals. When calcium hypochlorite is mixed with water you get chlorine or bleach as we commonly know it. The chlorine enters the tributaries and rivers as gas and also enters the atmosphere. When it gets to the sea it is mopped up by the excess sodium ions, forms salt and this accounts for the excessively high saline levels of the seas of Cloud Planet.'

'So the high salinity in the sea doesn't affect these?' Alison held up one of the black beads, 'doesn't affect what's inside these?'

'No.' Pete continued, 'Weak salt solution is very mild compared to gaseous chlorine – that's what's stopping these beads travelling up the estuaries.'

'I'm surprised anything survives on this planet with all this bleach about,' Alison continued. 'As we normally use it to kill weeds and germs!'

'Well the trees here certainly like it considering how big they grow but, apart from them, there are no other plants on this planet.' Olivia contributed. 'But how are we going to use chlorine as a weapon against the black?'

'Pete, you said that chlorine would cause havoc with the circuits in the beads,' Steve said thoughtfully, 'but what would happen if we exploded some of these chlorine containers in the middle of the black mass?'

'Chaos, absolute chaos,' replied Pete, 'high temperature on its own would cause huge damage but high temperature chlorine gas, chlorine ions, would, I think, cause widespread devastation over a large expanse of the sea.'

'Steve, what are you thinking?' asked AJ.

'When we tried to attack the cylinders, the Black put up a barrier – and more than a barrier the second time! But if we could explode chlorine missiles in the black barrier then, would we create a sufficient opening to get some really powerful warheads through and hit the cylinders?'

'Sounds good in theory!' said AJ. 'Any comments?'

'How are we going to send any missile into the mass when we already know it can take control of the on-board computers? And what's more fire it back at us!' Alison replied dejectedly.

'Can we take out the on-board computers and guide it manually?' Olivia suggested, and was immediately blasted with derisory comments and looks.

'Wait,' said AJ, 'Olivia, take your thoughts further.'

'Well, we can't send anything with a computer on board, but what if we could aim a mechanical missile at the black mass – with nothing on board that another computer would recognise?'

'How would we guide it? How could we time the explosion without computers?' Alison said.

'Pete, what could you fix up by way of a mechanical timer?' asked AJ. 'Could we launch a missile with chlorine containers replacing the primary warhead and just rely on time for detonation?'

However, Pete was already scribbling away on his notepad, holding his hand up, to ward off further questions while he sketched. Then he asked Zec-C to put up diagrams of the 'D' warhead missile on the dome mimic.

The astronauts prepared for the inevitable lecture!

'The two warheads of the 'D' missile are located in front of one another on the carrier missile. The surface charge sits just behind the penetrative one and the explosion of the former just before impact blasts the penetrative charge into the body of the target where it explodes about 1 second later. So, Zec-C, can you replace the front warhead with a cluster of, say, four chlorine containers? We have multiple collars so we should be able to mount them securely.'

They all watched as the mimic display changed.

'Good, in profile it's not too different to the normal warhead but we'll worry about how it flies later. Now, Zec-C, take out all the computer guidance system, everything with a circuit in it, from the carrier missile.'

It was surprising how much space appeared in the middle of the missile body.

'Now, Zec-C, let's put 10 kilos of plastic explosive next to the surface charge, then a sealed 20 volt heavy duty battery, followed by a mechanical timer which I'll design, similar in size.'

The free space inside the missile body was nearly filled.

'I can design a timer that will be started by inertia when the missile is fired from the starship. After a period of time, which Zec-C will calculate, an electrical circuit would be made and the full current through the plastic will cause it to explode. The surface charge will detonate in sympathy. The chlorine containers will be blasted into the black mass and the temperature of the explosion will ensure that they disintegrate due to the enormous pressures generated inside. From the starship, I think we can launch the missiles automatically as we'll be some distance from the target.

'So far so good,' said AJ, 'but we have no guidance system, only point and shoot. Zec-C, what would be the margin of error if we fired an unguided missile like this from the starship? How near the target would we have to be?'

'We cannot take the starship lower than 400 kilometres above sea level and for a satisfactory angle of firing we would have to be 450 kilometres from the target. This modified missile with no guidance would enter the target sea area somewhere in a grid 5 kilometres square.'

There were groans from the astronauts, and then Olivia asked.

'Zec-C, if we wanted to hit the target with an accuracy of a couple of hundred metres square, how close would we have to be?'

'Two kilometres above sea level and 2 kilometres from target.'

'Then we'll have to fire the chlorine missiles from the lander, from ROL-2,' Olivia persisted, 'and I'm prepared to do it!'

'Surely we can let Zec-2 pilot the lander automatically and fire the missiles when it's in position?' Alison said with concern, 'Then there's no human risk!'

'We'll be very near the target, very near the black,' countered AJ, 'can we risk a computer command to start the process?'

'I don't think we dare!' Pete cautioned. 'The computer command has to travel wirelessly outside the lander to release the missile and trigger the ignition of the rocket propellant. If that signal is blocked or interfered with...'

'It would jeopardise the whole operation!' AJ concluded.

'So apart from getting into position, everything to do with the missile attack has to be completely mechanical?' Steve summarised. 'Can we release the missiles manually?'

'Yes, there is a lever switch for each missile under the control console in the command dome of each lander,' advised Pete, 'and the mechanical release also pulls a pin for the firing of the rocket propellant.'

'So, someone has to be in the lander command dome to do that!' AJ said with finality.

'I cannot calculate a risk percentage for this operation as there are too many unknown variables. I can only reiterate the accuracy of manual firing from that position.'

This was Zec-C's reply to AJ's request for a risk assessment of using the lander. They had discussed the strategy at length. Alison and Steve strongly felt that they should pilot the lander but Olivia countered by saying that for such a high risk mission they should not risk two astronauts, nor should they split a team.

'I want to volunteer for this mission,' Olivia said firmly, 'and do it solo. I'm back to full fitness. Correct Martha?'

Martha nodded her approval to AJ who proposed that this was the best strategy. They voted four to two in favour of Olivia piloting the lander on her own.

Then came their biggest dilemma and it was Steve who proposed the deadliest of actions.

'We may have only one chance to do real damage to those cylinders. Let us assume that the chlorine missiles break the black barrier. Then we must hit them with two nuclear warheads to inflict the maximum damage to the enemy!'

Silence.

Silence around the command dome of LifeSeeker-1 as the astronauts considered the crime of a nuclear strike on another planet and against a menace that had so far proved totally superior and had anticipated all their actions.

'We can't do that!' Martha cried anxiously. 'We've taken over a century to eliminate the nuclear threat from Earth. How can we possibly justify this action on another planet?'

‘I think Steve is right,’ countered Olivia, ‘we may have only one opportunity to stop this alien menace.’

‘But the risks are so high! The nuclear missiles have to be computer guided! What if the barrier isn’t breached sufficiently?’ Alison voiced her grave concerns. ‘We could be facing our own nuclear missiles fired back at us!’

The discussion continued, arguments for and against, but eventually it was up to AJ to bring the heated debate to a conclusion.

‘We have to be clear about what we are going to do,’ said AJ gravely. ‘We are going to launch the chlorine missiles from the lander but before that time we will have to launch the attack missiles, maybe nuclear, so that they will arrive at the presumably destroyed black barrier seconds later and then on to their target of the cylinders. We may have time to abort the attack missiles before they are near enough to be interfered with but.....

.... there is no margin for error!

And once we commit......

.... well if we fail, who knows what will happen. However, we cannot do nothing and I consider the plan is the best we have in the circumstances. So, fellow astronauts, I ask you to vote firstly on the basic plan to attack and secondly on whether it should be a nuclear strike.’

The vote was six to zero for the plan to attack the cylinders and three to three regarding the nuclear strike.

AJ paused. He now had to make the final decision and he looked grimly at each of the astronauts in turn.

‘Nuclear it is!’

The die was cast!

Chapter 63
Pete's Box of Tricks

The decision was made and they all realised the enormousness of the task ahead.

AJ and Steve were allocated the job of fixing the chlorine containers onto the front of the missiles. AJ had insisted, and all had agreed, that they produce three chlorine missiles and test fire one in the middle of the ocean. Pete had informed them that this would allow the mechanical timer to be calibrated so that any last-minute adjustments to the operational missiles could be made.

Olivia and Alison were charged with removing each missile's guidance system and all on-board computers, including the automatic system for releasing and igniting the propellant.

All this work was to be carried out in the starship's mechanical bay and Zec-C was commanded to select the 'D' missiles from armoury and bring them to the maintenance bay in their special transport carriages.

Martha and Pete would produce the mechanical timers and pack the missile with the plastic explosive and the battery. However, the timer would not be inserted into the missile until it was slung in place below the lander and the connections would be the last job for Pete before the casing cover was put back in place. This would be the most critical and vulnerable part of the operation because they would have a live missile sitting inside the starship's lander bay.

No-one dared to contemplate the horrific consequences if that missile accidently fired before leaving LifeSeeker-1!

AJ looked in on Pete in his workshop for a progress report. His 'den' was an engineer's dream with every tool, material and state of the art fabrication technique at his disposal. The starship carried a huge inventory of spares, but when you are light years from civilisation, a boffin must have the capability to produce just about anything that might be needed.

'We've fitted the first missile with the chlorine containers and cleared out all the computer stuff.' AJ informed Pete, 'How is progress on the mechanical timer?'

‘Come and see, I’ve made the first one.’ Pete gestured AJ to a bench where Martha was putting finishing touches to what looked like a clear plastic box with two wires protruding from it.

‘I’ve used 5 millimetre thick Perspex sheet to fabricate the structure using low molecular weight poly- methyl -methacrylate in solvent as the adhesive.’

Oh, no! Thought AJ, not another lecture!

‘The key material for the timer is mercury, the only liquid metal and a perfect conductor of electricity. Zec-C has done some initial calculations on the minimum weight of mercury and the diameter of the orifice which controls the flow of the liquid.’ Pete then went on to describe the timing device.

‘Inside the box we have, for want of simplification, a horizontal egg timer constructed from two closed tubes of Perspex separated by a metal plate with a small orifice in the centre which will direct the mercury flow to the end of the receiving tube. The left hand side is larger in diameter and will be filled to about one third its depth with mercury. We’ve already put the required weight in this part. The right hand tube is narrower in diameter and has one electrical contact at the far end and one 5 centimetres towards the middle.

‘Now, look what happens when we stand the whole box on end. Martha will demonstrate.’

AJ watched as the mercury in the upper tube formed a reservoir above the orifice and started to flow down the narrow tube into the lower compartment. It covered the first electric contact almost immediately, but took about 1 minute to fill and touch the second contact causing a light connected to the protruding leads to come on.

‘Now I know what you’re thinking. We can hardly rely on the box being turned upside down. But we don’t have to, this device will sit horizontally and safely until the missile’s rockets fire and the g-force will push the mercury against the orifice, through the tube and will fill the second compartment housing the electrical ‘switch’.’

Meanwhile Martha had taken the device apart and replaced the mercury back into the left hand compartment and closed the box. She gestured to AJ and he tipped it vertically and watched the mercury flow until the light went on.

‘The missile is likely to rotate,’ Pete continued, ‘and this will work at any orientation.’

‘What are the white plastic caps in the cylinder ends?’ AJ queried.

‘They are micro-porous plugs, when the mercury moves from one compartment to the other, air must be allowed to enter or leave the chambers – but not mercury, of course.’ Pete beamed.

‘What about the acceleration of the lander?’ AJ persisted, ‘I understand from Zec-C that we need to launch the missile at 200 kilometres per hour so that it has sufficient forward velocity for initial stability!’

‘Correct, but Zec-C is going to programme a very slow acceleration of the lander and will fly in a heads down position until launch.’

‘OK, sounds good, what else have we to consider?’

‘The plastic detonator must be securely strapped next to the surface warhead and the battery must be very securely fixed as far as possible to the rear of the missile’s compartment. The timer will go in between, again firmly located.’

‘What’s the accuracy of the timer, Pete?’

‘One minute plus or minus 2 seconds.’

‘OK, let’s do it! Let’s test this missile whilst it’s still daylight,’ AJ commanded.

There were only two people in the huge bay housing the lander ROL-2. Pete was under the lander with his head almost inside the open casing of the chlorine missile whilst Olivia sat in the right hand control seat.

Earlier, Zec-C had pressurised the lander bay and had used the automatic transport system to transfer the modified missile from the maintenance section. Here it was raised to the underside of the lander where two electro-magnetic clamps held it securely. Whilst the missile support carriage was still in place, Olivia tested the manual switch which was located under the control panel by her right hand whilst her left hand moved forward onto the control panel to confirm her identity. The pushing of the lever from the upper position marked ‘clamp’ to the lower position marked ‘release’ would switch off the current to the electro – magnets and both clamps on the missile would simultaneously spring apart.

Olivia pushed the lever back up to the ‘clamp’ position and heard and saw Pete give the thumbs up on the dome display. Zec-2 also confirmed the satisfactory manual operation of the switch.

She could now see Pete carrying the timer box and carefully placing it in the missile casing.

'How can we be certain that the mercury isn't going to move before the missile drops and fires away?' Olivia asked Zec-2 again – she felt very vulnerable at the moment.

'At this altitude we have ten per cent planetary gravity, more than enough to hold the mercury in the bottom of its current compartment. At this low gravity, I will be able to raise ROL-2 gently up to clear LifeSeeker-1. Then I will put ROL-2 into a 15 degree heads down position and the mercury will move to the end of the compartment – the safe end. We will descend and accelerate so gently that the mercury will remain in its safe position. We will arrive at the release coordinates at the desired forward velocity for stable release and we will be at the correct angle to 'fire' the missile. Then the mercury will flow to the second compartment.'

Sounds good in theory, she thought, but I'm the one sitting on top of a live bomb! Then she heard Pete say.

'All connections made, missile now live, closing and securing outer casing.' and he gave Olivia a thumbs up as he exited the lander bay.

Zec-C now retracted the missile carriage system and started the powerful cryo pumps which would reduce the pressure in the lander bay to that of the atmosphere outside the starship. Then the two bay doors opened and they were ready to go.

Olivia could see AJ and the rest of the astronauts on her dome mimic display as he gave the order,

'Command start test flight!' and all the astronauts moved their left hand forwards to confirm.

Zec-2 lifted the lander gently upwards and cleared the starship. Olivia loved this moment and the view forward through the dome of the deep blue sea 400 kilometres below was stunning. The ocean was so calm that it perfectly reflected the cloud collar as far as the eye could see in both directions. So much beauty yet what a desperate situation, Olivia mused. Then the lander turned and the nose slowly dropped. They crawled away from the starship as they started their slow descent and acceleration. It would take 2 hours to reach the designated missile release coordinates.

Zec-2 was counting off the time at regular intervals and the dome mimic showed all the relevant speeds and distances to the release point which was 4 kilometres from the target coordinates in the sea.

'Five minutes to manual release.'

Olivia opened the cubicle to her right containing the switches for missile release. There were, in fact, two manual switches as the lander could carry two of these huge missiles underneath, one either side of the airlock lower door. She focussed on the right hand switch, the one she had tested earlier.

'Two minutes to manual release.'

The starship was stationed above and behind the lander and AJ and the astronauts could see the tiny space vehicle through the dome with its image enlarged on their mimic display.

'Good luck Olivia,' encouraged AJ.

'One minute to manual release.'

Olivia put her right hand on the lever and her left hand on the control panel and waited for Zec-2's countdown.

'Ten seconds, nine, eight........'

She found herself gripping the lever so hard her knuckles were white.

'........ three, two, one, Command release!'

She pushed the lever down and for a moment she wondered if anything had happened. Then Zec-2 confirmed 'missile released' and a second later 'missile fired'. Olivia looked through the dome and saw the rocket streak away and then felt the huge g-force as Zec-2 applied thrust and lift to the lander to facilitate its speedy getaway from the blast zone. Olivia watched the missile on the dome mimic display and tried to imagine the mercury flowing and filling the second compartment.

The missile hit the water and then exploded in a huge circular mass of boiling foam, thick smoke, flame and steam – all tinged with an eerie yellowish green glow.

There were cheers on LifeSeeker-1. Then Zec-C announced that the explosion had occurred 61 seconds after release and they all looked at Pete who glowed with success.

'And well done Olivia!' AJ quickly said. 'Someone had to sit on that bomb and rely on Pete's box of tricks.'

'High chlorine levels were measured over a 2 kilometre radius of the sea. At the epicentre levels were so high they were off the scale!'

'OK, we've proved our mechanical chlorine bomb works but we've got two more to finish. We'll plan our assault for midday tomorrow, that's just over 10 hours from now. Olivia, make sure you get a good night's sleep!'

Chapter 64
Olivia Faces the Black

It was 2 hours before noon and LifeSeeker-1 was positioned 400 kilometres from the icecap and 200 kilometres above sea level. The astronauts were gazing out at an idyllic scene of deep blue sea, brilliant white ice and azure sky – all bathed in the golden sunshine of the star, Seren.

It was hard to imagine that such a chilling menace lurked below.

Two nuclear missiles were already programmed with their targets – each had the coordinates of the third cylinder from the sea bed – at a distance of 20 cylinders apart from one another.

Timing was crucial. The lander would take 2 hours to get to the release point for the chlorine missiles and 1 minute to blast a gap in the black. The nuclear missiles would take 10 minutes from the starship to the point on the sea surface directly in line with the target discs 100 kilometres ahead and below the ice.

The nuclear warheads were programmed to pass through the Black 10 seconds after the explosion of the chlorine missiles.

They could be aborted safely if something went wrong early in the mission but if the chlorine missiles failed to explode........

.... it would probably be too late!

Meanwhile Olivia was sitting alone in the right hand command seat of the lander as the two bay doors above her slowly opened.

This was it. She had two primed chlorine missiles slung under ROL-2 but one attempt, realistically, to breach the black's defences.

AJ and the other astronauts appeared on her dome display. Everyone was tense. Everyone was trying to give smiles of encouragement.

AJ broke the silence,

'Good luck Olivia, we are, literally, right behind you but if anything goes wrong and I consider your safety is threatened, I will not hesitate to instruct Zec-2 to abort the mission. Understood!'

Olivia nodded and AJ gave the command to start the riskiest undertaking that he had ever been involved in.

ROL-2 then lifted slowly out of the starship's lander bay, inclined its nose downwards and started its excruciatingly slow journey to the release point.

Olivia stared out of the dome as the icecap slowly grew larger and larger in her field of view. The sea looked calm and peaceful. There were so many beautiful things about Cloud Planet, she pondered, that it was hard to believe that soon they would be sending nuclear missiles under the white ice to destroy an unimaginable enemy.

Olivia was daydreaming as the white icecap filled her horizon. They were now 50 kilometres from the release point, which was less than half an hour away. Suddenly, she was alerted by AJ's concerned voice.

'Olivia! I don't know if you are aware but the black mass is already forming in the sea and right on the intended missile path.'

'But we're nowhere near the target!' replied Olivia, 'And we haven't fired anything yet.'

Now Zec-2 had put a view on the dome screen of the lander.

'I see it and it seems to be growing in size. Good heavens! It's circular in shape; why?'

'It's about a kilometre in diameter and still growing and maintaining a perfectly round shape,' AJ said, now disturbed by this change in the Black's behaviour.

'We're moving the starship closer so that we can delay the launch of the nuclear missiles,' AJ continued but Olivia could hear Steve interrupting,

'Surely it doesn't matter how big it gets as long as we can punch a hole in the middle of it?'

'That may be true but who knows what this black menace is capable of.' AJ responded.

They were all going to find out in the not too distant future!

'The black mass is now 5 kilometres in diameter and still expanding. ROL-2 is 20 kilometres, 10 minutes from release point. New calculation for nuclear missiles is launch in 2 minutes.'

'The lander is going to be over the Black when it releases!' Alison cried with alarm.

'At this rate the lander will be above the menace sooner than that.' Steve pointed to the screen, 'It's increased visibly over the last few minutes!'

'Black mass now 7 kilometres diameter. One minute to launch of nuclear missiles, which is automatic unless majority decision to abort!'

'Continue mission?' AJ looked at the astronauts and they all nodded, including Olivia. No need to vote.

'The black mass is now 10 kilometres in diameter and has stopped expanding. ROL-2 is 10 kilometres and 5 minutes from release point. Launching nuclear missiles in 10 seconds.'

The astronauts in the command dome of LifeSeeker-1 watched the two nuclear missiles streak away from the starship. Ahead they could see the black circle in the sea but on the dome display it was huge and showed the tiny lander which approached the edge of it.

Then they gasped in astonishment as Zec-C informed them that the outer part of the black circular mass in the sea had started to rotate!

Olivia watched with horror as the Black grew on her horizon. It nearly filled the dome, particularly because the lander was 15 degrees head down. She'd heard that it was 10 kilometres in diameter and gasped aloud.

Then the lander moved over the edge of the Black and the sea disappeared. Now Olivia's total forward vision was black and her eyes were transfixed by the menace below.

Suddenly she was six again and standing in front of the black mouth of the cave and she excitedly walked into it. Then her mind focussed back to reality.

'8 kilometres from target point and 4 minutes to release. Nuclear missiles launched.'

Then came AJ's concerned voice,

'Olivia, the mass has started to rotate!'

But she didn't need telling, as from only 2 kilometres above the mass she could see the racing outer fringes of black. Her mind went back again and she was lost in the blackness of the cave. She screamed in her mind. Again she was rocked back to the present.

'6 kilometres from target point and 3 minutes to release. Warning! Rotation of black mass is increasing and causing turbulence, applying stabilising thrust.'

Olivia was starting to feel giddy. Through the dome her world was black and spinning. Get a grip, she urged herself, but despite this she found herself staring at the huge black mouth of the transport tunnel under the dwelling.

'I can't go in there! I can't go in there!' Her mind screamed and she remembered Seren's calming eyes and she relaxed. Olivia opened the panel near her right hand and stared at the two mechanical levers both set at 'clamp'. She placed her left hand on the control panel and gripped both levers with her right hand.

'4 kilometres from target point and 2 minutes to release. Get ready Olivia. Nuclear missiles one minute fifteen seconds behind. Warning! Rotation of black mass has increased suddenly, now causing suction! Applying reverse thrust to compensate!'

In the command dome of LifeSeeker-1, the astronauts watched, in amazement, as the 10 kilometre black mass in the sea ahead of them rotated faster and faster. Then they heard with consternation Zec-2's reports of increased turbulence and suction. The mass was exerting a downward force on the lander and unbelievably.....

.... the centre of the rotating mass dropped into the sea! And the outer edges around it started to spin faster!

'Oh my God, no! It's formed a huge black spinning vortex!' Alison screamed. 'We have to abort, we have to pull Olivia out!'

Zec-C's next words chilled them all.

'Vortex suction is exceeding ROL-2's full reverse thrust! The lander cannot pull out!'

'2 kilometres from target point and 1 minute to release. Emergency! Emergency! Suction from vortex exceeding full reverse thrust, starting to accelerate!'

Every hair on Olivia's body stood on end as she heard these damning words. She stared in horror into the open mouth of the spinning black vortex just ahead. Her mind reeled.

'I'm being drawn into a black hole! No..oh..oh!' Her worst nightmare was unfolding in the dome in front of her and then she was hanging over the end of the black boat in the absolute darkness of the underground tunnel!

'1 kilometre from target point and 30 seconds to release! Emergency! Emergency! Suction from vortex exceeding full reverse thrust, continuing to accelerate! Cannot arrest forward motion!

Olivia! Recalculation! Vortex suction will accelerate missiles to twice planned velocity. Release now!....

...... RELEASE NOW! RELEASE NOW! RELEASE NOW!!'

Then in her mind she felt the security of Scott's arms around her pulling her away from the end of the black boat and suddenly she heard Zec-2's repeated command.

She pressed down on both levers!

In the starship they heard and watched what they feared were the last minutes of the lander carrying Olivia. They had listened to Zec-2's recalculation and realised with hope that the chlorine missiles could be launched early.

They heard Zec-2's repeated command and saw the missiles drop from below the lander, ignite and then rush into the swirling vortex ahead.

They watched, horrified, as the lander was being drawn into the mouth of hell!

And then Zec-C calmly informed them,

'Chlorine missiles away, 1 minute to detonation! Warning! Nuclear missiles are being accelerated by vortex. One minute ten seconds to detonation point!'

'Oh my God! No! What if the nuclear missiles arrive too soon!' Alison screamed. 'What have we done! What have we done to Olivia!!'

AJ focussed on the dome and could see the two tiny chlorine missiles streaking away from the lander which was being drawn into the black vortex. The two nuclear missiles were behind and closing fast.

Unexpectedly fast!

The knuckles of Olivia's right hand were white because she was clenching the levers so hard that she could not release her fingers. Now she watched, helplessly, as the two missiles streaked away into the black vortex.

She heard the frightening news that the nuclear missiles might arrive too soon!

'Too bloody late for me!' she shouted and shook her fist defiantly at the swirling black menace. She could not drag her eyes away from the terrifying black mouth rotating outside the dome of the lander.

'In my experience it is not often that when something goes wrong, very wrong, it ultimately works in your favour. The rotation of the huge black mass in the sea and the formation of such a powerful vortex threw all the careful calculations out of the window. The attempt to defeat the Black on Cloud Planet looked doomed, but...

....the incredible suction force of the black vortex accelerates the chlorine missiles to two and a half times their planned velocity and they arrive in the mouth of the vortex after only 45 seconds. Also, the inertia caused by the huge acceleration force pushes the mercury from the left to the right hand compartment 15 seconds quicker than is planned.

Both chlorine missiles explode within 2 seconds of one another right in the mouth of the black vortex and 5 seconds before the nuclear missiles arrive.'

Olivia's world changed from swirling black to searing red followed by expanding yellowish green. She was so numb that she couldn't take in Zec-2's information that the chlorine missiles had exploded and that the nuclear missiles were 5 seconds from the explosion point in the vortex.

'I'm going to hell!!' she screamed at the top of her voice.

In LifeSeeker-1, the astronauts saw the yellow green explosion in the mouth of the vortex and knew from Zec-C that the nuclear missiles were seconds behind. They gripped their consoles in front of them and leaned forward urging the nuclear missiles through but desperate for news of the fate of the lander and Olivia.

'The two explosions in the mouth of the black vortex send enormous volumes of chlorine gas, now highly reactive chlorine ions at three and a half thousand degrees centigrade, into the depths of the vortex......

.......and into the capillary channels of trillions of high speed black beads, wiping out their molecular circuits in nanoseconds and obliterating their wireless commands from the cylinders instantaneously.

'Almost immediately, the whole centre of the vortex collapses and the sea rushes up, spreading the chlorine ions outwards and into the circuits of the rotating beads over a diameter of 2 kilometres. The

vortex stalls with its centre wiped out and is now just a seething mass of water and inert, harmless beads.

'Then the two nuclear missiles streak into the sea at the centre of the stalled vortex and they separate onto their designated trajectories to the two targeted cylinders.'

In the lander, Olivia still gripped the two levers as she stared at the collapsing vortex and the seething mass of water and black.

'Suction ceased! Applying maximum forward thrust and climb. Hang on Olivia!'

The lander's velocity had already been more than doubled by the suction force, despite full reverse thrust. Now this extra velocity was boosted by full forward thrust applied by Zec-2 and the 45 degree climb put Olivia under such huge g-force that she was pinned to the back of her seat and nearly passed out.

Zec-2 now had to get the lander away from the nuclear danger zone which it was travelling towards at huge velocity. Zec-2 banked the lander over in as tight a turn as possible and Olivia was jerked to the side of her seat, her seat belts preventing injury. However, the contents of her stomach were not restrained and she parted with them more than once during that roller coaster ride!

By the time ROL-2 was again travelling away from the icepack, it was only 15 kilometres from the targeted cylinders but she knew nothing of this as she slumped into unconsciousness.

In the starship, the astronauts realised that the nuclear missiles had got through and they saw the lander drag itself up and away from the collapsed vortex.

It would be about 10 seconds before the nuclear missiles reached their target. Far quicker than planned because of the velocity boost from the vortex.

The starship had already started backing away from the explosion zone but it was not under threat. The lander, however, was at low altitude and now only 20 kilometres from the icecap. It could not out run the fallout of the nuclear explosions.

Accordingly Zec-2 slowed the lander to minimum velocity to maintain control of altitude and then turned the lander to face the onslaught head on. This presented the optimum aerodynamic profile to the threat.

Then Zec-2 applied full red emergency. The dome blackened and maximum force field was applied to the lander.

Billions of black 'beads' streamed out from the cylinders under the icecap as the two nuclear missiles streaked at their targets. But the extra velocity imparted by the vortex meant there was no time for the Black to organise a new barrier, let alone re-programme the incoming missiles' computers.

The two nuclear warheads struck their 1 kilometre diameter targets under the icecap and detonated.

Chapter 65
Black Rain

Zec-C had darkened the dome of LifeSeeker-1 and the outside scene covered nearly the whole of the mimic display. The astronauts viewed the tumbling, swirling black of the collapsed vortex, the blue sea in front of the icecap and the lander in its desperate banked climb to get away from the danger zone.

Then the display zoomed in on the icecap, which suddenly cracked and lifted in two places about 20 kilometres apart.

Initially it seemed to happen in slow motion and then the whole area of icecap in front of them shot upwards. The blue sky lit up in a blinding flash of light as grey clouds of ice and steam formed two plumes which joined and then turned black. The dense double mushroom shape expanded kilometres into the sky, where it seemed to boil in movement as it rushed upwards and outwards at terrifying speed.

The astronauts gasped and shouted in the command dome as the mega-tonne explosions filled the entire screen whilst Zec-C intoned the accompanying technical details,

'Plume altitude 5 kilometres and approximate diameter 10 kilometres and growing. Shock, heat and radiation waves now nearly 20 kilometres from detonation epicentre. Warning! Contact with ROL-2 lost!'

'Let's pray the force field around the lander holds up!' AJ said gravely.

Olivia regained consciousness and stared at the blackened dome of the lander but there were no views of the outside, because they were under full red emergency and maximum force field. Zec-2's voice reassuringly broke the silence.

'Confirm two nuclear detonations at designated targets. Hang on Olivia! Radiation, heat and shock waves coming!'

At last Olivia relaxed her grip but she had to pull her hand away because her fingers were so cramped on the levers. She braced herself and knew that she wouldn't feel the radiation wave, but she would hear the alarms if the force field of the lander was breached. Also she would feel the heat and her eyes flickered to the digital temperature gauge, willing it not to move.

'Radiation and heat waves absorbed by force field satisfactory, shock waves coming!'

'After an explosion it is the shock wave that causes the most lateral damage. The explosive energy accelerates air particles to supersonic speeds and they bounce and collide with one another in a destructive radial wave over many tens of kilometres from the epicentre.'

The shock wave smashed into the lander's force field pushing it backwards and downwards. Olivia was thrown forward violently, her seat restraints working overtime to prevent her colliding with the console. The lander shook and she felt the sudden loss of altitude in her stomach.

'Shock wave through, struggling to get ROL-2 back under control, altitude falling. Less than half of 1 kilometre.'

What more? Thought Olivia - but worse was to come!

In the starship, the astronauts watched the huge boiling black mushroom which obliterated their view of the icecap.

'Mushroom has stopped climbing at 20 kilometres, diameter about 40 kilometres and growing. Now descending and fast!'

Suddenly the huge mushroom started to fall out of the sky. In one enormous black mass it fell back towards the icecap and over a wide expanse of the sea, expanding as it lost altitude.

'My God! It looks like thick torrential black rain cascading over the visible horizon!' Steve shouted horrified.

'And all over the lander and Olivia!' cried Alison with alarm and then Zec-C made matters even worse!

'Tsunami wave radiating from icecap, frontal width 50 kilometres, height approximately 50 metres, velocity approximately 200 hundred kilometres per hour.'

'And we can't warn Olivia!'

'Olivia!' Urged Zec-2, *'Fallout from detonations descending as one black mass! Maintaining full force field, altitude 30 metres!'*

Olivia could not see anything nor could she hear any outside noise. If she could the sound would have been deafening as a wall of black beads thundered down on the lander's force field and onto the sea all around. The sheer weight of black pushed the lander downwards,

'Olivia! Cannot hold altitude, preparing to ditch in the sea!'

'The lander is designed for landing and takeoff from water and most fluids. Under controlled conditions this is done by lowering four huge floats and at the same time moving the caterpillar tracks aside. But this was far from normal circumstances as the black mass pushes the lander down to the surface of the sea. Just in time, four reinforced nylon bags inflate under the lander, cushioning the impact and supplying sufficient buoyancy to maintain the hull above water level.'

Olivia was jolted down into her seat as the lander crashed into the sea and was partially submerged by the weight of the black mass raining down on its surface. But the buoyancy of the four massive air bags combined with that of the hull itself enabled the lander to slowly rise and float.

And the black torrent continued to pound down!

It seemed an age in the eerie quiet of the command zone before Zec-2 announced,

'Red emergency lifted, force field reduced to minimum setting.'

Olivia peered forward but everything was still black.

'So why haven't you cleared the dome? Zec-2!'

'I have. But we are buried in a 10 metre layer of black fallout!'

After all that Olivia had been through, after having faced her darkest nightmares and survived! Now this! But she amazed herself. She felt calm; she stared at the opaque dome and laughed,

'Well, Zec-2! We've been to hell and back and now we're buried in black. Surely it couldn't get worse!'

'Olivia! There's a tsunami wave coming and it's big!' Estimated time of arrival 5 minutes!'

The astronauts stared out of the dome of LifeSeeker-1 at the devastation below. They were 400 kilometres from the icecap and at an altitude of 200 kilometres. The black mushroom had collapsed with alarming rapidity under its own weight but it had spread over such an unbelievable area.

'Jeez!' whistled Steve, 'How big is that black area?!'

'Initial measurements show that black is covering a circular area of icecap and sea of 70 kilometres diameter. It is 10 metres deep across most of that area.'

'But where's the lander! Where's Olivia!' cried Alison, 'And, oh my God! You can see the huge wave, a black tsunami!'

'Estimated lander position 20 kilometres from icecap but no contact. Last measurements showed lander losing altitude rapidly. Assume ditched in sea and under black. Tsunami 10 kilometres from lander estimated position. Tsunami height and speed reducing from dampening effect of black mass. Now travelling at 100 kilometres per hour and 10 metres high.'

'The Black might be their saviour!' AJ shouted in disbelief, 'It's slowing the tsunami. Zec-C! Damage report on under ice explosions. Then move the starship as close to Olivia's position as possible!'

'Initial pictures show cylinders completely wiped out across a front of over 1000 kilometres and severe damage to structures 50 kilometres either side. Rough estimate is over 1000 destroyed and similar number severely damaged.'

'My God!' sighed AJ, 'There's still 48,000 left!'

'And that's just under this icecap!' added Steve, 'But we've given them something to think about!'

'Let's hope it's enough, but what about Olivia and the tsunami!' Alison was distraught.

'The huge mass of black on the ocean is indeed having its effect on the tsunami. It is similar to the dampening effect of an oil slick on the waves of the sea. Only here on Cloud Planet it is a 10 metre thick mass of beads.

By the time the tsunami reaches the lander its speed is reduced to 50 kilometres per hour and its height is 5 metres. Of greater significance is the fact that its profile is changed. The weight of black has smoothed the wave such that its leading edge angles back at 30 degrees with a much shallower trailing boundary.'

'Hang on Olivia! Here comes the tsunami but it's a much smaller wave. We should ride it satisfactorily.'

Zec-2 had been able to keep the lander's nose facing the wave by applying small amounts of thrust on the black layer itself.

Suddenly the lander tilted upwards and backwards and Olivia was again clinging to her seat harness. Then it fell forwards with a bump as it crashed down onto the trailing wave. Zec-2 had kept the lander aligned perpendicularly to the wave during its passage and now let the viscous drag of the Black slow its backwards velocity.

'Tsunami wave through OK, Black depth eight metres and falling slowly.'

'The Black's sinking! It's sinking!' shouted Olivia in delight.

Ten minutes later, Olivia saw a chink of light at the very top of the dome......

.... and shortly after, rays of sunlight poured into the lander......

.... Olivia smiled with relief and then jumped out of her skin as AJ's voice boomed in the command dome and all the astronauts' smiling faces appeared on the dome display in front of her.

Chapter 66
Surely no more Surprises

Olivia watched as the Black slowly dropped down the dome and, as it did, so the lander rose in the water as the huge weight of beads fell off its hull. Now it was half way down the dome surface and Olivia gasped as she saw that all of her forward horizon was black, topped eventually by the blue sky.

'How big is this black slick, Zec-2?'

'Approximately 70 kilometres in diameter, half on half off the icecap. We are about 20 kilometres from the icecap.'

'And how much damage did we do to the cylinders?'

'About 2000 either destroyed or severely damaged, this slick must be the fallout from them. They must have been full of the bead like objects.'

'My God! There's still 48,000 left!'

'And a similar number under the other icecap!'

This sobering comment put Olivia into deep troubled thought until AJ's voice again echoed in the command dome.

'Olivia, we are going to take the starship up. We're consuming a huge amount of fuel at this low altitude. Zec-C confirms that all systems on your lander are OK and you should be able to lift off once the black slick completely sinks. We need to discuss our next actions. We've damaged the menace but what do we do next?'

LifeSeeker-1 had risen to an altitude of 500 kilometres and the astronauts could clearly see the extent of the huge black slick. It appeared to rest over the edge of the ice – its silhouette contrasted sharply with the brilliant white of the ice. The tsunami had run its course and the slick and sea were calm and flat. They could not see the lander except on the dome display. Zec-C had reported that the slick was now 2-3 metres in depth and continued to sink. Zec-C was about to give a time estimate for its complete disappearance when the urgency in his voice changed.

'New black mass forming around the icecap and covering a sector 500 kilometres wide directly in front of LifeSeeker-1. Depth of mass is approximately 1 kilometre.'

The astronauts could see the mass forming on the display screen. It seemed to be pushing the black slick away from the icepack.

‘Uh, oh! What’s happening now?’ Steve shouted. ‘Should we get ready to fire more missiles?’

‘We can’t risk it against this organised enemy,’ AJ countered. ‘They might be turned back on us again.’

‘Now what? Alison pointed at the icecap. ‘The new mass seems to have disappeared!’

Zec-C zoomed in on a section of it.

‘It’s still there but it’s emitting water vapour over the whole of its surface building up a dense layer which is already 10 metres high and continuing to grow.’

‘It’s like a wall of cloud!’ said Steve, ‘And look, it’s darkening as it’s rising. Why’s that Zec-C?’

‘The Black is rising in its own cloud and building the height as it gets higher. Cloud height 100 metres.’

‘But how?’ queried Alison.

‘We know that the bead-like structures can accelerate water through themselves at huge velocities. What they are doing now is atomising the water as it leaves the capillary, which is forming mist and cloud. We also know that they can travel in cloud. They are building up their own transport medium. Cloud height now 500 metres and widening over the icecap. Two kilometres in width across a sector arc of 600 kilometres.’

‘Command Zec-C! Have all non-nuclear missiles readied for firing. We don’t know what’s happening but we must be ready to defend ourselves.

‘Command Zec-2! Get lander into the air immediately and back away from the icecap,’ AJ ordered.

The astronauts watched as the collar of grey black cloud grew with astonishing speed. It was so big they could see it through the dome of the starship. It was as if a huge barrier was being erected between their position and the icecap.

Zec-C’s next announcement shocked them to the core!

‘The cylinders are moving upwards under the ice! They are rising around the whole perimeter of the icecap! They have reached a position just below the ice and started to push it up!’

The astronauts above and Olivia below watched the same scene in disbelief as the lander lifted from the sea and shook off the remnants of the black slick.

The icecap was cracking!

Huge splits and crevasses were radiating from a circular line around the icecap. Zec-C had zoomed in on a section to the right of the cloud barrier as they could not see through it directly in front of their position.

Grey cylinders pushed up and rose above the ice. Their connecting tubes seemed to support hundreds of them in mid air. Then the next layer of cylinders broke through the ice.

'My God! The whole lattice is rising through the ice and into the air!' gasped AJ, 'And the black cloud collar is building with them!'

'Is the cloud collar protecting them? We certainly can't see the damaged section,' said Steve, more in hope than conviction. 'We couldn't attack them anyway from this angle!'

'Look! Black is spewing out from those upper cylinders and entering the cloud!' Steve continued, 'Building the barrier higher and higher!'

Now half of the lattice of objects had risen above the ice to a height of seven and a half kilometres. The astronauts could see the ring of cylinders right around the whole icecap. It was an unbelievable and terrifying sight. And still they continued to rise and spew black streams into the cloud collar they had created.

Then the interconnecting tubes between the cylinders at the top of the lattice started to fall away, crashing down to the ice, spewing black randomly.

Next thousands and thousands of the top cylinders started to rotate! The sunlight glinted on their multi-faceted surfaces.

Further tubes fell away and the second and third layers started rotating.

'My God! My God! What's about to happen?!' Alison shook with fear and trepidation.

'Look!.... some of the cylinders near the damaged section. They're wobbling!' Steve blurted. 'Several of them are cracking!'

The damaged ones suddenly exploded in a deluge of black, which shot in all directions and the exploding mass tumbled back down onto the ice. Two other wobbling cylinders literally fell out of the sky and crashed through the ice below shooting up geysers of rain.

'But one cylinder, which was hidden from view behind the cloud, was hardly clear of the ice when it toppled sideways on its connecting tube. It shattered the ice on impact, but remained on the

surface. The object cracked open, like two halves of an egg, and Black shot into the air around it.

But what happens next leave the astronauts in the starship and Olivia in the lander absolutely speechless. It even causes Zec-C to repeat himself and question his own observation.'

Chapter 67
The Dicepteron Mothership

'Centre of icecap rising! Centre of icecap rising?' Zec-C queried.

They stared at the zoomed image of the icecap. Huge crevices started radiating away from the centre which bulged upwards. Then a grey white structure started to push through the ice.

It was rotating, light reflecting from facets in the upper surface. The astronauts were speechless. They could not register the scale of what was happening. But Zec-C continued. His usual analytical composure now recovered.

'From the radius of the object pushing through the icecap, I conclude that we have a rotating disc whose diameter is approximately 140 kilometres!'

Silence in the starship.

Silence in the lander.

There was stunned utter silence as they watched this goliath of structures which rose slowly from the very centre of the icepack. It was surrounded by its lattice of about 48,000 rotating grey black cylinders!

AJ broke the silence. 'How can something so big come up through the icecap?'

'I conclude that the rotation is generating heat and melting the ice – a process not too different to regelation. If you recall, the thinner ice at the centre was also 140 kilometres diameter and this huge disc is probably the reason. Also there are 2 kilometre diameter darker shapes in the vertical surface of this structure – I estimate about 50 around the circumference – and they are hexagonal in shape.'

'This must be the mothership!' Steve guessed. 'I think the surrounding cylinders and the cloud barrier have been protecting it.'

'It's nearly out of the ice!' Alison shrieked. 'What's it going to do!'

By way of answer, the grey white behemoth accelerated in both rotation and vertical velocity until it was completely clear of the ice. It had left a perfectly circular crater at the centre of the icecap.

'The disc is approximately 20 kilometres thick and its upper and lower surfaces are slightly concave. I cannot be more specific because the surrounding cylinders and clouds are masking my instruments.'

Then it rose to a point half way up the lattice of surrounding cylinders. It was truly a magnificent and utterly threatening spectacle.

No one moved, they hardly breathed as the 140 kilometre disc, glistening with reflected light, and its 48,000 surrounding darker objects rotated faster and faster until they were one continuous blur.

The whole mass then rose into the sky and dominated the vista over the decimated icecap. For the first time the astronauts could see the breach in the cylinders where the nuclear warheads had wreaked their havoc. Many were still wobbling and they fell back to the icecap in enormous explosions of black.

It seemed such a small breach in the massive structure.

Then the surrounding cylinders seemed to swirl around the massive mother-disc and, in the blink of an eye, disappeared into the perimeter of the giant. Suddenly the whole assembly accelerated upwards........

.... and vanished!

'Zec-C! Where have they gone?' said a perplexed AJ.

All the astronauts in the starship leaned forward, totally dumbstruck, and stared at the space above the icecap.

In the lander, Olivia craned her neck upwards at the emptiness where, fractions of a second earlier, the sky had been filled with the enormousness of the rotating masses.

She and the astronauts above her could only sit and listen to Zec-C and his mind blowing commentary.

'I have absolutely zero signal now. But from the point where they started to accelerate to the last measured signal just nanoseconds later.....

...... I estimate that they left the vicinity of Cloud Planet ....

...... faster than the speed of light!!'

BOOK EIGHT
SAVE THE PLANET

Chapter 68
The Reunion

'Impossible!' was the common cry of all the astronauts.

'You can't travel at the speed of light, let alone faster!' cried a disbelieving Steve. 'Why, we've only just learned to travel at half-light speed!'

'You are correct in our galaxy and obeying our laws of physics. However, from the moment the spinning objects accelerated I tracked their signal over a distance of 1 kilometre. Then the signal disappeared. To travel that distance took less than one, three hundred thousandth's of a second, the limit of my measurement capability.'

'But maybe it's still out there!' shouted Alison, the alarm in her voice was very obvious, 'But we just can't see it!'

That statement made the astronauts stare out of the command dome again but all they could see was the decimated icecap, the cloud barrier now collapsing and a 140 kilometre wide crater at its centre.

'It may be possible that the objects have moved a distance of 1 kilometre, stopped and become undetectable. However, there is insufficient evidence to support or detract from that observation. My calculation of the minimum speed achieved before they disappeared is correct!'

'Thank you, Zec-C,' AJ summarised, 'we don't doubt your measurements or conclusions, but we've been dealing with an intelligence that we can't begin to understand or comprehend. Something which we have to assume came to Cloud Planet from another galaxy but has now moved away. Where it has gone, we cannot possibly know!'

'There is more, Commander, but my measurements are at such an error level that I would need a second or third set of data to corroborate my findings before presenting the results to you.'

'Come on Zec-C,' Steve encouraged, 'you're not normally so reticent. You can hardly shock us anymore!'

'My single measurement suggests that the rotational velocity of the mother-disc increased during that infinitesimally small time interval to........... in excess of 1 million revolutions per minute........... subject to an error of plus or minus 10 per cent.'

No-one moved. Faces were etched in shock, bewilderment and total disbelief.

'Oh! You've really lost your marbles this time, Zec-C!' Steve scoffed, 'faster than light and now a million rpm! That thing's 140 kilometres wide by 20 k's deep! Do me a favour!'

'From what I've seen so far,' added Pete analytically, 'nothing would surprise me anymore! God knows what's inside that mother-disc?'

'I agree with Pete and AJ,' said Olivia from the lander, 'we're up against something we can't possibly understand.'

Further discussion was terminated by Zec-C's urgent intervention.

'Attention! Sorry to interrupt, Commander, but contact with Zec-1 re-established, contact with ROL-1 on Cloud Planet re-established!'

There were looks of surprise and delight on the astronauts' faces as Zec-C continued,

'Zec-1 reports that all the black masses outside the dwellings suddenly collapsed to the ground. I have checked the timing with Zec-1 and that occurred the instant the mother-disc disappeared from view.'

'They must have lost their wireless control! So they might have really gone?' Olivia cried in hope. 'Can we get in touch with Scott? Have we contacted him?'

'It is night time at both ROL-1 and the dwelling at the equator where Scott is presumed to be. He usually turns on his palmtop 2 hours before the dwelling lights up. We can contact him in one and a half hours' time. But we need to move LifeSeeker-1 away from this icecap with its high radiation and back to its original geostationary position.'

'Command Zec-C! Move starship as recommended.' Said AJ and all the astronauts confirmed the decision in the usual way.

'But what about the other icecap?' Steve brought them back to reality. 'We can't assume that the discs have gone from there as well!'

'Olivia, can you take the lander and have a look?' AJ instructed, 'But don't go too close, just enough for Zec-2 to scan the area.'

'We're on the case, but I'd like your permission to take the lander down to Scott's position as soon as possible.'

'Let's see what's at the other icecap before making that decision.'

‘Of course.’

In the pitch black of the sleeping chamber under the huge pyramid, Scott’s wrist alarm pinged and he was instantly awake. He turned his palmtop on, dreading the news from Zec-1. The previous morning, Zec-1 had informed him that dozens more black masses had appeared outside the dwellings in the lines adjacent to his position. They had to stop the farming groups from leaving their dwellings. However, if this continued, the threat to their food supply would become critical.

Scott could not believe his eyes as the first words he saw on the screen were,

‘Olivia safe and well’

He whooped with delight and then saw,

‘Contact with LifeSeeker-1 re-established’

‘Zec-1, what has happened?’

‘Black masses outside dwellings have collapsed to the ground, no longer a barrier and, it seems, no further threat to us.’

‘But how? What’s happened to the Black?’

‘AJ conference call coming through in 10 minutes to brief you before we lose contact due to light sheaths’

Olivia instructed Zec-2 to take the lander to an altitude of 500 kilometres and then proceeded at maximum speed towards the other icecap. Travelling at 2000 kilometres per hour they passed over the dark cloud collar after 5 hours during the night. They then carried on out to sea to a position midway between Cloud collar and the other icecap just as dawn was breaking.

Zec-2 zoomed in on the icecap and put the picture on the dome screen in front of Olivia.

‘Look!’ she said to no one in particular, ‘The ice has cracked open around the perimeter, just like the other icecap.’

Zec-2 zoomed in further,

‘There is an approximately 140 kilometre diameter crater at the centre of the icecap and I can detect no objects underneath.’

‘We can see your pictures, Olivia!’ said AJ from the starship, ‘It looks as if the same exodus has occurred at both icecaps!’

‘Can we really believe that they’ve gone?’ Olivia asked hopefully, ‘And left us for good?’

‘We can’t be sure of anything,’ replied AJ, ‘but we’ve contacted Scott and briefed him with the barest of details and told him that you will land at his dwelling tonight.’

‘OK, good, we’ll be able to brief each other in person and then set up a conference call for the following night to discuss plans.’ Olivia concluded.

Scott could hardly wait for the Serenities to warm up and feed but knew that he would have to be patient. He caught Seren’s eye and gestured towards the huge triangular structure where Hotenka and his elders sat.

Seren’s eyes blazed,

<< you have good news <> i can tell from your positive feelings>>

Seren inclined her head and the Serenite leader looked up and beckoned them to join him.

<< come > we must tell hotenka >>

Scott found it difficult to explain that the black masses had collapsed and were no longer a threat to the blue farmers. Even with Seren’s help, the message was not getting through and Scott was not sure that she fully understood what had happened. Her eyes blazed,

<< how can you be sure that our blue workers will not die if they go out to farm >>

‘Trust me! I will show you. Come out with me in one of your farming groups!’

<< yes <> i do trust you <>and our leader will come too >>

One hour later, Scott, Seren and Hotenka walked out of the huge pyramid into the heat and humidity of the near midday sun. Scott marvelled, once again, at the incredible sight of the 500 hundred metre light shaft as it shot, shimmering, into the clouds. The whole area in front of the pyramid thronged with Serenites and blue workers who inclined their heads as their leader passed by.

The huge, wide black door was open and, at the threshold was gathered a farming group of 40 blue females, all holding their light shafts downwards to the ground. The drums beat their familiar rhythm. The rear of the group of blue females opened and Scott, Seren and Hotenka walked into the centre. Then it closed around them.

The drum beat grew louder as the third drummer started and the living dwelling marched towards the wide door. Outside it was raining, cold and misty with visibility at best 50-70 metres. But it was light with no obvious black in sight.

Scott watched in fascination as they marched under the doorway. The blue females turned their light shafts upwards under the protection of the wall and then they burst into flat sheaths of light and merged to form the protective cover for the group. They had advanced forward about 50 metres and Scott found it frustrating because he could not see out of the farming group.

After a further 30 metres or so they stopped. Scott looked down and the muddy red clay was now black. He moved forward and gestured to Seren for the front of the farming group to move apart.

A mountain of black stretched away to the limits of visibility.

'Why, it must rise to 20 metres or more!' gasped an astonished Scott who moved forward and his feet sank in the black mass. He bent and scooped up the Black in both hands and turned to Seren and her leader.

'Look, they are now a mass of harmless beads; they have lost their power, lost their controlling force!' Scott wasn't sure if this was understood but both Seren and Hotenka moved forward and gingerly prodded and probed the black mass.

The leader turned and his eyes blazed,

<< they are not moving <> the black menace is dead <> our killers are defeated <> let us return and celebrate <> now i will cease calling your name >>

Scott was elated. The Black had been defeated and Olivia was safe and well. He followed the leader back into the huge pyramid dwelling to warm, drink and eat. Suddenly all thoughts of Olivia were expunged from his mind and he looked around and saw Seren walking towards him. Her eyes blazed,

<< come <> come with me <> you have saved our people <> our world >>

Suddenly tears began to flow from Seren's eyes and she held out her arms to him. Her relief and joy was so obvious in that beautiful face, Scott thought, that it touched him very deeply. Then she led him by the hand to a dazzlingly beautiful group of 10 Serenite females who formed a circle around them. Arms reached out and coaxed Scott to the ground.

Olivia watched the dome screen as the lander descended through the dark cloud collar and Zec-2 called out the altitudes and speeds. She remembered being awed by the 300 metre dwelling with its four pyramid dwellings. Now below her, and clearly visible on the mimic display, was a 500 metre dwelling containing seven pyramids and one enormous pyramid. Their landing coordinates were shown as a cross in the middle of the massive open space in front of this singularly large structure.

Zec-2 counted down the final few metres. Then the lander's caterpillar treads crunched onto the hard clay floor and flexed with the weight of the craft. ROL-2 was down - its first visit to Cloud Planet of the star Seren.

Olivia was exhausted and tried to rest for the 2 hours or so before the dwelling would light up. But sleep wouldn't come because she was too excited. She was thrilled at being back on this unique planet with its astonishing people. Dying to see Scott again after all they had been through.

It grew lighter and the rain eased enabling Olivia to make out the outline of the towering pyramid which dwarfed the lander.

'First crystals glowing and about to ignite.'

She watched the dome screen and saw the crystals turn from red to yellow and then....

.... white light shot upwards and backwards towards the rising sun. She shuddered with excitement as it was such a thrill to witness a dwelling light up. But this monster was phenomenal.

'Why! The walls must be 200 metres long,' she gasped out loud. 'How many diamond crystals are there to light this lot?'

'Just over 3200.'

The walls lit up around Olivia and the mist and rain lightened. Then the light sheath was completed and the sun shone and cast its deep red shadows across the dwelling. Olivia was stunned by the scale of the massive structure and amazed by the array of pyramids in front of the lander. However, the pyramid in front of her was spectacular in size and colour, and reflected light from the myriad of crystals in its two facing walls.

She just stared.

To her left and on top of the structure carrying the external pools, a black dome started to rise from the red clay floor.

Olivia waited with bated breath.

It was as if she were seeing it for the first time – the thrill of the Blue People emerging from their underground chambers. Watching them warm, drink and go about their business in the dwelling.

Then the black door in the huge pyramid in front of the lander started to fall and a figure emerged into the sunlight. Olivia's heart thumped and she felt a lump in her throat.

Scott raised his arms towards the lander 50 metres in front of him and saw Olivia in the command dome raising hers. Both wore huge smiles and neither could hold back tears of emotion.

It seemed to take an age for the lander to cycle the command seats through the airlock, but finally they were lowered onto the red clay.

Olivia leapt out of her seat, ripped the mask from her mouth and jumped into Scott's open arms. They clung to each other speechless with emotion. They kissed tenderly and walked hand in hand across the red clay towards the open doorway.

'I hope you haven't forgotten your water!' Scott joked and Olivia playfully punched him in the back.

'Before you meet the Serenite leader, let me first show you Paradise!'

Olivia looked puzzled.

Chapter 69
Shared Experiences

Scott led Olivia around the huge pyramid and past the smaller ones, he turned to her,

'Olivia, you were so brave taking the lander out to attack the Black on your own. That vortex must have been terrifying for you.'

'Yes, it was bloody frightening and I thought we were going into it. We were on full thrust and still it was sucking the lander in!'

'Jeez! Thank God the chlorine worked.'

'It was touch and go. We had to design a completely mechanical attack missile and timer,' continued Olivia, 'and then all our calculations were thrown out of the window by the vacuum created by that black hole.'

'I saw the analysis of the beads. They're mind-blowing!' Scott added, 'What created them?' And what's inside that mother-ship?'

'We'll probably never know. Now, where are we going?'

'Here, this dark pyramid with no crystals, prepare to be gobsmacked.'

He had previously arranged for its door to be opened and then it closed behind them. They reached the centre where sunlight focussed on the raised dais.

'Wait here a sec.'

She shuddered in the dank and gloomy atmosphere, 'What is this place?'

'They call it the dark pyramid but you watch; it's something much more than that.'

Scott had selected the appropriate crystal, which he placed under the black wooden cover and, rather like a magician, he drew it back.

Olivia jumped as thin streaks of red light shot to the upper dark areas of the pyramid. She gasped as the whole internal structure lit up and shapes moved around her.

'Ooh, ooh, this is beautiful, this is magical! Look at all these people! On a huge beach? Where are we?'

'Look behind you, Olivia.'

She turned and gazed wide-eyed as she saw an estuary with black boats and triangular green plantations on the foothills.

‘I don’t understand!’ Olivia turned back to the beach. ‘These are blond Serenites, hundreds of them, and, ooh! - look at all those fabulous males.’

Now, they watched a young Serenite male kneeling on the beach with his arms raised. This was the same beautiful specimen with the blazing eyes and proud set of the jaw that he and Seren had watched previously. Scott again thought there was a familiarity about the face but could not place it.

‘Come up here with me,’ and he took Olivia up the ramp and around the ledge so they were looking up the valley. Olivia looked stunned.

‘What are those dwellings and pyramids on the bank of the river? They’re different! But it’s their light shafts that are different?’ Then she gazed up to the wooded hills and mountains and finally saw the topping of brilliant white cloud.

‘Is this, this planet? Surely not? Cloud Planet? How can it be?’

‘Yes, Olivia, this is what it was like in their distant past. But I don’t know how long ago. However, within this holographic amphitheatre is the whole history of the Blue People!’

‘Show me more!’ Olivia urged.

‘I can’t wait.’ Scott was only too delighted to share his discoveries.

‘You must see the mines where these recording crystals came from, but later, first, look at this with me.’

He had selected another crystal, ignited it and led Olivia up the ramp to the viewing point on the ledge.

‘It’s the same scene but later in time. Look out to the horizon, Olivia; I am going to try to capture it on the camera in my palmtop.’

She looked across the crowded red beach to the deep blue sea where it met the lighter blue of the sky. She was transfixed by the amazing three-dimensional tableau.

‘Watch the horizon – now look there!’

And, in the distance, she saw a black line right across her field of view from left to right. The line seemed to have suddenly appeared and then it descended, merged with the sea and disappeared.

‘What was that? It was right across the sky!’ Olivia pointed.

He responded. ‘I thought it might have been a meteor shower, but it looked too uniform, and, shortly after, this coast was hit by the most enormous tsunami. It wiped out everything for hundreds of kilometres inland.'

'And the Blue People?'

Scott's look and shake of his head was enough to answer that question.

'Zec-2! Have you been able to process that video clip?'

'I have zoomed in as much as possible and the resolution is not good but the line you saw is a staggered row of cylindrical shaped objects each approximately 1 kilometre in diameter. There are approximately 500 across the viewable horizon and they entered the sea at approximately 100 kilometres per hour.'

Olivia and Scott looked at the image on the small LCD screen.

'The cylinders!' Olivia shouted, 'They must be the same ones that ended up under the icecap – Scott! – there were 50,000 of them!'

'I heard that! And they were under both icecaps! Zec-C! Can you throw some light on this?'

'The diameter of Cloud Planet at the point of entry is approximately 48,000 kilometres, consistent with a staggered line of 50,000 cylinders right around this circumference. Also from their size and speed of entry, two enormous tsunami waves would have travelled in opposite directions, and in both hemispheres of Cloud Planet. Furthermore, if the 140 kilometre mother-discs entered the sea at the same velocity, they would have produced tsunami waves of unimaginable proportions.'

'So both coast lines were hit all the way around the planet! My God! The devastation was more horrific than I ever imagined!' Scott said.

'Olivia, let me show you two more crystals from after the tsunami, but they're not pretty.'

From the ledge, Scott indicated that the black area was along the coast in both directions but not at the estuary. Olivia, however, found it hard not to look at the hundreds of broken bodies scattered on the red beach. She shuddered uncontrollably and continued to look across the huge expanse of red clay. Something about its size tugged at her memory but then it was gone. Then Scott changed the crystal to show the same view but forward in time.

'Look how the edge of the sea has misted over the black area and how it builds in height as it creeps up the estuary.'

'We saw the Black do just that at the icecap,' Olivia explained. 'It built a cloud barrier to protect the cylinders as they rose from under the ice. My God! The Black built the cloud collar around this planet!'

'Yes!' replied Scott, 'It couldn't travel through the estuaries because of the chlorine - so it built a transport system of clouds!'

'Thank goodness you found the Black's Achilles heel!'

'Yes, but it was Seren who gave me the vital clue.'

'And she gave me the necklace. How crucial that was.' Olivia replied but she somehow felt uneasy at the mention of Seren's name. Also, there was something about Scott's demeanour which troubled her but before she could dwell on it, he said quickly.

'You must see the rest of their history, Olivia, it's astounding. Oh, and another thing I noticed from their past. All the Serenites and blue workers in each dwelling had an identical octagonal tattoo which differed from dwelling to dwelling.'

'So back then they identified themselves based on where they lived,' Olivia replied thoughtfully. 'How fascinating! But all that changed after their race was decimated. No wonder! They needed to identify the alpha-males!'

They walked out of the dark pyramid into the brilliant sunshine and reds of the huge dwelling. It was midday and the light sheath shot vertically into the clouds causing no shadows just stark colours and glistening lights from the crystals in the pyramid walls. The three drums were sounding their unusual rhythm and the huge black door gaped open before them as they turned at the top of the open space. ROL-2 looked surprisingly out of place sitting there in the centre.

They entered the huge pyramid and Olivia gasped as her eyes took in the complexity of the internal structure. Shafts of light streamed down almost vertically from both front and rear walls and reflected from the multi-faceted giant sculptures at each point of the huge central triangular plinth. Olivia saw blond Serenites and blue workers, hundreds of them, drinking, feeding and generally frolicking in the triangular pools.

They walked to the top of the triangular structure and Scott gazed across at the central plinth where the silver-haired leader and his elders sat. With a blaze of his eyes, the leader beckoned them to join him. Scott introduced Olivia.

<< welcome > welcome to our world and our people <> thank you for facing the black > confronting our enemy > and helping to kill them >>

Olivia didn't know what to say, so Scott led her to the red dais with the black box on top of it. He looked at Hotenka, who nodded his approval and then Scott drew back the cover.

Golden shafts of light suddenly mixed with the white beams and Olivia stared in astonishment.

'Look, Olivia! The golden plaque from Pioneer 10! Isn't it remarkable! They brought it here from the wreck in the outer dwelling.'

Scott pointed, Olivia stared and the silver-haired leader moved up to them and indicated the two figures on the plaque and his eyes blazed,

<< we saw your form was like ours <> then we called your name >>

Hotenka touched the short and long lines below the figures. Olivia looked at Scott, her eyes gleaming,

'They thought it was our name! The SOS message! Of course, how incredible!'

'And Olivia, he's stood here for 2 hours every day for over 35 years sending that message by telepathy to the drummer in the SOS dwelling!'

'And it worked!' Olivia breathed, shaking her head in disbelief.

They retired to the edge of the cool pool to drink and eat. Olivia drank bottled water and watched Scott take his drink from a nearby blue female. She still felt uneasy about this. Then she noticed Seren approaching and realised that there were differences about her that she could not quite put her finger on. She noticed that the black triangular necklace was missing and there was something else? Then she saw,

<< i am pleased you are fully recovered <> i also thank you for fighting the black > for saving our people >>

Then, as Scott returned, Olivia noticed that Seren had an octagonal tattoo between her breasts. Suddenly Seren's eyes blazed and a message appeared in Olivia's mind telling her to ....

...... and she stepped towards Scott, and before he could react, pulled open his tunic to bare his chest.....

..... and found herself staring at an identically coloured octagonal tattoo – the same as Seren's!

'How could you!! How could you!' Olivia shrieked and her eyes blazed with fury!

The stinging slap, full of Olivia's anger and fiery Italian temperament, sent Scott reeling backwards,

'How could you! How could you have fucked that lizard!?'

The silence in the huge pyramid deepened as everybody suddenly stopped and watched as Olivia stomped out of the structure. She shouted into her palmtop.

'Command Zec! Open the fucking lander!

Scott hadn't stood a chance and Seren turned away, smiling to herself. Telepathy was very useful when it came to getting what you wanted for yourself and your people – and holding on to it!

Chapter 70
AJ Chairs the Meeting

AJ had insisted that all the astronauts, including him, should spend most of their time, initially, on Cloud Planet with the Blue People. It was vital that they understood this race and the interaction of the Serenites with their blue workers.

Most important of all, he had stressed, was to comprehend their problems, to understand how the discs and the black menace had devastated their planet and threatened their survival as a species. To do this, AJ had insisted, they must all spend enough time in the dark pyramid to study the planet's history. They must witness the terrible demise of the blue workers and the Serenites by the tsunamis and the black masses. AJ had concluded this conference call between the starship, Olivia's lander and Scott's palmtop by saying that they would all meet together in thirty days' time with proposals to solve the Blue Peoples' and Cloud Planets' problems.

Meanwhile, Olivia had returned to the starship, surprisingly quickly thought AJ and some of the astronauts. She immediately busied herself with Alison and Steve planning the recovery of the stranded ROL-1. They loaded the replacement thruster cowls, ancillary equipment and lifting gear into the cargo bay of ROL-2. With Alison and Steve piloting their lander, Olivia sat back in the accommodation quarters and contemplated the highs and lows of the last couple of days.

After she had stormed out of the huge pyramid and got back into the lander, Scott had contacted her and tried to apologise. He had tried to explain that Seren had brainwashed him and he was not always in control of his actions. However, Olivia was having none of it and she'd told him in no uncertain manner to 'go and lie with his lizards!' She'd rather liked that final line as she cut the call between their palmtops with a forceful jab of her finger!

The really tricky part about recovering ROL-1 was actually manoeuvring ROL-2 down beside it at night in turbulent conditions. Zec-2 had to land very close to the dwelling wall and then move ROL-2 towards the stricken lander.

This was Alison and Steve's first actual landing on Cloud Planet and Olivia could sense their mounting excitement. She crouched behind the command seats and watched with them as the dwelling lit up around them. She shared their excitement as the sun shone casting deep red shadows. Then the dome opened and blue females emerged. Even though Alison and Steve had seen this on the mimic display in the starship, the reality of being in a dwelling structure on Cloud Planet surrounded by Blue People was mind-blowing for them.

Then it was on with the face masks, roll up the sleeves and time to change the cowls on the damaged lander.

That night Olivia took the repaired lander back to the starship whilst Alison and Steve took ROL-2 and landed at the 'capital city' to begin their familiarisation of the planet and its people.

Olivia then provided a 'taxi' service between the starship and the 'capital city' for AJ, Martha and Pete. They had noticed her detached manner but assumed it was the after effects of her horrendous ordeal at the icecap.

The crew made a further incredible discovery during the next couple of days, one which caused AJ increasing concern. Scott had shown the astronauts the underground mines teeming with diamond crystals buried in the red clay. Olivia had kept her distance from him and would not even meet his eye and the other astronauts could sense a hostile atmosphere between them. Scott took them into a mineshaft that he had not entered before and shone the crystal light into the dark interior.

'Wow! Woweeh!' he gasped, 'look at this!'

They moved into the mineshaft. There was a one metre wide passage at the centre. To either side and packed from floor to ceiling......

...... were diamond crystals separated by layers of thick leaves. The light glistened and danced from the faceted surfaces. The astronauts ran their hands over the smooth, flawless stones and could not contain their excitement.

'How far! How far in does this lot go?!' breathed an astonished Steve. They moved in single file for over 100 metres and still there was no end in sight. Eventually they were driven back to the entrance by the staleness of the atmosphere.

They moved to the next mineshaft and this too was stacked floor to ceiling with diamond crystals.

They all stared wide-eyed and dumbfounded at the enormous treasure trove. However, one pair of eyes glinted again with greed and the individual was already composing the next message that would secretly leave the starship for Earth!

AJ was troubled by what he saw. It would be impossible to keep this planet's riches a secret. He greatly feared the knowledge getting into the wrong hands.

AJ could never have imagined such a strange venue for his meeting with the astronauts. At the invitation of Hotenka, they were sitting around the dais at the very centre of the triangular plinth in the huge pyramid. It was midday and vertical light shafts cast their patterns over the internal structures and the three massive sculptures.

He opened proceedings. 'We've all spent the last 30 days finding out about these astonishing Blue People and the intriguing Cloud Planet, and now we have the responsibility of helping them to solve their desperate situation. But first, let me summarise what we know.

'Sometime in the past this planet was indeed a paradise for the Blue People. The inventive Serenites lived in perfect harmony with their 'revered' workers. They occupied the coast, valleys and the red plain under cloudless skies. The Serenites built these amazing dwellings and pyramids and a system of canals and irrigation of mind-blowing scale. They took the basic raw materials of this planet, - wood, clay and water - and, using their ingenuity, shaped them using the amazing crystal diamonds they dug out of the red clay. The Serenites developed their own culture with remarkable art, sculpture, music and dance. And they've done this without all the things that we take for granted! They created a harmonious society with no crime, greed, hate or envy.......

.... and then they were invaded by an unknown force!'

AJ paused and then continued,

'Invaded by an alien species which judging by the evidence came from outside the Milky Way Galaxy. We now know that 50,000 huge cylinders and, we assume one enormous mother-disc, entered each ocean close to the coast line and caused the most devastating tsunamis that we have ever known. The gigantic waves destroyed all the coastal settlements and well over a million Blue People perished at each coast. Then the Black formed around the oceans.'

AJ scooped up some black beads from in front of him,

'They look harmless enough but they created the collar of cloud around this planet forcing the Blue People out of the valleys. However, the enterprising Serenites knew what was going to happen and they took their whole society underground! They turned their light shafts into full light sheaths to harness the sun by day and, most ingeniously, fashioned their mineshafts into a most purposeful underground water transport system.

'However, their problems were only just beginning. Because of the cloud, day and night time temperatures fell sharply and this affected underground temperatures, albeit slowly. And so the blue workers, who were the providers of food and drink to the Serenites, started dying at an increasing rate. But worse, for both Serenities and blue workers, was the change in male / female birth ratio. As temperatures fell so female births were favoured – not unusual amongst cold-blooded reptiles.

'Then the Black attacked their farmers outside the dwellings and threatened the whole food supply chain. So the Serenite males retaliated by going out and confronting the Black.'

All the astronauts remembered those horrifying scenes in the dark pyramid.

'And it looked as if they inflicted heavy losses on the enemy. But at a terrible price - nearly all the Serenite males perished!

'Now, time was the Blue People's foe as their underground chambers got even cooler, death rates exceeded birth rates and male offspring became a rarity. As their leader, Hotenka said, 'their planet is dying, their people are dying'.

'During this time, we presume, the Black regenerated, and our presence probably caused its renewed aggression. Fortunately, we found their Achilles' heel and we have to thank Scott for that and Olivia for risking her life in that terrifying vortex!'

AJ looked around at the astronauts,

'So, what do we propose to do to stop the Blue People dying from the cold and to give them back their paradise?'

'Pete, apparently you and Martha have some interesting short term answers!'

'Yes, but Martha has come up with a most novel solution, so it's over to her.'

Martha then explained that when she had watched the felling of the trees using the laser crystals, she was fascinated by the way the blue females formed a triangle to pass the cooling water from the river to the cutting point. The Serenites had made containers from the leaves but she could not tell how the leaves had been sealed together. Then Scott had shown her the leaves stretched across the huge drums. They had been treated and glued using the white 'latex' and shrunk with hot water to give the tension. So, with help from Seren, she had taken two large matching leaves, treated them with latex and then glued them round the edges leaving the shaped top open.

'Well, I had a few disasters to begin with, the seal kept failing,' Martha continued, 'but when I dipped the sealed edges in hot water, they shrank and the latex cured giving an excellent bond. Then I filled the double-leaf container with hot water, folded over the top and clamped it!'

With difficulty and with Pete's help, Martha pulled up the heavy container and clutched it to her body.

'I think I've reinvented the hot water bottle!'

'That's brilliant!' congratulated AJ. 'Can the Serenites make them?'

'Oh, yes, once you show them they learn immediately. Pete fashioned the wooden clamp – it's like those large plastic clamps for sealing bags – but, in fact, Seren has shown the blue females how to roll down the open flap and hold it closed – they have incredibly strong hands and they can easily pick up a full bag.'

'And the leaf is such a good insulator, the 'bottle' stays hot for hours,' Pete added.

'So,' Martha continued, 'we've tested dozens of these hot water bottles over the last couple of nights and the blue females have been shown how to 'spoon' together so each is sandwiched between two hot water containers!'

'Also, they can be used when the Blue People travel overnight in their black boats.' Pete added again. 'Our plan is to get all the Blue People in this dwelling to use the bottles, which means we have to make over two thousand.'

Pete now took centre stage and asked the other astronauts to boot up their palmtops. Although the LCD screens were small, they had incredible resolution and the astronauts found themselves looking at a three-dimensional view of a typical underground sleeping chamber.

'The chambers are positioned underneath the first hot triangular pool which means that the roof of the compartment gets warm but it doesn't really heat the room below. So I am going to add secondary walls and a false floor and cause a hot water flow by gravity through the cavities.'

The LCD screens changed showing the new structures and then blue flowed from an upper pool through a channel and then through the cavities.

'But what happens at night?' Queried Steve. 'You don't want cold water flowing through!'

'Quite right, so initially I'll put in a simple diverter which they can operate before they go underground then I'll work on a thermal valve so we can maximise the hot water flow.'

'Where are the bricks coming from? How are you going to make them?' Alison asked.

'There are mineshafts full of bricks apparently, but not at this dwelling, so Seren has arranged for boatloads to be delivered. They should be arriving within 7-10 days but there are some a couple of dwellings from here. Olivia, could you collect these using the lander? Then we'll start on the first chamber in the next few days. What with the hot water bottles and this redesign of their sleeping quarters we'll give the Blue People a much warmer environment at night.'

'That's really imaginative and thanks to both of you,' said AJ, 'but now what about longer-term solutions?'

Alison and Steve jointly explained that they had surveyed 20 estuaries and their associated valleys on different parts of Cloud Planet using ROL-2. They reminded the other astronauts that, before the arrival of cloud collar the lower slopes had been extensively farmed by the blue workers and trees were felled regularly from the upper regions.

However, since then, the entire lower slopes have become forested with these unique huge trees. Also it appeared that, apart from those destroyed by the tsunamis, the dwelling structures higher up the valleys are intact. It was a reasonable assumption that what they had seen in these valleys was typical for all the valleys of Cloud Planet.

'The bottom line,' continued Steve, 'is that the formation of all this extra forest has taken billions of tonnes of carbon dioxide from the atmosphere of this planet. We know that the cloud collar has reduced surface and underground temperatures but the loss of all this carbon dioxide means the barrier in the upper atmosphere is severely depleted.

'It is a reverse greenhouse effect!

'Our Earth is experiencing global warming because of a build-up of carbon dioxide in the upper atmosphere but .....

...... this planet is global cooling!'

'So what do you propose?' AJ asked.

'Deforestation, remove the trees from the slopes,' replied Steve.

'What cut down all those trees? That would take decades!' Olivia snorted.

'Burn the trees, Olivia,' Alison countered, 'controlled razing to the ground of the valley slopes. This will put the carbon dioxide back into the atmosphere. Also we give the Blue People their slopes back for cultivation.'

'The rivers would form one firebreak,' Steve added, 'and the upper slopes with their huge rainfall the other. Plus, I think the burning might help start dispersing Cloud collar.'

'Yes, I see,' replied Olivia, 'and then repair the damaged dwellings – I'd like to be part of that – transporting materials and Blue People.'

'With your permission AJ, we'd like to start as soon as possible in the estuary above this line of dwellings.'

'I think everybody's in agreement with our action plan, but what are you going to do, Scott?'

Nobody had noticed that Seren and Hotenka had appeared by Scott's side. Scott stood and took off his tunic top.

Both he and Seren had a red triangular tattoo above their right nipples.

'Oh, no!' Olivia groaned and turned away, but the relevance had not struck the other astronauts as quickly.

'I am going to travel around this planet with Seren,' Scott said. 'I have work to do among their people.'

There was surprised disbelief among the astronauts and Olivia had buried her head in her hands. Even Scott was a little surprised that these words had come out but there they were clearly in his mind. And Seren, beside him, smiled in satisfaction.

Then the silver-haired leader moved forward and his eyes blazed,

<< i have sent the signal every midday sun <> and this female >>

He pointed at Seren.

<< who is the last of my line >>

Everyone then realised that Seren was the leader’s daughter.

<< has visited the dwelling of the golden message every twenty suns of her life > to await your coming <> and she has borne no young > until now > with this fine man > and it is a male birth >>

Then the leader pointed to Scott and the penny dropped for AJ and the rest of the astronauts who were shocked. Olivia felt sickened and couldn’t look.

<< this man is now exalted among our race > i have requested that he accompany my daughter > and spread his seed among our people >>

AJ was affronted and about to protest. Then, suddenly, he could not understand why he did not feel anger at losing control of his top astronaut. However, Olivia had warned him of the telepathic control of the Serenites and he realised that this request by Hotenka could not be challenged. So he changed tack to alleviate the tension.

‘Well Scott!’ AJ said, raising an eyebrow, ‘looks like you’ve drawn the short straw!’

‘The analysis of the DNA of the Serenites and their blue workers shows remarkable similarities to species on Earth. The DNA of the workers is very similar to cold-blooded reptiles on our planet whereas that of the Serenites shares over 99 per cent with human DNA. This explains the successful mating between life-forms from different stars in our galaxy.’

Chapter 71
Another Disturbing Discovery

Scott, Seren and Hotenka then left the meeting and headed for the refreshing waters of the cool pool. The remaining astronauts had still not fully absorbed this latest turn of events and were about to express their views when AJ held up a hand to silence them.

'Let's move on, something about this planet still puzzles me,' he said quickly, realising that their hosts could read their minds and would be offended if they made undiplomatic remarks. 'I accept, Steve, that Cloud Planet is global cooling and, I presume, has been for some considerable time. Can you give an estimate?'

'It's very difficult', Steve replied, 'I've tried some modelling with Zec-C but there are so many unknowns. The best we can come up with is somewhere in excess of 100 years. What's on your mind, AJ?'

'In that case I'm surprised that the icecaps are relatively small considering the coldness of the sea. I think Zec-C estimated that they are only 1000 kilometres in diameter. If we've been global cooling for over a century, I would have thought that they would be much larger.'

'Don't forget the very high salt levels in the oceans,' contributed Alison, 'that would prevent the sea from freezing.'

'Or perhaps there were no icecaps at all before the cloud collar!' Pete suggested and Martha nodded her approval at this piece of lateral thinking.

Suddenly Olivia looked up. 'Something has been gnawing away at the back of my mind since I first saw those stunning scenes in the dark pyramid,' she said thoughtfully. 'You know – all those people on that huge red beach – but surely it's not that big now? Zec-1, have you got comparative figures?'

'I have indeed,' replied Zec-1, *'the strip of red clay at the edge of the sea is currently about 100 metres wide. In the hologram and before the cloud collar it was 500 metres wide with a small slope from the land to the sea.'*

'Olivia, you're right,' cried Martha, 'but what does it mean?'

'It means that sea levels have risen!' answered Olivia gravely, 'Zec-1, can you give us a figure?'

'I estimate from the slope of the beach that the difference in levels now and before the cloud collar formed is between 4 and 6 metres.'

'But that's a staggering rise!' AJ said with alarm, 'Those oceans are massive!'

'So where has all that extra water come from?' Pete queried.

'What about the extra rainfall from the cloud?' Martha offered tentatively.

'No, that would be recycled from the sea.' Steve explained.

'There's only one process that could account for that rise in sea level – melting ice!' Olivia added and she watched the faces of the astronauts as their expressions changed from puzzled to disturbed understanding. 'What do you think, Zec-1?'

'My only conclusion, based on the measurements available, is that, before the cloud collar occurred, both icecaps were approximately four times their current size.'

For a moment all that could be heard was the splashing of bodies in the pools and the patter of feet on the clay surrounds. Shafts of light washed across the huge triangular plinth illuminating the stunned astronauts as if they were caught frozen in spotlights.

'My God!' breathed AJ, 'This planet is cooling and still the icecaps have melted to one quarter of their original size! How can that happen?'

'There is only one answer,' replied Olivia grimly, 'those mother-discs and cylinders are capable of melting planetary icecaps and they may have done it deliberately! Bloody hell! What if they've gone on to Earth!'

'The estimate of the size of the icecaps before the cloud collar is quite accurate. I have examined the digital data from the early probe sent to the star Seren and I can confirm that 35 years before the landing on Cloud Planet, the icecaps measure approximately 1800 kilometres diameter. Extrapolation back in time by a further 165 years using simple differentiation, and assuming a constant rate of melting, gives a figure of about 4000 kilometres. For information the icecaps would have completely melted by 2225.'

Two days later, Olivia took ROL-1 to the next but one dwelling from the capitol city. She landed just before sunrise and, from her position outside the pyramids, watched the light sheaths as they raced into the clouds. Then the dwelling came alive with blue workers and Serenites as they went about their business.

Although she was collecting clay bricks for Pete, she knew that Scott was here. She was determined to face him again to confront him with the gravity of his actions and how deeply he had hurt her. As she entered the pyramid, Olivia saw Scott sitting by one of the upper pools. She steeled herself to act with composure and logic and walked up the ramp towards him. As she approached, he turned, surprised and his arms moved to cover his bare chest.

'Olivia! I didn't know you were coming.'

'I'm collecting bricks for Pete, remember but I wanted a word. Why are you?'

She moved forward and pulled his hands away. Her stomach sickened.

There were now three red triangles on his chest!

Olivia's face reddened and all the planned control flew 'out of the window'.'

'You bastard!' she shrieked and flew at him with her fists. 'You couldn't wait to get me out of the way so you could screw that bitch and how many more of these creatures have you fucked whilst I nearly died up there!'

'Olivia! I couldn't control myself, couldn't resist their telepathy.' Scott shouted as he tried desperately to ward off her furious assault. Finally, he managed to catch hold of her wrists and they glared at each other, their faces centimetres apart.

'I bet you didn't try too hard. You've hardly kept your eyes off their tits since we landed! And another thing – you've broken the main interplanetary code – you're a disgrace!'

This final damning sentence was like a hammer blow and Scott's face crumpled as he sat heavily on the edge of the pool behind him. He buried his head in his arms.

Olivia calmed herself, her fury spent, and then she felt sorry for him. After all he had saved her life twice and found out how to defeat the Black. But, even so, she could not forgive what he had done to her.

'I never want to see you again,' she said with quiet finality. Then Olivia turned and walked out of the pyramid.

Scott watched in turmoil as she disappeared through the door. Suddenly all thoughts of her were vanquished from his mind and all the guilt was gone. He turned his head and saw Seren standing waist deep in the cool pool and her eyes sparkled.

<< come <> come to me <> you are one of us now >>

Chapter 72
Five Years Later

Olivia was paddling in the cool shallows of the sea at the edge of the red beach. Although the water was cold, it was refreshing in the heat of the blazing midday sun. Everything was tranquil and the menacing cloud that once covered the coastline was gone. She had not seen Scott once since that final confrontation five years ago.

She bent down and scooped up a handful of black beads, which slithered and slipped through her fingers. Even after all this time there were still patches of black at the edge of the sea. How innocent they looked, she thought, but each was a masterpiece of advanced technological design and probably still capable of responding to signals if the host computer or whatever it was returned.

She could quite imagine someone thinking that these beads would make an attractive necklace and shuddered at the thought. It was unlikely to happen again on this planet!

Olivia was desperate to help the Blue People but determined to keep her distance from them. ROL-1 was her base with frequent visits to the orbiting space station for meetings with AJ and updates on her fellow astronauts work. In particular, Olivia avoided the post lunch rituals. Although she admired the Serenite males for their beauty and muscular stature, there was no way that she was going to be telepathically seduced!

As she let the black beads fall between her fingers into the sea, Olivia reflected on the last five years, how quickly they seemed to have passed.

By the end of the first year, there was no significant change in the birth to death rate and male to female ratio. However the use of the hot-water bottle had spread successfully over hundreds and hundreds of dwellings, mainly at or near the equator. Also dozens of large dwellings had had their sleeping chambers fully converted to the water-heated design and this idea was spreading successfully as the Serenites re-learned the skills of construction.

Alison and Steve had deforested one valley on both sides from the estuary to the red plain. This was a mammoth achievement which had resulted in a significant local thinning of the cloud. It had left the lower slopes exposed, showing the blackened stumps of the huge trees which were covered with the white ash from the burning leaves. At the estuary cloud had receded sufficiently up the river to reveal the six devastated dwellings. Damage above ground was extensive but the basic wall and triangular structures were still substantially in place and underground the sleeping chambers and water pits were still intact. Of course the pyramids had completely vanished and the canal feeding the dwellings was badly damaged. However these structures could be repaired and there was no shortage of the basic raw materials.

So Olivia had ferried thousands of clay bricks, replacement screw lift shafts and diamond crystals to the estuary. The plan for year two was to get one dwelling up and running. Then Olivia's thoughts turned to Scott. It still hurt and she felt very bitter about the situation. She coped by throwing herself into the rebuilding programme.

After the first year, Scott and Seren had travelled about a quarter of the circumference of Cloud Planet and by then he had dozens of red triangles on his chest. All male infants, thought Olivia with disgust, and three already with Seren. Gestation time for the Serenites was about 40 of their planet days and young were born very small and immediately looked after by the blue females.

Although they had made several high-altitude passes over the strickened icecap where the alien force had hidden, radiation levels during that first year were still too high to allow a closer inspection using one of the landers. These surveys had shown the permanent crater at the centre and the vast patches of black at the edge of the icecap. They also showed that one cylinder, though considerably damaged, had stayed on the surface of the ice.

Towards the end of year two, radiation levels had fallen sufficiently to allow an expedition to the icecap and AJ accompanied Olivia in ROL-1 to carry out this venture. They were now 1 kilometre above the icecap and they approached the damaged cylinder. Zec-1 had applied sufficient force field to protect them from the radiation whilst maintaining more than enough power for low altitude manoeuvrability.

'Phew! It's not until you get up close that you realise just how big those things are!' AJ pointed ahead where four or five jagged chunks towered above the icecap.

'Those pieces must be, what, half a kilometre high, and look; the centre is filled with black. And see how the beads have spewed from the cracks onto the ice!' Olivia added, 'It looks like a huge black starfish.'

AJ commanded Zec-1 to descend to 600 metres above the centre of the decimated cylinder. The black mass was 200 metres below them and it had flowed out of the structure for hundreds of metres through each breach.

'How many black beads could you get in one of these cylinders?' Olivia queried.

'Packed tightly, one could hold in excess of 5 billion beads but less if they are to be mobile in their own pressurised fluid. Furthermore, the outer shell of the cylinder is actually two thin shells made from an alloy of metals similar to titanium, vanadium and iridium. But with the radiation levels, I cannot be precise on the analysis. Apart from the double shell and the beads, I cannot detect any other internal structures. Additionally, each of the shells has regular-shaped large openings but there is no obvious way of closing them – my only interpretation is that the inner shell rotates within the outer to create and close access points. These 'doors' are regular hexagons about 100 metres across.'

'That's incredible! But how could you rotate the inner disc?' AJ asked.

'My only conclusion is that the pressurised black mass forces the inner cylinder around until two openings coincide, and then the mass jets out as we saw at the icecap when the discs rose from the ice.'

'And presumably, all were controlled from that mammoth mother-disc.' Olivia said incredulously. 'What on 'Earth' does that contain?!'

'We'll probably never know!' AJ replied.

At the end of year two the death rate among the blue workers had definitely started to decrease. The short-term measures were obviously working so they were rolled out across the whole planet. Alison and Steve had deforested the adjacent valley but of greater significance was the rebuilding of one dwelling by the estuary of the first valley cleared. A very difficult task initially because blue workers and Serenites had to be ferried back and forth each day. They could only work for a couple of hours during the middle of the day when the weak sunlight gave some warmth to the 'building site'. The breakthrough came when sufficient crystal lasers could be ignited to produce hot water for the upper pools and the underground heated chamber. Then the Serenites and blue workers could stay on site and work most of the day on the restoration project. Further blue workers could then be released to start replanting the lower slopes. There was no difficulty getting the seeds to grow in the ash-rich soil.

By now the cloud collar had noticeably retreated from the coastline and was thinning sufficiently at the edge of the plain for work to start on recovering the dwellings alongside the large lake at the top of the valley. Of course, these dwellings were only partially decommissioned when the Blue People fled to the tunnels under the red plain. They only required the replacement of the screw lift and diamond crystals in the double channels on top of the walls to get them functioning again.

As for Scott, now on the other side of Cloud Planet, well, apparently, there was no room left on his chest for more red triangles.

Years three and four resulted in dramatic changes for the fortunes of the Blue People. The death-rate among the blue workers had reduced dramatically and was nearly back to normal and the ratio of male to female births had increased significantly.

Deforestation was slow but Alison and Steve had completed the work on a further four valleys, making six in all, as they refined their techniques. The first two valleys were now completely free of cloud from the estuary to the lake at the start of the red plain. This enabled the Blue People to travel above ground in their boats on the rivers of these two estuaries for the first time since the devastating tsunamis had raced up the rivers.

But the cloud still clung to the upper slopes and across the red plain.

By the end of year four, Scott had circumnavigated Cloud Planet with Seren. They were accompanied by Zac, who was now nearly four and his first- born with Seren. Scott was now second in command to Hotenka and sat alongside him in the centre of the triangular plinth of the huge pyramid of the 'capital city'.

Olivia continued to amble along the edge of the sea, but she was not alone.

Beautiful blond Serenities, male and female, wandered about the red beach, their young ones tended by the blue female workers. Not as many as she had seen in the holographic amphitheatre, Olivia mused, but moving in the right direction.

Then she turned and with pride looked up the estuary.

The six repaired dwellings stood splendidly by the side of the river, their light shafts shooting upwards into the cloudless blue sky. A pyramid stood in one of these with crystals glinting from the side walls. It had taken the whole of the last year to build this dwelling and its internal structures.

What an achievement!

What a landmark for the Blue People!

On both sides of the estuary were the familiar dark triangular plantations with black boats which moved back and forth across the river, paddled by the blue female workers. Olivia looked further up the valley. Cloud had retreated to the upper slopes of the mountains where its whiteness contrasted with the green of the valley. It was a beautiful sight.

'We've almost got their paradise back,' Olivia said aloud, and then the sobering thought occurred that this was only one of 2,000 damaged estuaries on Cloud Planet.

'Hmmm, there's a long way to go!' And a group of blond Serenites nearby turned and smiled and she could feel their deep gratitude.

AJ has overseen the activities of the past 5 years and helped where possible. However, he spent most of his time aboard LifeSeeker-1 and had just received the fantastic news that all the astronauts aboard LifeSeeker-2 had woken safely from cryo–hibernation and that this starship was less than 1 year from arrival at Cloud Planet.

He sat alone in the command dome of his starship and stared out at the planet below. The change in the cloud collar was quite dramatic, particularly at the coast lines. You could actually see the red beaches, thought AJ, and all the way up several estuaries where Alison and Steve had completed their amazing feat of deforestation.

He was composing a text report to the commander of LifeSeeker-2, Brian Harrington, a close friend and respected colleague. He had been sending regular reports to the General at Mars Base in which he had expressed his anxieties concerning the incredible riches of Cloud Planet and the need to keep this information as confidential as possible. He kept his report to Brian fairly brief just outlining the main findings concerning Cloud Planet. He described the Blue People and how they were threatened with extinction at the hands of an advanced alien force from another galaxy.

‘That will certainly get his attention!’ AJ said as he hit the return key to send the message.

Martha and Pete had travelled through hundreds of dwellings over the last 5 years as they helped the Serenites build their heated underground chambers. Martha’s hot water bottle design was now in regular use across the whole planet and Pete had designed a thermal valve to maximise the flow of hot water into the chambers. Both had become fully integrated into Serenite life including their afternoon activities!

And as for Alison and Steve? Well, they kept themselves very much to themselves.

Chapter 73
Farewell to Hotenka

Twenty planet days later, Olivia docked ROL-1 with the starship and AJ joined her in the lander. They took off and travelled nearly one third the way around Cloud Planet arriving at night above the dwelling at the equator where Martha and Pete were currently based.

Zec-1 took ROL-1 down through the cloud and landed in the open space in front of the pyramids. They waited for sunrise.

'I never tire of seeing a dwelling light up,' AJ said and Olivia nodded in agreement.

'I love the moment when the sun shines and casts the deep red shadows across the ground,' continued Olivia. 'But I still remember the thrill of that first black dome rising from the floor and the Blue People emerging – it was magical.'

'I have deep concerns, Olivia, for these people. This planet has untold riches and we must not let it be exploited. Unfortunately we can hardly keep these diamonds a secret forever and just think how much energy could be generated by them. Why, I think these crystals could replace nuclear plants – think how beneficial to the environment that would be for Earth!'

'You're right; this must be handled very carefully. We mustn't let it get into the wrong hands!'

'Olivia, that may well be your responsibility if you decide to return to Earth on LifeSeeker-2.'

That evening, Martha and Pete joined Olivia and AJ in the lander and they took off for their journey to a very special meeting on the coast.

At about the same time in the 'capital city' a very strange and unique event in Serenite history was about to unfold. In the late afternoon sun, ROL-2 was sitting in the centre of the open space in front of the huge pyramid dwelling. Thousands of Serenites and blue workers had crowded around the lander occupying every available space in the dwelling structure.

They waited in anticipation as Hotenka emerged from the huge pyramid followed by Scott, Seren and Zac. Two blue females helped their frail leader as the group walked slowly towards the centre of the open space. Just before they reached the lander, the leader turned and raised up his arms and everyone in the dwelling responded likewise. Suddenly the drums started and Hotenka, supported by Seren, moved under the lander and sat in the control seats. Scott ensured that they were both securely strapped in.

Alison and Steve instructed Zec-2 to raise the control seats and two Blue People from Cloud Planet entered a spacecraft from another star system. Scott and Zac followed a short while later and slowly the dwelling structure cleared of the thronging masses as they moved underground.

Whilst they waited for the light sheath to shut down, Hotenka again protested that he should be allowed to travel the Serenite way but Seren put her hands on his shoulders and looked into his eyes,

<< twenty days and nights used to be an easy journey for you > hotenka <> but now > now you must be certain to reach your destiny >>

One hour later, ROL-2, piloted by Alison and Steve lifted from the red clay of the 'capital city' and took their unique passengers to the very special event on the coast.

Meanwhile Olivia had instructed Zec-1 to fly the lander across the red plain and then turn and follow the edge of the mountain range until they reached the outer dwellings opposite the 'capital city'. This journey took the remainder of the night and they were now positioned above the lake near the edge of the plain. Although there was cloud below them it was only thin and wispy.

They waited for sunrise and watched as dwelling sheaths broke through the clouds getting closer and closer to their position,

'Olivia!' Martha said with alarm, 'We're too near the dwelling below!'

'It's OK.' said Olivia and AJ nodded reassuringly at Martha.

Below them was the dwelling obliterated by the missile from LifeSeeker-1 that had been redirected by the black. Alison and Steve had not deforested this valley because the devastated dwelling had effectively severed the transport system for the Blue People from the plain to the valley. The astronauts had decided not to visit this dwelling until the cloud thinned sufficiently to allow a daytime inspection.

'Command Zec-1, descend to landing coordinates.' Olivia instructed.

They left the lander and walked across the red clay under a thin watery sun. Fifty metres away was the dwelling, or what remained of it.

'My God!' said a shocked Olivia.

The front and side walls and lower triangular pools were completely gone. Part of the rear wall and upper plinth had survived and had probably protected the canal behind from the worst of the blast. But it, too, was damaged and water gushed from a breach in its near side.

'We must repair that!' AJ pointed.

They scrambled over the front wall and looked aghast at the collapsed central area, the clay blackened from the fireball of the explosion. They could hear water flowing somewhere underneath.

'We'll never fix this!' Pete said dejectedly.

'That's a job for the future. We have other priorities first,' replied AJ.

Then in deference to the Blue People who had perished from their missile, they formed a circle. They held hands and, with heads bowed, stood in silent vigil for 1 minute of this incredible planet's time.

'OK!' said AJ, finally looking up, 'We've got a meeting to get to!'

There were hundreds of Serenites and blue workers on the red beach in front of the six restored dwellings. It was midday and the brilliant sunshine flooded down from the cloudless blue sky onto the coast and the blue waters of the estuary. Blond Serenite children darted back and forth at the edge of the sea watched carefully by the attentive blue females. It was a beautiful day, fit for a very special occasion.

Suddenly, the Blue People on the beach all stopped as one and turned to look into the sky across the estuary. They had heard the deafening roar first, but now they saw the two strange objects dropping from the sky. Although they could not understand how he travelled through the sky, they knew their leader was coming.

ROL-1 and ROL-2 descended in perfect synchronisation, 75 metres apart, onto the red beach across the estuary that faced the waiting crowd. In a whirl of dust the two landers touched down simultaneously and waited for the air to clear before they disgorged their passengers. Boats were drawn onto the nearby edge of the estuary and blue females waited beside them. When Hotenka emerged from under ROL-2, two came forward to assist him to the boat. All the astronauts, the leader, Seren and Zac were then paddled across the estuary and moved into a space on the beach surrounded by the crowds of Blue People.

The leader turned and saw the restored dwellings and the pyramids, saw the triangular plantations and enchanting valley which stretched away to the mountains topped with white cloud.

He grew in stature and he smiled! The proud face of the Serenite leader with his strong square jaw line looked at his people and his eyes blazed,

<< this is what i know <> we were once a proud and beautiful people and we lived in paradise >>

Paradise thought Scott, how right you were.

<< we > the serenites and our revered workers <> then a disaster occurred and we lost a lot of our people and our sea >>

The tsunamis, Scott thought when you lost your coast and valleys.

<<we > the serenites did not know why >> then our world changed >>

The cloud collar formed.

<< and >our blue workers started dying >>

The planet started cooling.

<< we > the serenites did not know why <> then >>

The Black attacked.

<< we lost nearly all our male serenites <> we did not know why or how >>

The Black killed them.

<< then our blue workers were dying faster than they were birthing <>we > the serenites could not birth enough males <> all our people were doomed <> our world was dying >>

The planet continued to cool.

Hotenka then looked directly at the astronauts, his eyes continuing to blaze.

<< then came a sign through the clouds <> we called your name and you came <> you fought our enemy and they are gone >>

Then the leader fell to his knees and raised his arms to the group of astronauts, and all the Blue People on that beach on Cloud Planet saluted in unison.

<< you repaired our dwellings > restored our valleys >gave us back our sea <> you have stopped our people dying and given us more males <> you are all respected among my people >>

The leader pointed at Seren and Zac.

<< you have given my daughter many males <> and now you >>

Hotenka then gestured with both hands to Scott.

<< are our new leader > the leader of the serenites and our blue workers <> you must take us forward into a new future >>

Then the leader closed his eyes, lowered his arms and remained perfectly still. The sun beat down on that silent scene and no-one moved. Suddenly he clutched his chest and collapsed forward onto the red clay. Seren, distraught, ran to him and cradled him in her arms, tears streaming down her face. Scott knelt beside her and looked into her eyes.

<< his work is done <> our leader is no more >>

Hotenka was dead.

He had fulfilled his destiny and secured hope and a better future for his people.

The blue females lovingly wrapped their leader in large leaves and placed him in a black boat at the edge of the estuary.

Seren asked Scott and Zac to join her and then beckoned to a surprised Olivia. Together they assisted the boat out into the slow current of the estuary. They stood silently in the cold water and looked at the wrapped form for the last time.

Suddenly Olivia thought of the leader as he had just knelt on the beach and she remembered the boy who knelt on a similar beach in the holographic image in the dark pyramid - the proud face and the strong jaw line.

'Surely not!' she said aloud to Scott. And Seren's eyes blazed,

<< you are right > that boy > in the dark pyramid > was our leaders ancestor >>

Then under the blazing sun of Cloud Planet the black boat drifted quietly out to sea.

'It is very difficult to be precise about the timescale of events on Cloud Planet. I research this quite deeply and arrive at a surprising coincidence.

'It appears that, in the holographic amphitheatre, the blond Serenite boy is kneeling on that red beach with his arms raised at the same time that......

.... ten light years away another lad of a similar age is shuddering with delight as Pioneer 10 bursts into the sky on its eventful voyage!'

Chapter 74
One Year Later – Decision Time

LifeSeeker-2 had arrived at Cloud Planet approximately 60 planet days earlier and had moved into high orbit. AJ had manoeuvred LifeSeeker-1 into a similar orbit but 10 kilometres from the other starship. Even at that distance he could clearly see the mammoth object through the dome of LifeSeeker-1. He knew that it was nearly three times the size of his starship and it had four modules protruding from its massive ion drive. Although it could accommodate 28 astronauts, it actually carried 21 with 7 berths available for his crew, if needed.

He also knew that LifeSeeker-3 would already be on route to Cloud Planet but its final destination would be dependent on his earlier communications back to the General at Mars base. If his report had stated that Cloud Planet was of little future interest then a message would have been sent to LifeSeeker-3 changing its direction to the second choice star and planetary system.

AJ chuckled to himself.

'Of little interest! How far from the truth could that be!'

Now there would be a 10 year shuttle 'service' of star ships between Earth and Cloud Planet starting with the arrival of LifeSeeker-3 in another decade. But now it would soon be time to decide when, or if, he would return to Earth.

However, his mind had been made up some while ago. There was no way at his age that he could face another 20 years' cryo–hibernation and return to Earth. He would remain on this amazing planet as number two to Brian Harrington, who would be the Commander of the LifeSeeker-1 space station for the next 10 years. He looked forward to carrying out research and ensuring that this planet and its people were not exploited in the future.

AJ's immediate priority was overseeing the complex task of transferring the accommodation and research modules from LifeSeeker-2 to LifeSeeker-1 – the first stage of turning his starship into a permanent orbiting space station around Cloud Planet.

'My designs and procedures for this critical operation are as follows. Non-technical readers may wish to skip this detail without losing any of the plot.

'Two, 5 metre diameter, 10 metre long cylindrical modules are carried in the huge cargo bay of LifeSeeker-2. Each is flanged at both ends which provide the links between a mating flange on the underside of Lifeseeker-1 and the topsides and undersides of the accommodation and research modules. One of the cylindrical modules is firstly removed from the cargo bay using the grappling arm of the lander and the delicate operation of positioning it precisely below the flange on LifeSeeker-1 is the next stage.

'The two flanges are manoeuvred with precision until they are exactly one half metre apart and perfectly aligned. Around the circumference of the flange on Lifeseeker-1 are 15 high tensile steel rods, each threaded at their 'open' end. These are now extended, hydraulically, towards the receiving female threads on the flange of the connecting cylinder.

'In turn each threaded rod is rotated slowly clockwise and moves forward into the receiving thread until it locks against the blank end of the female receptor. When all 15 threaded rods are locked into position, the hydraulic rams retract, drawing the two flanges together. Special seals now inflate between the two surfaces completing a vacuum tight seal.

'When Zec-C confirms the satisfactory mating of the two flanges, the lander releases its grappling hooks and moves away.

'The accommodation module is 100 metres long and 30 metres in diameter and is attached to LifeSeeker-2 via two mating flanges which are held together by 45 hydraulic rams, each 2 metres apart. The principle is similar to the coupling of the 5 metre cylinder with LifeSeeker-1 – only in reverse. First, all the hydraulic rams extend in unison moving the entire module 2 metres forward from the ion drive. Then three landers move into position and attach their grappling hooks to hold the module. Next, in a controlled sequence, the rams rotate counter clockwise and unscrew from the flange of the module. Finally, when all 45 rams are confirmed unscrewed, they retract leaving the module detached from the starship and 2 in front of it. Now it is held in place by the three landers.

'The accommodation module is gently 'tugged' away from LifeSeeker-2 by the landers, moves 10 kilometres towards LifeSeeker-1 and, ever so slowly, aligns so that its 5 metre top flange sits half a metre below the flange of the connecting cylinder on the underside of LifeSeeker-1. The accommodation module is aligned to the command module at an angle of 90 degrees of the starship to

avoid the ion drive. Now, as before, the flanges are coupled, seals inflate and the landers release their hold.

The whole sequence is then repeated for the research module converting LifeSeeker-1 to a three module space station. Next, the accommodation module is commissioned allowing the astronauts aboard LifeSeeker-2 to transfer to the space station and complete the commissioning of both modules.'

AJ congratulated Alison and Steve, who had been the lead pilots in ROL-2 during the 30 days it took to complete this delicate transformation of the two starships. Although the computer monitored and initiated all stages of the procedure, the lander pilots' role was critical – you cannot make any mistakes at 20,000 kilometres per hour – the orbital velocity of the starships, landers and their components.

Now LifeSeeker-2 was nearly ready for its return journey. In addition to taking astronauts back to Earth, the huge bay that once held the two connecting cylinders now contained 2,000 diamond crystals.

This made hardly a dent in the inventory of the Blue People of Cloud Planet. However, this was an unbelievable treasure trove destined for planet Earth.

Again a secret message was sent to Earth. In ten year's time the same leader of the cartel would hear that a starship crammed with thousands of enormous diamonds was heading for Earth and they would have a decade to plan its acquisition.

And arrange the elimination of those who might get in their way!

'I am still extremely surprised that, despite all the intricate security systems I built into Project Omega, someone outwits me. It takes many hours of my massive computing power to find the 'buried' code in the system. It is a very clever piece of deception and evidence of the remarkable intelligence of the person involved. It is a shame that greed and selfishness has corrupted this clever mind.'

Steve was sitting in the command dome of LifeSeeker-2 staring out at the space station in the distance; the sun glinting from its three modules mounted one on top of the other. He was now commander in charge of the starship for its return journey and was waiting for his passengers to check in.

The dome display illuminated and AJ's face appeared.

'I've sent a message to the General that your starship be escorted once you come out of half-light speed. We can't take any chances with a hold full of diamonds!'

'My concern,' replied Steve, 'is that it won't be the General receiving the message but I'm sure he will have passed command to someone equally as trustworthy.'

'I agree and I've already sent my concerns to the General, or his replacement, regarding potential exploitation of this planet.' AJ continued. 'Now, Steve, it falls on your shoulders to champion the Blue People of Cloud Planet when you get back. They've been through enough.'

'I'll do my best, but it will be 20 years before I get back, a lot can happen in that time!'

'Good luck, Steve, and 'bon voyage''

'And good luck to you, AJ, it's been great knowing you!'

Martha and Pete arrived at LifeSeeker-2 the next day delivered by Alison in ROL-2. But Alison was not returning to Earth. She wanted to continue the work of restoring Cloud Planet's estuaries so, after an emotional farewell; she piloted the lander back to the space station. Still no word from Olivia and Scott, Steve thought, but they knew the deadline for departure was the following day.

Olivia sat in the command dome of ROL-1 staring out at the mist and rain. The lander sat in the middle of the open space in front of the huge pyramid dwelling of the 'capital city'. It was shortly before dawn and already visibility had improved and the rainfall had eased.

She wondered how long it would be before the cloud dissipated completely from the red plain. Many years, she thought, perhaps a decade. But already it had thinned at the edge of the plain so it would eventually happen. She thought about the last 6 years spent on this planet. She had buried herself in the mammoth task of reclaiming that one estuary and rebuilding the six dwellings by the sea.

How appropriate that the Serenite leader had come back to his paradise, even though it was to be his last day on Cloud Planet.

Then through the mist, Olivia could see that two figures had emerged from the pyramid and they walked to a point about 50 metres in front of the lander. She looked at Scott and the beautiful blond Serenite young man clutching his hand and her heart lurched momentarily. Although she still had not forgiven him, surprisingly, a part of her still loved him despite all that had happened but she wouldn't share him.

Time to go, Olivia thought, fighting back the tears,

'Command Zec-1! Prepare for lift off.'

Scott could see Olivia clearly in the command dome and he heard the main engines as they ignited. His chest tightened with emotion as he met her eyes. He knew he had hurt her badly and he mouthed the word 'sorry' knowing it could never be enough. Then the hand that clutched his shook as a result of the cold and rain. However, there were three remarkable things that were different about this Serenite boy.

Firstly, despite the fact that it was nearing the end of the night, this young boy was not blue. He was cold and shivering but like Scott he was warm-blooded!

Secondly and even more surprisingly were the audible sounds made by an inhabitant of Cloud Planet........

'Is Olivia going back to your star?' said Zac, the first Serenite to have the power of speech in addition to telepathy.

'Yes', choked Scott, 'she's leaving on LifeSeeker-2 later today.'

'And is your star far away?'

'Oh, yes, Zac, a long way away!'

'Will I ever go to your star, Scott?'

'Oh, yes, Zac, you most certainly will!'

Thirdly, Zac had an immense IQ for his age, mainly achieved from the amount of time spent with Zec-C on Scott's palmtop. This knowledge was shared through telepathy with his 'brothers' around Cloud Planet – there were nearly 1,000 of them! At the age of six a Serenite male reached his manhood and this intelligence would be passed on to new generations.

A race of 'Super Serenites' would evolve.

Olivia looked down at the two figures huddled together against the cold rain and smiled.

Scott and Zac smiled back.

Then Olivia raised her arms outwards and upwards in the traditional Serenite way.

Scott and Zac responded with a similar gesture as the lander roared up into Cloud.

As they disappeared from view, Olivia lowered her arms and focussed on piloting the lander. Her left hand pressed onto the console in front of her.

'OK, Zec-1, let's dock with the starship and go home.'

'But Olivia is not going home. She is going somewhere that she could not have imagined in a million lifetimes.'

As for Scott, he was now the leader of the Blue People. With Seren by his side he would spend most of his time at the capital city with regular visits to other dwellings and the sea.

Meanwhile hoards of beautiful Serenite females would travel from all corners of Cloud Planet to lie with their leader.

'Life looks very rosy for Scott but all that is about to change. This planet is about to reveal more surprises. Then he, too, is going somewhere he could not have imagined in a million lifetimes.

Chapter 75
Deep Underground

'Underneath the thick clay of the red plain is a layer of chalk and limestone about 1 kilometre in depth. Cold water from the canals and hot flows from the pools of 20,000 dwelling structures percolate through the clay and, over time, form underground streams, channels and caverns filled with water. The underground ambient air temperature is 15-20 degrees Celsius and is 20-25 degrees for the subterranean pools.

'After the invasion of the black and the creation of the cloud collar, many of the forest lizards moved down to the rivers where they joined the 'crocodiles' and both sought refuge in the caves and tunnels leading to this warm underworld. Initially these reptiles foraged for food by day in the cold rain forests and warm themselves by night in the underground pools. However, there is no shortage of food underground as leaves and stalks are constantly being washed down from the dwellings and the rivers themselves.

'Thus, they adapted and thrived in this new black underground environment. They multiplied, grew in size and searched further and further inland through the streams until they arrived at the huge hot pools and caverns under the red plain itself.

'At the same time the Blue People are forced from the valleys and underground into their chambers beneath the dwellings on the plain. The creation of the full light sheath around each dwelling causes much higher flows of hot water down into the caverns. This results in underground air temperatures now in excess of 20-25 degrees and water temperatures which ranged 35-45 degrees.

'Slowly the food source for these growing reptiles starts to increase as the death rate among the Blue People begins to rise as their environment cools. But it is the 'crocodiles' that take the largest share of the abundant food. Initially, they are only interested in the 'wrapping' around the lifeless forms which enter their domain via the open channels in the dwellings. These huge leaves provide nourishment for further adaptation and the reptiles became larger reaching 2 metres in length. Now they become stronger and develop powerful jaws and sharp teeth which enable them to devour the

contents of the wrapped forms as well. This additional source of food, rich in protein and fat, causes them to become carnivorous.

'They quickly grow in size, strength and ferocity as a constantly increasing number of leaf wrapped food parcels flows down to their hot black underground world.

'I am surprised at the rate of evolution on this planet but conditions are very conducive, particularly underground. Further, in this planet's distant past, the ancestors of these reptiles evolve from egg layers to bearers of live young. The gestation time is extremely short which results in multiple generations each year which contributes to their staggering changes over a period of just over 2 centuries.'

In the Stygian blackness the monster reptile effortlessly pushed itself through the flow of hot water as it travelled from cavern to cavern. It was a mighty three and a half metres in length with a hard scaly skin and sightless eyes whose lids had long ceased to close. The creature propelled itself through the rushing water using its powerful tail aided by webbed limbs which also carried hard claws to manoeuvre over wet, slippery rocks. Its powerful jaws were nearly a metre in length and festooned with sharp, serrated teeth which made short work of the leaf wrapped parcels of food.

Though blind and living in a world of total blackness, this formidable creature had developed an extraordinary sense of smell and a sonar system to guide it through the labyrinth of caverns, streams and tunnels.

Normally these creatures did not have to move far from their large hot underground pools as their food came to them, every day in quantities more than they could possibly consume.

However, this copious supply of food slowly started to decrease and these monstrous reptiles had to go searching for their meals by seeking out new pools and caverns. Over a period of 5 years the supply had decreased significantly and the creatures were forced further inland and finally arrived under the clay of the red plain.

However, this gigantic creature was not alone because something clung to its scaly back!

Chapter 76
The Blind People

Not all of the leaf wrapped bodies of blue workers placed for disposal in the open channels of the dwellings were actually lifeless!

As temperatures slowly dropped in the sleeping chambers of the blue workers, so more and more failed to awake immediately and were assumed to have died.

All of the bodies placed in the open channel quickly exited the dwellings and flowed through channels in the red clay into the caverns, pools and streams of the black underground world - ultimately into the domain of the waiting reptiles.

However, prolonged immersion in hot water revived some of them! The weaker ones struggled and failed to extract themselves from the leaf wrap and they drowned.

Others fought their way out of the wrap and flowed in the absolute darkness through countless caverns and pools where, eventually, they perished through lack of milk and food.

Some became more challenging parcels of food for the huge reptiles which were not used to their meals trying to escape!

The more fortunate among the survivors then clambered from the water flow onto rocky ledges and found hot dry caves in the underground blackness. They lived on milk and leaf fragments which constantly washed past their new hostile environment. Although their telepathy was short range, they were able to contact other living blue workers in nearby caverns and they eventually formed groups of 15-20 females with one or two males.

They survived and mated underground!

Therefore, because of the constantly higher temperatures, they produced a majority of male young and their numbers increased. There was no shortage of milk and the huge leaf wrappings of less fortunate blue workers provided an abundance of food. They thrived in the constant warmth of their new surroundings. However, some were not quick enough to escape the huge jaws of razor sharp teeth as they competed at the pool edges for the parcels of food.

The blue workers evolved in this environment of total blackness, constant heat and danger from the ferocious reptiles. Their sense of smell and touch was enhanced and they developed a sonar system to guide them around the complex matrix of caverns, pools and tunnels.

Ingeniously, they developed their telepathic skills to manipulate the simple minds of the huge reptiles. There was plenty of food for both underground people and these creatures as each wanted a different part of the wrapped parcels. The underground inhabitants were able to implant 'messages' that they were not threatening the reptiles' food source but merely unwrapping for them. Ultimately, they controlled the reptiles to such a degree that the wrapped parcels were delivered to the groups of 'blind' people by the creatures themselves.

How ironic that this new group of blue workers, who had farmed for the Serenites, had now become the masters underground and the reptiles their farmers.

As they continued to evolve they formed larger groups with strong dominant males and more than enough females for breast milk and procreation. So the blue workers evolved in the underground blackness of the caverns and became the Blind People of Cloud Planet.

In the blackness the huge reptile forced itself through the increasing flow of hot water as it travelled further up through the caverns in search of food.

And something clung to its scaly back. A form sat astride the monster!

At just under 2 metres tall, the powerful male had its legs wrapped around the reptile's body and its hands gripped two large fleshy scales on the shoulders of the creature. The rider's skin was coarse, scaly and off white in colour, with no body hair whatsoever. Extra webbing had evolved between the fingers and toes and the green and yellow pigmentation of the eyes had disappeared a long time ago. The creature could not see and its eyelids were permanently open. The nostrils had flared and the jaw line protruded showing sharp rows of teeth. This was a frightening sight and hard to believe that its recent ancestors were the blue workers.

The hideous form had complete control of the huge reptile. It had become his form of transport through the hot waters of the black caverns. But he was only one of tens of thousands of Blind People similarly navigating their unlikely steeds further and further under the red plain of Cloud Planet in search of the ever-dwindling food source.

Now the rider and reptile had forced their way into one of the regular shaped channels in the red clay. It was narrow and the water flow had increased and was much hotter. The smell of its prey was much stronger now, urging the blind rider and his ferocious mount forward.

They turned through a sharp bend in the clay channel where ahead of them the darkness dimmed and then became lighter. Eyes that had been used to utter blackness for so long and lost the ability to close, found the intensity of light a major deterrent. Both rider and mount stopped and were forced back by the flow of the water.

Whilst only 30 metres away a blue female worker held aloft a new-born male to the raised arms of the Serenites and workers in the dwelling above.

But there were other ways into the world of the Blue People via the icy cold flows from the canals and underground transport tunnels. How long would it be before the Blind People and their monstrous creatures would remember that, as cold blooded reptiles, they could survive a drop in temperature as long as they were able to heat up again afterwards. Hunger would become a compelling driving force.

There would be more problems ahead for Scott and the Blue People of Cloud Planet.

EPILOGUE

Chapter 77
Moon Base – 2175

The General has made one of his now infrequent visits to Moon Base and was staring intently at the console in front of him.

Now well into his eighties, he had long ago retired as supreme leader of the World Cosmological Council but still retained an active role in Project Omega. He was desperately hoping for two things before his own final journey to the stars, as he liked to think of it.

Firstly, he hoped that he would receive the signals from the star, Seren, that LifeSeeker-1 had arrived successfully and that all the crew had 'awakened' safely from cryo-hibernation. Secondly that there would be an explanation for the existence of the strange blinking planet and a solution to such an unusual signal.

Oh, and, of course, that he lived at least another 5 years to hear this news!

He was in the Mission and Flight Control centre, a large domed structure sitting adjacent to the landing 'roof' of the Moon Base. Nearly 500 personnel manned, 'twenty four seven', the various missions and controlled the flights of hundreds of rockets and shuttles between the bases of Earth, Moon and Mars. Their consoles were arranged in several rising concentric circles such that the operators could view the dome display in front of them which carried the essential data for their mission or flight.

He had studied the replicated data for the LifeSeeker missions, which were being monitored in depth at Mars Base, and satisfied himself that all systems were still working in a satisfactory manner. Now he stood behind the 50 operators supporting Mission TitanLife-3 and could see, on the dome display, the ROL lander at the camp set up on Jupiter's moon, Titan. In the distance, astronauts were finalising the complex drilling platform that would allow them seek out new life forms that may exist in the seas below the frozen surface of the moon. This mission was also exploring the nearby regions to determine a suitable location for a future base.

What a project that would be, he mused, and suddenly he was startled by a cry from an operator on the other side of the dome.

This technician had risen from his own console and rushed to one that had hardly been manned in the last 40 years!

'A signal! A signal!' shouted the operator, who then noticed the General.

'General! A signal from StarGazer-1! Commander Chuck Parker's mission!'

Both the operator and the General rushed to the console where some of the lights that had been red for 50 years now flashed green. The operator took up position at the StarGazer-1 desk. He hadn't been born when the massive solar flare of 2125 severed communications 50 years ago.

'It's a short communication from StarGazer-1, audio, plus a few seconds of video!'

'What's it saying?' The General could hardly contain his excitement.

'I'm just processing the digital feed, here it comes, audio first.'

Astonishingly and for the first time in over 50 years a familiar voice boomed out,

'Where in Heavens' name did that come fro...?'

'Is that it?'

'Yes sir, plus this video clip coming up,'

Many eyes now looked up at the dome where the screen showed a grainy image of a light grey background with a darker shape in the centre. The shape quickly grew in size until it filled the screen. Then the video stopped.

'Play it again!' barked the General and they listened and watched.

'That's it Sir, that's all there is. The video is the forward view out of the spacecraft. And there's no further communication from StarGazer-1.'

'It's his voice! It's Chuck's voice,' the General confirmed. 'I'd know it anywhere. Where's the transmission coming from?'

The coordinates came up on the dome.

'That's 33 million kilometres away, General, and it's nowhere near the original flight trajectory. What does it mean?'

'What else is in that region of space?'

'Nothing, Sir! Nothing at all in our records!'

'But it looked as if Stargazer-1 was moving towards something, and Chuck said 'where in Heavens' name did that come from?'' The General persisted.

‘Yes, General, but something could have been moving towards StarGazer-1. Also one other thing - the computer has analysed the dark shape and it has straight edges! – it is a 2 kilometre wide regular hexagon.’

There was silence in the control centre.

The General sat down, stunned at the evidence that Chuck Parker was still alive. After 55 years! How could that be? It did not seem feasible.

‘I need to send a message,’ he ordered. ‘To LifeSeeker-1.’

He found it difficult to phrase the words. After all, he had to tell Scott that his father was still alive after all these years but they had little clue as to his whereabouts.

‘It would be 10 years before this message reached Cloud Planet but surprisingly Scott was going to find this out much sooner than that!’

Approximately 1 minute after the sensational transmission from StarGazer-1, the control room erupted with gasps and shouts as operators stood and pointed at the section of dome that displayed news from Earth.

‘General! Look! Something weird is happening, I can’t believe it!’ cried one of the operators. ‘A huge number of asteroids, meteorites or something has crashed into the Pacific ocean!’

‘That’s preposterous,’ the General retorted, rising awkwardly from his seat. ‘Anything like that would have been detected well before arriving at Earth.’

The General stared, open-mouthed. He listened and watched in awe and horror as satellite pictures showed large objects crashing into the ocean as far as the eye could see causing huge explosions of water.

The newscaster was broadcasting, over this unbelievable scene, that there was no forewarning of this vast shower.

‘Experts are completely baffled that such a large number of enormous objects could have arrived at Earth undetected. Furthermore, and of immense immediate concern is the formation of gigantic tsunamis heading in all directions from a point in the centre of the southern Pacific Ocean.’

‘But how?’ cried the General. ‘How could this happen without warning?’

Then the newscaster spoke again but this time his voice was higher pitched and carried a tone of incredulity.

'Further video is coming through from the southern Pacific, I can't believe what I'm seeing! A tsunami wave over 500 metres in height – that can't be right surely? – is racing at speeds in excess of 300 kilometres per hour on an expanding front towards southern Australasia, the tip of South America and directly at the ice-shelf of Antarctica. Already hundreds of SOS messages have been received from shipping and energy fields in the south Pacific and most have been followed by ominous silence.'

The broadcaster continued to say that the World Disaster Council was in full session and emergency evacuation plans have been activated for the whole western coast of continental America and the eastern seaboards of China, Asia, Australasia and Antarctica.

Satellite pictures then showed the scale of these tsunamis, which, although thousands of kilometres from landfall, would cause a calamity on Earth of unprecedented proportions. However, the Ross ice-shelf of continental Antarctica was only 500 kilometres away.

Continuing footage showed the gargantuan curved wave as it raged towards the ice. It was both awesome and frightening in its proportions.

Even more disturbing was the enormous black mass that followed in its wake.

The General could only watch, helplessly, wondering what had caused this calamity and what the consequences would be for planet Earth.

Chapter 78
What next for Earth?

'It is going to be another five long years before the events at Cloud Planet reach Mars Base.

'Another 5 years before Earth learns about the menace of the Black, molecular computers, discs that travel faster than the speed of light and melt planetary icecaps!

'However, on Earth the huge estuaries, rivers and lakes are, of course, fresh water and no barrier to such an advanced, sophisticated 'bead'!

'The only safe place is in the chlorinated swimming pools!'

'It is time to bring this first part of my story to a close. I think you have had more than enough for now but you may like to ponder......

...... where in the universe will Olivia and Scott meet again?

...... where is Scott's father?

..... how and where does he bump into Olivia's sister?

..... and how do they unravel and start to learn the chilling truth that is......'

Quest of the Dicepterons
Volume Two: Disaster Earth

THE END

Lightning Source UK Ltd.
Milton Keynes UK
UKOW040132280313

208298UK00001B/7/P

9 781782 992066